UNDER THE Orchard's Spell

UNDER THE *Orchard's Spell*

A NOVEL

ANN ADAMS

DELL BOOKS
NEW YORK

Dell
An imprint of Random House
A division of Penguin Random House LLC
1745 Broadway, New York, NY 10019

randomhousebooks.com
penguinrandomhouse.com

A Dell Trade Paperback Original

Library of Congress Cataloging-in-Publication Data
Names: Adams, Ann (Romance fiction writer) author
Title: Under the orchard's spell : a novel / Ann Adams.
Description: New York : Dell Books, 2026.
Identifiers: LCCN 2026029429 (print) | LCCN 2026029430 (ebook) |
ISBN 9798217095452 trade paperback | ISBN 9798217095469 ebook
Subjects: LCGFT: Magic realist fiction | Romance fiction | Novels
Classification: LCC PS3601.D326 U53 2026 (print) |
LCC PS3601.D326 (ebook)
LC record available at https://lccn.loc.gov/2026029429
LC ebook record available at https://lccn.loc.gov/2026029430

Printed in the United States of America

1st Printing

BOOK TEAM: Production editor: Annette Szlachta · Managing editor: Saige Francis · Production manager: Meghan O'Leary · Copy editor: Whitney Bak · Proofreaders: Hope Clarke, Frieda Duggan, Emily Zebrowski

Book design by Betty Lew

Title-page butterflies: Владимир Феофанов / Adobe Stock
Pear tree watercolor: Florabela / Adobe Stock
Pear art by Grgroup / Adobe Stock
Butterflies on pages 3 and 327 by thawats / Adobe Stock

Also by Ann Adams

Racing Hearts

For Cam,

a world without you wasn't made for me.

UNDER THE *Orchard's Spell*

Fourteen Seasons Ago

I'm considering tying myself to a pear tree in a desperate ploy to stay on this orchard forever, but my mother has a talent for ruthlessly cutting through knots and dreams. When the woman has her sights set on a new move—in this case, Fairbanks, Alaska—she's like a honey badger in a beige turtleneck. And after today's phone call in which she informed me of my new fate, and then hung up when I started to cry, I need the comfort of the trees.

Climbing one will have to be good enough.

I brace my hands against the flaky bark of a thickly curved bough, mapping my ascent. A strong, steady branch crawls skyward, disappearing into olive-colored leaves and miniature bobbling pears. Casting a final glance over each shoulder, I hitch up my dress and hoist myself aloft, my sandals slipping for purchase. Then, with as much grace as I can manage, I swivel to a seat and throw my arms around the trunk.

Every ounce of tension dissolves from my chest as I hug tight and the wind carries the leaves in a whispered song. Here, in a tree, I'm not the girl who gets funny looks when she can't remember her mailing address. I'm not the only high school student with an immaculate yearbook, a naked locker, or blank bedroom walls (because what's the point of tacking up a poster if you're going to take it down in a few months?).

I am a person with a past and a place. I have roots. I belong.

The wind picks up again, riffling my dress against my bare knees. Next to my fingertips, a caterpillar pauses its ascent of the trunk. It twists to administer a beady stare, like it's here to report my misdeed to Uncle Martin. As much as my uncle might relate to my love of these trees, he'd still be disappointed to see me risking a branchful of product, particularly given we're so near picking season.

Imagining a firm look in Martin's usually twinkling eye is more than enough to make me consider climbing back down, but then—

"Ali."

Crap.

I try to spin to see who said my name, but I can barely move my torso, wedged as I am into this U-shaped branch. Thankfully, the voice is male, so it's not my honorary aunt (and uncle's forewoman), Val. If Aunt Val found me up here, she'd tell me she doesn't care that I'm in high school—if I'm young enough to be climbing a tree, I'm also young enough for a good spanking.

A figure ducks under the canopy.

My heart stills.

Because not only have I been caught, but I've been caught by *him*.

Logan.

I'm so used to watching him from far away, usually separated by rows of trees or a rolling hillside. Up close, I have to remember to breathe as I take in his face. His serious brown eyes, rimmed by dark eyelashes. His defined chin. The firm press of his full lips, like he's holding in a secret.

"Oh, it's you," I say, striving for cool and indifferent even though my heart beats out the same words in a different rhythm.

Oh. It's *you*.

Logan's eyebrows pull together as he scans my spot among the branches. He must be done with the barn for the day because his T-shirt is damp with sweat around the collar, and he's got a sketchbook tucked under an arm. It draws my attention to his biceps, where his skin transitions from light to honey tan, accentuating the rough edge of his muscles.

"You're in a tree," he observes.

I wince and scrounge around for a reasonable explanation for my behavior. But I can barely think. Logan's presence is like a chemical bloom flooding this tree's understory.

Which is probably why my next words are, "I'm looking for caterpillars."

Now I want to kick myself. What am I going to say next? I'm planning to run them off with hand-to-hand combat?

Logan's gaze brushes past my bare knees to the daisies on my sandals. "Without a ladder."

This, I've noticed, is how Logan asks questions—without a question mark. Like they are a frivolous adornment at the end of an otherwise perfectly utilitarian sentence.

"What are you doing?" I ask. "Shouldn't you be off on a hill somewhere, glaring at the trees while you draw and then rage-erase everything five seconds later?"

He blinks. "Specific."

Warmth glances up my neck. "Just, uh, something I've noticed."

Logan's lips work like he's silently tasting the words before he speaks. Then he says, "Maybe I'm just surprised *you* aren't parading through the orchard with that speaker, half shouting, half singing about how you were born this way."

Now it's my turn to blink. "Only the trees are supposed to hear my singing voice."

He chuckles. "And deprive the rest of us of those high notes?"

Before I can flush or protest, he takes a few steps toward me, that sketchbook still clasped under his arm. "Tell me why you're really up there."

Briefly, I consider climbing down, but this floral-print dress isn't exactly modest attire, and the only way to embarrass myself further is by showing Logan my underwear.

"I'm not telling," I say.

He crosses his arms. "Now I have to know."

Logan does, in general, seem like the kind of person who gathers information in the same way a magpie might amass shiny scraps of nothing.

"You'll think it's silly."

My mouth makes these words against my best intentions to remain cool and indifferent. Who am I kidding, though? I'm a puppy rolling around in the summer grass, belly exposed. I'm never cool or indifferent.

"Try me." Logan braces an elbow against the trunk. "I won't leave until you do."

Again, I consider staging an escape, but then I remember that this morning's underwear selection was neon orange.

So, instead, I say, "I'm connecting with my roots."

Logan holds his expression so neutrally it looks like he might have pulled a jaw muscle to keep everything in place.

I bury my face in my hands. "See? I knew you'd think it's ridiculous."

"I didn't say anything," he protests.

"You thought it, though!"

"You can't hold my thoughts against me." He nudges a shoulder against my shin. "Besides, I don't know what you're saying. You have to explain."

"No," I say, but I tuck my chin so I can look down at him. "I've been traumatized enough."

"Please," he whispers.

And, oh. He's so close.

Our conversations this summer have often been interrupted, usually by my uncle who needs me on the mower or Logan's mom reminding him there's sawdust to sweep.

Or they've happened entirely from afar, like that time his gaze caught mine over a long wooden board. Or the time I heard him playing tag in the trees with his two much younger brothers, and I paused behind a trunk to listen to his laugh. Or when I was on a ladder thinning and Logan was diligently jotting down measurements as his mom called out numbers from the rafters. Except his face kept lifting toward my ladder, like he was trying to memorize two things at once.

But now? Now I can see the flecks of gold dancing across his irises. A suggestion of facial hair along his jaw. The rough edges of his worn cuticles against large, flat fingernails. And his expression, so full of studied interest, that the last of my resolve ebbs away.

"Fine," I say, but I still brace myself like my tree might topple. "You know how me and my mom move around a lot?"

"Yes."

It was a sticking point of our first conversation at the beginning of the summer. We were standing outside the gravel pad where Uncle Martin introduced me to Logan and his parents, waving his hands like a magician revealing an empty box.

"Get used to this lot," my uncle told me, "because they're building us a new barn this summer."

Hands in his pockets, Logan asked where I was from and I said everywhere and he said a person can't be from everywhere, so I followed it up with nowhere, which seemed just as accurate. Then Uncle Martin patted my shoulder while Logan squinted at me like I was an especially difficult trigonometry problem.

"Well," I say, "the summers I spend here, on my uncle's orchard, it's the only time I feel connected to anything. Like, four generations of farmers in this valley grew and nurtured these trees from rootstock. And when I was little, I'd climb their branches and imagine they were part of my family. They aren't going anywhere, and I didn't need to go anywhere either. So sometimes, when I want to remember that, I climb a tree and I feel . . . I feel grounded."

I don't admit the rest—the most ridiculous, secret part—that sometimes the trees feel like more than trees. Sometimes they feel like they're watching me. Listening to me. Breathing with me.

Even still, Logan is so quiet I can hear the distant growl of my uncle's mower as he prowls the northern edge of the land. Even still, I've said too much.

"I don't think I've ever heard anyone say something like that before," he says.

I wince.

"No. Wait," he rushes to add. "That's not . . . that's not how I meant it."

But this fumbled reassurance isn't enough to stem the sting of angry tears against my eyelids. Not only because I've blathered and made a fool of myself. Also because I've just remembered why I'm up here in the first place. I don't want to spend my sophomore year in Fairbanks. I don't want to, yet again, be the new girl parting waves of attention down a hallway. I don't want to, yet again, stare at an unfamiliar ceiling in an unfamiliar bedroom as my classmates pile into cars for homecoming. And in three years, I don't want to graduate surrounded by strangers.

All I want is to *stay*.

Or, at the very least, to push away this crushing avalanche of emotion.

I'm about to beg Logan to leave me alone when I feel a creak against the trunk. I open my eyes to find his boots and sketchbook discarded on the grass. He push-presses himself upward. The tree groans a low protest, but he adjusts himself onto the branch until his eyes are level with mine.

"There," he says.

Even though my nose is still stinging with repressed tears, I'm stunned to silence. Because I'm me, that silence doesn't last.

"Where?" I ask.

"I'm in the tree with you."

My lips crack in the slightest smile. "So I don't have to feel ridiculous?"

He lifts a shoulder. "Or so we can be ridiculous together."

A soft wind ruffles his hair, carrying the trace smell of cut grass and earth. Everything prickles with awareness: the bark under my thighs, the cool breeze over my knees, and Logan's eyes across the tree.

"I'm still the only one," I say quietly. "Because you're only humoring me."

"Fine," he says, "you want to hear something ridiculous about me?"

"Please."

"I've never left Apple Valley."

I gape at him. "You're exaggerating."

His eyes shift. "A little. I've been to Maplehurst."

"And?"

"And that's it."

I rest my head against the bark. "I won't tell you I'm jealous."

He mirrors me. "And I'll avoid saying the same to you."

Temples on the trunk, we let that sit between us: a difference so intense it feels an awful lot like it's the same. The breeze moves over us again, as if the orchard is exhaling its own delicate sigh. I think about the funny look Uncle Martin gets when I point things like this out to him, the way his bobbing sun hat will go still before he changes the subject.

"Do you ever think—" I start. Cut myself off.

Logan tilts his head. "What?" he encourages.

I look into his eyes, feeling like I'm edging up to the side of a cliff. And then I let myself fall. "Do you ever think there's something different about this land?"

"Different?"

I nod, trying to find the right word. *Strange* feels too negative and so does *unnatural*. *Special* doesn't seem strong enough. "Remarkable, I mean."

He rubs at his jaw. "Other than the fact that it's the only pear orchard in Apple Valley?"

Apple Valley was given its name for a reason. It has the ideal soil, weather, and climate for (you guessed it) apples. It's always been strange that only pears flourish on our land, while our neighbors can never grow any of their own, a fact that has garnered whispers and stories. Some people claim my great-great-grandfather had a feud with a neighbor and, out of spite, my ancestor pulled up every apple sapling in reach. Other people say we Reids grow pears because we have a flair for novelty and anything dramatic. And once, in an ice cream shop, I saw a girl point at my uncle and whisper to her mom about the ghost who inhabits a felled apple tree. Yet whenever I repeat these stories to Uncle Martin, he only tweaks my nose and winks before Val barks out that microclimates do weird shit.

"Other than that," I press, letting my feet swing. "Even more than that."

On the next arc of my legs, Logan's foot catches my ankle. Doesn't let go. "I can only think of one other thing that makes this place remarkable."

My scalp tingles. "Oh?"

He nods slowly. All the heat in my body has gathered at the point where Logan's foot is hooked around my ankle. A butterfly wanders between our noses. Its wings catch the light with an iridescent sheen before it trips upward toward the dark canopy. And I have this feeling of infinite expansion, like maybe I could hang, suspended, in this moment forever.

"Want to hear a secret?" Logan asks, foot still unmoving, like we're just accidentally holding on to each other, neither of us fully aware of the contact.

Even though I can barely think about anything else.

"Always," I whisper.

"This job—building the barn for your uncle this summer—it's supposed to be an apprenticeship. My parents want me to follow in their footsteps. Start working with them. Become a carpenter, too."

"Is that the secret?"

He shakes his head. "The secret is I'm going to leave."

I watch him, half perplexed and half mesmerized by the reverential way he's talking about wanting to do the exact thing my mother is forcing on me. "When?"

"After we finish this fall. I'm turning eighteen in a couple of weeks. Though I don't know exactly where I'll go. Portland, maybe? Seattle? I've found these communal living places for artists. I want to see if I can get someone to let me trade woodworking labor for room and board."

"You want to be an artist," I say. "Like for real."

His mouth lifts into a smile. "Or at least rage-erase something other than fruit trees."

The tiniest part of me feels confused by the idea that Logan would want to leave this beautiful, perfect place. But another, much bigger part of me is awed by this forming picture of him: a boy with the hands of a carpenter, the heart of an artist, who will soon have the freedom to break away from the limits imposed by his parents. Grounding himself in the life *he* wants.

But maybe I consider it for too long because Logan releases my ankle. "You think that sounds like a bad idea."

"No," I insist. "I think that sounds like a remarkable idea."

His lips part before spreading into another smile, this one full and eager. It gives me a kick of pleasure as a second butterfly lands on the trunk between our faces. Its wings are transparent, but for a series of black geometric lines edged in auburn and silver. It's beautiful, like a scrap of heart-shaped stained glass.

"That's no sawfly," I whisper as the butterfly flits upward.

We tip our faces to follow its flight. And let out twin gasps.

Above our heads, a sea of tiny wings ripples, pulsing open and closed. They're cascading over the branches and leaves, winking in every possible color and pattern: bright streaks of cerulean, stripes of seafoam green, whispers of harvest gold. Their antennae dip and rise, punctuated occasionally by sudden flutters.

"Oh my god," I say. "Have you ever seen anything like this?"

"Never." Logan's voice is tinged with awe.

I reach up as if to brush the closest pair of wings with my fingertips. They are far too high, but the movement still disturbs a few of the creatures perched on the trunk.

Suddenly, they all take flight. Wings beat in a flurry that scatters across the leaves. In the next breath, we're surrounded by a shimmering, swirling mass—a vortex of color that runs and falls like kaleidoscope glass. I shouldn't be able to hear them, yet the rustle of wings roars like far-off ocean waves as the cyclone spins and morphs.

Eyes wide, Logan reaches out. A butterfly perches on his open palm. It's the most unusual one I've seen yet, with electric-blue wings rimmed in flecks of silver. He lifts it toward me as his lips unfurl in an unbridled smile.

And that smile? It's just as beautiful as the iridescent wings.

His full, round lips. The way his mouth folds around the edges. The glow in his eyes. It's . . .

"Remarkable," I whisper.

He catches one of my curls between his fingers, then tucks it behind my ear. "Not just the butterflies."

And my heart can't help but answer in frantic pulses.

Stay, it beats. *Stay. Stay. Stay.*

"You'll only be in Apple Valley for another couple months," I say.

Logan edges closer, ignoring the goldenrod wings that glance off my cheek and the cobalt pair that rests on his shoulder.

"And in two weeks," I continue, "I'm leaving for Alaska."

"Which means . . ." Logan's nose tips forward, so close it brushes mine. So close that when he exhales, I can feel the warmth of his breath. "For the next two weeks we'll both be here."

Stay, my heart keens once more.

I can't, I tell it. *He won't.*

And yet. Even though it can't last, because nothing in my life ever can, I edge forward. He closes the rest of the gap between us. And with a thousand beating wings circling our bodies, Logan kisses me.

Chapter One

THIS SEASON

"Well, if this ain't weirder than a scarecrow on a trampoline."

Ahead of me, Val storms down a row of trees, white hair spiking like a wild crown. She skids to a stop and glares at a branch in her eyeline, reminding me of the time she suspected she'd caught Uncle Martin counting cards.

"Do orchardists even use scarecrows anymore?" I ask as I hoist a ladder off the Gator and hurry to her side, brushing past branches that slap my shoulders like they're urging me along. It's still late afternoon, but the whole orchard is steeped in that golden hour light that September always brings a touch too soon. "Those machines with the percussive sounds seem much more effective."

"Cherry guns, you mean." Val claps her fingers against a palm to marshal me and the ladder to the spot where she wants us, then digs a pressure gauge out of her back pocket and scales the steps. "Sure, but it wouldn't have been so funny if I'd said it was weirder than a cherry gun on a trampoline."

"I mean the scarecrow thing wasn't that funny, either," I tell her.

She frowns down at me, brown skin breaking into even more lines than usual. "Because you have to picture it. Did you picture it?"

"I'm trying."

"And?"

"And it's a bit unclear. Is the scarecrow, like, bending its legs or—"

Val plucks up a half-rotten pear and chucks it at my forehead.

I snicker as I duck. "But I was right? Something is wrong with the color."

I noticed it this morning. The pears looked like . . . green bananas. When they should be the color of a honeydew rind, right near the flesh.

It's a color seared into my mind from the year Mom and I moved to Grand Rapids, Michigan. That fall, I didn't start school until after Labor Day, so I walked this exact row with Uncle Martin at this exact time of year. He asked me what the fruit reminded me of, and when I said "a honeydew rind," he wheezed out a laugh before cupping one of the pears in his hand and shout whispering: "Very good, but don't let them hear you comparing them to a buffet fruit."

Now, Uncle Martin is gone and the orchard is mine—far, far sooner than either of us would have wanted—and I'm always looking for that exact shade of greenish yellow, as if finding it might bring back an echo of his wheezy laugh from halfway down a row.

Val nods as she picks a fresh pear, expertly angling it upward to snap the weakest part of the stem, then flattens it against a ladder step while she spears it with the pressure gauge. The reading loads as she lumbers down.

"You sure were right." She tips up the face of her gauge. "See it now?"

With a glance at the needle, realization dawns. What's off isn't just the color; it's this pear's color relative to the others.

"These should be the first to go," I say, "but the pears in the Thompson block had higher readings."

"Exactly right," Val says, dropping the fruit to the base of the tree and dusting off her hands.

I look back at her, considering this. Fruit turns in stages on any orchard, including ours, depending primarily on the rows' exposure to heat and sunlight, and the age of the trees. Those schedules should be predictable, though. Trees that get more sunlight one year will pretty much be the same as the next.

"That's strange, isn't it?" I ask.

Val lifts a shoulder. "Weird microclimates around here. Makes things unpredictable."

It's something I've heard her say a thousand times to explain all manner of oddities, including why my orchard remains the sole pear farm in a valley filled with apples. Or why our picking season always starts on September 30—a date that is both later and more clockwork precise than it should be.

Before I can ask about it, though, Val says, "You knew that because of the color?"

"Yeah."

She arches an eyebrow.

"What?" I ask.

"Nothing," she mumbles, stooping to hoist the ladder onto her shoulder and starting back down the row. "It's just subtle, that's all. Hard to see with the naked eye. That's why we use the gauge."

"Val. Did you just tell me you're impressed?"

She spins, but she's not laughing. "It's something Martin would've noticed."

And this time the compliment is loud and clear.

My throat tightens. "He taught me everything I know."

Or, rather, everything I *feel*.

The weight he placed on feeling, not knowledge, is the reason Uncle Martin never showed me how to use a pressure gauge—much to Val's chagrin—opting instead to get me to compare the fruit to fennel and zucchini blossoms. It's why, when I was in eighth grade, he taught me to prune by running my hand along the branch, feeling where the growth was thin or crowded and instinctively finding the right place to cut. Feeling is how I knew last summer, when I came to visit right after he told me about his diagnosis, that a new disease had taken root on the north side. There wasn't anything visible, really. It's just that the branches seemed tired.

When I pointed it out, Martin clapped me on the back and said, "Ali, my dear, you're going to make one remarkable orchardist."

I only grimaced, not ready to hear it. I was convinced he'd pull through and farm this land for decades more. I was sure the pancreatic cancer wouldn't—couldn't—take him.

A few months later, he admitted he was starting hospice. I scrambled onto the next flight from Miami to Portland, a foolhardy attempt to convince him to keep fighting. But when I saw him, hollowed out and frailer than I could have imagined, I finally started to accept the truths I'd been railing against for too long.

I was going to lose the only adult who ever made me feel safe.

I was going to be the next owner of this land.

We—me and the trees—were going to have to face the world without him.

Over the next few months, these ideas turned from abstract concepts to practical inevitability. I told Mom I'd be moving onto the orchard and was met with a silence even sharper than usual. I gave notice at my consulting firm in Florida and transitioned my contracts and clients to another project manager. My uncle and I signed deeds and probate orders and transfers of water rights. Then, in a whirlwind, I packed all my belongings and rented what I hoped would be my last U-Haul.

Only, when I returned, I wasn't alone.

My uncle's farmhouse—so recently consumed by stillness—filled with new kinds of sounds. Tape ripped off boxes. Voices drifting between rooms. Glasses clinked, toasting what had been and what remained. I went to the hardware store to have three sets of keys made, all with matching heart-shaped fobs. At that time, just about everything came in threes: laptops on the kitchen table, mugs of coffee with cream, pairs of work boots by the front door.

But that was a month ago. Now there's only one.

One laptop.

One mug.

One pair of boots.

And a new kind of silence. At least I still have the trees.

"So, how big of a deal is it that the fruit is ripening at weird intervals?" I ask, pushing out thoughts but also already bracing myself for a fresh round of bad news.

To my relief, Val lifts a shoulder. "Not at all. We've just gotta adjust our picking schedule."

"The start date?"

"Nah. We'll start the last day of September, same as always. I just mean the order we'll go. You have your uncle's aerial photos up at the house?"

"In the kitchen."

"Good, we'll just—" Val stops short, her gaze caught on a branch just above the parked Gator.

I follow her eyeline to a pear. Like the others, it's still small since it's only early September. Unlike the others, it's coated in a white-looking sheen.

"Wax bloom?" I ask.

Val reaches toward the pear and rubs her thumb against its surface. Oddly, the film doesn't budge. Eyebrows pinched together, she studies her thumb, then her eyes flash to me. "You notice anything off lately?"

"Off?"

"About the land. Unseasonable weather. Unusual temperature changes. Since I was last here a month ago."

A month ago. When three pairs of boots turned to one.

When they left.

The woman I called my best friend.

The man who was always, always, *always* supposed to be there for me.

I swallow, sorting through memories of those hazy, sticky-with-grief days that followed. In my bleary state of semiconsciousness, I barely registered what was happening outside the darkened bedroom, but . . .

There was the fog. The one that prowled over hills and across grass. Crept up trunks, swallowing my trees into silhouettes. Grew so thick that, when I leaned a temple to a cold window, I could barely see more than a yawning wall of gray.

"There's been some fog," I say evenly. "Especially in the mornings."

Val's eyes dart between me and the tree trunks, lips pressed. Then she shakes her head as though clearing it, wipes her hands against her Carhartts, and hoists herself onto the driver's seat of the Gator.

"Hey," I say, scrambling in next to her. "Are you going to tell me what that was?"

She shrugs and punches the gas, throwing us both backward. "Nothing," she yells over the roar of the engine. "Someone wasn't paying attention to the sprayer."

After we get back to the house, we kick off our work boots in the mud room—damp with grass and dew—and head to the kitchen, with its gingham wallpaper, ancient Frigidaire rattling in the corner, and Formica countertops riddled with stains from hundreds of tea bags. The early fall weather is temperate enough that I can throw open the windows and allow the sheer curtains to dance over the sink. I pour us each a glass of iced tea and Val tugs off her pilled neckcloth so she can dab at her sweaty brow while helping me unroll an aerial photograph of the farm.

When he found out I wouldn't be moving onto the orchard alone, Uncle Martin paid someone in town to take these photos with a drone.

"We might know every rock and tree and creature on this land," he'd whispered as I laid out the photos on his bedspread. "But not everyone can paint with all the colors of our wind."

And though his face had taken on a waxy pallor, purple bruises tracked up his forearms, and he could barely sit up even with the stack of pillows wedged behind his too-thin back, he tweaked my nose and grinned.

In times like these, despite the evidence, my mind still whispered, *He's going to pull through. There's no way this man is going to die.*

I swallow past the tightness in my chest and tap my finger to the block of trees Val and I surveyed this morning. "So, Thompson the first week. And then we'll move onto the Dethman block?"

My aunt takes a big swig of tea and plops in a chair, rattling the ice as she squints at the photo. "Thompson block first sounds right, but I don't know about a week. How many other people do you have picking?"

"Just you and me. I thought I told you that?"

We had the conversation a month ago.

Alone and desperate, I had called Val and begged her to come out of retirement, just for this one season. She showed up at the farmhouse an hour later, took one look at my hollow eyes, and agreed. Besides, she'd said as she patted my arm, she loved my uncle—and this land—far too much to say no.

"No," Val says now. "You did not. You said you needed my help and that you wouldn't ask if you weren't desperate. You didn't say a word about not getting other pickers."

"I don't have money to hire anyone," I say. My uncle didn't leave the farm in great financial shape—it's been losing money for years, and Martin was using loans to make ends meet. "So, it's just you and me. We'll do as much as we can."

She balloons her cheeks as she blows out a breath. "Fine, but in that case, the Thompson block'll take us at least three."

I drop my glass to the counter, nearly do a spit take. "Three *weeks*?"

"It's not going to take three afternoons."

"But . . . Uncle Martin said that once the trees turn, we only have six weeks max to get the pears down."

She nods. "Otherwise, they'll see to it themselves."

I spare her a smile, but I don't like where this conversation is going. "Right, so we need to go faster than that."

She squints at me. "How fast do you think the two of us can pick fifty acres of fruit?"

"I mean, I've never picked pears before—"

Val snorts. "That much is clear."

"But I do know there are seven blocks on the land. So, if we want to get most of it down, we'll need to finish the Thompson block in a week. Less, ideally."

"Not possible."

I stare at her because this math isn't mathing. "I'll work as hard as I need to. I won't sleep. I'll eat in the trees. I'll wake up before dawn. Keep picking in the dark with a headlamp."

She shakes her head. "All of that is impossible." I open my mouth to protest, but she puts up a hand. "Ali."

She angles a slightly crooked index finger at a family portrait above the kitchen table, a shot from harvest decades ago. It features my grandmother, her third husband by her side, and my mom, already a blank-faced teenager. Between them, Martin holds up a pear with the mischievous grin he carried into adulthood. He's the only one smiling, though. My mom, grandmother, and her husband struggle to stay upright in their picking bags—apron-like contraptions filled with pears from shoulders to knees.

"This work is harder than anything you can imagine," Val says. "The damn bags weigh fifty pounds when they're full. You have to scale a ladder dozens of times every day. You can't wear gloves lest you damage the fruit. Your back will hurt so bad you'll cry yourself to sleep. You physically can't do it for more than a few hours a day. You'll break yourself otherwise. You might even break as it is."

Uncle Martin already told me all this. Once he understood the reasons I was resisting taking over the orchard—not because I didn't want the land, but because I hated the idea that he wouldn't be the one farming it—he asked me a million times if I'd still want to do it, even if it's the hardest thing I could imagine.

I told him yes, over and over. It's six weeks. I can handle six weeks of torture in exchange for the other forty-six I'll live here.

Here, where every new leaf remembers the ones that came before. Where the fern green of summer always yields to white—powdery snow in the winter and blossoms in spring—proof that even change can be steady if you stick around long enough to see it. Where the wraparound porch and wicker chairs still bear the faint outline of where I used to sit, shoulder to shoulder with Uncle Martin, scraping up pasta sauce with forks, our arms aching from a day of thinning.

The porch boards remember where we sat, the orchard where we worked. I've left my mark here and this land has marked me, too.

Faced with Val's skeptical frown, I cross my arms.

"I'll figure it out," I say.

"You know you're not going to *positive think* your way out of this problem," she says.

Years ago, I told Martin and Val that I was joining a change management firm that helps organizations navigate business transitions and build resilient teams by harnessing the power of positive thinking. Uncle Martin chuckled and told me it sounded like a perfect fit.

From the background, Val yelled, "What the fuck is the 'power of positive thinking'?"

"I'm not trying to *positive think* my way out of anything," I retort, even though that is at least partially what I'm doing. But only because it really can work. "I'm making a commitment. It will work because it *has* to. I might be the fifth Reid to farm this land, but I most certainly will not be the last."

Val gives me a once-over, lips pressed like she's torn between warmth and skepticism. "I like your conviction, girl."

"Why does it sound like there's a but coming?"

"*But* picking fruit has a way of breaking resolutions. And I don't think you're facing facts."

I feel slightly unsteady, like the kitchen floor is seesawing, an airplane jostling in turbulence. "I can face facts."

"Good. Fact is you need three pickers."

My stomach washes. I was supposed to have three pickers, but now I have a tan line on my ring finger, and I have Val.

"I don't have enough money," I say, pointedly avoiding a glance toward the pile of bills that has been accumulating on the kitchen counter.

Val drains her glass and yanks her phone out of her back pocket. "I have to go, chicken. Poker night."

"But Val—"

"We'll find someone else," she says over her shoulder because she's already plowing toward the door. "Someone you don't need to pay so much. We'll call in a favor. Or maybe there's some kid that needs work for the summer."

"But who?" I ask, scrambling to catch up as she forges across the grass. "You said yourself it's hard work. It's not something a kid can do for pocket money, and even if we do find someone like that, there's no guarantee they won't quit on us and leave halfway through the season."

Val pauses her clomping steps, a funny look in her eyes. "Is that what you're really worried about? Getting left?"

An image of the barn strobes through my memory. An open door, hanging loose on its hinges. The scuttle of a black-furred body across the weather-stained floorboards. Hay bales—

I shove the thoughts away. "I can handle it. We can handle it. Together."

"Well, that's where you're wrong," she retorts as she ducks under a branch and beeps her key fob. "Sorry to be blunt about it, but Martin—god love him—left you with more debts than fruit trees. So, if you want to save this farm, you'll find another picker instead of clinging to that irrational—"

Val stumbles. A root I hadn't noticed a second ago, one that should never have been above the surface to begin with, seems to have materialized in front of her.

Her ankle buckles.

I'm already rushing toward her as she slams against the ground. And howls with pain.

Chapter Two

After four hours, two sets of X-rays, and a chunky new boot, the hospital staff cede to Val's demands to be discharged. The good news is her ankle is sprained—not broken—and the doctor expects her to have the boot off in two weeks. My aunt interprets this to mean she'll be ready for harvest when it starts in four. (When the doctor leaves, I ask her who is "positive thinking" now. With a withering stare, she retorts that this will be her sixty-first year on earth and forty-seventh on a tree ladder. No kid with a stethoscope will tell her to stay off it.)

The better news (according to Val) is that the near miss was the final push I needed to try to find a third picker. As she says, we're hanging on by a thread and I don't need another sprained ankle—mine or hers—tipping my farm into the final stages of ruin.

So that's why, the following Saturday morning, I'm forging through flapping white tents at the Apple Valley farmer's market, beelining past baskets of heirloom tomatoes and sweet corn stacked in crates. After a brief detour to buy myself a maple-pecan donut, I locate my destination. For some reason the rickety old sign is missing—the one promising LOCA APPLES and ICY COLD BEV. Fortunately, the cheerful red wagon behind an A-frame menu board is distinctive enough.

Of course, I'm not here for the hard cider. I'm here for the cider maker's nephew.

He's the third (and last) person on the list Val gave me from her bed a few nights ago, where she was propped up with her boot elevated and a cigar she definitely shouldn't have been smoking seesawing across her face. Personally, though, I'm most hopeful about this one. I've only met the guy once, but he's so freakishly tall I bet he makes ladders feel insecure. Even better, his aunt, June, told Val he's taking the year off before starting college, which means he might be interested in some pocket money in exchange for a month or so of extremely hard work.

I'm still licking sugar glaze off my fingertips when I reach the red wagon's open window. On the ground by the wheel, a new wood sign sits nearly finished, rimmed with tools and declaring that this is BROKEN HART'S CIDER CO. It's pretty—certainly a big upgrade to the one with missing letters.

"Hello?" I say as I ball up sticky paper and peer past empty cider bottles being used as vases.

"Be there in a sec!" a high-pitched voice calls from inside.

A moment later, a short woman with fair skin flushed to pink and laugh lines around her eyes materializes in front of me, a tiny baby slung across her front.

"Ali!" she says like we're old friends, though we've met only a couple of times.

"Hey there," I say. "It's June, right?"

"You've got it," June says warmly. "June Hart. And this is Teddy, short for Theodore. You're fast—most new folks don't pick up names that quick."

She tips her temple to the top of her baby's head, and smiles in a way that draws one from me right back. She has the same kind of infectious familiarity with perfect strangers that Liv always had. Has.

I don't know what tense to use for a woman who is very much still alive but will never again be part of my life. I shouldn't be thinking about Liv, anyway.

"I'm good with names," I say. "Former consultant and all that."

June grins. "I'll be honest, that job always sounds kind of fake. Like something an uptight career woman brags about before she falls for a guy in a pickup truck and discovers the meaning of Christmas."

I chuckle. "Does it sound more or less made up if I tell you I worked in 'change management to help organizations navigate business transitions by guiding culture shifts'?"

She raises an eyebrow. "Must have been quite the change to go from all that to this."

"I don't have to account for my days in fifteen-minute increments anymore, so I'd tend to agree."

She laughs before her face firms. "Hey, Ali, I've been meaning to stop by."

She says it in that hushed, conspiratorial whisper that folks around here always use to talk about our farm. Like it's a little strange, a little off, and maybe safer not to speak of too loudly.

I blink. "Why would you?"

"To see how you're doing?" she says. When I don't say more, she adds in a stage whisper, "Val told Kristi what happened. And she mentioned it to my mom. About Blake and Liv, I mean."

My smile falters. I suddenly register the fact that my thumb has been running laps over the empty place my engagement ring used to occupy. After a year of wearing one, my fingers still feel naked without it. I force them to relax.

"Oh," I say.

I don't want to talk about Blake and Liv. Don't want to think about them, either. Or the front door snapping closed. The lapse of silence as I fell into a fitful, sweaty sleep. The days I spent cocooned in my grandmother's black-and-white quilt.

Shallow indents in the wallpaper. Rows of lifeless hangers.

I never knew emptiness could feel so full.

"I'm sorry I didn't come by on my own," June is saying. "But if you ever need anyone to talk to about everything, you can count on me."

I know she means well (mostly, I haven't missed the signs of curiosity), but I'm suddenly seasick and trying to keep myself from flagging.

Not every emotion requires immediate action or deep focus, I remind myself. It's something I used to tell middle managers in the workshop I taught on leading teams through corporate mergers and major restructures. It used to help my audience in business casual, and I'm sure it can help me, too. Sometimes emotions can be acknowledged and then released. Or, more to the point, shoved into a box and stashed in the deepest recesses of my mind.

"To be honest, I'm doing really well," I say, steadier now. "It was a big change, but it was also for the best. So, there's no need for an apology."

June smiles, and as is so often the case when I announce that, actually, everything is fine, relief washes over her features. "I'm so glad to hear that, Ali. Let me get you a cider. On the house."

Before I have a chance to say no—or redirect the conversation to her very tall nephew—she stoops with some effort to retrieve a glass demijohn. In an impressive display of forearm strength, she single-handedly pours golden liquid into a mason jar.

Despite many previous attempts to thwart them, people in this town will never accept the fact that I don't like apples, so I keep my smile in place as she fills the glass. Under her watchful eyes, I take a swig, swallow as fast as possible, and bob my head enthusiastically as I wipe my lips with the back of my hand.

June beams.

"So," I say, looking around my shoulders for real customers but finding only people with overflowing tote bags milling around the fruit and vegetable baskets. Hopefully I've come early enough that I can have this conversation without interrupting her actual business. "I wanted to ask you about something."

"Shoot."

"Well, because of everything that happened"—I gesture vaguely—"I'm looking for some extra help picking."

June nods knowingly. "Ah, yes. Mom mentioned Val was coming out of retirement for the season. I bet she's grumbling aloud and secretly thrilled."

I chuckle. "I think complaining might be Val's love language. But yeah, she also said you have a nephew who might be interested in helping us pick? I think he just graduated high school this year?"

"Mack, yes!" June says brightly. But then she shakes her head. "But no. He's just joined AmeriCorps."

"Oh," I say, heart sinking.

"But," June says. Teddy has clearly woken up because I can hear burbling noises emanating from the sling. His mom increases the pace of her back-patting and toe-to-toe-jumping. "I have another idea for you. That is, if your deal includes housing?"

I pause, not overeager to invite a stranger to live with me. Then again, I'm not sure how many more names Val can supply.

"We don't have any cabins for pickers," I hedge. "My uncle sold the tract of land they were on a while back. But depending on who it is, I could offer up a room in the farmhouse."

With an encouraged nod, June drops her cheek to Teddy's bald head. His babbles are now interspersed with hiccupy whimpers. "Well, then, my husband and I have this friend. He lost everything to a fire a week or so back, and he's been sleeping on the couch and helping out at the stand in the meantime. He's too polite to complain, but I can't imagine this little guy is doing wonders for his eardrums."

I smile, but when I don't rush to agree, June hastens to add, "I wouldn't offer this if he weren't a really good guy, super trustworthy." She nudges her chin toward the sign by the wagon's wheel. "He's the one who's been carving that for us."

My eyes find the nearly finished wood sign again. I take in the smooth, meticulous cuts. The way the letters are raised just enough to play with light and shadow. The careful flourishes at the edges—miniature broken hearts littered with apples.

And, in the corner, a tiny butterfly.

June is still talking in a confidential murmur. "And I'll tell you, Ali, he could use a break. Life sure has had a way of kicking him down. First he lost his mom when he was barely grown, then his dad a few years ago, and now the fire and— Oh, here he is now."

I whirl to find a broad figure, shadowed by the sun. My heart stalls into that weightless sensation you get at the apex of a roller coaster or a playground swing. Right before you start to fall.

Logan Wright is striding toward me.

He's taller than I remember. His jawline, once bare, is covered in the scruff of a slightly unkempt beard. He's wearing a plaid shirt, crisp enough to look ironed. The sleeves are rolled to the elbows, the fabric tapering over his now very broad chest. There's still a serious intensity in the stroke of his mouth and the curve of his eyes, but it's all hardened now, etched into place by fine lines.

One thing hasn't changed a bit, though. He's still the most attractive man I've ever seen.

And now he's in front of me, a loose grip on some kind of metal-tipped tool, gazing back at me with the same *Oh shit* expression I think might have come over my face.

"Ali Reid." Logan's voice is maybe a touch deeper now, but my name sounds just the way I remember on his tongue. A fullness around the vowels, a deep baritone on the consonants.

Somewhere I register that a customer has approached the counter and June is chatting brightly with them. But I'm trying to figure out what to say.

I'm trying to remember how to breathe.

If Logan registers my awkward silence, he doesn't show it. In fact, he's looking at me like I'm the first green shoot following a hard winter.

"Hi," I finally manage. It's not revelatory, but at least it's a well-known word in the English language.

Logan takes a small, almost unconscious step toward me. "You came back."

The words dredge up memories. An idling car in the driveway. A tearstained kiss. Sobs racking my shoulders as I dragged my feet across asphalt.

"You, too," I manage.

"Never left, actually."

I blink, itching to ask him about that, to resume a conversation that's more than fourteen years old, picking up like we've gotten a phone call disconnected. But instead, Logan says, "And you cut your hair."

I touch the ends of my curls. I started chopping it short a few years after college. One of the partners said it made me look *brighter*. "After fourteen years, I can't imagine that's the only difference."

"Nope. I count six so far."

Warmth rides up the back of my neck. "Hopefully not too many for the worse."

His gaze hasn't released mine. "Haven't found one yet."

And maybe it's because June's customer has cleared off and

she's turned back to us—bouncing from foot to foot with a bemused expression—but the way Logan's looking at me feels intimate enough that warmth spills over my cheeks.

I clear my throat. "You're in the sign business now."

He blinks, a microscopic reorientation behind his otherwise controlled expression. Then he says, "Only circumstantially." He nods toward June. "A small installment on a second debt to the Harts."

"Hush," June tells him. "There's no such thing as a debt between our families. Besides, you're welcome to stay with us for as long as you need. But Ali here might have alternative lodging for you and I think you'd be perfect for her job. Besides— Oh gosh, Logan, do you mind?"

Despite his mother's rhythmic rocking, Teddy has let out a bleating wail just as a customer steps up behind me.

Before she's finished the sentence, though, Logan is tucking his metal-tipped tool away and rounding the stand to take her place. June disappears with a grateful squeeze of his shoulder and the man at the counter orders two apple-blackberry ciders. Logan checks the guy's ID before pouring out liquid into mason jars. As the customer gathers up his glasses, my eyes graze Logan's flannel shirt again—the spot where it's open at the top, and the buttons straining slightly against his broad chest. He looks indecently good. Like he belongs in the October photograph of a wall calendar featuring shirtless lumberjacks and firefighters. Instinctively, I feel guilty for the thought before remembering that I have nothing to be guilty about. More than half a decade of monogamy will do that, I guess.

"So," Logan says when the customer has cleared off. "Do the pears know you're drinking that?"

He tips his chin toward my barely touched glass.

I grimace. "Everyone here always tries to force-feed me their fruit like some kind of conversion therapy into a cult of apples."

Logan presses his lips together like he's repressing a smile. Then he gently guides the glass off the counter and tips it into a flowering bush by my feet. "Not today, Satan."

I gape at him. "Surely you don't have a problem with apples?"

"Never liked them much."

"Never?" I ask. I have a distinct memory of Logan balancing an apple on his knee, eyebrows drawn together as his pencil furiously worked over his sketchbook. When he finished, he tipped the page toward me with a bashful smile. And maybe this was teenage hormones, but I remember thinking it was a masterpiece. Logan might not have had expensive paints, canvases, or a dedicated workspace, but he could draw out shadows and light with nothing more than ink and paper, like a window to another world.

He considers for a beat. "I guess there was a time I felt differently."

"And you changed your mind? But you're *from* Apple Valley. Negative opinions about apples are pretty much blasphemous."

"Says the woman who called them cultish."

"Right, but I hate apples for good reason, like lifelong bias imbued by five generations of pear farming."

Logan's lips twitch and I try not to be too pleased with myself. "Tell me. June said something about lodging and a job?"

I sense movement by my shoulder and find another customer—this time a woman in a comically wide sun hat. Logan pauses our conversation to card her, too, and remains impassive as she huffs and makes a big show of fishing out her wallet.

I'm grateful for the moment to organize my thoughts—in particular about asking *Logan Wright* to move into my farmhouse and pick fruit in exchange.

Of course, my brain hijacks the moment to replay memories instead. The smell of late-summer pears as Logan and I wandered through the trees, fingers braided together. A kiss while pressed against the barn doors. Lounging on the moss by the south-side creek, Logan's sketchbook flung open in the grass, our bare feet trailing eddies through clear water.

The goodbye that felt like I was carving my heart in two.

The phone calls that started out raw but eventually succumbed to silence.

"Ali?" I look up to find Logan leaning a corded forearm on the counter, customers gone.

I have to decide whether I'll ask him. There's a clear answer, though. As Val has bluntly put it, I need another picker. Logan might be available. And so, even though this could end in familiar disaster, I need to try.

"I don't know if you know this," I say, "but I inherited my uncle's orchard. Moved onto it earlier this year."

"I didn't." His chin dips. "I did hear we'd lost him."

My shoulders rise as I wait for Logan to fire off one of the statements posing as questions that have become familiar over the last few months.

He didn't even tell me he was sick.

It must have happened so fast.

I heard no one in town was invited to the funeral.

Instead, though, I hear Logan say, "He was a good man." I nod, jaw clenched, as my chest pulls tight—that old ache rising again when I try to think about my uncle in the past tense.

"He might not have been around much in the final years, but his death was a huge loss for the valley," I find myself saying. It's easier to recite the lines I've taught myself than to give voice to anything deeper. "My uncle's legacy will outlive him for generations."

Logan tilts his head. "But it's also a huge loss for you. You and Martin . . . I remember how close you two were."

"Right," I say, without letting myself remember it with him. I cough into my hand. "So, June mentioned a fire?"

He blinks but doesn't question my abrupt non sequitur. "Lost both the shop and my apartment."

"The shop?" I ask.

Another infinitesimal recalibration. "For woodworking."

A breeze moves over us, fluttering the edge of my pin tuck dress against my knees.

"You're a carpenter."

"Family business and all."

Not only did Logan stay in Apple Valley, but he became a carpenter.

A second breath-hijacking surprise.

How many times did we lie with our backs in the clover-pocked grass, gazing up at shifting clouds, and imagine our futures? How many times did we take turns on that tire swing, whispering about our dreams between swings of the creaking rope?

Up.

My mom would finally let me stay in one place for more than a year at a time. I could belong somewhere.

Down.

She'd let me stay in *Apple Valley*.

Up.

Logan would get an email back from a shared artists' residence. He'd have paints and canvases in a sunny studio in a big city.

Down.

One day, he'd see his name on the wall of a gallery.

Unlike my dreams, this wasn't supposed to be a fantasy. It was meant to be his future.

I search Logan's face for a hint of regret, but his flat-lipped expression betrays nothing. It's another subtle difference, that guardedness. Or maybe we're just strangers now and I don't know how to read him. Either way, I can't ask what I want to know. "And you're looking for a place to stay?"

He nods. "Apparently my insurance company is facing some backlog. The investigators keep hinting that the settlement process will be lengthy."

"Right, good." I kick myself. "Shit, I mean that's terrible."

But Logan, still unfazed, nods as if to say, *Go on.*

"Well, good because I might have a solution? I'm looking for pickers. I know I should have found someone a while ago, Val keeps saying so, but the truth is I don't have much money to pay so I didn't think it would be possible to—" I cut myself off, grimacing. I'm rambling. I ramble when I'm nervous. "Anyway, June mentioned you might appreciate having a different place to live. We could trade."

On cue, Teddy lets out another shrill, high-pitched wail and June tries to soothe him with enthusiastic cooing noises. Logan has gone still, but for his fingers that open and close on one hand.

When he still doesn't speak, I add, "You'd be welcome to stay at the house as long as you want. I'd just need your help in the orchard for a few hours a day. Early mornings and hard work, but . . . You get the idea. What do you think?"

Logan rubs at the back of his neck. There's a shift in his neutral expression. The lightness in his eyes has darkened into something I can only describe as wary. It's the same face he made when his dad unveiled a new logo decal on the family's truck.

"Much more professional, don't you think?" I heard his dad

ask as they stood in front of the new words: *Wright and Son*. "Really instills a sense of continuity and trust."

In front of me now, Logan swallows in the exact way he did when his dad patted him on the shoulder. There's something strangely surreal about this moment. Although I can read the emotion with almost perfect clarity, fourteen years have erased all context to tell me what could be going on in his head. It's like being able to hum the melody of a song without knowing any of the words.

"On the farm," he says, as though this is meaningful.

"Right. Is there a problem with the orchard?"

"I have some—" He clears his throat, shifts his weight. "I haven't been there since before."

"Before?"

"Since I was eighteen."

"I see." I have no idea what he's talking about. "Well, is there anything I can do to convince you? For example, I can assure you there isn't a single crying baby in earshot. In fact, in the evenings, it's so quiet you can hear the frogs in the creek." Not just quiet. Silent. "And you can stay as long as you want. You could even move in now. Harvest won't start for almost a month, and early fall on the orchard is downright languid."

Logan's fingers tap on the counter, but at least he looks like he's considering. "I only need a place until my insurance money comes through. They're saying it could be around two months."

"That's no problem," I assure him. "We'll have the bulk of the work done by then. And any help you can give in the meantime would be extremely appreciated."

Still, he hesitates. "Let me think about it."

A desperate feeling claws up my throat. I don't want to push him too hard or demand to know what happened—I'm well aware of how it feels to have people ask questions with uncomfortable answers. But, at the same time, I want to give myself a fighting chance. June's nephew was my last lead. And Val's warnings keep pounding through my mind.

"Do you want to maybe think about it on the farm?" I ask. "Might be easier to do with frogs and silence instead of a crying baby."

His eyebrows rise. "A trial run?"

"Yeah, exactly. Come back to the orchard, see how you feel about it. If you don't want to be there, you can leave at any time, no hard feelings."

Logan considers this for long enough that I wonder if I've offended him. Long enough that a guy in a puffy vest pauses to study the chalkboard menu and, when Logan doesn't greet him, moves on.

Before I have a chance to wonder what June might think about that, he says, "All right."

"All right?"

"All right, let's do a trial run."

My lips lift. "Yeah?"

"I can be there tomorrow."

And for the first time in weeks, my chest unknits. "As early as you'd like. I get up with the sun."

Chapter Three

The next morning, as the sun gilds the white-capped mountain, I shove a wide-brimmed hat low on my forehead and tug on a pair of boots underneath a dress. That first pull of damp early autumn air hits my lungs as I step into the rows. Dew catches the sunlight in sparkling prisms and the scents of soil and pine waft past me on the next gust of wind.

These early mornings in the rows feel both like a solemn duty and a heady privilege. Not for the practical reason I'm out here (surveying for problems), but rather because every corner of this land holds my roots.

There's the row of trees I helped plant when I was in fifth grade on a rare spring break that Mom let me visit. I still remember the smell—fresh rain on warm dirt—and the formidable weight of the post driver in my small hands. At the time, the root stock barely reached my temple and I could scarcely imagine a day that these trees would rival the barn. Now? They arch above me like summer antlers, casting dappled shadows over the same patch of ground where I once knelt.

And here's the stump where I tripped and scraped my elbow. I still have the half-moon scar where Uncle Martin pressed a Bob the Builder Band-Aid before rubbing a callused thumb against my cheek.

"They've marked you," he said. "Just like you've marked them."

I ducked my face, hiding the tears shining on my cheeks. "Like we're hurting each other?"

Uncle Martin pressed a knuckle to my chin and lifted my eyes to his, studying me without flinching from my tears or brushing them away. "Maybe sometimes," he said. "Love often does that. But no. I meant the trees will always know you've been here." He gently tapped the spot that would eventually become my scar. "And you'll always know they've been with you."

I'm still rubbing the raised skin at my elbow, my heart heavy with his absence, when I hear the rumble of tires against gravel. Shielding my eyes from the rising sun, I find a cloud of dust kicking up behind a clean truck with red paint.

I jog out to the driveway and Logan rolls down the window, leaning a tanned forearm on the sill.

"Morning," he says.

He's trimmed his beard since yesterday. More of his face is visible and it's unfairly good—the line of his jaw sharper, his lips easier to read. One side of that mouth hitches higher. His familiar half-crooked smile, framed by the sweep of my trees, triggers something deep and primal inside my brain.

Oh. It's *you.*

"You're here early," I say, lifting my hat just enough to slide my fingers underneath and push my curls off my face. "Calling my bluff?"

"I know better than to think you'd joke about these trees."

"Good." I grin. "Farmers don't mess around about sunrises. It's in the standard operating procedures."

Logan's eyes move to my knees, the slice of exposed skin just between the hem of my flowy midi dress and the top of my boots. "And are florals part of those procedures, too?"

I gesture at my hem. "This is what we call a 'temporary modification to protocol.'"

For most of my life, I've worn clothes that blended in—when you're new to a place, the goal is not to stand out any more than you already do. Even though I stayed for years in Florida, I kept the same wardrobe of beiges and neutrals, partly because it was what I had and partly because I worried other people would find it jarring if I started wearing polka dots.

On the orchard, my attire has always been as loud as I've wanted.

It started the day I found a vintage dress in the back of a closet—possibly something that had belonged to my mom or, more likely, my grandmother. Tentatively, I asked if I could have it and Uncle Martin clapped his hands and told me, "Wear it now if you want!"

"But we need to work," I said.

He guffawed. "Who's going to care? The trees?"

That year for my birthday—in July, so I nearly always got to spend it on the orchard—he bought me four more dresses. And I never went back to pants.

"Ali," Logan says. "Did you grow up to be a lawyer?"

"Consultant, actually," I say.

He studies me. It's the same unbroken concentration he used to bestow on his notebooks when his parents called out measurements, or on his sketchbook as he frowned at a curling leaf, half shadowed in dappled light.

"Unexpected," he says without elaborating.

I cross my feet and lean against a tree branch to steady myself. "Did you have something else in mind?"

"I've pictured you in all sorts of careers," Logan says. "But none of them quite fit."

And there's something about the way he says this—*I've pic-*

tured you—that makes my next breath feel sharper in my lungs. Maybe because I've pictured him in a thousand lives, too. Although none of them were here in Apple Valley.

"And how about as a farmer who gets up at dawn and confuses the neighbors by wandering around her orchard in a sundress and boots?"

Once more, his gaze drags downward, tracing the A-line of my dress, and pausing briefly at my waist. Heat trails in the wake of this path.

"Yes," he says evenly. "I can picture that one just fine."

My insides curl like I'm that leaf, half-baked in sunlight. I clear my throat. "Want me to take you back to the house? Or are you hungry? I got some extra scones at the farmer's market yesterday."

Now his gaze clears my shoulders, pinging down the rows that lead to the barn and the farmhouse beyond it. His expression changes again, shifting from the crooked smile to a quiet wariness. I've noticed this too has become more pronounced with age: Logan takes his time to think. He never answers a question, even a simple one, until he's examined it from every angle.

His energy firms, like he's readying to yank a splinter out of his palm.

"How about company, instead?" he asks. "With the wandering."

"That works, too."

After Logan parks his truck in the grass, we start down the nearest row. Side by side, we steer around the sprinklers, boots crunching over the occasional dry leaf and snapped twig.

As we angle between branches, I find myself searching Logan for all the details I used to know by heart: the faintly metallic smell of graphite that clung to his shirts. The ink stains that never fully left his fingertips. His quick, easy smile. A million particularities I thought I'd left behind when I moved to Alaska.

After I piled into my mom's station wagon, Logan and I planned never to talk again. By then, I'd already learned long-distance relationships always have a way of fading. Still, it took only a few eerie twilight evenings in that strange new home for me to slip up and call. Logan answered after a single ring.

At first, our conversations flowed as easily as the orchard's south-side creek—we could sit on the phone for hours, usually talking, sometimes just listening to each other exist. But over the weeks that followed, something shifted. He started taking hours, sometimes days, to respond to my texts. When he answered my calls, he'd tell me he needed to go ten minutes later. When we managed to talk for more than a few minutes, Logan was quiet and withdrawn.

The distance was pulling him away, that much was clear. I was too familiar with how miles can erode just about everything, not to notice. So, I hastened the inevitable. I stopped texting so much and started letting some of his calls go unanswered. Within a few weeks, we lapsed into complete silence.

Now he's here again, carefully setting his boots to avoid the sprinklers and the occasional fallen pear, sparing me a quick sidelong glance as I direct him up a new row. When I try to catalogue him, I find more differences than similarities to the boy I once knew. He's much taller than me—I still have to tip up my chin to make eye contact with him, just the way I remember. But his posture is straighter, his hands clean of ink, his smile slower to come. Despite these tangibles, something indefinable makes Logan's presence feel like a barometer change. Or like hearing a song I swore I'd stopped playing. One I haven't listened to in years but with a baseline that yanks me back to moments long forgotten.

"So," I say, sidestepping to avoid the circular spray from a sprinkler, which still manages to fleck my knees from afar. "I have to admit I lured you into this stroll under false pretenses."

Logan glances at me. "Did you."

A question without a question mark. I like that he still does that.

"We're not wandering. We're looking for unusual pears."

"As in, a new variety?"

"As in, there's this white stuff on some of them. Like a coating? I'd like to figure out what it is."

Yesterday, after I got home from the farmer's market, I noticed more of those affected pears. At the time, I shrugged it off with Val's excuse—likely the sprayers. We use kaolin clay, a natural pest deterrent that leaves a white, powdery coating that bugs don't like but washes off for consumers. Blake was in charge of running the sprayer this summer. He could have gotten distracted and ended up with too much on some of the pears.

I didn't think more of it until late last night, when unsettled weather rolled through the orchard. Lying in bed, I found myself kicking my sweaty sheets and twisting through snippets of involuntary thoughts, the kind conjured only in the liminal wilderness between sleep and wake. Blake and Liv. Picking strategies. Val's warnings about the farm's financial situation. Somewhere along the way, my jostling thoughts landed on those unusual pears again.

And then my eyes flew open wide as it hit me: The pattern doesn't make sense for spray. In addition to helping with the bugs, kaolin clay is used to protect the fruit from sun damage, so I specifically instructed Blake to run the sprayer on the southern slopes and in the corners. But Val and I were in the interior of a north-facing row when we saw that whitish film first. And Blake might have many flaws, but the man follows directions like a caboose clinging to a train car.

"I'm no arborist," Logan says, as he lifts a branch away from his face and stoops out from under a canopy. "But 'mysterious white pear disease' sounds uncomfortably like the beginning of a movie that ends in widespread crop failure and space exploration to save humanity."

I chuckle as I squint up into the nearby branches. "I suspect this is a lot more mundane. Irrigation water and pesticide sprays can leave a similar-looking residue."

"But you don't think that's what it is."

"No," I admit. "I don't think that's what it is."

"What, then?"

The truth is, I don't know. What I do know is that if Uncle Martin were here, he'd tell me to try to listen. "The fruit will talk, you know," he once said, a pear balanced on his knee as he rooted through his deep pockets, pulling out handfuls of seeds and twine until he landed on a paring knife he called *flicker*. He scowled at a branch above our heads, as though about to admonish it. "Sometimes they prattle so much you'd wish they'd clam up."

"Like aloud?" I asked, back ramrod straight as I leaned forward, watching him carve off a shiny slice of fruit.

His head cocked, that wide-brimmed hat dusting over one eye, and I thought he looked a bit like he was considering whether or not to let me in on a secret. "Tell me, Ali. How do you know a high-quality fruit?"

"Size, color, sugar content," I said straightaway.

"Good." He handed the slice of pear to me. "And what can go wrong?"

The better question was what couldn't go wrong, but my uncle wouldn't have wanted to hear me being so pessimistic. "Disease. Fungus. Equipment failure. Late frost. Sunburn. Pests."

A pleased nod. "And . . . ?"

"Hail," I said, leaving the worst for last.

Hail is a death sentence for fruit.

He tweaked my nose. "There you have it. That's how the orchard talks. You just have to listen."

"I'm worried about a disease," I say to Logan now. "Or maybe a fungus."

Although voicing this feels so at odds with our surroundings—the sparrows rustling in overhead branches, a chirr of crickets accelerating as the sun climbs, the dusty smell of sunbaked bark on a row of trees my grandmother planted when she was a teenager. How could a place this beautiful—this *steady*—possibly have something unseen going wrong?

"What diseases turn pears white?" Logan asks.

"Powdery mildew. *Maybe* pear rust. It could also be something else, something new. Val is always saying— You remember her?"

"No one could forget Val. Your aunt, right?"

I nod. "Not biologically, but yeah. Val was my uncle's forewoman, her dad was my grandfather's foreman. She knows this land just as well as anyone with the name Reid. Better, actually. Anyway, Val's always reminding me that the valley is constantly turning up new diseases. Climate change and all."

Logan's lips firm and he lifts a low-hanging branch for me to pass under. As I do, I'm bathed in his clean scent, the proximity of his features. His probing eyes. Strong jaw. Barrel-wide chest. It's unfair how attractive he's gotten in the last fourteen years. No one should be allowed to age this well.

"Why does 'some new disease brought to us by climate change' still sound like the beginning of that science fiction movie?" he asks.

I lift a shoulder. "Nah. If one of America's crops ends up screwing over humanity, my money's on corn or soybeans."

"Not a fan of commodity farming, then?"

I snort. "'Farming' isn't the right word for what they do. It's basically just data entry with dirt."

Logan chuckles and I grin back at him, but as I turn, I nearly run headlong into the barn. My entire body freezes as pleasant orchard rhythms are choked by memories.

Moving through the broken door, hanging loose on its hinges. The dark shadows resolving to hay bales as my eyes adjusted. A squeak, and the clicking of paws as a furry body, streaked with white, scuttled across weather-stained floorboards. And then—

I swallow, fighting to erase the images along with whatever is showing on my face.

This story isn't serving you, I remind myself like I'm a small-team leader resisting a digital transformation initiative. Abruptly, I turn to Logan.

But he's not looking at me.

He's staring at the barn, too.

His eyes have gone hard, big hands limp by his sides. Is it because the barn looks so different now? We've had some hard weather since that summer, and my uncle didn't have the funds to keep up on repairs.

But no. Logan's expression is deeper than that. Like he's seen a ghost. A ghost that just hit him in the face with a folding chair.

Chapter Four

Logan?" I ask tentatively. "Did something— Is everything all right?"

Logan scrubs a hand against his beard, moves it to massage the back of his neck. "Not exactly."

I'm officially too tempted not to ask. "Is there something wrong with the barn?"

Nails still raking, he glances at me as though deciding something, then blows out a long breath. "You remember my parents built it, right?"

"Of course. And you helped."

"Barely. I had only started learning at that point. That summer we were here, it's . . ." He shakes his head, clearing it. "My family built that barn fourteen years ago, and then my mom was gone. The last time I saw her was the day we finished."

My hand flies up to my mouth before I have the good sense to drop it. Holy shit. I have no idea what I was expecting him to say, but this was certainly not it. "She *disappeared*?"

"She left," he corrects.

"What happened?" I whisper.

I wonder if Logan will answer. His eyes are hard, his expression closed off in a way I never saw when we were kids. But then he says, "I don't know. Maybe my dad did but . . . Well, he was never much good at talking about hard things and he only got worse about that once she left. And my brothers were too young. They barely remember her at this point, let alone know her reasons. So, I never found out."

"I'm so sorry." Suddenly my own barn-related trauma feels mild. "That's awful."

He nods, once and sharp, like the acknowledgment can shake it off. "Anyway. Now you know why I've hesitated about coming back. I should've told you yesterday."

"You didn't owe me an explanation."

We stand for a long moment, still facing the barn, me waiting for— What? Him to turn his back and return the way we came? To start searching for my strange pears again?

"Would you rather silence or a distraction?" I ask.

His eyes cut to mine and he considers. Then he says, "I would take a distraction."

"Okay." I flash a smile. "A month ago, I was engaged."

He double takes. "I didn't know that."

"Yeah, well, I haven't gotten to the distracting part yet."

An eyebrow rises. "Go on."

"I moved here earlier this year with Blake, my fiancé, ex-fiancé now, and my best friend, Liv. That all happened really fast. My uncle was only diagnosed last summer—pancreatic cancer. Just after Thanksgiving, he started palliative care . . . and he died in February."

Even living it, I struggled to keep up with the speed at which things evolved. After his diagnosis last summer, he tried to talk to me about taking over the orchard, but I shut it down. It all felt far too soon. When I visited in the early fall and found him still laughing, I let myself cling to relief. But by Christmas he had stopped chemo and the inevitable settled in my chest the way frost hardens soil: I would be the next Reid to farm this land, long before I was ready.

Logan's fingers twitch and for a sudden, irrational moment I wonder if he's going to reach for me. "I heard there was no funeral."

"Martin wanted to keep it small."

In fact, tiny. Just me and Val. As far as I know, even my mom wasn't invited. Uncle Martin wouldn't tell me why, although I overheard Val arguing with him about it.

"Damn it to hell," she said, punctuating the curse word with the bang of a fist against a table. "They'll come if you ask them. The whole valley will show up tomorrow if you give them the say-so."

He sighed. "There's no point, Valentina. You know they won't. Can't."

"Martin Charles Reid, don't you dare try to distract me with that name. That's all a crock of shit and you kn—"

"Val, please." He sounded tired all the time in those days, but this time there was a heavy finality in his tone. "I don't want to fight about this with you again. Not anymore."

I shake my head, setting aside the memory. "I gave notice at my firm a month before he died. We didn't have much time left together and there was a lot we needed to work out. Honestly, I was pretty prepared to come here alone. But, somehow, Blake and Liv wanted to move, too."

Taking over my uncle's farm wasn't part of Blake's five-year plan or his fifteen-year plan for that matter, but when I nervously brought it up, he paced around the room, hands thrust into pockets, before declaring, "We've lived our whole lives on a schedule. So, what if this one time we threw it all away?"

Liv took no convincing at all—in fact, I think she was the one who first proposed coming along. It was in the final month of Martin's life, and she was only here for a weekend, but she insisted I take a break from peppering my uncle with questions to spend an afternoon on Main Street. As we strolled in silence, the world seemed to pare down to essentials: the silver crust of ice along the curbs, the fogged window of a bakery glowing gold against the gray afternoon, the faint smell of woodsmoke from a chimney.

We stopped to admire the scene above the snow-dusted rooftops, where two mountains rose sharply against the pale winter sky. Liv grabbed my hand and shout-whispered, "Ali. This is the place we should spend the rest of our lives."

That promise—that possibility of a shared future—was the steeling thought that got me through the wreck of grief in the weeks that followed.

Logan's looking at me now like the barn has stopped existing. At least I've accomplished that distraction.

"And then?" he encourages.

"And then, a few months later, I got home early from a trip to get irrigation supplies and I thought I heard an animal in the barn."

I'd nearly cleared the red siding when I paused. The wind kicked up, and the rafters groaned, low and ominous. Another sound spiked the air—the telling scrape of claws on wood that could have been anything from a raccoon to a possum.

Trying to save the floorboards and picking bags, I tiptoed inside.

My eyes adjusted to the dark.

And there they were. Against the hay bales.

Two pairs of work boots, staggered. Big boot. Small boot. Big boot. Small boot. Liv's cracked fingernail paint digging into Blake's shoulders. His hand pressed into the straw next to her arching neck. Her porcelain cheeks rising red.

She moaned. And my world toppled.

"I found them together," I say now, and because it seems like the best way to handle it, I smile.

Logan takes an almost involuntary step toward me. "And you're still here."

"Yeah."

"You never thought about leaving?"

My fingers find my half-moon scar. "I could never abandon these trees."

Logan considers this, something unreadable passing over his expression. "Well, thank you."

I drop my hand. "For?"

"Using all that as a distraction for my benefit."

I let out a humorless laugh. "Only because what happened to you is *much* worse. My thing is practically a stroll through a park in comparison."

He frowns. "My scars don't cancel out your pain."

I force another smile. "It was for the best, honestly. Now I have all the fridge space I want and I never have to worry about my antique water tank running out of hot."

I wait for his relief, that emotional reprieve that always happens when I've turned a conversation from *serious and heavy* to *light and manageable*. But, instead, his gaze holds mine, like he's searching for something hidden in the freckles that splash across my cheeks, the bridge of my nose. My neck tingles with awareness, a feeling like I'm not just being watched, but seen.

Then Logan says, "You didn't use to do that."

"Do what?"

"Smile over the pain."

My head feels light. "It helps, though."

Logan's jaw works like he might say something else, but he doesn't. He just nods. "Okay, then. If it helps."

This conversation feels jagged, the same sensation as running a hand against an old board and finding splinters embedded in my palm. My chest screams for an escape.

So, I shift away, forge back toward the tree line, searching again for those strange pears with enough intensity that it will let me forget, let me—

There. A spot of white in the leaves. My shoulders hitch to my ears as I careen toward the unusual pear, then pluck it from its stem, turning it over in my hands, brow furrowing.

"This is it," I say as Logan shadows my shoulder.

It has the same coating as the one Val noticed, but thicker. So thick, the fruit's skin is overly smooth, like it's been dipped in icing. In my hands, sunlight runs across the white coating, and it shifts in color, going deeper.

I scrape my thumbnail across the surface. Again, the coating doesn't budge.

"Hey," Logan says. "Here's more."

A few paces away, he's gazing up into a canopy dotted with white. A splotch here, a splat there. Like a careless artist tossed a bucket of paint into the branches.

"Holy crap," I whisper.

"Powdery mildew?" he asks.

I shake my head, like, *I don't know.* It's definitely time to bring in Val. A call is unlikely to go through out here, at least not without a lot of skipped words, but a text should be fine. So, I swipe open the camera on my phone and snap a photo.

Look at this, I type. Like the one we saw a few days ago, but thicker.

The message whooshes away.

"And here too," Logan says.

I hurry toward him, and we peer into the thick canopy. The breeze stirs the leaves and high up—strangely—a pear gleams. It's not matte like it should be or waxy like the others. At the base, that coating is shiny, like a pearl.

"What the hell?" I mutter.

My phone buzzes. **That the only one?**

No, I type, frowning. **Many. Different trees, too.**

Her dots bounce immediately. **Need to see for myself. Be over in a sec.**

"Can you reach it?" I ask Logan as I tuck my phone back into the shaft of my boot.

The pear with the pearly underside sits well above my arm's length, but Logan is much taller. Yet even standing on his toes and reaching, he can't skim it with his fingertips.

"I'll do it," I say when he gives up. I hitch my thumbs skyward as I click my tongue. "You can lift me up."

Logan arches an eyebrow. "Lift you. Like with my hands."

His wide palms have gone still by his sides. And then I'm picturing it—those hands, both unknown and achingly familiar, spanning my waist.

"Right, okay," I stammer out. "Maybe you'd rather not . . . I have a ladder at the—"

He steps toward me, his gaze feathering with mine. "I'll do it. If you want."

Warmth rides up my neck. "That would be easier. Quicker, I mean."

Logan takes another step and suddenly he's towering over me, so close. Close enough to wrap me in his arms. We've been like this before. We've kissed and touched before. In the trees. Next to the burn pile. Under the old equipment shed during a thunderstorm, my shirt clinging to my back, his breath warm against my cheek. He used to trace the freckles on my shoulder like he was mapping an escape from Apple Valley. Once, we shared a pear from cold storage, so perfectly preserved that juice dripped down my chin and onto my forearm. Logan licked it off my wrist before kissing me, grinning like he couldn't help himself.

But that was a different Ali. A different Logan.

Not this version of me, the adult with a college degree and a former client list and a broken engagement.

And not *this* Logan, with a rough scratch of beard, a slow smile, and lines around his eyes.

Still, I lift my arms and he reaches toward my hips. But then, as though thinking better of it, his hands rise to my waist, still hovering inches away.

"I, um." He takes in a breath. "Please tell me how I should touch you."

Heat singes my cheeks and a tingle traces the circumference of my waist. "I can . . ." I set a hand on his shoulder. It's practically solid under my touch, and noticeably wider than I remember. "Okay?"

"Yeah," he breathes.

Slowly, Logan squats and wraps an arm around my hips. My heart jackknifes as he squeezes close. Thank god he's not looking at my face right now because I'm pretty sure my eyes would give away every one of my tortured thoughts.

"I'm going to stand now," he says.

I nod in hurried little motions that he must see because he's looking up at me now, and those golden flecks in his eyes are practically glowing.

He presses higher. I wouldn't say that I am anywhere near weightless, but my mass doesn't seem to bother him because soon he's fully upright. Ignoring the squeeze in my chest, I reach as high as I can, skimming the smooth underside of the pearly pear.

The branch wobbles, the fruit darting in and out of my fingertips.

"A little more?" I say.

Logan's shoulder sways, but he presses higher. With shaking fingers, I manage to grab hold of the pear. It glints as it snaps free.

"Got it!" I exclaim.

Logan curses, then staggers.

We both fall. He reaches for me, grasping for my shoulders, but it's too late. I land on my back, Logan on top of me.

"Shit, I'm so sorry!" I nearly shout at him. "I— "

I stop short when I realize his hand is cradling the back of my head, his nose hovering just above mine.

Neither of us moves.

We're chest to chest, mouth to mouth. As close as we were that summer afternoon when Logan yanked me behind a stack of picking bins to avoid getting assigned another job by his mom. We ended up pressed together in the shadows, breathless and still as we waited for her to pass. So close I could feel his heartbeat knock against mine.

Just as it did that day, Logan's gaze travels from my eyes to my mouth. I feel his thumb twitch against the back of my head, a shadow of a stroke.

My heart thumps: once, twice. And, oh no. It's been fourteen years. I ended an engagement only a month ago. I'm barely holding the line against an avalanche of grief. All of that should speed bump my heart's reckless careening down these memory-slicked tracks. Yet the way I used to feel about Logan—that intense bleating in my teenage heart—seems to be pure muscle memory, just as familiar as riding a bicycle or driving a tractor.

Because all I can think about is how he smells like the orchard: musk and earth and something just on the edge of sweetness. All I can think about are his lips.

A rumbling sound reverberates through the trees. We both twist to find a Subaru peeling up the soft driveway.

"My aunt's here," I say, throat tight.

Logan swallows and pulls himself away.

Chapter Five

Show it to me," Val demands as she hurtles toward us, ignoring the booted limp that's threatening to slow her warpath. Her hair is a wild mess and damp at the ends, which I assume means she skipped blowing it dry before she careened over here.

She smacks me in the chest with a book called *Arbory Health in the Pacific Northwest* and wrestles the offending piece of fruit from Logan. Her scowl deepens as she turns it over, catching the pearlescent tint in the thick, white coating.

"Definitely strange, right?" I ask. "Like for sure this isn't irrigation water or residue from a pesticide."

She doesn't answer right away, still too absorbed by the offending fruit. "This is the first you're seeing this?"

"Well, no. You and me saw that one odd pear last week."

"That was—" She cuts herself off. Swallows. "Was that the first you saw of it? Last week?"

"I . . . Yes? But I haven't been out here as much as I should have been in the last month. Why do you ask?"

She mutters, not by way of answer but more to herself, "'Cause it turns out I might have been wrong about something."

"What do you mean?" I ask.

She doesn't answer, just keeps her lips pressed tight. I don't like the look in her eyes. It reminds me too much of the face she made when Uncle Martin told me he needed a CT scan. Val was hovering in the background of our video call, shooting sharp glances into the screen, even as Uncle Martin assured me that everything was going to be okay.

I believed him for a long time—well past the time he stopped believing it.

"So, you know what it is?" Logan asks.

Val startles and squints up at him like she's just registering his presence. "Logan Wright. How you doing, kid?"

He nods. "Shouldn't complain."

"And your brothers?"

"Both healthy."

They watch each other for a beat longer and I'm reminded of what Val told me when I texted her last night to say I might have found a third picker. I'd expected her to be elated, but instead she wrote: He's moving onto the farm? Not sure that's a good idea.

Why not? I asked. He needs a place to live and you said yourself we needed another set of hands. It's not for sure yet, though. He hasn't committed.

She didn't respond to that, and I wrote it off as Val's inherent skepticism of change and new people.

She tugs fingers through her damp hair, pulling one section into an upright spike. "Haven't seen anything like this before. Show me the rest?"

We trudge back the way we came, Logan and I a few paces in front, slow enough that Val's booted gait doesn't grow too labored. Fortunately, with my aunt here and my new growing anxiety about this mysterious disease, I can't process the complicated and possibly inappropriate emotions that came up when Logan landed on top of me.

Instead, I focus on Val, who is circling the first set of affected trees like a prowling jungle cat. She selects a piece of waxy fruit from one of the lower branches, sniffs it, and scrapes a thumbnail along the waxy coating.

"How bad is it?" I ask.

"Don't know yet." She snatches her book from me and braces it against her thigh as she trips through pages. "Quit interrupting my process."

For a while we continue like that—Logan and I watching as Val gathers choice pieces, discarding most to the base of the trees but keeping some bundled in one arm. Occasionally, she fishes a pocketknife out of her fanny pack to cut through the wax coating of a pear and sniff its insides.

Finally, what feels like an age later, Val straight-arm points toward the farmhouse and shouts, "We're done here!"

In the dining room, my aunt arrays her pears on the white linen runner. The one on the leftmost end has a waxy surface, like it was sprayed to keep fresh. The one on the far right is the one Logan and I picked: unusually smooth and firm. Under the dining room lights, it remains solidly matte. The ones in the middle, I realize, hover between—dull and pale in spots with a faint granular sheen.

Val sinks into an antique chair and steeples her fingers. "What are your theories?"

I take a chair across from her as I run through every fruit malady Uncle Martin ever lectured me about. His lessons weren't exactly linear, especially when it came to diseases and pests. Until I was a teenager, I thought powdery mildew was "ghost dust" and I hadn't understood that we are the only farmers who call aphids "juice weasels." Still, even as I plumb the deepest recesses of my mind, I can't think of any disease or pest that would turn pears pearly white.

"Maybe a new disease or fungus," I say finally. "Something we've never seen before."

Val nods. "Unfortunately, I think that's right."

"And there's nothing like this in your book?" Logan asks from his station where he's leaning against the doorjamb, stretching out his long body.

"No," she says as she digs a thumbnail into the fruit with the hardest shell but barely leaves an indent. "But I'm thinking we might find something about this somewhere else."

"Where?" I ask.

Val pushes herself to her feet but instantly winces and slams a fist against the table. I rush forward to support her elbow, but she glares at me until I back off. From his side of the room, Logan's eyes shift between us.

Val blows out a breath, looking down at her boot. "Might have overdone that a bit."

"What do you need?" I ask.

Her eyes lift toward the ceiling.

"Your uncle's journals. He kept careful notes on the land for years. We've had our fair share of afflictions around here and if this is something he saw before, he'd've made note of it. Maybe he even has a remedy."

"Of course," I say, straightening. How many times did I see Uncle Martin traipse through the trees with a leather-bound journal tucked under his armpit? Or scribble on some pages from his perch on the John Deere? They were packed with his observations, the same way his pockets were stuffed with twine, buttons, and anything that could someday be useful. If there's an answer to this problem, it will be in those pages.

"Where would they be?" Logan asks, pushing off his wall.

"The attic," Val says. "Unless it's cleared out?"

I shake my head. Blake, Liv, and I barely had the bandwidth to go through the generations of belongings in the house's actual living space. The attic and basement are untouched, except for the boxes of Martin's belongings that I crammed on top of the others.

"Good. In a box somewhere, then. Probably. God knows what all he was hoarding."

"We can get it," I say.

She frowns at her boot again, rolling her lips between her teeth. "Go on. But bring them straight down, you hear?"

"Of course."

"Ali," Val warns. "I'm not messing around. Do not read those journals without me."

She has her jaw set in that protective way of hers. It's the same energy she brought that time I overheard my uncle arguing with a neighbor about a Berkshire pig that had wandered onto our orchard. Even though Martin had been caring for the pig for months—named her Daisy Mae and dressed her up in a hot-pink harness—the neighbor insisted she be returned for "processing." Martin, floppy hat wobbling with each wave of an arm, tried to argue that he and Daisy Mae had become fast friends! And friends simply do not let their friends be murdered. Just as the neighbor had grabbed the pig by her pink harness and started to tug her away, Val marched up, clapped a steadying hand on my uncle's shoulder, and planted herself squarely in the neighbor's path, finger pressed to the man's chest. She growled out something inaudible. The man's confident sneer faltered, and he released the pig.

"I promise," I say, more serious this time. "We won't read the journals without you."

The creak of ancient wood fills the silence as Logan and I scale the stairs. The attic smells of earthy musk and something decidedly less pleasant. Mildew? A caked window lets in only a pitiful glow of afternoon light. When Logan tugs on a string pull, the ceiling light flickers alive and casts a yellowish sheen over the towers.

And now I remember why I haven't been up here since the early spring—in the first few days that Blake and Liv joined me in the house. Blake dove straight into making checklists of everything we needed to do to transform my uncle's house into ours, and assigned me and Liv with the attic. We skittered up these steps, crashed into each other at the top, and our mouths dropped open.

Then Liv dusted off her hands and said, "Well, this looks like a problem for future us." We laughed, traipsed back downstairs, and slammed the attic door closed.

Now, they've left, and it's a problem for only me.

I grimace and push off thoughts of Blake and Liv. Unfortunately, I can't push off what's staring me in the face. This attic is cluttered and not in a cute way. Narrow paths carve through towers of boxes sagging with mold. Electronics are piled on top of furniture parts—a headboard resting on a desk, chair legs sticking out at odd angles like broken limbs. Dust-covered bins are overflowing with cords and gadgets that belong in a museum.

I'd like to blame the clutter on the four—now five—generations of Reids who lived in this home, but the truth is that my uncle and I have always shared a key characteristic. If a box looks too full or a pile too difficult to sort, we just . . . don't.

To my side, Logan's shoulders are tight, hands stuffed into his pockets. His gaze has snagged on something fluffy and white, which is either an old wedding veil or some kind of nest. I shudder. My brain is screaming at me to run back down those stairs, to leave this entire mess behind.

"Shit," I say helplessly.

Logan's mouth firms before he squats in front of a set of boxes wedged between the wall and an antique crib. "What do those journals look like, then?"

I grimace as he lifts a moldy lid. "No, this is so disgusting. You don't have to do that. I'm not even sure *I* want to do that."

He grunts. "I get my hands dirty for a living, Ali. You're not scaring me off with some old boxes."

"*Moldy* boxes," I correct. "And there are about six hundred places those journals could be."

Logan's long fingers work over the contents of his box—chipped coffee mugs interspersed with string lights and plaid bedsheets. When he slides the lid closed, he looks up at me. "Now there are five hundred and ninety-nine."

I chuckle and feel myself relax minutely.

"Okay," I say as I lift onto my tiptoes next to him, reaching high for a box precariously teetering atop a tower of junk. "They're brown leather. With a strap to— *Aaargh.*"

Something dark splashes down my arm, painting my shoulder and chin and pulling an inhuman sound from my chest. Logan bolts to his feet like I might be in mortal danger, reaching for me just as he notices the sludge on my shoulder.

"Gross," I say meekly as alarm dissolves from his expression, softening into something more like endearment. I try to squeegee my arm with my fingers, but the ooze is as thick as motor oil. "I told you this is *so* gross."

Logan fishes a red handkerchief out of his back pocket and gestures at my wrist. "May I?"

I go still. "You don't have to."

But of its own volition, my arm lifts toward him. Logan smiles softly before reaching for me, taking my wrist in his warm hand. His grip is gentle as he starts to lightly dab at the dark liquid.

"Now you're getting that nice bandana all dirty," I whisper as he scales my arm with his cloth, picking up droplets from my thumb. The line of my forearm. The crease inside my elbow. I shudder.

He hums as he bends closer, scrutinizing his work. "That's what this particular bit of material was made for, you know. Cleaning up messes."

In the feeble overhead light of the attic, his eyes seem darker. The shadow of his beard more pronounced. The rough cut of his jaw and the long line of his throat more angular.

"Still," I say, "this isn't the trial run you signed up for."

He grunts without breaking his concentration.

"Plus," I add, probing, "I know you weren't exactly eager to come back here."

Logan brings the handkerchief to my neck, uses a thumb to gently guide my chin upward. With a delicate sweeping motion, he wipes grime from the underside of my jaw. My heart seems to have lodged itself in the exact spot where his hand is lightly cupping my throat. Another shudder moves through me.

"Being here . . ." he says carefully, "is complicated for me."

I don't know how to read that, especially not with his hands on me in a way that is either completely innocent or, as the trembling of my heart would suggest, entirely indecent. "As bad as you thought?"

He considers as he folds over his handkerchief, then leans back in to work out a stubborn bead from my collarbone. "I've tried to put that part of my life behind me. Coming back here . . . I guess I'm realizing I haven't gotten as much distance as I thought."

"I'm sorry," I say, trying not to sound affected by the brush of his fingers against my clavicle. He's telling me he doesn't want to be here, but all I can think about is the way he gently moves aside the strap of my dress to wipe the top of my shoulder. "I don't want you to do anything that makes you uncomfortable. You can leave right now if—"

"Ali. I'll let you know when I need to leave."

I swallow. "Right. Okay. Thank you."

Still holding my wrist, he looks me over again: my chin, my neck, down the length of my arm. Checking his handiwork. I feel like my entire chest has moved north to my throat. My heart is thundering so loudly I'm sure he can hear it in this deafening quiet. Then Logan clicks his tongue, pleased, and releases me.

"Done," he says, dusting off his hands and easily turning back to searching a new box.

We get back to work in silence, although it takes several minutes for my heart to return to my chest where it belongs. As we search, we're accompanied only by the creak of floorboards and soft thumps of shifting boxes. In the quiet, Logan's words start to register—not just his discomfort about being here, which I still regret imposing on him, but also the differences between what has to have been replaying in his brain since he arrived, versus what's been in mine. Over the last few hours, Logan has probably been singularly focused on his life's central trauma. Meanwhile, my mind has been splatter-painted with our shared memories, kicked up like mud behind the spinning wheels of a tractor. He's been in pain, and I've been thinking about his lips. Embarrassing, really.

The problem, I think, is that past and present have easily blurred for me. Too easily. Logan was my first boyfriend, the first man I ever loved. Although we never said those words to each other, I know that now in retrospect. We have too much emotional residue.

It's possible—likely even—these flares of attraction I keep feeling aren't even real. It's been only a month since Blake and

Liv left me. Maybe what I've been feeling is loneliness. A desire for the comfort of something familiar. Nostalgia.

Besides, given what I now know, I'm not sure how much longer Logan's trial run is going to last. Frankly, I'm surprised he was even willing to try coming back to the orchard.

"Can I ask you something?" I say.

"Go on."

I hesitate. "It's personal."

He glances over his shoulder. "That never used to be a problem for us."

Our eyes meet and that tire swing flashes through my mind so clearly, I can feel the worn rope under my fingertips. Damn, nostalgia sure is a hell of a drug.

I avert my attention to the wooden chest by my feet.

"After high school," I say, "you were supposed to move away."

The floorboard creaks as Logan shifts his weight. "That's right."

"Did you stay because of what happened with your mom?"

He frowns and moves to a new set of boxes, lifting and replacing lids, looking so absorbed I think he isn't going to answer. But then he swallows and says, "When she left, Dad needed help with the business, another set of hands. And my brothers, Andrew and Mason, they were little. Someone needed to help them get dressed in the mornings and brush their teeth at night. Make sure they weren't eating cold cereal for every meal."

I frown, trying to picture teenage Logan putting away his pencils so he could pack lunches and build barns. It's easy to envision. Too easy.

"I'm sure that was a big adjustment for your dad," I say. "I can't imagine losing your wife like that is bearable, let alone easy. But he figured it out eventually, right?"

Logan lets out a hollow laugh. "Not so much. He'd always had this tendency to check out when things got hard. He'd stay out late, sometimes shut himself in the shop for hours. When she first left, I thought maybe, well, at least now Dad would have to stick to the house. But it only got worse. He started disappearing for days at a time. He'd come hours late to our jobs without a word of explanation. Eventually, he stopped showing up entirely. But we still needed money, so he 'retired' and I took over."

I blow out a breath. "Damn, that's not fair."

Logan exhales as he squats, controlled but audible. "I did what I had to do."

"Still," I say, thinking of that sketchbook. His dreams. "You should have been allowed to live your own life. They left you without any choices."

Logan doesn't say anything to that, but he does look at me. His attention is so steady, exacting, I start fumbling with the closed lock of an antique box, just to give myself something else to focus on.

"How about your brothers? Were they able to help?"

"I wanted them to be kids. They're not anymore, of course. Well, at least Andrew isn't. He enlisted in the navy when he turned eighteen. Mason is in college now, PNU in Maplehurst."

"What year?"

"Junior. With the maturity of a kid in braces."

I smile. "And your dad?"

Logan pries open the brass clasps on an old suitcase and sifts through the contents, although it appears to contain only musty wool scarves and bulky, knitted sweaters. "He's gone now, too. Fully. A couple of years ago."

I hardly remember Logan's dad—Ron, I think his name was? Richard, maybe?—even though we met many times that summer. I do remember Uncle Martin was skeptical of him, which was notable because Martin liked everyone except men in tailored suits and animals with sharp claws. There was this one day when

Logan's dad was late with some supplies from Portland, and every time we drove past the barn site in our Gator, we'd spot Logan and his mom, sitting on a stump, waiting.

On the fourth pass, Uncle Martin leaned over and muttered, barely audible over the engine, "Funny how that man never shows up when it matters. Almost like he's got somewhere better to be."

I had no idea what that meant. When I asked, Martin told me he shouldn't have said it.

"I'm so sorry," I say.

Logan lifts a shoulder. "They both left, just in different ways." Before I'm able to respond, he closes the suitcase with a click and glances around like he's looking for something else to focus on. "Tell me about you."

"What about me?" I ask, slightly distracted because I've just found the key to the locked antique chest, inside an envelope and taped at the back. When I click open the chest, I see it's filled with ribbons grayed with age. Odd, I think, to have that locked.

"It's been fourteen years," Logan says. "And all I know is about the last few months."

"Right. Yeah." I lift a ribbon and squint at the date—and, damn, it's a prize from a county fair that's quite literally a hundred years old. "Well, you already know that Mom moved me to Anchorage after that summer. It was supposed to be Fairbanks, but she changed her mind at the last minute."

"Did it ever get any better?"

I arch a surprised eyebrow. "You remember I was unhappy there?"

He scoffs. "Of course I remember."

"I wouldn't blame you if you didn't. Those phone calls were a long time ago and—" And now that I'm thinking about it, that must have happened right around the time his mom left. "And I'm sure you had other things on your mind."

Logan's eyes are dark as he opens the top of a chest, revealing a set of dusty, brightly colored rocks. Almost like gemstones, but too large and slightly dull. Then he says, "That fall, it started snowing in Anchorage in early October, which everyone warned you could happen, but you didn't believe it until you saw it yourself. The nights felt unnaturally long and the days weren't just short, you called them 'feeble.' You said the sun didn't so much 'rise' as it 'hovered along the horizon for a few hours before ducking back under the mountains.' And you were most annoyed by the wildlife. People kept saying it would be exciting, but the neighborhood moose broke your neighbor's porch swing and once you were late for school because he was napping in front of your garage door."

My mouth falls open.

Logan's lips quirk. "I remember it all, Ali."

There's a sharp twang in my chest, like the low ring of a bronze bell. I have to clutch at the broken leg of a four-poster bed to steady myself.

"So," he says into the resulting silence. "Did you eventually learn to enjoy the wildlife like they all said you would?"

I swallow thickly. "I would say I got used to it." The novelty certainly never erased the ache of homesickness I felt at the sight of evergreens instead of pear trees. Or the shot of discomfort when I realized I was the only one wearing a shiny new winter jacket and boots with no traction. "Like how the deer are like rats in Pennsylvania or you'll find alligators sunbathing on golf courses in Florida."

"And after Alaska?"

At my feet, another chest overflows with Christmas lights and a garish array of Santas that would have delighted Liv.

"Mom dragged me to Georgia for junior year," I say, closing the chest and thoughts of Liv with it, "and Florida the year after.

She kept moving, but that one stuck for me. I graduated from high school there, so I stayed for the in-state tuition."

"As warm and sunny as people say?"

"All tanned bellies and sunglasses."

"That why you didn't leave?"

I don't quite know how to answer that. I've kept the door shut on this particular room for a long time. "I stayed because it was easy. And it was sunny all the time. Consistent. Predictable. That makes people happier, I think. Plus, I got a job offer at the firm where I interned, and . . ."

I let myself trail off. The truth is I stayed in Florida partly because I wanted to stick with Blake.

Unlike Liv, who steamrolled into my life in a single afternoon, Blake found his place in my heart slowly, bit by bit and day by day. A game of inches and perseverance. I probably wouldn't have let him in any other way.

We met at orientation in college. With the last names Reid and Reilly, we ended up in the same academic advising group, and we were down the hall from each other in our freshman dorm. After I nearly failed a particularly hard midterm in my Introduction to Microeconomics course, Blake started giving me copies of his pristinely organized notes and extensive deck of flashcards. The year we graduated, we both got internships in the same building: me at the consulting firm on the tenth floor, Blake at a law office on the sixth. Four years after we met, he was still there—a continued, unflagging presence in my life.

We went on our first date after that, when I was finally convinced he had the potential to stick around for the long haul. When we got engaged, I thought the matter was sealed.

How wrong I was.

Instead of finishing my thought, I focus on sliding open a lid on the box of serving dishes with at least four different patterns and, underneath, a a small stack of yellowing envelopes, each addressed to my uncle.

"Anyway." I force a smile, although it instantly makes me self-conscious. I wonder if Logan will call me out on it again.

But, no, he's watching me evenly, one of those broad shoulders braced against a antique rolltop desk.

"So, you stayed there," he says, finishing my thought. "But you belong here."

"Yeah," I say. "Exactly."

I'm tempted to ask whether, at some point, he started feeling like he belonged in Apple Valley. I can't, though. It's far too intimate of a question—a stolen scrap of this stranger that I shouldn't have.

Instead, I ask, "Do you still draw?"

Without answering, Logan slips open the lid to an old Bankers Box in faux wood grain. His face snaps up.

"Hey," he says. "I found those journals."

Chapter Six

With a heavy thud, I let the box drop to the dining room table. Val startles from her seat by the windowsill, where I see she has not been idle. She's got a pocketknife in one hand and a pile of brown leaves accumulating beside six of my house plants. My monstera appears to have been repotted.

"Good work," she says as she dusts soil off her hands and yanks the weathered box across the table. She flings open the lid before stilling, and letting it slowly drop in place again. Then she frowns at me. "I could use a drink."

"Something stronger than water?"

"Black tea, if you've got it."

With a nod, I forge to the kitchen. Logan, perhaps taking the hint that Val wants to be alone with Martin's words, goes to retrieve his bags from the truck.

While I wait for the kettle to boil, I listen to my mountain of unopened voicemails, which is something I should have done days ago when my phone alerted me that my voicemail box was full. I have a couple from my rep at the packing house who, apparently, has been trying to touch base with me for the last few days. I wasn't ready to talk to him until I had better news to share about the crop, and I don't yet know whether Logan is staying, so for now I decide to leave that call unreturned.

I also have a voicemail from Mom, which I received at exactly one o'clock Pacific time. Mom's phone calls arrive with mechanical precision—probably because "Call Ali" is one of her recurring calendar events, sandwiched between oil changes and dental cleanings.

Truthfully, I haven't picked up one of her calls since the breakup. I waited two weeks to tell her what happened, when I could be sure I'd get through the call without crying. Even still, she was silent and wary afterward, as though bracing for the tears I hadn't shed yet. When I didn't disappoint her, she let out a breath and said, "I'm sorry to hear that. When do you think you'll move back to Florida?"

My shoulders hitched. "Why would I move back to Florida?"

Her long silence suggested the answer was obvious. "Or wherever you'd want to be instead."

I squeezed my fingers to the bridge of my nose, flushing with annoyance. She might have hated it on this orchard and hightailed it out of Apple Valley as soon as she was legally allowed, but I'm not like her. I don't abandon a place at every minor inconvenience and displeasure. I don't have such impossibly high standards that I can never be content no matter where I am.

I wanted to tell her: I *choose* to be happy.

"I'm not going anywhere," I said.

Another long pause. "I see."

After a few more minutes of stilted small talk, we hung up.

Standing in the kitchen now, I erase her voicemail without listening beyond the words "Hello, Ali." I already know how the rest would go. *This is your mother. I had a moment free and thought it would be appropriate to try to talk. Please return the call when convenient.*

The phone rolls into the next message, this one from an unknown number.

"Hi, Ali, I miss—"

Adrenaline shoots through my limbs. I panic-drop the phone and it clangs to the bottom of the sink.

"Everything okay?"

I wheel to find Logan in the doorway, a line etched between his brows like he can hear my heart thundering against my rib cage.

I shouldn't be having this violent reaction to someone's voice. Proportional responses are the key to preventing minor issues from escalating into major distractions.

"Yes, I'm . . ." I fish my phone out of the sink, and force on a smile as I use a sleeve to wipe off the screen. "I'm okay."

Clearly this is not convincing because Logan takes two swift steps into the kitchen. "What's going on?"

I grip the counter to keep from flagging. This is not a proportional response. "It's just Liv. She's been texting me a bunch. Calling. I blocked her number and I deleted all my social media accounts because she kept messaging me from new ones. But I guess she used someone else's phone and . . ." I shake my head. "It's not a big deal. I'll just delete it."

Logan's expression darkens, as if a fast-moving storm cloud has rolled over it. "Why would she do that?"

I lift a shoulder, unsure of how best to explain Liv.

I've never been quick to warm up to new people. In college, my closest friends were the ones I'd had the longest—my roommate from freshman year and the one girl I knew from high school, even though we'd barely been more than acquaintances before. It took me years to go through the stages of friendship that most people breezed past in a few months.

Liv steamrolled over all of those stages in an afternoon.

The day we met there was a power outage at my office, and I was sending emails at a coffee shop. She asked to borrow the chair across from me. We started talking and that was it. In the weeks after, she began showing up at my apartment in the evenings, carting plastic bags stacked with squeaking takeout boxes. She'd plop herself down on my secondhand couch, flick on the TV, and start prying open lids. On the weekends, she'd schedule appointments for wine tasting or manicures without asking if I was free. My clothes showed up in her closet. She started introducing herself as my best friend.

"This is just how she is," I manage.

Logan's jaw tightens, something oddly protective in his expression. "That doesn't make it okay."

The teakettle whistles. Unsure whether I'm grateful or not, I turn away.

Back in the dining room, the vintage table is now blanketed in leather-bound journals, each flipped open to a seemingly random page of garbled handwriting. Val is hunched over one, biting at her cuticle.

I peer over her shoulder.

April 12, 2011

07:10—Weather's in a mood and the trees seem to agree. Branches tossed, mulch everywhere. Val showed up with her coat zipped to her chin. Said it felt like the wind had teeth.

10:45—Aphids in the Rummel block again (of course). Not spreading.

13:20—No sign of mildew or rot. Bark looks good. Buds opening like they've decided.

18:05—Spotted a beetle near the old gate. Bright green, faint glow along the back. Unusual. Will check again tomorrow.

Visitors—Val, of course. And Bobbie stopped by for tea.

"The beetle was *glowing*?" I ask.

Val startles, one hand flying to her throat. "Jesus, Ali," she mutters, then twists to side-eye me. "I won't be able to pick fruit if you've put me six feet under."

"Sorry." I plop into the old, squeaky chair next to her and hand her the mug of tea.

She sniffs it skeptically. "What's this?"

"Black tea."

"It smells funny."

"It's flavored. Sweet harvest pumpkin. I like to drink it in the fall."

Her lip curls as she takes another skeptical sniff.

I roll my eyes. "Try it. You'll like it, I promise."

Logan, who has taken a seat across the table from us, says, "The journals mention glowing beetles?"

Val tentatively sips. "Sure. We've always had weird critters on this land."

I raise an eyebrow. Yes, our land is different—and, yes, I've seen my fair share of fireflies on the East Coast—but I wasn't aware there was anything like a faintly glowing beetle in Oregon.

Brows knitted, Logan picks up the journal in question and starts reading for himself.

Val slurps from her mug. I resist the urge to say I told her so.

"What other 'weird critters'?" I ask.

She lifts a shoulder. "Some black fox was hanging around the barn a while back. Martin and I saw an albino deer when we were kids."

Logan looks up from his journal. "And how about multicolored butterflies?"

Our eyes meet and my mind leaps to a razor-sharp memory: a whirl of butterfly wings circling Logan's awestruck smile. Then, a kiss. *The* kiss. My first ever.

I blink hard.

"Could be," Val says. She chases her tea bag with a spoon. "Like I said, farm's got weird fauna."

"But *why*?" I press.

"Bizarre microclimate. Same reason this land shits out nothing but perfect pears while they won't take anywhere else in the valley. Probably something about the soil. Could be a geothermal vent underground, or some old hot spring. Maybe we're on a terminal moraine."

Eyebrow cocked, I cross my arms and lean back in my chair. The back rest, which has been hanging on by a thread for years, screams a protest that's almost exactly the pitch of my next question. "And that makes beetles glow?"

Val frowns at my chair. "You ought to get rid of these nasty old things."

"I helped Uncle Martin pick them out at an estate sale when I was twelve," I say, "and they have pears on the backs. Explain the beetles, please."

She shrugs. "Funny soil makes weird plants, and weird plants make even weirder bugs."

I regard her skeptically and she crosses her arms.

Logan pushes the journal toward her and taps a finger against the word *visitors*. "And do you know why Martin was making notes on this?"

"Why wouldn't he?"

"The rest of the entry is about the land, the trees, the weather conditions," he says. "All directly relevant to the fruit. This isn't."

Val chews at her lip like she's checking the flavor of her answer. "There wasn't always accounting for what was in that man's head."

This, at least, I know to be true. Still, Val is being cagey.

Logan can clearly tell, too, because he hums, flips the page, and starts reading again. Then, his shoulders go stiff.

"What?" I ask.

When he doesn't answer, I lean over, arching my neck to read the entry in his hands.

May 14, 2011

06:42—Sky cracked pink like it was trying something new.

11:15—No pests. No wilt. Trees humming with me. Not sure which of us started it.

Visitors—Rick and Lydia came out to have a look at the old barn site (work starts next month, weather willing). They seem competent enough. Hired them on the spot, though Rick hurried us along like he was late for something else.

I have to read it a second time before I understand the significance.

Those are his parents.

Lydia is his mom.

Logan's expression betrays nothing, but I can't help but wonder if he's experiencing anything like the jump scares I endured in the days after Blake and Liv left. Blake's magazine subscription showing up in the mailbox. Liv's discarded toothbrush head in the bathroom trash can. A calendar reminder popping up about our monthly bookstore and brunch date.

So many things, once impossibly mundane, suddenly terribly consequential.

"You don't have to keep doing this," I say quietly. "I'd get it if you were over this trial period."

I desperately need his help, of course. I want nothing more than for him to stay on this land and help me pick pears so I don't lose a third of my harvest—and the income to pay off some of the farm's debts. But he's well within his rights to leave. It's a wonder he hasn't walked away already.

His gaze catches mine. "You haven't scared me off yet, Ali."

My stomach jolts, even though I'm not entirely relieved. "All right, then."

We decide to split the stack of journals, each taking a handful to comb for mentions of white pears. Val hefts hers—the early years, right after Martin inherited the orchard—to the couch by the fireplace and elevates her still-booted foot with a stack of folded blankets on the ottoman. Logan remains upright at the dining room table to read the middle ones, ending around the time his family built the barn. I take the later years, which include the final entries Martin kept in the months before he died. In an armchair, I curl up with a journal against my knees, hoping his words will tell me what he never got the chance to.

February 5, 2015

08:10—Irrigation line burst on the Dethman block. No warning. Loud as a marching band full of excitable geese. Soaked the whole slope.

09:40—Pipes looked fine. Too fine. Maybe the trees flinched.

Visitors—Just me, Val, and the mess.

This irrigation mishap is the first in a host of strange problems: late frosts that stop at the edge of the property, sawflies with a penchant only for pears, a storm so violent it shatters the barn's windows. I'd already known about some of these issues—I distinctly remember Val shouting about the "damn freeloading bugs" in the background of a call with Martin. But I hadn't realized the problems were so numerous. And I never knew that the crops had been worn down by these problematic conditions for so many years—even as early as 2019, my uncle is lamenting how thin the crop is and how few props the trees need.

We read in near silence, occasionally calling out highlights from our entries, and only take a break a few hours later when our stomachs start growling. My fridge is embarrassingly empty, but I still manage to scrounge up a tin of sardines, a family-sized bag of hot Cheetos, and a veggie platter with carrots that are only a bit chalky. Fortunately, neither Val nor Logan complains.

I resettle at the dining room table, dip a hunk of broccoli into ranch dressing, and prop my next journal against a glass of ginger ale.

June 20, 2021

07:15—Mist hanging low. Air closing in.

15:40—Codling moths in the pears again. Too many for traps, sprays did nothing. The trees seem resigned. We might have to cede this round.

Visitors—None.

A lump rises in my throat as I try to think back to our sparse phone calls from this time. I remember my firm had just landed its first contract with the State of Florida, Blake and I had finally moved in together, and Liv was storming into my life like she was laying siege on a fortress. I still called Uncle Martin as often as I could, and when we did talk it always felt like no time had passed since our last conversation.

Still, I could tell something was off. When I visited later that summer—the first one in a couple of years—more than one person stopped me in the grocery store to ask if Martin was well.

"It's not long COVID, is it?" Midge Pritchard said in a hushed whisper after she'd cornered me by the parsnips.

I told her Martin was perfectly healthy, which was true at the time. When I asked Val about it later, she coughed out something that sounded distinctly like *busybody*.

I wrote it off, figuring if Val wasn't worried, I shouldn't be, either.

What I've come to learn is that Val doesn't tell me her concerns.

By the following year, my uncle's entries take another turn. Problems of biology turn to the problems of finance that Liv started sorting through when we moved onto the farm.

December 10, 2022

07:30—Heavy sky. Air thick, like it knows something I don't.

9:40—Moths again. I fear I'll never be rid of the fluttering freeloaders.

14:10—Accountant came by. Will need another loan to replace the tractor. I smiled like it was fine.

Visitors—The fellow with the briefcase doesn't count.

My mind flicks to the stack of ledgers and bills in the office, where the door has been firmly shut since Liv left. She was the one with the head for the numbers, not me. And I haven't had the bandwidth to pry open that door yet.

Best not to think about that right now.

Instead, I keep reading.

It's past midnight when I set down my last journal. These pages document more problems than I'd thought possible, but I haven't found a single mention of white pears.

"Anything?" I ask Val. Logan is still hunched over a set of pages, but she's staring into the empty fireplace.

She startles. "You done?"

I nod and she heaves off the couch to join me at the table. By my side, Val is quiet as she thumbs through a span of pages from my journals, lingering on some of the later ones. Then the last one. Uncle Martin stopped taking notes last November, shortly before he decided to stop chemo.

Her thumb rubs over the words *Visitors—None.*

"I didn't realize he was so lonely," I say quietly.

She swallows. "Feels worse than when we were living it. Reading it back-to-back."

"What happened?" I ask. When I was a kid, there was always a steady stream of friends and neighbors stopping by for tea or rhubarb wine. "Did he have a falling-out with a friend or something?"

Val sighs heavily. "Nothing like that. He sequestered himself up here. Refused to go into town. Stopped seeing any of the old crew. It got worse and worse, until eventually he was damn well convinced it was happening *to* him, not because of him." She purses her lips, looking like maybe she's just said something she shouldn't have. "Doesn't matter now, anyway."

As painful as all this is for me, I know it's a thousand times worse for her. So, I let that topic drop. "Things were bad for longer than I realized. I don't remember the farm having problems like this when I was a kid."

"For what it's worth," Logan says, looking up from his open pages, "the entries I've been reading weren't nearly that bad. Martin is mostly reporting full trees, some unusual flowers. Hardly any pests, and most of them benign. Although it does get worse toward the end."

"When exactly?" I ask.

Val frowns. "Why's it matter?"

"I know it's a long shot," I say as Logan flips through his pages, skipping around by weeks, then months, "but we haven't found any mention of white pears, so maybe we need to pivot. Maybe if we can figure out what went wrong for my uncle, the source of it, we can also figure out what's going wrong for me."

"Don't see how they're related," Val grumbles.

"You're the one who said it's all connected," I argue. "That the soil is unusual and that encourages unusual flora and fauna."

Her jaw flexes.

Logan stops flipping, turns back a few pages. His expression darkens as he reads.

"What?" I ask.

Mutely, he slides the open page toward me.

September 3, 2011

06:40—A day that never really began. Just that cold, suffocating gray mist. Thick enough to blur the barn from view.

11:15—Storm hit without warning. Wind screamed. The orchard screamed back.

14:45—Tree outside the window split right down the middle, like it let a giant take an axe to its core.

16:00—Barn hasn't made a sound since.

"A new pest shows up the next day," Logan says, voice unusually low.

I read and reread the entry, trying to make sense of it.

"There's no visitor logged here," I say, turning toward Val. There's nothing logical about this statement or my accelerating thoughts—the weather described in this passage can't be affected by soil, and it's certainly not affected by some visitor—but the woman *must* know something I don't. "Do you remember who was there? Did something happen that day?"

She opens her mouth like she's working out the answer, her fingers twiddling with the thin strap on my last journal. But Logan speaks first.

"I know."

We both turn to him.

"This is the day after my mom left us."

Chapter Seven

"What?" I say, without expectation that Logan will repeat himself. My mind is still stumbling as his declaration hangs in the almost silence of the ticking grandfather clock.

Logan smooths a finger over the spine of a journal. "That day we finished the barn, she was supposed to come home a few hours after us. Dad and I were ferrying all our tools back to the shop, and Mom was sweeping out. She'd be home for dinner, she said. But hours later, she still wasn't. That wasn't like her."

"Did anything happen that morning?" I ask, reading over the entry again, my eyes hiccupping on the description of the empty barn. There's something hauntingly familiar in Martin's words. "Or the night before?"

Logan answers the question like he's already recited it a thousand times. "Mom was quiet. Dad came home late. But none of that was strange."

I wince slightly. Of course he's already asked himself these questions, replayed those final days a thousand times in his mind, hunting for scraps.

"Maybe the journals say more?" I ask, trying to find a new avenue. "About your mom?"

He thumbs through a few pages. "Not from what I've seen. She's mentioned as a visitor a lot, but so is my dad. You. Me. And

Martin's entries don't have much in the way of detail or editorials. I'm not sure how this is connected."

My chair squeals as I sit back, trying to think. At this point, the most likely explanation is that it's all a coincidence. The second most likely explanation is that something about the orchard—or something that happened here—made Lydia leave. Although that wouldn't explain why the bad luck started up after she left. Right?

I rub a temple and look to Val, who is idly picking at her cuticles. She's been silent. Too silent.

"Val?"

"What?"

"Do you have something to say?"

She plucks up a half-dried carrot from a nearly empty plate and bites off the end, chewing hard. "Nah. I hardly knew Lydia."

My eyebrows draw together. "But you know something else."

She drops the rest of the carrot and dusts off her hands. "Yeah. I know there's a big problem at hand and digging around the past isn't going to help."

I level a stare at her. Challenging my aunt is not something I enjoy doing—or, for that matter, ever do. At the same time, this seems way too important to just let go. "But you clearly know something. And if you—"

Val pounds a fist against the table and Logan and I both jump. "No. What I know is that you need to focus on what matters if you want to save this farm."

Then she crosses her arms, expression pinched, and leans back in her seat so far I think the antique backrest might snap in two. The shift is swift and immediate. Something has shut down behind her eyes, like a door slammed, locked, and boarded over.

I've always known Val to be obstinate, sometimes a bit harsh, but I've never seen this kind of cold finality from her. Not in the dozens of arguments she and my uncle had about irrigation schedules or pruning rotations. Not even when she found out Martin had stopped chemo without telling her.

I glance at Logan. He's watching Val, brow furrowed, but he seems to feel my gaze because his eyes track to mine. A long moment passes in which we negotiate a silent conversation. His chin lifts, like, *It's up to you.* I shake my head to say, *It's really not.* After he considers for a beat longer, he nods.

"Fine," I say, putting up my hands. "We'll let it go."

Val unwinds her arms and leans forward on her elbows. "Good. Then we can discuss some solutions to your two problems."

"I have only two?" I ask, trying to lighten the tension that's still thick in the air.

She snorts and slides a few journals aside so she can grab up a waxy pear.

"Two big ones," she says, rubbing at the white coating. "The packing house won't buy fruit like this."

That much is obvious, although I'm not happy to hear it said out loud. The packing house has strict quality controls, and I wouldn't try to sell them cull fruit anyway. I have a legacy reputation to uphold.

"And second?"

"It's spreading."

I probably could have predicted that, too, although it's deeply worrying. As Uncle Martin would have said, the wind blows hard in this valley, and you can't quarantine it, no matter how hard you want to try. "How can you tell?"

"The pattern in the trees. Though, we won't know how fast 'til you watch it awhile."

I let out a tiny sigh. Also, not good. At the same time, it was already going to be a bit of a long shot to get all the fruit down, especially considering my inexperience and Val's injury. "So, when we pick, we'll focus on the unaffected trees."

Val frowns and drops the problematic pear. "Sure, but you can't start for at least a few weeks."

The implication is clear: By the time we start picking, the rest might have turned. Or at least enough to severely cut down my harvest. Possibly by so much I won't be able to afford the minimum payments on my debts.

The bills.

The thought has my spine straightening, as though I can feel that closed door to the office. The ledgers I haven't opened since Liv left. The stack of envelopes stamped with words like URGENT and OPEN IMMEDIATELY. My head starts to spin.

Prioritize the possible, I remind myself. *The rest will fall into place when you're ready.*

It's good advice. I've repeated it often to harried-looking men with ties askance and women in wrinkled blouses, with papers scattered everywhere as they furiously click between tabs. The issue is that in those cases, the problems were solvable—reports to file, emails to send, forms to fill out.

Mysteriously diseased pears aren't like spreadsheets and emails because I don't know what is "possible" to prioritize. We could change up the sprays, but it'd just be guesswork. I could hire a pesticide consultant, but that will cost money I don't have and, besides, it's unlikely they'd know more than Val.

I swallow and shut my eyes.

Uncle Martin trusted me with his legacy and now he's gone and I can't be the reason it all falls apart.

"Maybe it won't keep spreading," I say.

"'Course it will," Val says with the overconfident pessimism of a disgruntled team lead complaining about new performance metrics.

"The disease is new," I argue, opening my eyes to meet her confidence with my own. "It's only affected a few trees so far. There's no guarantee it will spread to the rest, or even much more at all. We can hope for the best here."

Val rolls her eyes. "You sound like Martin when he'd had one too many whiskey sours."

"Optimistic?"

"Delusional."

I flinch.

Val grimaces and shoots me an apologetic look. "Sorry. Didn't mean it. Those journals . . . I'm just sour is all."

"Yeah," I say, because I get it. My uncle's words have been replaying for me, too, especially *Visitors—None.* "It's fine."

"But what I said, less gently than I should have, is still true. We need a better solution than *hope.*"

I wince, confronted with the sudden, almost physical urge to grab the waxen pears littering the table, march them across the property, and hurl them into the burn pile.

But then Logan asks, "What about a backup plan?"

We turn to him. He's been quiet for a long time, running a callused thumb across the surface of one of the pears. Taking his time to think.

"What do you have in mind?" I ask.

"I don't think we've hit the worst-case scenario yet." He tilts his head toward me, a reassuring glance. "But we can't stop the disease from spreading, and we can't start picking until the end of the month. Maybe we need a contingency plan. Diversification."

I nod because I like what he's saying—or maybe the steady, logical way he's saying it—even if I don't know what he means yet. "Like leasing or something?"

"Leasing isn't an option," Val cuts in. "I'd sooner break both hips than see someone without the name Reid farm this land."

"Nothing that drastic," Logan reassures her. "But there has to be another way for the orchard to make money."

It's a good idea. Besides, the weeks before harvest are quiet. It'd be great to have something productive to do while I'm waiting for the pears to finish growing.

"I could make jams," I offer. "The freezer in the basement is basically a fruit vault."

Val hums noncommittally. "Not bad, but you'll have to sell a shitload of pear jam to make a dent in the lost revenue. What about a wedding?"

"A wedding?"

"Sure," Val says. "They're huge around here lately. Rich couples from Portland shell out tens of thousands for a few hours of these views."

While it sounds appealing, it's also hitting an uncomfortably sore spot. Blake and I were engaged for more than a year, so you might think that I'd already had everything from a wedding band to a color scheme picked out. The truth is that every time things were settled enough to start planning, I'd get overwhelmed by the scale of it all. Besides, Martin got sick a few months after Blake proposed, and between my uncle's illness and our subsequent move across the country, Blake and I barely had time to think about a wedding. We hadn't even brainstormed destinations for a honeymoon, at least partly because the idea of getting on a plane and leaving Apple Valley—even temporarily—felt wrong to me. All that said, long before I met Blake, I had pictured the venue. I wanted to get married with a row of trees as my aisle and a mountain as the altar.

It's still vivid enough that I can't watch someone else have that moment.

Val doesn't seem to have noticed my hesitation, but I think Logan does because he says, "Likely not enough time. Couples book venues months if not years in advance, especially for high-end weddings."

"True," Val says.

I let out a breath.

"But . . ." Logan continues, still in that quietly considered voice, "something like a big party might work."

"What kind of party?"

"Right after Mom left," he explains, "Dad had to cancel a bunch of big jobs and things got . . . a bit rough financially. But the Harts—they own the ciderhouse in town—threw us this fancy dinner. Like a charity, although no one called it that. Folks paid for tickets. They served hard cider and someone else chipped in for food. The Harts pulled in pretty good money on it—and they had plenty to cover their expenses and give us the rest. It got us by for a while."

Val snaps her fingers. "I remember that night. The three of you boys ran around in matching jackets and ties. The little one caught his sleeve on fire."

"Mason always has been good at blowing things up," Logan concedes with the shadow of a smile. "So, what d'you think?"

They both look at me. The relief is practically staggering.

"It's a great idea."

Val bangs a palm against the table. "Excellent. We'll make it fancy like the Harts did. Call it a 'gala.' Charge an arm and a leg for tickets."

"We'll need to do it before harvest starts, though," I say, pulling up my calendar on my phone. Provided that the orchard continues operating like clockwork, we'll start picking on September 30—a Monday. "And we should pick a weekend day for the gala, plus give ourselves a buffer so we can prep."

Val leans over to squint at my screen. "How 'bout two Saturdays from now? It's not much time, but it's also the equinox. We can call it an Autumn Gala. People always pay extra for shit that's fall themed."

"First of all, rude," I say. "And second, also true. I'll happily pay double for anything pumpkin flavored."

Logan's mouth ticks.

Val rolls her eyes. "Like I said. What about drinks?"

"I bet we could buy some discounted cider from the Harts," Logan offers. "I wouldn't usually ask, but June was just complaining about a batch that's about to get too old to sell. As long as we pay them cost for it, I'm sure she'd be happy for us to get it off her hands."

"Excellent," Val says. "And I'll shill tickets and get a food truck over here."

"I'm sure I can scrounge up some serving dishes and flatware in the attic," I say, thinking of the panoply of both I just saw, "but we'll need furniture. Folding tables and such."

"I'll get some on loan from the neighborhood," Val says, an oblique reference to her retirement community for active seniors, words she never actually uses in conjunction with the place she lives. "All we need is a venue."

"The orchard," I say.

"Right, but the house is too cramped and god knows what the weather will do. How 'bout the barn?"

The barn.

The words slide through me like the rough edge of a dull blade. I haven't stepped foot on those dusty wood floors since that day a month ago.

And, just as quickly, I remember that Logan has this much worse than me. I glance at him, but his expression is neutral, unreadable.

He hasn't even agreed to help yet, I remind myself. Picking will be hard enough. I don't want to force him to also spend the next two weeks fixing up the barn his parents built—the last place he saw his mom before she disappeared.

"It's not enough time," I say. "The barn isn't in great shape anymore."

"Sure," Val says. "But you have a couple of weeks. Throw up some lights. People will think it's rustic."

"But it needs real work," I protest, "not just lights and furniture. The door is off its hinges and there was a leak in the roof that half rotted the floorboards. I can't fix all that in two weeks."

She looks between us like she's missing something. "Logan is a carpenter."

"Yeah," I say, "but he still hasn't decided whether to stay or not."

Logan glances toward the window. It's dark now, but moonlight catches the swaying branches. Beyond them, the barn sits like a stubborn sentry. When he looks back, something in his expression has settled.

"I'll stay," he says. "Fixing up the barn won't be a problem."

The words loosen something in my chest. I'm about to ask Logan if he's certain when he starts speaking again.

"But also"—he cuts a glance at Val, flat and deliberate—"I intend to go digging into the past."

Chapter Eight

Early the next morning, Logan and I begin work with an intensity that belies either of our emotional states.

The hardest part was getting started. An hour ago, we stood shoulder to shoulder in front of the barn's door, which was still gaping like a haunted eye. Every urge in my body screamed to run away, to turn back before I'm met with the sticky-sweet smell of hay, the creak of floorboards.

I was already leaning back on my heels, preparing to bolt, when Logan's gaze found mine. And his head was tipped not with an answer, but a question in return. Like: *You ready?* Or *So, can we do this?*

Like, maybe confronting these demons wouldn't be so bad since we both have them.

He held out an elbow.

"Together?"

I hesitated—just a breath, long enough to feel the pull and push of wanting and knowing better—then looped my arm through his. "Let's go."

And we stepped through the broken door.

We've started by clearing out junk. The barn is full of equipment and gear that need to go to a storage shed before we can even think about the rest of it—sandblasting the floor, repairing broken windows, rehanging the door.

So far, I think we're each handling this fine, although we keep throwing glances at each other from across the dusty wood floor, like we're both monitoring the other for a reaction. Once, I gently elbowed Logan out of a daze by one of the wood beams, where he had his hands shoved in his pockets, staring as though he were questioning its structural integrity.

A few minutes later he caught me frozen by three picking bags—side by side on pegs, each personalized with Liv's iron-on patches: *Blake, Liv, Ali.* Liv had been practically bouncing on her toes when she showed them to me. And I'd thought, *How could hefting a fifty-pound bag be so bad when I have these two people to do it with me?*

Logan bumped my shoulder. I startled, realizing I'd been staring limply, tracing my thumb over the bare spot where my ring used to sit.

"Doing okay?" he asked.

I relaxed my thumb. Felt my lips stretch. "I'm fine."

Fortunately, since then I've done what I do best: I shoved all the memories into imaginary boxes and stuffed them into a mental attic so deep they can't hurt me anymore.

After we finish loading a pair of twin propane tanks onto the bed of a Gator, Logan wipes his forehead with a sleeve and asks, "How much do you think she's not saying?"

It takes me a moment to realize he's talking about Val. Given how late it was when she left, Logan and I haven't had a chance to talk about what she said—and, more to the point, what she refused to tell us.

"I hate to say this," I tell him, "but I think it's very possible she knows what happened to your mom. I have no idea why she wouldn't share, though."

Logan frowns as he pushes loose a half-rotten bale of hay, revealing a damp spot underneath. "Did she seem . . . upset when you asked?"

I move closer to help push the bale on its side, make it easier to roll out. He's not wrong. Val can be gruff and stubborn as hell, but she rarely gets angry. "You're wondering if that's why she wouldn't say? Like, she was involved, somehow?"

He nods, and I shake my head as I consider. "Maybe. It's possible. I don't know. She was here on the farm when your parents were building the barn that summer."

We don't say any more until we've gotten the Gator loaded and Logan has driven it down to the storage shed.

"There's something else to keep in mind," I say when he's back.

"Yeah?"

"There were two other people on the orchard that summer. Your dad. And my uncle."

Logan squints slightly. "Were the two of them . . ."

"Friends. Partners. They worked together nearly every day from the time they were teenagers. My uncle always used to say that farming has a way of forging the tightest of bonds—and sometimes breaking them."

"But not romantic," he says.

"Never. Val's not attracted to men. But she did love my uncle as much as a person can love another."

Logan rests an old tractor tire against the wall as his thumb traces a rusted hinge on one of the barn's beams.

Long silences in the middle of conversations usually make me uncomfortable, maybe because, with my mom, they were rife with land mines. But there's something different about pauses with Logan. His silences don't feel like disinterest. Just the opposite. Like he cares so much, he wants to think carefully before speaking.

"Maybe I'm looking for information where there isn't any," he says.

When he doesn't lift his eyes from that scrap of rusted metal, I say, "And maybe you'll find clues in these old beams?"

He drops his hand. "Not sure I should admit it, but yeah."

I consider that for a beat before saying, "A few days after Blake and Liv left, I spent a full afternoon digging through every trash can in the house. I was looking for . . . I don't know. Evidence."

I close the distance between us, partly to stand by his side and partly to avoid looking at *the corner*. Even with the hay bales cleared out, I have to fight to keep from picturing Liv's light-colored hair tangling with straw.

"Don't ask me *evidence of what*," I continue. "Or how I thought I was going to find any useful information in dryer lint or empty soda cans. But that's where I looked."

Logan tucks his chin to study me, and there's something in his expression that makes it feel like a string has been pulled taut between our chests. A tingle works through my shoulder blades.

Not real, I remind myself. *Just nostalgia*.

"You wanted to take back control," he says.

I clear my throat. "Right. That's it. So, that's all to say, I will not be judgmental if you think you can find information about your mom's disappearance in some rusted hinges."

He smiles gently. "Fasteners. And maybe it's nothing, but that's exactly the problem. They shouldn't be rusted."

"The roof leaked a while back."

"You said." Arms crossed, he glowers between the ruined floorboards and the roof. I shouldn't admit this, even just to myself, but frustration looks good on Logan. He's all narrowed eyes and flexed jaw and pursed lips. Serious in a way that's not severe. "That shouldn't have happened, either. When was it?"

"I'm not sure." I turn to get back on task and grunt as I awkwardly lift a hedge trimmer. "Maybe a few years ago?"

"Not the work quality I'd expect."

"You're saying something was different?" I ask.

Logan lifts a section of tangled rope and, even though his shoulders are still tight, he works it over in his hands with smooth, practiced movements. "I've thought about that a lot over the years. That job feels different than the others they brought me onto, but it might be because it was the first time I'd worked with them seriously or, more likely, because all my memories were messed with by what happened after."

"What do you think you remember, though?"

He frowns at a knot in the rope and then starts pulling it out with a careful precision that's difficult to look away from. Despite my best intentions, the slip of the rope pulls a memory loose. Logan and I were alone and we'd scraped together dinner from whatever we could find in the fridge. My head was on Logan's knee, curls splayed across his lap, and his fingers were combing slowly through my hair—steady, patient, like he was working something free.

He blows out a breath, and I startle. Kick myself for letting my mind wander again.

"My parents often weren't on the same page," Logan says, fortunately oblivious to my reverie. He weighs a knot in his palm. "They had worked together for almost two decades, but it was never smooth. Mom loved the work, but Dad wasn't fully there. It caused a lot of fights. Mom would be up in the rafters, focused and precise, and Dad would be down on the foundation, half listening or distracted. She'd snap at him, telling him to pay attention, but it never seemed to stick. I know it caused a lot of mistakes, too.

"But that summer felt worse. It wasn't just that they weren't on the same page. They were rarely in the same room. Mom was *always* up here working while Dad almost never was. Like he'd run to the lumberyard or whatever, drop something off for her, and immediately head out. They weren't even arguing about it anymore. I thought maybe it was because they had me to pick up the slack—to stay up here with Mom. Or maybe that's just how bad it had gotten."

He shakes his head and leans against a beam. "But, also, I don't know. She'd always been deep into the work, much more than Dad. And breaking things up was a perfectly normal part of their routine. Especially once I came on board. Maybe there's nothing significant about any of that. If I'm being honest, what actually strikes me as different about that summer is that it was the first time I really connected with her."

"How so?"

"Mom always seemed most herself when she was building something, like she only felt fully whole when she was holding a hammer and a fistful of nails. Me and my brothers never interrupted her when she was working, even Mason knew not to. But working with her that summer, I saw it up close—what the work meant to her. And for the first time, I guess I wasn't in the way of that. I was part of it."

My back stiffens as I register how eerily familiar it sounds. Not because my mom threw herself into work—she was a travel nurse and her job wasn't so much a passion as a convenient means of excusing all our moves—but rather the idea of unspoken expectations. And the way he's describing that distance. Like you're standing across a ravine from someone you want to love and, even though they're close, you have no way of reaching them.

"I get it," I say.

"Do you?" he asks, genuinely.

"I know what it feels like to miss a parent who's right in front of you."

Logan's gaze on me is unsteadying. I feel like it's rocking through me, a tractor crashing over a ravine. I take a small step back.

"You must have theories," I say. "About what happened."

He rubs at the back of his neck. "My dad never talked about her after she left. Honestly, he never talked about much at all. I'd try to ask him about her, or even Andrew's grades or whatever, and he'd just stand up and walk away. But there was this one night, when Andrew had just won this huge soccer tournament. Dad managed to show up to the trophy ceremony, had cake with us. After, we were sitting in the living room—Mason and Andrew had gone to bed—and he looked over at me, and right out of the blue, he said it was his fault. 'Maybe she's punishing me,' he said. 'Maybe I deserve it.'"

I blink. "What do you think he meant by that?"

"I don't know. I tried to ask and he shook his head."

My mouth goes dry. I have way too much experience with a parent shutting down for that not to hit hard. And here Logan experienced it with both of them.

"Hey, I think we should read the journals again. Maybe Uncle Martin wrote something that can give us a clue of what happened to your mom. I think we'll find something. We just have to look harder."

He stays quiet for a moment, and then one side of his mouth twitches—not quite a smile, more like he's noticing me.

"What?" I ask.

"You have the same look you got when Martin told you he'd need to pull up that old tree."

My lips lift as I remember the one: planted by my great-grandfather, which made it older than color television and the microwave oven, with the perfect central branch for climbing. "I told him I'd tie myself to it to keep him from cutting it down. Dramatic, I know. But he relented. Let it hold on another year."

Logan's eyes flick back and forth between mine. "I've always liked that about you."

"That I'm optimistic?"

"That you hold on so tight."

My stomach backflips, betraying me before my mind can shut it down. Then I swallow because, even though Logan's gaze is heavy and certain in a way that feels almost like physical touch, I can't help but think about my mom's purse-lipped stare.

"That tree died a few years later. I didn't save it in the end."

He lets my words hang in the space between us, one of his deliberate pauses. Then he says, "When you care about something, you hold on to it. Even if it doesn't ultimately work out, you don't abandon what's important."

I'm not sure what he means by that. I don't think he's talking about me, or us as teenagers, but I still can't help but think about our phone calls that faded into silence. The end that I hastened along when I stopped returning his messages. The timing of it all.

"You, uh . . ." I busy myself by stacking up some five-gallon buckets, buying time to find the right phrasing. "I guess your mom must have left around the time we stopped talking."

"A bit before but yeah."

"Is that . . ." I fiddle with the handle on one of the buckets. "I'm sorry. I should have been there for you. Helped somehow."

"You didn't know," he says. "I didn't tell you, and I'm sorry for that."

I hesitate before asking, "Why didn't you? Tell me."

He frowns. "I didn't know how to talk about it, to be honest. I was young and everything was changing so fast and . . . I barely knew how to handle any of it."

I nod because I get it. Probably more than he knows.

"Thanks for telling me now." I stack my pile of buckets onto a crate and squat to lift the tower, tall enough that it obscures most of my field of vision. "I can understand why being here is complicated for you."

Arms loaded, I waddle toward the open door. My pile teeters, buckets rolling precariously. I stop short just as Logan materializes to steady us both.

He lifts my stack of buckets, revealing his face, closer than I was expecting. Darkened eyes. Firm mouth. That jaw. "I said it was 'complicated' to be here because it's not all bad."

Oh. "It's not?"

"I would say I'm glad I came."

I fidget by rubbing a finger against the corner of my crate. "We do have a nice view of the mountain. There's that creek. And it's quiet. No screaming baby, I guess."

Logan's lips hitch, carving out that now familiar half smile. "I think you know that none of those are the reason."

"I do?"

His head cocks. The smile sharpens, turning full on for the first time since the farmer's market. Logan is attractive enough with his level stare, but this smile? It rearranges my atoms.

Then, as though this wasn't enough, Logan says, "It's good to see you again, Ali Reid."

Heat spreads from my temples to my toes. My freshly rearranged atoms reach for his.

"It's good to see you, too, Logan Wright."

He steps back, expression turning serious. "Ali, I should—"

Before he can finish, something bright—as startling as a camera flash—catches my eye. We both wheel toward it. For a split second, all is dark and still: just a pile of dried leaves that must have blown in at some point, and a thick netting of cobwebs where the wall meets the floor.

But before I turn away, it happens again. A glint of light. Like the edge of a knife catching the sun.

It came through a small, jagged hole at the base of the wall. The kind that an animal with sharp teeth and claws might use to get into this barn and ransack my picking bags.

Cautiously, we both set down our armloads, and as we step toward it, a whiskered nose pokes out of the hole. It's pink and small and far too adorably round to belong to an opossum.

The nose twitches. A single dark gray paw follows.

"Oh, it's a *bunny*!" I squeal before clamping a hand over my mouth.

Logan glances at me, amusement ghosting his expression.

"Sorry," I say through my fingers. "That was my last high-pitched outburst. Probably."

"Please," he says, "don't hold back on my account."

Fortunately, I haven't thwarted our new furry friend because the rabbit takes another few steps out. Its coat is the most unusual color I've ever seen—like the blue-steel reflection of an overcast sky in a shallow puddle.

Nose thrust in the air, the rabbit hops forward. And then the fur, er, catches the light?

Like . . . it's . . . silver?

I grab Logan's arm. His whole body has gone rigid.

The astonishing rabbit turns. Its eyes gleam in the dark.

Holy shit. Its eyes are silver, too.

For a long moment, the three of us are immobile, a triangle of frozen awe and confusion.

Outside, a magpie caws.

The rabbit bolts. Its body streaks away like a minnow just below the surface of the water, disappearing under the wheels of the Gator.

"Holy shit, holy shit, holy shit," I say, my fingernails digging half moons into Logan's forearm. "Is it just me or was that a silver rabbit?"

"I saw it, too," he says, although he sounds like he isn't sure he did.

"Do you think we're having a stroke? Do you smell anything strange? I've heard people smell strange things when they're having strokes."

He side-eyes me. "A *joint* stroke?"

I drag a hand down my face, from temple to cheek. "Maybe we're hallucinating. Or I don't know, did we get a contact high from my uncle's patchouli stash?"

Logan raises an eyebrow. "How strong was his patchouli?"

"I don't know." I throw up my hands. "Very? Sometimes the man wore two kinds of hats, right on top of each other, and I once caught him giving a downed branch a stern talking-to."

Logan grunts out a laugh, but he hasn't turned away from the wheel.

"We need to get it out of here before we can do anything else," I argue to his stunned silence. "Where there is one, there are a hundred more, and I don't want them getting into the picking bags."

"'They might get into the picking bags,'" he repeats flatly, "is not the slam-dunk argument you think it is."

"It is if you know just how bad I am at patching."

He shakes his head. "I'm fairly certain I've seen this exact episode of *The Twilight Zone.* If I remember correctly, the rabbit is a messenger from the underworld, and the story either ends with an alien invasion or an eternal punishment time loop." He frowns. "Possibly both."

I snort. "You should watch more rom-coms. Also, in less than two weeks from today, there will be about a hundred guests in this barn. We can't have a silver bunny—nightmare-world messenger or not—darting across the dance floor."

This does seem to sway him because he considers for a beat longer, then nods. "Fine. But I'll pick up the rabbit."

I arch an eyebrow. "Why? Because you're tall and manly and have burly muscles?"

"You think my muscles are 'burly'?"

My cheeks warm, but I still manage to gesture at his broad chest and the sleeves of his flannel, where the fabric pulls across the ridges of his biceps. Logan's muscles—the ones clearly wrought over the last decade and a half of hard manual labor—are an undeniable fact. I don't need to be remotely nostalgic to notice them.

"I'm not telling you anything you couldn't see for yourself with a mirror or, I don't know, a really shiny plate. Actually, come to think of it, our underworld friend would probably work, too."

A smile hitches up one side of his lips. It's a small triumph, getting him to make that face.

Another glint of light hijacks our attention and we both turn abruptly back to the problem at hand.

"How about if neither of us touches it?" I offer. "We could chase it into a picking bin."

After Logan agrees to my idea and we spend another minute or so coordinating (though perhaps it's not quite enough logistical planning, considering the unusual circumstances), we prop a big, white picking bin on its side and I get on my hands and knees to try to shoo the bunny into our makeshift trap.

Under the shadow of the Gator's carriage, the rabbit's fur is nearly dark as it remains stock still. I flap a hand toward it, but just as my fingers edge closer, the rabbit moves again. Not a hop or a jump.

It *blurs*.

The rabbit bolts out from the wheels, sprinting across the floor so fast I can barely track it. Logan, apparently thinking faster than me, grabs a picking bag and rushes forward.

I point at the last place I saw a flash of silver. "There!"

He wheels. I lunge in the opposite direction, trying to hem the moving body between us.

Suddenly, there are more.

Rabbits pour out of the crack, fur flashing in hues that can't possibly be natural. One the color of a sunflower careens around me, glancing against my ankle. I twist to find another, this one electric blue, vaulting through the wheels of a tractor. A third appears on top of a toolbox—at first presenting as natural brown, but when it moves, I realize it has a sheen like a copper pipe.

"Logan?"

Behind me, I hear a bang followed swiftly by a loud curse. I whirl to find Logan rubbing at his elbow as he ducks under a ladder. The magenta rabbit he's chasing after scurries away but rounds a corner and hits a dead end. He lunges and manages to close his hands around its tiny torso.

"Got you," he whispers with endearing triumph as it wriggles against his broad chest.

"Picking bin!" I say, pointing to the corner.

Bolstered by Logan's success, I whirl toward a soft rustling noise by the only remaining hay bale. As I approach, the creature stills. It's nearly shrouded in darkness, but I can make out a black nose and a tuft of white as it steals behind a shovel. At least it's not moving as fast as the others. I jog toward it.

The bunny must spot me because it changes course. I bank to cut off its path, cornering it in the shadows between a metal shelf and the wall.

The creature stalls, then spins.

Even considering how unusual these rabbits are, this one is

especially odd. Not only because it has a wide tail, but the way it stomps its feet and lifts onto its front paws . . .

"*Skunk!*"

Logan drives into me from behind as the animal launches its tail toward the rafters.

A noxious odor slams against us both, like we're driving headlong into a putrid cloud of burning rubber.

We stagger, backs slamming against the upright bin. It topples, freeing the only rabbit we managed to catch. Tiny paws patter over our limbs as we hit the ground.

I can't worry about that, though, because the rotting-egg smell is so intense it's like my lungs have caught fire. It coats my skin in a sticky film. Clogs my throat until it's hard to inhale.

I stagger to my feet and start plowing toward the exit, but find Logan is still on his knees, blinking like he's underwater. Coughing and spluttering, I backtrack to tug at his forearm, trying to haul him upright. He's so solid and big, it's like trying to wrestle with a piece of wall. Still, I manage to yank him hard enough that he stumbles with me toward the doors and then outside.

The sun washes us in bright light. Hands on our knees, we both rack out spluttering coughs. I suck in air, desperately willing seconds to tick away and the stench to abate.

We're outside. In fresh air. It should get better.

Instead, my lungs splutter on the thick smell, and I convulse with another hacking cough. Even from a few feet away, I can see Logan's eyes have started to water.

"What the hell?" I manage with my next sip of air. "Why isn't it going away?"

Chapter Nine

Nothing helps.

In the upstairs bathroom, I plunge myself into a stream of piping hot water and viciously scrub my skin with lava soap and a bleach-stained washcloth. My arms and legs turn a scraped pink, but the smell doesn't dampen. If anything, it intensifies, like water is bringing it more life.

Logan's outdoor shower is still running when I get out of mine.

"How are you doing?" I call through the shutters.

No response. Maybe he didn't hear me. But then he says, "I think it's worse."

He sounds miserable.

"Yeah, me too," I say. "Regroup in the living room?"

Two hours later, Logan and I have changed our clothes four times and tried three different at-home remedies—including soaking our hands and forearms in the cans of tomato juice I found in the basement. We still smell as acrid as burning batteries.

Back in the living room, we plug search terms into our phones with increasingly nonsensical and alarming undertones. I've managed to sit down, but Logan is still pacing the carpet like he's trying to run out of his own skin.

"There has to be a better idea out there somewhere," I say, rubbing at my forehead. "Surely someone on Reddit has dealt with skunks this unholy."

Logan's face snaps up. His eyes are still bloodshot. "Unholy."

"What?"

"Why did you call them that?"

"I—I don't know. Something my uncle used to say?"

He closes his eyes and sways slightly, like he's having trouble forming coherent thoughts. Probably, he is. As miserable as I am, Logan dove in front of me. He got the brunt of the spray.

Finally, he says, "There's something about skunks in the journals. Martin called them that. Unholy."

We blink at each other for another beat before hurtling into the dining room.

"It was spring," Logan says, flipping through pages. "I started skimming these passages when I saw they barely mentioned pears, but I remember the skunks."

"What year?"

"Sometime in the—" Logan's next breath abruptly turns to a cough that rocks him off balance, forcing him to grip the side of the table.

"Logan?"

"The late 2000s," he finishes before pushing himself upright. "Sorry. Mason and I had a bad experience with a skunk. When he was a kid."

I want to ask about it, but the way I can help is by doing, not talking.

"Okay," I say, refocusing on my pages. "We can fix this. Try not to breathe in the— Oh, wait, look at this."

I flatten the heel of my palm against the journal's binding, spreading the pages wider.

April 9, 2009

06:30—Warm morning. Was out pruning and startled a skunk. In hindsight, shouldn't have been wearing so much purple.

07:00—Tried the usual suspects: baking soda, tomato juice. No improvement.

09:05—Used the hose for a good, long soak. Didn't help, but I'm wetter than I'd like.

15:45—Val suggested rose water. Now she says I smell like a garden full of abandoned eggs. A rare compliment?

Visitors—Was supposed to have the lot over for poker, but I've advised them to steer clear.

April 10, 2009

07:10—Woke up still reeking. Possibly worse.

11:30—Tried a vinegar bath. Smell's turned to an ancient pickle hot-boxing a minivan.

14:25—Spent the afternoon by the creek, dreaming up violent deaths for those unholy scent merchants. If I come upon another, I'll stab it in the neck with a grapefruit spoon.

16:45—Clouds rolling in.

Visitors—Just me and my revenge fantasies.

April 11, 2009

06:30—Waiting it out also useless.

09:30—World might be ending. Not a bang nor a whimper, but the slow, suffocating smell of rotting gym socks.

14:10—In my final act of desperation, I'm going to crawl into the backwater pool in the south-side creek. Hoping the shock of cold water will revive my spirits.

15:10—An hour soak, and dare I say? Smell is abating.

16:25—Kissing everything. The earth. The grass. Val. (Have a black eye now, but nothing can break my spirit.)

Visitors—Celebrating a second chance at life. There will be too many to count.

We finish reading at the same time, look up at each other, questions lurching in the lingering odorous fog.

"Do we try it?" I ask aloud.

"What do we have to lose?" Logan says.

Shoulder to shoulder, sulfur smell still wafting from our skin, Logan and I take in the backwater pool at our feet. And . . . new problem.

It's tiny.

The so-called pool is basically the size of a clawfoot bathtub and barely large enough for Logan to fit alone. It's certainly not big enough for both of us. At least not without me, say, straddling him.

Logan is taking in slow, shallow gulps of air as if threading a delicate balance between not breathing and not passing out. "You go first. I'll wait."

I squint at him. "That's ridiculous. You're miserable. I'll wait."

"For an hour?"

Okay, yes, that sounds like torture. My skin has started to burn, like maybe I scrubbed off too much and, instead of removing the skunk's noxious oils, I only gave them an avenue to seep deeper. It'd be hell to sit on the grass with relief within reach.

"Fine." I take a deep, steadying breath. We're both adults here. "We'll get in together."

Logan, clearly still in both physical and some kind of mental agony, closes his eyes and swallows so hard I can see it trace down his throat. "Right. But I don't know how much clothing we should wear."

Um. Crap. Despite my fresh change of clothes, the smell has already seeped into the fabric. "Underwear?"

I've already seen Logan in a bathing suit—that time I dared him to jump into the irrigation pond with me. This should be the same thing, right?

He nods, jaw tight.

"You get in first," I add. "Because you're bigger."

Logan stares fixedly for another moment before stepping toward the pool. Then he pulls off his shirt. And I try my best to look at the sky because I can't trust my brain not to wander. Plus, it's the respectful thing to do. Then again, I'm human.

My gaze drops. And my next few heartbeats flicker instead of thump.

This is nothing like that day in the irrigation pond.

Logan's hair is still damp from our several showers, the droplets tracing the slope of his wide shoulders. His back muscles are defined, his frame fully grown, every line different from the boy I once knew. Moisture licks along the prominent ridges around his spine, soaking the waistband of his shorts as he loosens them. His plaid boxers sit low on his hips, clinging to defined hamstrings.

And shit.

This . . . this sure doesn't feel like nostalgia.

I close my eyes and silently swear.

Logan plugs a foot into the pool, then another, and sinks down. He draws his knees toward his chest, like he's trying to take up as little space as possible with that massive frame of his, but he's too big for me to get in next to him.

"I think, um." This was a terrible idea. "You're going to have to straighten your legs."

Logan's jaw throbs, but he silently complies.

"Right." My cheeks are as hot as a burn pile now. "That'll work."

Logan has his face pointed toward the sky as I tug off my pale blue linen dress. Underneath, I'm wearing white cotton underwear and a bra, both old and almost threadbare. Despite the heat in my face, I shiver as wind stirs the branches nearby, sending goosebumps racing across my skin. Then I move toward the pool, radiating in bright sunshine.

Fortunately, warm water scales my leg as I slide a foot into the surface. I bring the second leg in, and this time, my toes glance off Logan's thigh. He tenses. I almost recoil but instead press forward, lowering myself until I hit the silty bottom.

Then, I settle into his lap.

Familiarity, I tell myself, clenching my teeth so hard I can feel my jaw popping. *Emotional residue.*

I can't get caught in the riptide of the past.

But, right now, the past isn't so much the problem as the way Logan is incontestably *present.* The backs of my legs are pressed against his quads. My hip slots into his torso. The creek's faint current twirls around us, bringing with it warm silt that runs over my skin and slips between our bodies.

But also.

My lungs feel . . . They aren't burning?

I take a tentative sip of air. It still tastes of sulfur, but dampened. Dare I say this is working? I draw in another breath, deeper now. My first real inhale since I was in the barn.

Definitely working.

Logan's shoulders relax beneath me. With his head tipped back to the rock, the line of his jaw is even more prominent. His breaths are steady and deeper. His rib cage expands to meet my own, our skin touching in a new place.

"Logan."

His chin lifts. His gaze meets mine. It sends an electric zip between my shoulder blades.

Two minutes down and fifty-eight to go. "What the actual hell just happened to us?"

There's a long pause, filled only by the gentle rushing sound of water running over rocks. Finally, Logan says, "I've only ever seen something like that once before."

I hesitate before whispering, "The butterflies."

One of my damp curls has sprung loose from my ponytail and now rests on my forehead. Logan lifts his hand to sweep it out of my sight line, a gesture that was once so rote he still seems to carry its muscle memory fourteen years later.

And now there's no stopping it—my mind slips back in time, skimming directly from turquoise and amber butterflies fluttering around that first kiss . . . to the dozens that followed it. Against the barn door at dusk, Logan's skin smelling faintly of sweat and sawdust. Behind his mom's pickup truck, the metal radiating heat through my sundress, our knees bumping. Next to an old oak tree, my finger winding through his belt loop, his breath stirring the fine hairs at my temples.

I blink and teenage Logan is replaced with this very adult one. With a beard instead of that youthful roundness in his cheeks. With an expanse of muscles across his shoulders and chest. With so much more hair dusting his arms and legs.

More guarded. Fewer easy smiles.

But still the same steady eye contact that leaves me both grounded and unmoored.

My throat is sunbaked dry. I clear it. "And that's not to mention that skunk. No skunk spray should last like that, not through that much soap and water. And now"—I take another long draught of air—"this pool should not be helping, but it is."

But as I say this, I feel the shift. We're suddenly talking about something else, something more significant, and it tolls between us with the low, purposeful ring of a bell that cannot be unrung. It's a shift into something entirely new and, frankly, terrifying.

"Something here is . . ."

I can't say it.

Logan apparently can because he says, "Supernatural."

The word sits between us. Despite the heat and the silt and the way Logan's body is rubbing against mine, I'm only thinking about one thing.

My farm is remarkable.

The butterflies and the glowing beetle and the bunnies and maybe even the problems Martin dealt with over the years. It wasn't all natural. It means something more than I'd realized.

I should be more unsettled by this idea than I am, though. But I suppose it could be because I've always known, deep down, that something about this land is different. I've always had questions that my uncle wouldn't answer directly. Sometimes about mundane things. But also about deeper things. Like why the trees felt like they were breathing with me. Why they seem to be more than unconscious life.

"Could that be what's going on with the fruit?" Logan asks.

I turn to him, startled anew by how close he is. Droplets cling to his beard and eyebrows. A bead of water traces a tendon in his neck, tucking into the depression at the base of his throat.

"I think it has to be," I say, trying not to look like I've been staring. "Whatever is wrong with the fruit isn't natural." Could this be what Val has been hiding? The reason she got upset yesterday? In some ways it would make sense. She's most defensive when it comes to two things: the land and my uncle. "Why wouldn't she have told us, though?"

"Martin never said anything, either?"

I rub at my temple, trying to think. "Not exactly. He always had this flair for the theatrical, and he was prone to, I don't know, exaggeration? He used to say stuff like 'Never forget that this land's special, Ali.' Or 'You'll never step foot on an orchard like this one.' Or he'd talk about how you have to respect the trees so they respect you back. But when I asked him to explain, he'd just tweak my nose. And . . . I don't know. I always figured that was how he talked, you know? He was just like that."

"I remember."

"Right. I keep forgetting about that steel-trap mind of yours."

"Only for some things," Logan says.

I swallow. "Maybe he was hiding something."

It's not a pleasant thought. Why would Martin have hidden this from me, especially considering the weight of the responsibility I was taking on? He knew how important it felt for me to get this right. He would have wanted me to have all the information so I'd have the best chance.

Right?

"Why not tell you, though?" Logan asks, mirroring my thoughts. "Before he left you the land? Surely, he must have figured you'd find out on your own."

I blow out a long breath as I reflect on our conversations from last winter, when I finally stopped fighting the idea that my time with Uncle Martin wasn't just finite, it was filled with lasts. The last time we'd walk through the trees together. The last time I'd hear his wheezy chuckle. The last time he'd tweak my nose.

I had so many questions for him—about soil management strategies, the mountain of debt, legal logistics, contacts at the packing house. I clung to his answers like they were precious beads of his own soul. And even though his advice was often peppered with his trademark irreverence, it was also underlined with an uncharacteristic realism. Like Uncle Martin was emphasizing every possible problem, and constantly checking in with me to see if I was really sure I wanted to take them on.

Yes, I kept telling him, *I'm sure*.

It doesn't seem possible he could have been holding back.

I shake my head, pushing away that uncomfortable thought.

"No," I say more confident now. "Uncle Martin was full of secrets, but they were the harmless kind. Like, the man had a whole box of hats he 'wasn't allowed' to wear on certain days of the week and he always smelled like cinnamon even though I never once saw him bake. When it came to the big stuff, he would have told me everything. Especially about the land. He must not have known."

Logan hums. Despite all this talk of something so big and, frankly, terrifying, he's at ease again, that relaxed confidence shawling his wide shoulders. Now that he's powered down, I can see just how worked up he was earlier.

On the south-side creek's opposite bank, a white bird with long pale legs bobs like a teeter totter, pecking intermittently at the shoreline. I shift. My hip skates against Logan's torso, drawing another electric tingle up through me that I can barely keep from showing on my face.

His head dips to the side. "Go on."

"How did you know I have something to ask?"

"You get this kind of round-eyed look when you're about to ask me something you think is too personal."

I lower my chin. "Round-eyed."

His lips lift. "Well, you would have been offended if I'd said doe-eyed." Then he tips his head back again, eyes closed, exposing the long line of his throat in a way that's downright distracting. "Ask your question, please."

I watch his beard. "Don't answer if you don't want to, but what happened? With the skunk, I mean."

Logan opens his eyes slowly and takes in the wisps of clouds cruising across the sky. He's silent for long enough that I'm sure he's not going to answer. But then he lifts a hand until the current sends ripples across his fingertips and starts to talk.

"It happened a few months after our mom left. Mason couldn't stay asleep—he never slept well back then—but that night was particularly bad. He kept waking up screaming, soaked in sweat. Inconsolable no matter what I tried. I figured I needed to get him out of the house, you know? I took him to the park."

He pauses. "It was late, but he was having fun running laps down the slide. I dozed off on a bench, listening to him play. When I woke up, he was screaming, on the other side of the tennis courts. I sprinted after him and I could already smell the skunk.

"I don't know if it was the smell or the dark or sleep deprivation, but he kept running away from me—right into the road and in front of a pickup truck. The guy slammed on his brakes, but it was a moment too late, and Mason got hit."

I cover my mouth with a hand as Logan's face tightens.

"I held him against my chest, his little broken body still smelling like that fucking skunk, and I screamed at the driver to call 911."

"He was okay, though?" I ask.

"He had a concussion and a wrist fracture, but nothing physical that didn't heal."

"I'm glad."

Logan blows out a long, controlled exhale. "That night was the first time I really let myself feel angry at her. It hit me in the hospital, when I was waiting for the results of the CT scan. When I still didn't know just how bad it would be. Because she was the reason it was happening. And I was alone."

I repress a shudder. "Your dad wasn't there?"

"He didn't answer his phone. Later he said the battery had run out or something, but who knows."

I grab Logan's arm, and his forearm is tight under my fingers. When he looks at my hand, I don't pull away. "They shouldn't have left you alone with that. Neither of them."

He nods, jaw tight. "Yeah, I figured that out later. At that time, I blamed her for all of it—Dad checking out, Andrew's problems in school, how hard it was to pay for everything. But that stuff was his fault, too. It was unfair to blame her alone for so long."

I tighten my grip. "No. You were a kid still, basically. You had just lost your mom. Nothing you did or felt was unfair. None of this should have been on you to handle in the first place." I squeeze again, then let go. "I learned that one the hard way."

"How so?"

"My mom—" I cut myself off. I shouldn't. "You know what? I don't want to compare our situations. My mom might have her issues, but she didn't leave me. And I might have grown up without a dad, but that certainly wasn't his fault. I'm sorry for bringing it up."

Logan catches my wrist with his fingers, smooths a thumb against the soft skin on my forearm. His mouth firms. "Ali. We've talked about this."

"What?"

"These comparisons."

Warmth radiates outward from the spot where he's holding me, and I tell him: "You're going to say your scars don't erase mine."

He smiles softly. "I don't mind being predictable. It's a good quality, I think."

"Criminally overlooked, as far as qualities go."

A chuckle shakes loose. "So, then, tell me. About your mom. I already remember some, anyway."

If his memory is as good as it seems, then I guess it's true, he does. He knows about the moves. The tears. He knows my dad died in a car accident when I was in diapers and that everything I know about his face comes from a set of evenly spaced photographs in matching frames—one of the rare decorations Mom bothered to haul around the country. He knows that, once, when I asked for a hamster, she gave me a mouse-shaped plush instead. He knows I cried every night in Anchorage and she pretended not to hear.

But that was *then*. A different Logan who listened to my whispered pain. And I am most definitely a different Ali. One who should be stronger, more resilient. One who should not feel a twist like a corkscrew through her gut when she talks about her mother.

And yet. Logan's focused gaze feels steadying instead of off-putting. It's the same look he gave me outside the barn when he put out his elbow and said, "Together?"

The rippling jewels of early-fall sun run across the creek beyond his face, encouraging me with their winks and divots. There's a reason, I think, that my uncle used to visit this spot at the creek for his late-afternoon "thinking sessions" as he called them. There's a calm—a *space*—here that's downright comforting.

Maybe that's why I clear my throat, brace myself. "It's hard to explain, but did you ever know something your parents expected of you, even if they never said it out loud?"

"Yes," Logan says without hesitation. "Like taking over the family carpentry business."

"Right." I smile. "Well, with my mom, I was expected not to feel things."

He tilts his head in wordless question.

"Like, she'd get tense when I'd cry during a movie. Or when I got upset about a fight with a friend. Or worst of all, if I reacted when she said that, yet again, we'd be uprooting our lives and moving somewhere new. We were always leaving something behind, rejecting some place that wasn't good enough and moving on to the next place that was surely also not going to be good enough. But I was supposed to just lift my chin and tighten my shoulders and take it.

"But I was so bad at that, you know? I was that kid whose parents expect A's but they're still getting C's. Except in my case it was that *Bridge to Terabithia* made me sob and I still wanted to watch it over and over. Or how I'd cry when saying goodbye to some new friend. She didn't yell or tell me off or anything. But she'd get this *look*. I always knew when I was disappointing her."

My fingers curl before I realize why.

"That's why you started smiling when it hurt," he says.

My breath trips, one over the next, and there's a tremble in the walls around my mental attic.

"Yeah. I—" Honestly, I had never connected those dots before. "Yeah. Maybe it is."

Logan hooks my chin with a forefinger to lift my face. Our eyes connect. His gaze is sharp and settled, and a flush of warmth spreads through my chest. And, shit.

What I'm feeling isn't nostalgia or emotional residue.

My attraction to Logan—*this* Logan—is very real.

"You get to feel whatever you feel," he says.

"I don't know," I whisper, because right now we're pressed so close together that all I can feel is the heavy, staccato beat of his heart. The stuttering, pining answer of my own. His finger on my chin. Our skin running together. "I tend to feel a lot of stuff."

He lowers his hand. "Tell me."

You, I want to say. *I feel nothing but you.*

I shift, angling our bodies together, chins aligned. Between the water and the silt, it's so easy it's practically frictionless. I breathe in, he breathes out, and our lips hover less than a foot apart. It's a line we've crossed before, dozens of times, and yet—

"I feel like I'm circling back to something I forced myself to forget," I say.

Logan draws in a breath. The water picks up its pace, the current seeming to circle us, nudging us together into a tightening eddy.

"And you?" I whisper. "What do you feel?"

He hesitates before his forehead lowers to mine. "Like everything I thought I knew is changed."

My next breath trembles into my lungs.

The eddy swirls faster, cinching our limbs together. Maybe Logan closes the disappearing distance between our lips. Or maybe I do. Or maybe it's just the spinning current, but, in the next breath, I feel his lips brush against mine. A butterfly of a kiss. So soft it might not even count.

But then, his mouth presses tighter and I part my lips. And suddenly that invisible line is a thousand miles behind us. His mouth is on my neck and my hands are climbing into his hair, my fingernails grazing down his wide back.

It's familiar and effortless—the shiver of his exhale when I run my tongue against his jawline and the firm press of his fingers against my neck. Like, despite all the years and changes, this kiss is pure muscle memory.

But, also, entirely new.

Because the last time I kissed Logan, he wasn't yet the man who'd been left by one parent and then the other, trying to fill both the roles they abandoned. And I wasn't this Ali—broken and mended and broken all over again.

Or maybe it's both. New and old. The way it would have been if, through some miracle, I had spent the rest of my high school years here instead of the farthest reaches of this continent. Like I'm closing an open circle I hadn't fully appreciated was incomplete.

Somehow, we've changed positions again, because I find myself straddling Logan's torso, both legs wrapped around his middle. His hands run up the backs of my legs, cup my backside, and he drags me closer. My hips roll against his torso and our skin runs together, made glossier and silkier by the warm water and twist of silt.

Logan moves his lips along my throat. My skin feels like it's tightening against my bones, a cling wrap of pleasure. I roll my hips into him again, aching to get closer despite the way we are pressed together. I feel his erection twitch against my thigh and it sends a low rumble of pleasure and want through my center.

My breaths are coming in harder. Like every time he kisses me with conviction, I want to respond with nothing but recklessness. The creek seems to swell with it, with us. Water rushes faster, crashing over the rocks and frothing in eddies. Logan's hands explore my back even as the current tightens and grasps, trying to pull us together or down. I'm losing myself in this torrential, dizzying moment, and it's so intense and overwhelming that just for the briefest of seconds, I need a breath, a bit of air, so I release myself from Logan and a single word slips from my lips:

"Wait."

He's off me so suddenly it's like he ran headlong into a low-hanging tree branch. His body is strung tight, his eyes roaming over me with some realization dawning.

"This is—" He pulls even farther away, difficult considering the bathtub-sized space we're wedged inside. "We need to slow down."

The creek stills like ice.

I blink. "Okay? Like right now or in general?"

Logan doesn't answer, but his eyes drop to my left hand, where my fingers are still squeezing his forearm. My empty ring finger. I withdraw, curling a fist into my chest. "Because of Blake?"

He frowns. "Blake?"

"My ex. You're saying this is going too fast because I was engaged a month ago."

"No, I certainly was not thinking about Blake." He says the name like he's just tasted an ancient pickle hot-boxing a minivan. He raises a thick eyebrow. "Were *you* thinking about Blake?"

"*No.*" The word bursts out of me. Maybe I should have been? Is it weird I wasn't? "Absolutely not. But then, sorry, can you tell me the problem?"

Logan closes his eyes, massages a temple. "The problem is that I'm an ass."

"I doubt it."

He opens his eyes, but he's still wincing. "There's something I should tell you. Something I should have already said before we . . . before we did all that."

"Okay?"

He takes a steadying breath. "I'm not planning to stay. Once my insurance money comes through, I'm leaving Apple Valley."

Chapter Ten

Now it's my turn to back away, although Logan's thighs are still pressed to my legs, my waist on his rib cage. The words—he's leaving, he's *leaving*—are substantial enough to occupy the slim space between us.

He grimaces at my expression, then drags his fingernails across his beard. "I've inherited a lot—a business, duty, expectations. But not once in my life have I said, 'I want this.' That's what Mason says, anyway. And he's right, unfortunately. Somewhere along the way, I stopped letting myself imagine a different life than the one I already had. There was work to do, my brothers depending on me. No use wanting something I couldn't have.

"Then, after the fire, Mason started asking all these questions. Ones I didn't know how to answer. Stuff like: If I could start fresh, where would I go? What did I want for myself before Mom left? Questions I haven't let myself think about in a long, long time."

Logan swallows, glancing at me again. "I'm sorry I didn't tell you sooner. I should have. I would have if things didn't . . . Like I said, this moved fast."

I nod, stomach twisting, even though I understand what he's saying. His life has been shaped by tragedy, by burdens thrust on him by the two people who were supposed to make his life easier, not harder. He's forfeited his entire life to theirs. It's only fair that he should choose his own path—or get back on the one that he would have been on, if it hadn't been taken from him.

And he's right about something else. This has moved too fast. He's been back in my life for only a couple of days. I just broke off an engagement.

"Where will you go?" I ask.

"As many places as I can, I guess. Maybe start driving west, and when I hit the ocean, go south. I've never been to California or Mexico. I've never seen the Pacific Ocean. When the insurance settlement comes through, I'll have the money to do it."

"Oh," I say. "And, um . . ."

He tilts his head.

"I just thought . . . I was thinking about your art," I say. He hasn't mentioned it since he came back to the farm, so it feels slightly awkward for me to be the one to bring it up. But it still seems too important not to ask. "Drawing. Painting, I think you said you wanted to try, once you could get better supplies. Is that part of the plan?"

He reorients, then exhales, like an uncomfortable laugh. "Sounds a bit juvenile now, doesn't it?"

"I don't think so," I say quietly. "I mean, maybe it could use some refinement. Specifics. But I don't think being passionate about something is ever juvenile."

"No?"

"No. I fell in love with this land when I was a kid and, well, like you said. When you love something, you hold on to it."

Logan stares at me for a beat too long, and despite the warm water, I shiver. "Well. Either way. It's a bit late for that particular dream."

I smile back even as my stomach twists and I want to insist—

insist—that my body stop reacting this way. I have no hold on this man. He gets to decide what dreams he has or doesn't. He has the right to drive straight to Mexico without an ounce of reaction from me.

Clearly my throat does not find this convincing because my voice comes out tight as I say, "You deserve it. You deserve to be happy."

Logan blinks hard and his hand rises like he's going to reach for me, but then he thinks better of it. He drops his arm. "I want you to know that no matter when I get the money, I'll wait to leave until picking is finished. I've made a commitment and I'm a man of my word."

I nod, glad for this, but the truth is I wasn't even thinking about harvest. I should be, though. My family's legacy is riding on me.

"Right." My nose pricks. This is ridiculous. I'm being ridiculous. "Thank you."

My phone alarm screams, startling us both.

Grateful for the distraction, I leap out of the now still pool, bolting onto the bank to retrieve my towel. I shiver as I wrap myself in the material, made stiff and coarse from years of line-drying. My skin is goose-pricked all over, maybe not only from the breeze.

When I turn, Logan is standing more than an arm's length behind me, his towel slung around his shoulders. "I'm sorry, Ali."

"You did nothing wrong," I say mechanically.

"I shouldn't have let myself get close to you like that. Not without telling you the truth." He inches toward me and I clutch the towel tighter. Logan tenses, then retreats. "I never want to hurt you. I'm worried I already did once, when my mom left and I didn't know how to talk about it. And I'm sorry about that. And now I'm doing this again, when you're in a difficult place—"

"No, please." I shake my head, and even though I know exactly what I'm doing, this, too, is pure muscle memory. My lips stretch into a smile. "You haven't. I'm fine."

Logan's eyes tighten as he watches me.

It's absolutely fine that Logan is leaving.

Not in a "smiling over the pain" way, which I guess, sure, is something I do. Rather, because it should be fine. What I just went through with Blake and Liv was objectively worse. Logan is a long-forgotten childhood crush. We've spent, what, a few days together? Kissed once since I was sixteen?

Meanwhile, I was engaged to Blake for more than a year and we dated for five more before that.

My feelings about Logan should be a single raindrop in a flood.

Yet the truth is that my relationship with Blake never felt like a storm—and that was the point. Blake was a person who went to college an hour away from the town where he grew up and spent every Sunday with his parents. He had five-year plans. Shared his calendars with me. Always refilled my wiper fluid. When we moved in together, he started making me the same banana and peanut butter smoothie every morning, insisting that it was just as good as a cup of coffee. Sure, I usually ended up dragging myself into a coffee shop an hour later, still half asleep because bananas do not, in fact, have the "waking up power" of a French vanilla iced coffee. But still. I liked that the smoothies felt repetitive. I thought that meant something.

When he proposed, saying yes felt like the right choice, but also, the only choice. We were both in our late twenties, and we'd been together for half a decade. Our friends were buying houses and having babies. Casual acquaintances had begun to ask when it would be our turn, and Blake's dad had long moved past good-humored teasing. A few weeks after we spent Christmas and New

Year's with his family—and a few months before my uncle's diagnosis—Blake proposed.

I said yes because it felt like the inevitable—the *right*—step on the path I was walking. But I knew it was the right choice for certain nearly a year later, when Blake agreed to move to Oregon to take over my uncle's farm with me. I might have seen his five-year plans and weekly visits to his parents' house as signs of dependability and trustworthiness, but his willingness to set them aside and return to my home meant even more.

As it turns out, I was wrong. Maybe it never meant anything at all. And if I can't count on my own sense of certainty, what can I count on?

So, Logan?

He's leaving. And that's fine. There's too much else on the line.

Over the next week, we return to work in earnest. Back in the barn, Logan and I resume our efforts to round up the bunnies. This time, instead of lunging at the rabbits, we try to lure them to us by testing out a variety of enticements. As it turns out, our furry friends are quite partial to unsweetened apple cider soaked with allspice.

"Little traitors," I whisper affectionately as I dip my finger in dark liquid and hold it out to the hole in the barn's wall. "I still can't believe they turned up their noses at my pears."

Within moments, I have a highlighter-yellow bunny tucked into an elbow and apple cider dribbling down my wrist. It's striking just how quickly I've gotten accustomed to these ridiculous rabbits and, perhaps, the broader idea that this land is supernatural. Maybe because this place has always been remarkable to me. Its further strangeness isn't a shock. It's just a deeper layer of the familiarity I've always held close.

"Terrible taste," Logan agrees before letting out an exaggerated sigh. For the last five minutes, he's been trying to lure out a rabbit cowering behind a ladder, but it has staunchly refused a single lick from his outstretched bowl.

I deposit my catch into our makeshift crate and crouch next to his shoulder.

"You have to be enticing." I make a gentle cooing noise as I hold out a hand with more apple cider on my fingertips. "Try not to glare like you're about to give them a stern lecture."

"A stern lecture," Logan repeats flatly.

"You know what I mean."

"I really do not."

I swivel to look him up and down. He's hunched over, frowning, his big frame taking up twice as much space as it should. "Rabbits respond better to positivity."

"How would you—"

The cowering rabbit takes two tentative hops toward my outstretched hand. Moments later, I have its soft, wriggling body in my arms, licking at me with a bristly tongue.

"Like I said." I steer my triumphant grin toward Logan. "They like it when you smile."

With obvious effort, his gaze lifts from the rabbit, nuzzled against my fingers, to my face. "I see that."

Our eyes meet, and something sparks like static up my spine before Logan turns away.

He's leaving, I remind myself sternly as I cuddle my bunny closer. *And that is fine.*

We use Logan's truck to transport the rabbits to a rescue outside of town, and although Logan fretted about this decision—What would the people say when we showed up with blue and silver rabbits?—his worry turns out to be needless. As soon as the creatures are off the property, their colors revert to natural ones: gray, brown, white. Another miracle of the mundane.

Then, the real work begins. We clear out piles of broken equipment and replace the barn's cracked, foggy windows with clean glass. The fresh sunlight makes me acutely aware of Logan watching me as I balance on the stepladder, stretching on tiptoes to wedge the last windowpane into place. When my foot slips slightly, he lifts his hands to steady me—reaching as his shoulder brushes my thigh—before he catches himself and steps back, fists tightening at his sides.

"Sorry," he says, eyes fixed somewhere on the floor. "I know you're perfectly comfortable on a ladder."

"I am," I manage, although, at this moment, even solid ground would feel unsteady.

By the time we're buffing the floor with an industrial sander, I notice that I've stopped flinching every time I walk into the barn. As we start in on the stain, it's getting easier to glance at the corner where the hay bales used to be. This, at least partly, is because it's so effortless to watch Logan instead. Like the way his shirt rides up as he lifts the new barn door onto the track. Or the pull of the muscles across his back as he hooks it over the rollers.

He glides it back and forth, testing that smooth, soundless movement. Then he looks up at me like he's waiting for my assessment.

"Nicely done," I tell him.

Logan peels off his gloves and stuffs them in his back pocket, the fingers peeking out like a burly pocket square. He wipes at his brow with his forearm and steps back to appraise his work.

"I wish they'd done this job right from the start," he says. "But at least now I can fix what they broke."

I frown and bump his shoulder with mine. "Hey, I'm sorry that even now, you're still cleaning up their mess."

"I don't mind."

Something catches in my chest as he smiles softly, but I push it aside.

In the evenings, we search the journals together, as promised. Usually, I'll prop myself up with floral-print pillows on the couch, a journal held aloft until the weight of my exhaustion takes over. I'll wake hours later to find the lights off and a blanket tucked around my toes, even though I don't remember covering myself with it.

Logan will nearly always be where I left him: hunched at the dining room table, lamplight pooling over the pages and his clenched fists. Sometimes I'll find myself watching him—his furrowed brow, the careful way he turns a page, that etch of his mouth—until I stir.

And turn away before it can go anywhere else.

Sunday comes and goes and, yet again, I let Mom's call go unanswered. Forty-two seconds later, her voicemail pops up. It's the same formal, stilted message, and I can feel my stomach steeling itself against that wall of indifference in her voice.

Meanwhile, I haven't yet managed to look at the farm's books. I also haven't brought myself to open my near-weekly letters from the bank and creditors, but I have started putting them in a shoebox in the dining room, one step closer to the office, instead of letting them pile up in the kitchen. Progress?

Who knows, but I'm certain I'll have the fortitude to tackle all that once I've gotten some good news about the crop.

Which hasn't happened yet, because so far, the mysterious pear affliction has only gotten worse. And now it's undeniably supernatural. The coating that began as white and waxy has started to turn to *glass*. It's like the pears are covered in clear, hard polish.

Or like a late frost crept across the branches and claimed the fruit in its icy grasp.

The first time I see one, I freeze. Logan, a pace behind, stops just short of my shoulder. Then he takes a measured step to the side, putting about a grizzly bear's worth of space between us.

We stare at the fruit.

"They look like *crystals*," I marvel.

A crystal pear turns in the orchard's constant breeze, sending dappled light in pink and yellow across my pale-colored sundress.

I turn to find Logan watching the speckled lights spin across my waist. When our eyes meet, my toes go numb.

"Even Val can't deny this," he says, low.

I nod and swallow past a constriction in my throat. "I think it's time to push her. I'll try alone this time, though."

I have my opportunity a few days later when Val barrels through the new barn door, waving her ticket sales like a winning bingo card.

I nearly capsize off my ladder when she starts shouting out numbers. "I'm sorry. Two hundred?"

It's double what we discussed.

She rubs her palms together. "Folks in town are *eager*. Could be because this farm's always been a bit strange and they're just looking to sate their own curiosity, but I'm not going to spit a gift horse in the face."

"You mean 'look a gift horse in the mouth.'"

She shrugs. "I wouldn't do that, either."

"But how about food?" Logan asks. "Seating?"

"We'll call in a second food truck and folks will be too busy dancing to sit!" she says. "The only thing we cannot run out of is cider."

Surprise aside, doubling the revenue is a huge win. Maybe

even enough to convince me to open some mail. Especially if the gala goes without a hitch.

"I think we might also need another server," I say. "Someone to pour all that cider."

"My brother can help," Logan says.

"Andrew?" Val asks.

"Mason. He's in his junior year at PNU, and he's got a new job at a bar in Maplehurst. Not even old enough to drink legally, but he's already got someone paying him money to tap a keg."

Val snorts. "Sounds about right."

"I'm sure he'll be happy for the excuse to show off his skills, as long as I can be sure it doesn't interfere with his exams."

Val smacks her palms together and rubs them tightly. "This is shaping up."

She's already clomping toward the door when Logan meaningfully lifts his eyebrows toward her disappearing back.

Right! The pears.

I scamper down my rungs. "Val?"

"Walk with me," she says over her shoulder, moving surprisingly fast for a woman still in a boot. "If I'm late for this game, they'll let Bernie deal, and she flashes the bottom card like it's a damn peep show."

"Right," I say as we spill onto the moist grass, just long enough that it clings to my boots. I suck in a breath, steel myself. "Well, I know you've noticed the pears by now."

Val glances over her shoulder. This patch is one of the most advanced—the glassy pears are iridescent, and when they catch the wind, the hues shift like the whirls in a soap bubble.

She grunts. "Strange. My money's on a new sort of pear rust."

I splutter a laugh but she doesn't so much as twitch.

"Come on," I say as she starts walking again. "Logan and I

found multicolored bunnies in the barn. Like, not brown and white—blue and green."

She shrugs. "Maybe someone dyed them. Could have been a prank."

"Val."

And maybe this time I've been forceful enough because she pauses mid-stride.

"This is not pear rust and we both know it," I insist, motioning at the closest tree. As if on cue, the wind breathes over the branches and the hyaline pears clink together, making the gentle tinkling sound of forks tapped against a sea of champagne flutes. "This is *supernatural.* I inherited this land. I'm responsible for this farm. I think it's only fair for you to tell me what's going on."

I brace myself as Val runs her tongue over her teeth. Her gaze drags from my face up the hill toward where the house sits and back down. She swallows, and her shoulders are still stiff, but she doesn't shut down again.

"Fine," she says. "You're right."

"I'm right," I repeat, feeling like this needs to be marked with an audible record-scratch. "You agree it's supernatural."

She throws up her hands. "Yeah, whatever. Supernatural. Afflicted. Cursed."

I squint at her. "Cursed?"

She flinches. "Or whatever."

"You didn't say 'or whatever,' you said 'cursed.'"

Val crosses her arms but zippers her mouth shut.

"What kind of curse?" I press.

Her fingers twitch against her overalls. Again, her focus flicks between me and the house, as though she's half expecting someone to come loping down the hill.

Wait. Is she *literally* expecting someone to come down that hill? "Not . . . ghosts?"

She scoffs. "No, of course not ghosts."

"Then what? What kind of curse?"

But Val shakes her head, whirls away, and yanks open her car door. But just before she slams it, she says through the crack: "It's not my place to say, all right? Try asking your mother."

Chapter Eleven

It's not my first choice to talk to Mom about this.

Frankly, it's not my sixty-seventh choice. A couple of months ago, she barely knew how to respond when I told her I'd chipped my favorite *BRANCH MANAGER* mug. And that's not to mention the disastrous conversation we had after Blake and Liv left.

So, I'm not particularly eager to broach the subject of our family's cursed pear orchard, not least because Mom has spent her entire adult life putting physical and emotional distance between herself and this land. Which is at least part of the reason that I don't make the call right away.

In my defense, every time I intend to call, something gets in the way—usually because Logan and I are buried in gala prep. I finish every day exhausted, palms buzzing from gripping a power sander or shoulders sore from hauling joint compound. The thought of adding emotional taxation on top of the physical is overwhelming.

I'll do it once we're done with the construction work, I decide.

The only problem is that once that's finished, the pace doesn't slow—it merely shifts. There are pear-themed pastries to bake, tents to set up in case of rain, centerpieces to put together. I promise myself I'll call after this batch of puff pastries cools. Or once

I've put the finishing touches on the garlands. Or after I'm done digging through the attic for serving platters and table runners.

But every time, something new comes up. I forgot to candy pear slices. My grandmother's serving spoons are tarnished. I don't have enough extension cords for all the string lights, and I need a last-minute trip to the hardware store. My phone is dead again.

"Tomorrow, I'm calling her," I tell Logan, three days before the gala. I even had the phone ready to go this evening, propped against a bag of flour, although I was elbow-deep in poached pear filling. But the tart shells took longer to bake than expected and its midnight in her time zone now. "Hold me to it, okay?"

The next night, he steers me away from the pear crumble, which I'm still trying to figure out how to beautify (cinnamon sticks, maybe?), and presses a mug of tea into my hands.

"What's this?" I ask.

"Get comfortable," he instructs.

"But my pear crumble still looks all ugly and crumbly."

"I believe 'crumbly' is, in fact, the point."

I harumph. "The photos made it look more appetizing."

"Sit," Logan says sternly. Then he adds, "Please."

I shoot him a skeptical look but comply, holding my mug aloft to keep it from sloshing as I sink into the worn couch and kick my feet onto the ottoman.

"How's the tea?" he asks.

I take a sip. Clearly, he used a bag from my pumpkin spice tin and topped it with cream and brown sugar—exactly how I make it for myself—but after I swallow, an extra note of spice lingers at the back of my throat. Like he's also added cinnamon and cloves or . . .

"Is that cardamom?"

"Do you like it?"

I slurp another greedy sip. "It's heaven, actually."

Logan smiles to himself before humming under his breath and tucking a fleece throw blanket, still warm from the dryer, over my legs. Then he steps back to appraise me like he's checking the alignment on a door.

Something about the scene, which feels perfect to me, seems to displease him, though, because he closes an eye and puts up a finger before disappearing into the kitchen. When he returns, he wordlessly holds out a tin of my favorite cookies—pumpkin spice snickerdoodles. I take one and dip it into the tea, and the crumbs soften instantly.

"Okay," he says. "Now you're comfortable?"

I've forgotten about the lumpy crumble. I've nearly forgotten that anything exists beyond this couch.

"I'm wearing pajamas and a warm blanket," I say, motioning at my flannel nightdress topped with a robe. "I have tea and cookies. This is the literal peak of comfort."

He nods, finally satisfied, and sets my phone in my lap. "It's fully charged."

I stare down at the scuffed device, suddenly overcome with the acute urge to leap off this couch and find something—*anything*—else to do but make this phone call.

"Sneaky," I call as he eases from the room.

"Drink your tea," he says before clicking the door shut.

I'm down to the last spicy dregs when I finally have the courage to dial. It's Thursday, not Sunday, so when the video call connects, Mom says, "Ali. It's a surprise to hear from you."

Through the screen, I can see she's in her sunroom, a spotless gardening apron over her pressed button-down. Her shoulders framed by a row of clean, terra-cotta pots and pristinely green plants. When I was a kid, there was never much room for decor in our U-Hauls. Our apartments stayed bare but for the basics: utilitarian furniture and that series of framed photos of my dad. The only other exception was Mom's plants. Her one indulgence.

Mom's looking into the phone now, her usual, obligatory eye contact at the beginning of our calls.

I sit up straighter. "Hey there, Mom. Is this an okay time to talk?"

She sets down the phone so she can peel off her suede gloves, revealing manicured nails—somehow always pristine despite all the gardening—and her plain, silver wedding band. She's worn it every day I can remember, even though my dad died almost thirty years ago.

"You haven't answered my calls recently," she says as she busies herself with her African violets, drawing the pot onto the coffee table and plucking up a pair of tweezers to remove dead buds. I'm unlikely to get more than another couple of glances for the rest of the call.

"Right, yeah. I'm sorry about that. I've had a lot going on."

She raises an eyebrow. Plucks another bud. "Oh? In September?"

She means because the weeks before harvest are supposed to be languid. Of course, she didn't think I might mean I've had a lot going on emotionally.

But I'd rather not go down that rabbit hole with her.

I close my eyes and take a sip of Logan's tea, pull the blanket tighter. "I'm calling because there have been some, uh, unusual happenings on the farm lately and I wanted to get your take."

Without answering, Mom lifts a glass bottle and spritzes her leaves with a fine mist. I expected this. I also have anticipated the string of questions that will come next.

Which is why I nearly spit out my tea when she says, "I've been wondering when you might come to me with this."

I cough to keep from choking.

Mom brushes a fleck of soil off the rim of her pot.

"I'm sorry. What?" The word comes out too high and loud and I nearly flinch, then modulate my tone. "Sorry. You're saying you already know?"

She sniffs and looks at me. "I grew up on that farm, Ali. The land has been strangely afflicted since long before I was born."

"Why didn't you tell me?"

"When?"

"When what?"

"When would you have liked me to tell you about it?" she asks pointedly.

"Uh, when I was a kid and spending summers on the farm? Last winter when I told you I was moving here?"

She purses her lips and gives her plant a quarter turn. "The family always had a rule about discussing this matter with children. Children are too unpredictable, too liable to let the secret slip. And by the time you were an adult, well . . . I did try to warn you."

"You did?"

She nods. "When you called me to say you were taking over for Martin. I told you to be careful about what you were getting yourself involved in. I reminded you that I left for a reason, and it wasn't just your father."

I remember the conversation because it was one of those rare occasions she spontaneously brought him up. I seized the opportunity to talk about him, redirecting the conversation to how they met when he was in Apple Valley on assignment. I know little about their early history except that my dad was a photojournalist with a fellowship to work on a story documenting the slow decline of family-run farms. But as much as I pushed, Mom refused to budge. Instead she kept circling the conversation back to what I assumed would be the same laundry lists of complaints about the farm. Eventually, I ended the call, trying to avoid getting upset in front of her. I hadn't realized she was trying to tell me something else entirely.

"You were determined to make the decision you wanted to make," Mom adds. "My input was irrelevant."

I sit back, trying to work that over in my head. Meanwhile, Mom busies herself: wiping dust from leaves, checking moisture levels with a slim meter. As a kid, I would resentfully watch her devote hours of meticulous attention to those plants, wondering what they had that I didn't. Now I know it's more about what I have that they don't.

"Okay, then," I say. "Are you still willing to tell me what you know?"

She resumes tweezing buds. "The farm's affliction changed over the years. It was never precisely the same from season to season. But that was what it was: mercurial. A sunny day could easily turn to a thunderstorm. Pears straight off the trees would change flavor—sweet in one bite and too bitter in the next. Even the birds were erratic. Some days they'd sing in a kind of harmony, but on others their song would turn jarring and discordant."

Huh. That doesn't sound anything like what I read in my uncle's journals.

"My pears are turning to crystal," I say. For the first time in the conversation, I let a twinge of powerlessness creep into my voice. Mom doesn't look up. I force myself to keep talking. "Have you seen anything like that before?"

"No, but I wouldn't have." I tilt my head and even though Mom isn't looking at me, she continues, "The land reacts differently to different people."

I sit up straighter. Now we're getting somewhere. "Really? How so?"

A long pause stretches between us and I immediately worry that I've asked the wrong question.

"I mean—" I start.

"I realize I haven't told you much about my mother."

I blink. I can't remember the last time Mom voluntarily talked about my grandmother. Wait, no, I can. I was in high school. Mom came home from some work function having had more than her usual two glasses of wine. She kicked off her heels and made an uncharacteristically off-the-cuff comment about how she never could have pleased her teetotaler mother and even "settling down with a man" didn't win her any points.

Meanwhile, I hardly have enough of my own experiences to understand my grandmother. I recognize her from her portraits all over the farmhouse—stately and commanding in her frames—but I met her only a handful of times. My lasting impressions were the contradictory observations that she ruled the house with an iron fist but would cry if the pie didn't set.

"Yeah, not much," I say.

"She was married several times."

This I did know—there are portraits of her four husbands hanging in chronological order along the staircase. Technically, Mom and Uncle Martin were half siblings: My mom was my grandmother's child with her first husband, who passed away. Martin was the product of her second and, as I understand it, shortest marriage.

"Right," I say.

"The farm's afflictions were different for as long as each of those husbands were part of the family."

Okay. Maybe I see where this is going. "How so?"

"There were field mice everywhere in the months she and Martin's father were married. The soil was always cold to the touch while her third husband was living with us. And when my own father was alive, the trees' leaves would turn golden for a week, right before the pears were ripe, and sometimes the soil turned up rocks so bright they almost looked like gemstones."

I sit back, eyebrows raised. Are my crystallizing pears connected to a particular person? I noticed the first signs of them before Logan moved onto the land and after Blake and Liv had already left. And *my* presence couldn't have been the cause, because I'd already been here for months.

So, I'm not sure. However, this does explain why Martin kept logs of visitors alongside notes about soil and weather.

"So, where does the curse come in?" I ask.

"Curse?"

"That's what Val said. I don't think she meant to."

"Val said that?" Mom asks, uncharacteristically sharp.

"She said it's not her place to say more."

Mom's back somehow goes even straighter. "I couldn't tell you why she said that. Martin called the orchard 'charmed.' 'Afflicted' is what I said. But it's been years since . . . Well, I suppose the last time we discussed it, we were teenagers."

She's stock-still, shears frozen. I wonder if she's thinking about her brother. They barely had full conversations when I was growing up, at least not beyond cursory words exchanged while Mom idled in the driveway and I stuffed my duffel bags into the trunk. I got the sense that their distance only grew in the years after she stopped dropping me off for visits. I'm not even sure if she reconnected with Martin at the end, although I told her he was sick.

"Val said I should talk to you about it," I insist. "She must have said that for a reason."

Mom tenses again. "Val told you to talk to me?"

"Yes. So, maybe you can think of something?" I'm gripping

the bunched-up blanket in a fist, teetering on the edge of pushing too hard. But I can't help it. I'm so close to learning useful information. "Was there something that happened or did you—"

"I couldn't tell you," Mom snaps. "And I need to go. I'll try you again at our normal time."

She ends the call.

Frustration boils in my chest as I blink at the blank screen. I should have known it would end like this. Even in a world where she admitted I'm right, she couldn't connect with me about it. Of course, she shut down when I needed her.

I sigh, detangle my legs from the blanket, and wrestle myself off the couch, pushing open the double doors that separate the dining room and den. I find Logan where I expected him: bowed over the dining room table, an antique lamp scattering tessellated shadows over the pages of an open journal. From this angle, I'm met with a full view of his details. The horizontal lines on his shirt, pulled tight between the slopes of his shoulder blades. His focused gaze. His facial hair forming precise lines around the sweep of his cheekbones.

For a sudden, irrational moment, I have the urge to push his chair away from the table and wedge myself in the resulting space. What would he do? Study me with the intense concentration he's bestowing on those pages? Push me away? Kiss me before pulling back, like he did in the creek?

Maybe Logan feels the angles of my ping-ponging thoughts, because he glances up at me. His brow furrows. "That bad?"

I balloon my cheeks on a sigh. "That obvious?"

"I'll say no, if that's the answer you want."

I slip inside the room and sink into the chair by his side, let my temple fall to my crossed forearms. A curl cascades along my cheek. Before I can blow it away, Logan reaches to tuck it behind my ear.

My breath goes still just as he seems to realize what he's done, because he freezes, then retracts his hand and clenches his fist on the table.

I straighten, leaning back into the chair instead. Then I rock back another time. It's quiet?

I eye Logan. "Did you fix this chair?"

"You said they were important to you."

Goose bumps rise across my arms.

Leaving, I remind myself. *He's leaving.*

I clear my throat. "Well, to answer your question, it turns out my mother—usually more granite sculpture than actual human—believes in the occult, so I nearly flatlined from surprise."

Logan chuckles, but his gaze hovers around my nose instead of meeting my eyes.

"She said she doesn't know anything about crystal pears," I continue. "But I do think I found out why my uncle was keeping track of visitors in his journals. Apparently there's a connection between the orchard's phenomena and the people who are on it."

Logan's forehead wrinkles as an eyebrow rises. "How so?"

"Like, my grandmother had four different husbands, and the soil or the animals were different depending on which man was here."

His frown deepens, and even though I tell myself he's just thinking, there's something overwhelming about that expression. Like it's not my mysterious farm that's the subject of his intense focus, but *me*. It draws a flash of yearning through my chest, a sensation so fast and intense I almost flinch away.

"What are you thinking?" I ask.

Logan's attention moves to the journals, and he starts leafing through pages slowly, then more quickly. He stops, reads, and raps his knuckles against an open page.

"Does this mean anything to you?" he says, splaying out his fingers to swivel the entry toward me.

June 2, 2011

06:15—Sky the color of dishwater, but clearing.

08:40—Scorpion grass everywhere. Hate the stuff—smells like wet envelope glue and clings like regret.

09:30—Tried to pull it up by its stubborn roots, but they snap easy and come back twice as thick.

Visitors—Lydia, Rick, Logan working on the barn in earnest. Tried to get Val to help with the weeds, but she told me it was more fun to watch me flail.

"What am I looking at?" I ask.

"The scorpion grass. Here." He leans closer to turn the page and his shoulder—far too solid to be human—presses against mine. "It keeps coming up."

June 10, 2011

07:10—Scorpion grass spreading low and sneaky. Stuff slips past the trowel like it's avoiding a debt collector.

"And another just a few days later," Logan says. He thumbs over a couple of pages, guides the journal back.

June 15, 2011

06:55—Stuff's blooming now. Pale blue, all over. Looks harmless if you don't know any better.

Visitors—Plenty, but none with good ideas. Val (wants me to try a sledgehammer next time), Rick (left too quickly to survey properly), and Lydia (thinks it's dreamy and I should let it be). Ali gets in tonight—won't force her to weigh in until we've celebrated properly.

"There are a bunch of days it isn't mentioned," Logan says, "but those entries are focused on your uncle's other work. But then . . ."

July 5, 2011

09:10—Scorpion grass is thick as a rug in the lower rows, buzzing with bees. Lydia called it a ground cover and smiled like she'd just won the argument. Maybe she has.

Visitors—Lydia and Ali

"Or this one."

July 23, 2011

07:20—It's blooming again—blue as a crack of sky after a hard storm. Lydia brought tea. We sat in the middle like it was a blanket. Didn't itch once.

Visitors—Lydia

I look up. "It's connected to your mom. He mentions it whenever she's there."

"Exactly."

"Does it disappear after she leaves?"

"Yes. With one exception. Well, Martin doesn't name it, but I think it's clear."

He skims through pages, clearly passing some months, before landing on an entry in messy black pen.

December 1, 2011

07:30—Chilly, plenty of morning frost. No snow yet, but I'm sure it's on the way.

08:20—It's back. Blue flowers under the rusted old gate. Thinner, like it doesn't want to take up too much space. Color's softer now, too.

14:45—Orchard's been quiet. Birds quieter, too. Clouds rolled in but haven't done much.

16:35—Stopped by the gate to see the blooms one last time.

Visitors—None.

I read it twice before looking up. "But what does that mean? If the flowers are linked to your mom, why would they have been here if she wasn't?"

"Maybe she came to see Martin."

"But she didn't see you, right?"

He shakes his head, expression tight. "That was the day we went to get a Christmas tree—I know because it was tradition to pick one up on the first of December and that was our first holiday season without her. I tried to make the most of it, but Andrew wouldn't say a word the entire car ride there, and Mason was still asking about her, wondering when she was going to show up. 'Maybe she'll meet us at the tree farm,' he kept saying."

Before I can even think twice about it, I reach for Logan's forearm and squeeze the tight muscles that run toward his wrist. "She couldn't have come here, then. My uncle wasn't meticulous about everything, but he was about the orchard. If he thought the visitors were important, he would have been honest about them in the entries."

Logan stares down at my hand for so long, I pull back. Clench my fingers in my lap.

He takes a steadying inhale. "Maybe I'm wrong. The scorpion grass could be a coincidence."

I don't think it is—there are just too many entries like this. But if it is tied to Lydia somehow, how could it have shown back up without her?

"My uncle said the flowers were thinner and less vibrant that last time," I say, thinking aloud. "Maybe she was here without really being here. Or only some part of her was here?"

"Like . . . she came and left quickly?" Logan asks.

"No, because then she'd be listed as a visitor."

"Or he didn't know."

I shake my head as my eyes roam the dining room, as if I'm looking for answers in the wood-paneled walls, on the face of the grandfather clock.

"Maybe the land was reacting to something that belonged to her. She left something here." My eyes land on that shoebox filled with my unopened bills. I straighten. "Or what about a letter?"

"A letter?"

"There are letters in the attic."

Logan's eyebrows jog up. "It's worth a shot."

I push back my chair. Usually I wouldn't go digging through my uncle's personal correspondence, but these seem like extenuating, and fair, circumstances. "I know where they are. I'll be right back."

I've sifted through the attic so many times this week, collecting various odds and ends for the gala, that it takes me only a moment to find the letters from the dusty wooden trunk. Back in the dining room, I hold out the stack to Logan. "You should be the one to look."

He doesn't move. I watch him swallow. Then, I pull back my hand, prickling with a sudden awareness of what's unfolding right now. For Logan, this isn't just about the mystery of my quirky uncle, some blue-flowering weeds, and a curse that's turning my pears crystal.

This, for him, is about potentially hearing from his mom one last time.

I hug the mail to my chest. "We don't have to do this. I can put these back in the attic. Until you decide otherwise."

"We need to know why your pears are crystalizing."

I drag out a chair across from him. "We're not reading a potential letter from your estranged parent unless it's what *you* want to do. My pears are just pears. This is bigger."

Logan raises his gaze slowly, like he's giving himself permission to do it. When our eyes meet, his jaw tightens, and I feel that point of connection settle low in my belly.

I bite the inside of my cheek.

Logan clears his throat.

"I want to read them," he says, definitive.

I nod, slide the bundle across the table. Logan eases the letters apart, one by one, until he stops. Pauses. Sets aside the rest of the stack.

He's holding an envelope now: plain, standard letter size, but yellowish with age. The front is addressed to my uncle in clean, looping handwriting.

I watch as he carefully unfolds the flap and pulls out a single sheet of paper so deeply creased its marred with divots. Clearly, it's been folded and unfolded over the years, tattered by scrutiny.

The grandfather clock ticks away in the corner as Logan's eyes glide back and forth. A furrow inches between his brows. Several minutes later, he sets down the page.

He opens his mouth. Closes it again. Takes a deep breath.

Then he asks, "Does scorpion grass have another name?"

I blink in surprise, but quickly recover, and fumble for my phone. After a few seconds of typing, I look back up at him.

"Forget-me-nots."

Chapter Twelve

Dear Martin:

I've started this letter more times than I'll admit. Every version has sounded too finished, like I might sign my name and be done with it. But I'm not finished. That's the problem, really.

Now I'm forging ahead. Mostly because, yesterday, I saw a patch of forget-me-nots coming up through the sidewalk. You would have called it a sign.

I'm somewhere on the coast now. Smaller than Apple Valley, if you can believe it. The kind of place where the sea eats at paint and a lonesome cafe closes by three. I don't think I'll stay long, but it's the first place I've found—apart from your orchard—where I've finally been able to hear myself think.

I can practically hear what you'd ask if you were standing over my shoulder, watching me write this.

"But Lydia, have you stopped feeling like you're disappearing?"

"Can you feel the edges of your life?"

"Is this the place you truly belong?"

And to those questions I would say: yes, maybe, and no.

(You're the only one, by the way, who would have asked me any of that. No demand for my return. No insistent questions about why I've left. Just . . . "Are you okay?" Your questions were a gift. As were our walks, where you gave me the space to answer. It's rare, you know, to have someone stay truly present when you unravel.)

To answer the last question I know you would ask: No, I don't miss the version of myself who was playing a part. But I do miss the heft of cedar. The shavings that curled like question marks. Sometimes, when I'm out walking on the beach, I'll pick up pieces of driftwood and turn them over in my hands, like I'm checking for grain. There is a clarity in that work, something honest that doesn't need explaining.

I worry, sometimes, about what I've left behind. But the more time I have to think, the more I'm certain that this is the cleanest version of love I can offer. You showed me that. And your extraordinary orchard. I wonder if you're right, that it played a role in us. It pulled us in the same way bark splits when the season turns—slow, then all at once. I can't say for sure what was real and what was spell work. But I know what I felt was true. My revelations are true.

I hope you're well. I hope the barn is holding. I hope the pears are as bitter and sweet as ever. If you're inclined to write back, well, please don't. Besides, by the time you're reading this, I imagine I'll have moved on from this salty town.

Yours,
Lydia Holloway

PS: Going by my maiden name again. Strange, but right, don't you think?

Chapter Thirteen

As I lower the trembling leaf of paper to the table, Lydia's words cycle through my mind.

Our walks.

Your extraordinary orchard.

It played a role in us.

A role in what, exactly?

Obviously, she and Martin were close. Plus, there's the forget-me-nots. Maybe it doesn't get more obvious than that.

Was it the same as what happened with Blake and Liv? A friendship that deepened until it crossed a line?

Without my consent, my mind starts replaying Liv's voice, muffled against a closed door, and words I've been shutting out for more than a month. *We didn't mean for it to happen, Ali. It was just so fast.* Even through the wood, I could hear the sob caught in her throat. *We were going to tell you after harvest.*

There, cross-legged on my bedroom floor, with Blake's watch still charging on the end table and his face still smiling at me from frames on the dresser, I screamed.

And now.

Is it truly possible Martin could have done anything like that to anyone else? That he could be like them?

My uncle was a man who told me hard truths with a wink and a gentle smile. Who would always correct falsehoods, no matter how trivial. Who admitted fault, even when no one would know any better. I once saw him apologize to a hose, for god's sake.

And what did Lydia mean when she said the orchard "played a role" in what happened between them? Does this have to do with the curse? Is that the secret Val's been keeping?

Suddenly it all feels too big. The thoughts are so intense I have to force myself to breathe slowly. Get a grip. Try to keep it all from spiraling out of control. Keep myself from toppling over some emotional cliffside.

I glance at Logan. His face is carefully neutral, but his shoulders are hunched, his mouth set tight. One fist is clenched above the table.

Although it's been fourteen years, we've barely been apart for the last week and a half. Maybe that's why the contours of his body language have come back to me with astonishing clarity, like once-beloved lyrics tripping effortlessly off my tongue. This—bracing, impossibly tight—is how Logan looks when he's shaken.

I exhale and round the table so I can take a seat by his. Nudge his knee with my own.

"Hey," I say. "How about we take a walk?"

His face lifts toward the darkened window. "A walk?"

"It usually helps me. To be in the trees."

He considers, then nods.

After slipping on jackets and boots—I'm still feeling warm enough that I don't want to change out of my nightdress—we spill out into moonlit grass.

The air is unusually still, like the orchard is holding itself as taut as Logan. As we pick our way into the trees, the crystal pears catch the moon's silver touch, reminding me of candles flickering in glass orbs. They'd be beautiful, I think, if they weren't threatening my home.

I need to find some words of comfort for Logan, but all I can think about is my uncle. How entranced he'd be by these pears, glowing with borrowed moonlight. How he'd wink and whisper that the land is *special*, hinting at the truth that he was clearly keeping from me.

Another secret. Another silver lie.

"How are you doing with all this?"

Logan's voice cuts into my thoughts and I wheel toward him. He's walking a few paces away, carefully positioned so our shoulders won't accidentally brush. But I can still feel the gentle concern in the question.

"*Me*?" I ask.

He gives me a once-over, as if to quickly reassure himself of something he's already seen. It's been like this throughout the last week. His measured half looks, always putting space between our bodies. He's not wrong to do it, but it still makes me want to grab his hand and force him to look at me properly.

"You have that look," he says softly.

I touch my cheeks, wondering how they've betrayed me. My lips part, ready to stretch into a reflexive smile, but then I think better of it.

"No look," I say, dropping my hand and the corners of my mouth.

"You don't have to talk about it. But you can."

I try to inhale, but the tightness in my chest is making me slightly winded. Or maybe it's just that I'm walking too fast, like I'm sprinting away from the house and that letter. I force myself to slow. "I want to stay focused on you. What are *you* thinking about?"

We crest a small hill. Light bounces over dry fissures in the ground—like the soil has cracked open by the roots. Eventually, Logan says, "I keep coming back to what she said about how this is the cleanest version of her love."

It takes me a moment to remember what he's talking about. Lydia's letter didn't explicitly mention her family, which, come to think of it, is disconcerting. But there was an oblique line about my uncle staying present for her—because her husband didn't? And what she'd left behind, which must have been a reference to her kids. Then there was the part about the cleanest version of her love.

"What do you think she meant by that?" I ask.

"Do you remember when you asked if I had any theories about where she went?"

"You said your dad blamed himself."

"And I didn't answer," he points out.

"Oh," I say. "Right. What, then?"

"I used to have this hope that . . . that deep down she had an altruistic reason."

"Altruistic?"

He blows out a breath. "The year after she left, Andrew read *A Wrinkle in Time* for school. Do you know that book?"

"I saw the movie. The dad disappears and the kids go to find him, right?"

"Exactly. It took me forever to get Andrew to read it—all his schoolwork was a fight that year—but when he finally started it, he wouldn't put it down. For months after, he carried his copy around and kept asking me questions about it. Like whether I thought tesseracts could be real. Or if there was any chance Mom was working on a top-secret government project." He sighs. "It was a child's interpretation of the loss, but also . . ."

We're walking fast again, nearly at the end of the property, but this time Logan is setting the pace, a half step in front of me. I touch his elbow, intending to slow him down, but his entire body tenses. He wheels, back stiffening as he faces me.

I pull back my hand.

"But, also, you hoped something like that could be true?" I ask.

The crystal pears cast shimmering light across Logan's expression, highlighting the ridge of his nose, the clench of his jaw. Distantly, I wonder if the pears will still be glowing like this two nights from now, and how on earth we're going to hide them from two hundred guests.

"I was always angry with her for leaving us," he says. "But sometimes, when I got tired of being angry, I let myself believe that it wasn't her fault." He pushes out a breath. "I know that doesn't make any sense."

My mind flashes to something my mom once said. We were in the car on a long stretch of highway, parabolas of the orange-and-white trailer visible in the rearview mirrors. I was crying, but we were in some expanse of arid desert—going through Utah, maybe, or Nevada—with no exits, no rest stops, no escape.

Her knuckles were nearly white as she clutched the steering wheel and she said to me, "Can't you see I'm doing this for you?"

Sometimes, later, I'd think about that. It was always when my chest was wrung dry of tears, when I was too exhausted to rail against her wall of indifference any longer. I'd give up instead. I'd tell myself that exact lie.

She's doing this for me.

Sometimes, I almost believed it.

"Sometimes," I say now, "you get so tired of feeling something that you just have to shut it off."

He swallows, eyes on mine. "Yeah."

Wind gusts over the branches and they shiver in response, drawing the crystal pears into a tinkling harmony. I don't know how we ended up here, but this row has always been one of my favorites. The trees are old—planted by my grandmother when she first took over from her father—and the limbs nearly crowd together, carving spaces beneath that feel like secret dens.

Logan leans a wide shoulder against a branch. He's still watching me, intensely enough that I feel my heart skip its next beat.

"See?" I say.

"See what?"

"Being in the trees, it helps."

"It's not the trees that are helping," he says.

My chest tugs, like it's reaching for him.

Logan clears his throat. Looks away. "Anyway, you asked what I was thinking and that's it. The letter might not say why she left, but it does rule out that theory."

My mind flits back to our other scraps, fledgling bits of information. "My uncle seems to have contributed to her decision in some way."

Maybe this is what Val is keeping quiet. Not just whatever was going on between my uncle and Lydia, but the role he seems to have played in the unraveling of Logan's family. Val is so protective of him, I'm sure she'd want to protect his memory, too. And she wouldn't want this secret to change my opinion of him.

Well, if that's it, then she was right. It has.

Uncle Martin was the only adult who ever made me feel truly safe—and now I'm not even sure who he was.

Logan hasn't spoken yet, like maybe he's waiting for me to continue. And, somehow, I do have more to say.

"I always knew I'd find out secrets about him when I moved into his house, but I never thought they'd be the painful kind. Like, it turns out he had a hidden penchant for apple preserves, despite our family's bias. He had a whole shelf of the stuff in the basement, hidden behind his bottles of rhubarb wine and fermented hot sauces." My chest twinges with affection, and it's replaced swiftly by another bolt of anger. "God. I'm sorry for what it looks like he did to your family."

Logan's eyes catch the light as they rise. "She was the married one."

"Then I hate what they *both* did to you."

"My brothers were the ones that grew up without a mother."

I step toward him. I don't dare come too close. Not with the way he's holding his body stock still, his arms crossed over his chest. Not with the way he's so purposefully put space between us since what happened in the creek. But I want to underline what I have to say with more than my voice.

"And it was *you* who stepped in to take care of them," I say fiercely. "Maybe she abandoned them, but she *left* you."

He blinks once, slow. When he speaks, his voice sounds like it's been dragged over my gravel driveway. "Ali."

"Logan."

The wind picks up, tossing a curl loose from my bun and into my face. Logan's hand rises and he brushes it back, tucking it behind my ear. This time he doesn't flinch away.

"Only you would say that's worse," he says.

"It is," I insist and I can feel the hot sting of tears behind my eyes, even though I'm not completely sure why I'm getting emotional. "You had the weight of *everything* on your shoulders. You had plans, you had a whole life decided, and she took that from you."

Logan's gaze lingers on mine. He's closer than he has been in over a week, expression dark in the moonlight.

"I hate that they hurt you," he says.

My next breath hitches. "Me?"

"You had weight on your shoulders," he says. His voice is low and rough, but I don't miss the purpose in his tone as he returns my words to me. "You had plans and a whole life decided. *They* took that from you."

Something twists in my ribs and, for a second, I forget to breathe.

The wind picks up, bringing with it a chill. I shiver, hug my jacket closer.

"I liked it better when we were focusing on you," I say, with a shaky smile.

Logan steps toward me—for the first time in days drawing closer instead of farther away. He's close enough that I can see the flecks of gold in his irises, gleaming in the soft glow of crystal pears. He brushes his thumb against the lifted corners of my lips. Like he's wiping away a tear.

"It kills me that I can't fix it for you," he says.

My heart seesaws. "I'm sorry that I'm not as easy as a barn door."

"I didn't say I want to fix *you*." Logan's next inhale is slow, deliberate, but when he shifts again it's to bring himself a hair closer, like he's being tugged by the inexorable pull of a distant gravity. "It's not you that needs fixing."

He's leaving, I try to remind myself again. But the thought quivers, breathing its last breath.

Because he's warm and close—his wide back and steady presence shielding me from the wind, carving out our own personal microclimate.

"Can I touch you?" I ask, then add quickly, "A hug, I mean."

His jaw tenses, but he doesn't pull away. "I don't think that's a good idea."

Now that I've put the thought out into the night air, I'm aching for his touch. I can't stop thinking about the way his skin felt against mine when I was curled in his lap in the pool. The way he held me in his arms, steady and unyielding. The way he kissed me, careful and exploring.

I'm aching for it so much I can't help but ask, "Why?"

He's silent, holding back an answer I can see flickering on the tight set of his lips.

"Logan, tell me."

His jaw works over a swallow. "Because I don't have enough self-control around you."

These words draw a ripple of heat across my skin, a pool of desire that tugs low through my belly.

"But not," I clarify, as I inch closer, "because you don't want to touch me."

"Ali," he says, and it's a clear warning.

"Tell me why we shouldn't."

"Because I don't want to hurt you."

My chin lifts. "I can handle it."

"You've already been through enough," he says softly. "With your uncle. Your ex. I know you can handle it. The question is whether you should have to take on more."

"Or maybe"—my hands close into fists—"the question is whether I want to."

Logan's holding himself so taut he might as well be a tree trunk, braced against the valley's relentless wind.

"Maybe it will hurt," I say pointedly. "Maybe at some point in the future, I'll have to experience the pain of losing you for a second time. But that's my choice, right? And that's not happening now. Right now . . ."

I tip my face toward him. The flicker of a tremor passes over Logan's lips, and in that moment, I see his resolve crack.

"Right now I'm saying I want you," I finish. "Whether or not it's going to hurt. I say *yes.*"

For a split second, even the trees seem to hold their breath, as if the orchard, too, is waiting for his answer.

Then, without a word, without looking away, he gathers me into his arms.

Chapter Fourteen

Logan's hands span my waist and a weightless sensation soars through me as his arms draw me onto tiptoes. I cling to his shoulders and burrow my nose into the soft, worn collar of his shirt. When I inhale, I find a smell that is more than Logan. Or maybe it's fully him: deep and earthy, like sweat and sagebrush, tinged with sweetness.

"You smell like an orchard," I tell him, twisting in his arms so that we haven't separated, but I can still lift my face to his.

Logan's eyes are all shadow and weight, framed by dark lashes, but for those flecks of gold, still glowing.

He smooths back a wisp of my hair. "If I didn't know you," he says, "I would wonder whether that's a compliment."

"Hmm," I say thoughtfully. "You know that's one of your best qualities?"

"My smell?"

"Knowing me."

His eyes trace my face with an attention I can't escape. It's the same way he's holding me—deliberate, warm, and impossible to ignore.

"Ah," he says carefully, "but I'd like to know you even better."

For the space of a heartbeat, we stare at each other, bodies still pressed together, touching for the first time in days, caught in shifting light and shadow under the canopy of a pear tree.

Then I lift my chin. And his mouth descends onto mine.

Logan hauls me against his body just as my hands fist his shirt, yanking him closer. Heat pours through my limbs, lighting my blood on fire. His kiss coaxes my face higher, his mouth hungry on mine, and a sigh loosens from my chest.

With one arm around my shoulders, he eases me backward until I'm pressed against the tree trunk. The backs of my shoulders scrape against bark and Logan's beard scratches my cheek. They're both rough, not enough to hurt, but to build friction.

There's an urgency and purpose to our movements that we didn't have in the creek—and certainly never had as teens. His fingers in my hair. My teeth at his bottom lip. Our panting breaths between tongues. It's like the last week of his physical absence, but persistent presence, is lancing me with a sharp pulse of need. Need to be closer. Need to close some gap that's been opening for days. Need to close the distance that's stretched over years.

"Logan," I murmur.

I arch like a bowstring, bending my body into his. His hand skims up the back of my thigh, lifting the hem of my nightdress with it. The air is cool against my skin, and I shudder—not from cold, but from the way his touch wakes something under my ribs.

"Your outfits drive me crazy," he says, voice so rough it's almost dazed. "It's September in Oregon and here you are in a dress."

"A nightdress," I correct for reasons that surpass understanding. Maybe it's just the frenzy of my brain, the pool of heat between my legs as Logan works his lips along the base of my throat, the back of my ear. "And when it's cold, I wear leggings."

He grunts a laugh and his hand dances higher, drawing a trail of fire with his touch.

"Not tonight, though," he says.

I gasp as his fingers glance along the edge of my underwear, so near where I want him. And still not nearly close enough.

I try to press into his hand just as Logan's lips drop to my ear. "Can I touch you?"

I shiver, a week's worth of desire lifting my hips with unconscious thought. "Yes. Please."

Logan groans, low and urgent, one elbow inching my legs apart as he swipes my underwear aside. His finger barely brushes against me, but even with that touch, I can tell I'm embarrassingly wet.

"I'm sorry," I stammer out. "I've just wanted this."

His fingers trace in a tight circle, coaxing pleasure through me.

"I don't think I've ever wanted anything more," he whispers.

I shudder at his words, torn between the aching pleasure of his touch and the echo of his absence. "But you've been so far away."

Logan's mouth is on me again, his lips urgent. His finger hooks inside me, moves slowly, in and out, and I feel myself moan, another locked room inside my soul unfastening for his key. Every swipe is devastating, pulsing, infinite pleasure. I'm wobbly and jelly in his arms, like nothing is holding me upright except Logan and the tree trunk.

"I never stopped wanting you," he says.

"Didn't you?" I ask.

Something soft trips against my shoulder. In the pale light of the crystal pears, a blossom descends the length of my dress—a shock of white against plaid. Before I can wonder about that I hear Logan say, "I tried to forget." His voice is rough, pulled tight. "I'd lie in bed at night, staring at my ceiling, thinking about nothing but you. Wondering where you were. Missing you is the only part of my life that has felt fully mine."

For a second, I can't breathe.

"*Logan*," I say, strumming and needy.

Suddenly, it's still not enough. He's not close enough, could never be close enough. With one hand, I fist the fabric of his shirt and use the other to tug at his belt.

"Ali," Logan says, and to my consternation, there's a warning in his voice again. "Unless you've got a condom in that nightdress, we might need to take a pause."

My hand stalls, but there isn't a single chance I'm willing to walk back to the house, putting distance between us in the meantime.

"Okay, but," I say, "hear me out."

Logan waits.

I duck my chin. "I was hoping to come up with an idea by the time I stopped talking."

He grunts out a laugh and then with the barest of smiles, drops to his knees. With one arm around my backside, he hitches me onto tiptoes, my back braced against the trunk. His lips travel higher, kissing the inside of my knee, then the soft, sensitive skin along my thighs, up and up, until—

I gasp with pleasure, my hips arching. This. *This* is finally close enough. Enough pressure. Enough heat. Enough Logan.

My fingers dig into the soft bark, and I'm sure I've just ruined my nails with dirt, but I can't care. My spine arches and my hair tangles in bark. My breaths come faster, heaving in and out of my lungs as Logan's tongue moves, driving me with the force of a cresting wave.

His name rips out of my lips. My fingers twist into his hair, and maybe I'm pulling too hard, but I barely know what I'm doing because I'm close to bursting, exploding, radiating. Like I'm lost in the movement of his mouth as he unshackles each nerve ending from its muscle.

Then Logan adds his finger, too, and everything clenches. Explodes. A bright pulse of white.

I'm opening, relaxing like a bloom. I tip my head back, and Logan is still nudging his nose against me, murmuring encouragements as the wave ebbs.

My eyes open toward the branches. They should be filled with nothing but leaves, dark silhouettes against the starry sky, but my vision spackles with white.

I blink as my back relaxes against the trunk, limp and boneless. Logan eases me to the ground, gathering me into his arms. Vibrations still race through me, but they're subsiding now. Still, the white filling my vision doesn't fade.

"Logan," I say and shake his elbow.

"Hmm?" he says distractedly.

"Logan. Look."

I tip my chin higher. Our faces travel upward.

Impossibly, so impossibly, the tree has bloomed. Where, minutes ago, these branches were only green, they've erupted in a riot of glowing buds, silvered under the moonlight. A breeze catches a branch and blossoms scatter in a million disintegrating pieces. They drift and rise in the shallow breeze, shimmering down on us like a rainstorm of flowers, decorating my curls in specks of white.

A laugh catches in my throat as I lift my hand. Delicate petals collect in my open palm. "Logan. Tell me this is real."

His eyes are wide with awe—an expression of wonder I haven't seen since we were children, didn't even realize his adult face could still make. Our gazes connect as a blossom settles on his cheek.

I pinch it off his beard, and his hand rises to catch my wrist.

"As real as the butterflies," he says, thumb tucked into my palm.

My mind sheers in half, splintering a jagged edge between *then* and *now.*

His barrel chest. Probing eyes.

A worn pencil in his fingers, his back against a tree trunk.

The line of his jaw. The rough pads of his fingertips.

His pinky finger anchored to mine as we follow the drift of clouds through a cornflower blue sky.

I'm straddling a line, living a refraction. I see him as he was: open and young and standing in the light of his biggest dreams. And here. The man who can steady, or unravel, me with a single glance.

"Remind me why you're the one leaving this time," I say quietly.

Logan rests his chin on top of my head. "Sometimes it's hard to remember."

I swivel so I can look up at him. "What times?"

His thumb runs against my cheekbone, and even though the eye contact is so intense my veins hum, I let it ride. "Anytime you're looking at me."

My breath hitches and now it is too overwhelming, so I motion like I'm going to turn away.

"Well, let me just—" I say as Logan grunts out a laugh and catches my shoulder, keeping me pinned into his side.

He rests his temple on top of my head again, lifts his head to smooth back some of my unruly curls, and replaces his cheek.

"When I was eighteen," he says, tracing the inside of my palm with his thumb as he talks, "I stayed in Apple Valley because my mom left and my brothers needed me. When I was twenty, I took over my family's business because Dad stopped working and someone needed to pay the bills. I'm thirty-two now and until it burned down two weeks ago, I was still sleeping in the same bedroom I had as a child."

He pauses. "I've never gotten to choose any of my life for myself. Until now."

I feel the words twist in my chest.

"Those are good reasons," I say.

"You think?"

"I really, really do." I consider how much practice I have with goodbyes. "And maybe I deserve it at this point. Some kind of karma. Now that I'm finally staying put, it's—"

I cut myself off. Bolt upright.

Logan swivels, his eyebrows pulling together in concern. "Ali?"

My mouth drops open, working over words I haven't even put into thoughts.

"Blake and Liv," I say. "My mom. Your mom. *You.*"

"What about us?"

"The curse," I tell him. "I know what the curse is."

Chapter Fifteen

"It makes people leave, doesn't it?"

The next day, I corner Val, freshly out of her boot, when she shows up with folding tables and chairs.

I've barely been able to think about anything but the curse since last night when Logan and I made our way back to the house together, although I was still vibrating from his nearness, my brush with something beautiful and fleeting. In the cold light of day, I'm already wondering if, last night, I was acting more on impulse than logical thought. Under that tree, I wanted him so much that I told him it didn't matter if it would hurt later. Maybe that was wrong. There are too many logical reasons we shouldn't have done what we did. He's leaving, for one. He's barely been back in my life for two weeks. And less than two months ago, I was engaged.

At the same time, being with Logan, drawing myself close to him once again, feels right in a way that it never did with Blake.

Although if I'm right about the curse, I might soon regret that, too.

When I brought up my theory to him, Logan didn't seem entirely convinced. Whether this was a product of his reflexive skepticism or because my explanation wasn't that compelling, I don't know.

"Might not be what it is," he said.

I found myself wondering if his doubt was a kind of false hope. Either way, I need to know.

So, the question practically explodes out of me as Val rolls open the door of her overfull rental van.

She turns slowly. She's supposed to be taking it easy now that her boot is off, but I don't think that has anything to do with the way she's still clutching the door handle.

"The curse," I repeat. "It makes people leave the orchard. Maybe it's circumstantial or maybe it's a suggestion or maybe it's a full-on push, but that's the result. People who spend time here end up leaving."

Val's shoulders hunch. Her tongue runs over her teeth as her eyes dart like she's searching for the exits.

"I would really like to know the truth," I plead quietly. "It's my land. Uncle Martin entrusted this place to me, and I'm supposed to take care of these trees for the rest of my life. I'd like to understand exactly what that means."

Val sighs and rests a temple against the van. Then she slides the door closed and loops an arm around my shoulder.

"If we're going to have this talk," she says heavily, "I'm going to need to a drink."

In the kitchen, Val sinks down to the table while, at her instruction, I forge to the basement to retrieve a dusty bottle of rhubarb wine from the shelf filled with jars of preserves and dill pickles. When I return, I pour pale blush liquid into two crystal glasses.

Val eyes them, then me. "Just us, right?"

I nod. "Logan already left for Maplehurst. He had a meeting with his insurance company, and then he's going to bring Mason back for the gala tomorrow."

"Good." She lifts her glass and takes a deep swallow, then

wipes her pressed lips with the back of her hand. "I guess you've got the gist of it, then. Mostly."

I squeeze the bottle in my hands, watching the sediment spin as my head does the same. "People who come here end up leaving."

A curt nod. Her eyes remain on her glass, now clutched tightly between her callused fingers. "The way Martin would say it—it drove away the people he loved. The Reid who tends this land is cursed to a kind of solitude."

My next few heartbeats flicker as I try to digest the words *drove away* and *cursed to solitude.*

Val sighs again and takes another long swig of wine, draining her glass. She slides it toward me and I refill it before stepping away, taking refuge by a countertop.

"I didn't believe him for a long while," she continues. "For years I wondered if Martin didn't make it happen himself. He was always talking about how he was meant to be alone, always so goddamn convinced of it, that he holed himself up in this house until that's exactly what he got. I didn't want that for you, too."

"That's the reason you wouldn't tell me the truth?"

She frowns. "No. I didn't tell the truth 'cause I promised the man I wouldn't. Before he died, Martin made me swear not to tell you."

"He *what?*"

A fresh round of betrayal rises up in me.

We had a whole month together, at the end. We played pinochle and did about six hundred puzzles. I'd wake up in the middle of the night—plastered with sweat from those heavy quilts—and my cheeks would already be wet because I couldn't imagine how this world could exist without him. How these trees could thrive without him tending them. I asked him a million questions about watering schedules and irrigation systems and clung to every word of his answers. Yet he didn't tell me this.

This. The most important thing.

Val fiddles with one of the lace doilies on the kitchen table. "He said he was worried you'd hightail it out of here if you knew the truth. And . . . you know how he felt about this land. What it would have meant if you weren't the one to take over."

I suck in a deep, steeling breath as my mind flicks back to those last days. He was oddly insistent about educating me on the land's problems. I haven't understood why he seemed so adamant—usually it was Val who told me I needed to be more realistic, not Martin. But now I wonder. Was it guilt? Did he feel conflicted? Maybe it was his attempt at honesty, like emphasizing all the other problems would make up for withholding this big one.

That doesn't make it right, though. He should have told me. I deserved to know.

"Like I said," Val continues, "up 'til recently, I wasn't so sure the curse was real. Just some self-fulfilling prophecy he'd laid on himself. But then you came here with those two. . . ." She blinks like the names are on the tip of her tongue.

"Blake and Liv."

"Yeah. Them." Even though she doesn't know the whole story about what happened—I've only told Logan about what I saw in the barn—her expression tells me exactly how she feels about them both. "And not a few months after, they were gone. And the land started acting up almost right away."

My jaw clenches. "And you *still* didn't tell me."

"I gave the man my word," she says. "And I tried to tell you what I could. Without breaking that last promise."

"Some things are more important than a promise."

"Not to me."

I look at her flatly, arms still crossed.

"I have my flaws, Ali," Val says, and her voice is rougher than usual. "I know that. I haven't got much patience. I never seem to know the right thing to say when folks are hurting. And I've been called 'bullheaded' from time to time, maybe even rightly. But if there's one thing I've always been good about, it's keeping my word. Especially when I give it to good people. And your uncle—god love him—was one of the best men I've ever known."

I rub at the bridge of my nose as I push off my counter, then lower myself to a seat next to her. My jaw is throbbing from clenching my teeth so hard. At the same time, the person to blame for that isn't here.

"That's why you told me to talk to my mom," I say heavily. "Because she's one of the ones who left."

Val swallows hard and her gaze goes distant. "She sure was."

In half explanation she adds, "That's how Martin got on this whole idea the first time. When Nora left, everything went haywire. Cold frosts, colors draining out of the leaves. A few years of crops so thin we barely thought we'd survive to the next season. Martin took all that real hard. Got convinced it was connected." She sighs heavily. "Maybe he was right though. Maybe it wasn't just the shock of her leaving."

I glance at the family portrait hanging above the old, cast-iron radiator. Mom's standing off to the side. A picking bag weighs her shoulders, and she has her hands on her hips, lips pinched. That photo isn't an aberration. In fact, I can't think of one in this house where Mom doesn't look tense or withdrawn.

"I thought she hated it here," I say.

"I suppose she did," Val says, expression curiously blank as she swirls wine around in her glass. "For the most part."

"And my dad was only in Apple Valley for a short time."

Here, I'm certain Val's eyes flash. "Yup. Probably the reason she wanted him in the first place."

I blink. "Like she married him for a ticket out of town?"

Val rubs at the back of her neck, the spot where her short hair fades into skin. "No. Forget I said that. She loved him all right. I'm sure of that. But she was looking for an escape, and your dad was everything that Apple Valley wasn't. Educated, a traveler. He walked into our town with that big camera and an even bigger smile, started taking pictures and asking questions like he already had us all figured out and he'd be ready to get on out of here by Tuesday."

This is the most I've ever heard Val—or Martin for that matter—talk about my dad. When I was a kid, they both acted like they knew nothing about him, and I had no reason to question it. But that wouldn't be right. He was in Apple Valley for at least a few months, working on that photo series, before my mom left with him. They all must have met at least a few times.

"It sounds like you didn't like him."

She presses her lips even tighter. "I don't want you to take that from it. He was your father and you didn't even get to know him. All I'm trying to say is that I can see why he was appealing to Nora."

"So, you couldn't have been surprised she left."

Val reaches across the table to grab the wine bottle again, leaving new fingerprints against the dust. She swirls her freshened glass a few times before taking another swallow. "In retrospect, I guess not. But at the time, it was a shock. Nora was always supposed to take over, you see. Was groomed for it from the beginning. She might have been—well, she might have been *Nora*, but that's just it. How she was. Never one to make a fuss. She had high standards. And she took the work seriously. The land listened to her, too."

There's a distant, maybe begrudging kind of admiration in Val's voice. I think about Mom patiently clipping at dried buds or measuring lukewarm water into one of her brass watering cans. "She was a good orchardist."

Val nods. "Very. Your grandmother—I always called her Mrs. Reid—always said her daughter was born with two green thumbs and a green pinky, although she still watched over Nora's shoulder like one of them might fall off. The woman was devastated when your mom left. She had lost her daughter, but also, I think she knew what the land was losing, too. What this meant for her legacy. She threatened to come after your father with her shotgun, even though Nora was legally drinking age by then, and there was nothing to do about it. Then she pulled out about six fistfuls of hair and screamed herself hoarse every night for a month."

My eyebrows tick up. "Dramatic."

But Val's shaking her head, as though clearing the memories. "That's how your grandmother was. High highs and low lows. Anyway, Mrs. Reid probably wasn't wrong to be worried." Val's eyes flash before she brusquely moves forward. "I never would have breathed a word of this to Martin when he was alive, but Nora would've kept this place running smooth as clockwork, even with all the bad luck piling up. She wouldn't have gotten distracted with some specialty irrigation system or a fancy new tractor. But it's not a fair judgment, I guess. Martin wasn't the one raised to be in charge."

"Why was she the one?" I ask. Mom's life on the orchard wasn't something she ever talked much about, despite my many attempts at asking. "If she didn't seem to like it."

Val lifts a shoulder. "She was the oldest. Mrs. Reid saw it like I did—Nora was damn good at growing things. And Mrs. Reid was a hard woman to impress."

"But that can't have been all," I say, "if it was always planned that way."

"Well," Val concedes, "I think it's also 'cause Nora was the daughter from Mrs. Reid's first marriage. The one who died. 'The soulmate,' she called him, even after she remarried. None of the others lived up."

My eyebrow ticks. I hadn't put my grandmother's long list of ex-husbands on the list of people who have left the orchard, but it certainly fits the pattern. "Was that the curse at work, too? My grandmother's husbands?"

"That was Martin's theory, yeah. And there were others, too. In those years when he started shutting himself up here, he went looking farther back in the family tree. Turns out every Reid who farmed this land—starting with your great-great-grandfather Ransom, who lost his wife in childbirth—died here alone." She rubs at her forehead. "I sbould've listened to him when he told me all that."

My breath stills as her words sink in. *Cursed to solitude. Cursed to die alone.*

"And every time a husband left, the magic acted up? Like when my mom did?"

"Right. Things were always weird around here when we were kids, but when a husband was out of here, it all got worse. Big swings in weather. New pests coming and going. Noises at night that we couldn't always explain."

"But no crystal pears."

"Not that I know of, no, but it wasn't like that for Martin, either, after—" She cuts herself off with an aggressive swig of wine.

"Subtle," I say.

She frowns back. "Yeah, well, this particular secret doesn't have nothing to do with you."

I sigh. "I already know about Lydia."

Val startles. "Excuse me?"

"We found a letter she wrote to Martin."

Val crosses her arms and even though Logan fixed it, she still manages to elicit a creak from her chair as she pushes back in it. "You shouldn't be nosing around other people's mail, girl."

"To be fair, we also shouldn't be reading other people's journals."

"That's different," Val protests. "I already knew the gist of what was in those, knew they wouldn't have direct references to the curse or . . . anything else Martin would have wanted secret. He always kept those professional—well, professional for him, anyway—just in case he needed to show something to the packing house or some pesticide consultant."

"Fine," I say. "But Lydia's also Logan's mom. So maybe this secret had nothing to do with me, but I think he has a right to know what happened to her."

Val relaxes minutely, tipping forward in her chair again. "Yeah. That's true. I reckon he does."

"And Uncle Martin was in love with her," I press. "That's why the farm had so many problems after she left. The codling moths and the sudden explosion of the irrigation system and all the rest of the stuff I read about in those journals. It went on for years."

I'm guessing, of course, but it fits. And I'm hoping that if I frame my question as a statement, Val will be more likely to tell me what I want to know.

My tactic seems to work because she nods. "That's what he thought, yeah."

I hold my breath as I craft my next question-posing-as-a-statement, aiming for nonchalant but possibly missing the mark by a mile. "And the two of them had an affair."

This time Val either catches the strain in my voice or she isn't fooled by my tactic. She purses her lips. "I don't know about that. Martin never told me exactly what happened between them."

My heart pounds low in my ears as Val watches me for another long beat.

"I'm serious, Ali," she says. "Now you know every bit that I do."

I nod and spin my glass of my otherwise untouched rhubarb wine, mostly to give my hands something to do. I can't dwell on my uncle's mistakes. What matters is the curse, the reason behind the crystal pears. Unfortunately, this new explanation fits better than I'd like.

The pears started crystalizing after Blake and Liv left. That's also when all kinds of other weird stuff showed up, like the persistent fog. And the skunk with the spray that was impossible to clean off. The multicolored rabbits, too. To be fair, those were more nuisance than malicious, but I suppose not every aspect of the curse has been problematic. My mom mentioned golden leaves and gemstone rocks from when she was growing up—and I can't see the harm in either of those.

Val's still watching me. "You've always been like him, you know."

I startle, try to reorient. "Delusional, you mean?"

She winces. "I shouldn't have said that. But, no, that's not what I'm talking about, although you do both have a way of focusing on the bright side. I was talking about the way you both love—loved—these trees. Like they're part of the family."

And even though I'm still angry with him, her words stir a memory that's now tinged with both fondness and grief. That summer Uncle Martin and I found fire blight on the main trunk of one of his oldest trees and knew we'd have to pull it up, roots and all. He hid the chainsaw away from it as long as he could, like he was shielding the tree from its own fate. Then he patted the limbs and whispered a goodbye before making that first cut. He was so kind. So earnest.

But now I don't know if I can see him like that anymore. Not after everything he kept from me.

I shake my head, bottling up these thoughts. I guess my entire childhood with Martin is also going in a box.

This mental attic of mine is getting about as full as the actual one.

"I told him," Val continues when I don't say anything, "that he should trust that in you. That he could tell you the truth and you would still want to stay."

She eyes me significantly as I turn that over.

Cursed to a lifetime of solitude. Staying put while all the people I love eventually leave. It's one of the worst fates I can imagine.

In fact, I can imagine only one that's worse.

Leaving myself.

Because this place? It's not just where I belong; it's where I began. Every hill holds proof. The branches remember my small, determined hands. The stump still bears the ghost of my fall. The old Deere tracks have long since blurred into soil.

These days I walk the rows with steadier steps, my boots pressing into the same furrows where I once ran barefoot. But some mornings, when I'm cradling a mug of coffee and the light filters through the leaves, I can practically feel it: the quiet exchange between what I've tended and what's tended me.

My trees—my roots—remind me that I am part of something living and lasting. That I'm allowed to settle. To exhale. To grow here, too.

"Yeah," I say. I've been rubbing at that scar on my elbow. I drop my hand. "You were right. It doesn't change my mind."

Val pats my wrist. "Martin would be proud."

The words feel like an ice pick to my rib cage. I blow out a breath. "As long as we can get through this season."

"Not long now."

"Yeah," I say. We have ten days until the end of September, and even though I can't see the fruit from here, I know what's happening outside the kitchen window. The pears that haven't crystallized are on the edge of ripe: the color developing, the pieces full and round, good sugar content. The problem is that, at this point, the ones that have turned are just as numerous as the ones that haven't. "I just have to hope it's enough."

Val eyes me sharply. "You have some reason to think it won't be?"

"Not . . . specifically," I say. I might not have stepped foot in the office or familiarized myself with the exact contours of the numbers, but increasingly, avoiding them has felt like delaying something inevitable rather than holding out hope.

"Well," Val says, patting my hand. "The gala replaces about half your crop. You've got the other half ready to pick. Given how long Martin hung on with things like they are, that will be enough to get you through to next season. You might not get ahead, but you'll be keeping it all afloat."

I blink at her, doubt still worming around my heart, and for a fleeting moment, I wonder when our roles reversed. But then I push away the thought. This will work out.

The gala will be a success.

We'll start picking in a week and a half.

Everything will be okay.

Chapter Sixteen

I'm not sure how to tell Logan I was right about the curse. Nor do I know how to talk to him about us. I'm also worried that, by the next time I see him, he'll have retreated into his protective armor of restraint and self-control.

Fortunately or unfortunately, between his trips to Maplehurst and then to pick up the cider kegs from the Harts, about forty-eight hours pass before Logan and I have a chance to talk again. Nearly every minute of that is filled with my own final preparations for the gala—arranging the fall-themed centerpieces on our tables, plating my panoply of pear desserts, setting up signs for parking—so I also barely have time to think about what I'll say.

Less than an hour before the guests are set to arrive, Val directs two food trucks to their spots next to a pop-up canopy and then perches herself on a stool by the barn doors, where she'll collect tickets. Meanwhile, I duck into the house, change into a dress appropriate for the evening, and swipe on some mascara.

When I stride through the barn's new doors, I'm finally able to appreciate what we've pulled off.

Dozens of string lights drape from the rafters, casting a soft glow across the dance floor. Wine barrels serve as high-top tables, each adorned with taper candles in amber glass holders. Beyond them, the room is rimmed with hay bales and tables on loan from

Val's retirement community, disguised beneath plaid bedsheets and centerpieces of pumpkins and pine cones. It smells like cinnamon, orange, and a hint of sawdust, and the stereo hums with a song that's romantic but restless.

And I don't recognize it? I could have sworn I started this playlist with "Uptown Funk." When I make my way over to the phone to investigate, I find *mason's no skips, all bangers* has taken over my Spotify.

"You must be Ali!"

I spin to find a tall guy releasing a dolly behind the bar and then driving across the room for a hug. He breaks it off only to hold me at arm's length and inspect me from head to toe. "I've heard *a lot* about you."

He grins in a way that can only be described as shit-eating.

Obviously, this is Mason.

In features, he's a near replica of his older brother, with the same strong jaw and chin. Mason's an inch or two shorter, though, with slightly longer hair and softer, more youthful features. The biggest difference between them is their expression: Mason's wide smile is the near opposite of Logan's serious countenance.

"What exactly have you heard?" I ask as Logan, metal tap handle and rubber mallet held in one hand, strides up to clasp his younger brother around the back of the neck, dragging him a few steps backward.

"We've talked about this," he growls.

Mason grins back. "Talked about not repeating your compliments to attractive women in purple dresses? Because I can assure you, we have not. In fact, I don't think you've ever said so many nice things about—"

"No," Logan cuts in. "We've talked about respecting personal space and asking before touching."

Mason ducks his head. "Right. That."

They break apart, and I realize that Logan is . . . wearing a suit. I've never seen him in anything but cotton or flannel, yet it fits him beautifully, hugging his shoulders, tapering at the waist. Sharp lapels form clean lines that frame his wide chest. It's perfect but for one detail: the sleeves are a hair short for his long arms. It's a little flaw that makes him more Logan—and somehow more perfect—than any expensively tailored jacket ever could.

"A suit," I say. "This is a first."

He clears his throat, tugs at those slightly too short sleeves. "We agreed this event should be formal."

I smile, still unable to look away, even though the words *cursed to solitude* are ringing in my ears. "I'm not complaining."

Logan's gaze runs down my dress, lingering on my waist and hips. Usually, I wear dresses that flow and breathe—bohos in bold patterns, swing dresses made of cotton or chiffon. But this one is reserved only for special occasions because it's not like the others. It's a rich shade of burgundy that plunges at my neckline and hugs my curves.

Logan's grip on the mallet tightens. "I'm not either."

Our eyes meet and it's so intense that I can almost feel the echo of the blossoming tree. His lips crashing onto mine, like a dam breaking—hungry, flooding, no pause. His shoulder anchoring me against the trunk as his hand worked up my dress. His fingers finding me.

I shudder.

"Soooooo," Mason says, "just to recap: Logan is wearing a suit, Ali has a banger of a dress, and I'm standing here, continuing to draw breath."

"We're all very impressed," Logan mutters.

"Well, you should be," Mason says, "considering the suffocating tension in the room."

My cheeks warm. "Can we circle back to my dress?" I stuff my hands into the velvety material that clings to my hips. "Because I haven't yet had a chance to point out that it has pockets."

"Why do women always need to say that?" Mason asks.

"I think it's in contract law," I tell him. "A woman wearing a dress with pockets is obligated to mention the existence of said pockets upon receiving a compliment on said dress."

Mason laughs.

"I really appreciate you coming all the way down here to help," I add. "We desperately needed you."

"No problem at all," Mason says over his shoulder as Logan nudges his brother toward our bar—a wooden plank laid across two hay bales, wrapped in burlap to soften the edges. I follow in their wake and help arrange glasses as Logan slides the last keg off the dolly and Mason rocks another into place.

He glances up as he twists in the coupler. "You know, my eldest brother was a bit vague about why you're having this fundraiser in the first place."

"It's a thin crop." I repeat the line Val gave everyone while selling tickets. "And China had a big year. It was looking like we wouldn't break even."

"Huh." From his squat, he slants his eyes at his older brother. "Logan didn't mention any of that."

I raise an eyebrow as Logan murmurs to me, "I don't lie to my brothers."

Mason, of course, doesn't miss this, and shoots to his feet, eyebrows leaping into his hairline.

"Explain," he demands.

"It's your choice," Logan tells me. "But he'd take it well."

"He'd take *what* well?" Mason asks, voice climbing to a fever pitch.

I tip my head and stare at Logan for another meaningful moment, silently questioning, *You sure?*

He nods. "He's always been into this kind of stuff."

Before Mason can shriek out *What kind of stuff*, I say: "My orchard is cursed."

Mason's shoulders deflate. He blinks, looking between us. "Oh. That's all?"

"What do you mean 'that's all'?" I ask as Logan mutters, "As expected."

After checking around my shoulders for guests who might have started filing in early, I whisper to Mason, "Let me be clear: It doesn't surprise you that the farm has glowing beetles, flowers that grow only when certain people are present, and pears turning to crystals?"

I decide to leave off the part about how it curses people to leave. I'm not about to have that rather loaded discussion in Mason's presence.

"Wait." Mason's eyes widen toward the windows, his mouth splitting into another smile. "Val said those were decorations."

"I'm glad to hear you found that convincing."

"And here I thought you were just very committed to theme. Impressive. The rest of it is exactly what I would have expected, though."

I squint at him. "The rest is what?"

He slings a towel over the shoulder of his suit and splays his hands out on the bar's burlap, grinning like he's savoring his own nonchalance. "How old are the trees on this property?"

"Uh, well, it varies, obviously. Most of our trees live for decades, some even a century. My uncle used to say the oldest one was planted by my great-great-grandfather. Supposedly, the first tree ever planted on our farm."

"And your family has owned this land the whole time?"

"Yep. Five generations of Reids."

Mason swings a hand like I've proven his point. "There you go. The whole concept of a family-run orchard? We're just asking for one of these suckers to get mystical."

"Because . . . ?"

"Because trees are like snakes and ravens. Across nearly every culture worldwide, they're some of the most common symbols ascribed with spiritual or mythological significance. And trees are most mystical when they're connected to ancestry. There's a reason we call it a *family tree*, and it's not just because it looks like one."

Behind us, the door rolls open and Val heaves off her stool, welcoming the first set of guests. They wander into the space, and I enjoy the way they survey the light-strung rafters and centerpieces with obvious awe.

Logan is still frowning. "As appealing as it is to have an explanation for Ali's cursed pears, I can't help but wonder if the reason *trees* are a common mythological symbol is just that trees are pretty much everywhere."

Mason rolls his eyes and jerks a thumb at his brother. "Don't listen to him. Just a complete failure of imagination on this one."

Logan snorts. "Says the kid who started telling me I have 'heavy Saturn placements' when he was nine."

"Well, you do," Mason says. The door rolls open again and he drops his voice to a conspiratorial whisper. "But this I learned in a religious and cultural anthropology class. We spent a whole lecture on trees as cosmological anchors, sites of ritual, and metaphors for kinship, ancestry, and transformation."

I tilt my head. "Really."

"Yep." His attention darts to my side. "But also, I've got four kegs of hard cider and our first thirsty guests."

I glance over my shoulder to find a couple has lined up behind us. Logan shoots me an apologetic look before stepping behind the bar to join Mason, who is already fishing out a pair of glasses.

As I move away, Logan asks for IDs and Mason elbows him in the rib cage. Smiling, I take a lap around the room to say hello to the guests starting to trickle in, rearrange a few of the dessert trays, and straighten a pine cone centerpiece.

Most of the attendees don't bother to hide their looks of patent curiosity as they circle the room. I expect most of the town is relishing the opportunity to see this quirky little pear farm up close. But I don't mind. These people are saving my livelihood. This gala is happening, already a success. I can't be mad if that's due to some errant curiosity.

"Stunning decorations," someone murmurs as I pass by Val's stool. "I just love the lights outside."

Val winks at me, and I can't help but grin back.

Sometime later, I fill a plate with desserts—a ginger scone, two tarts, and a pear and goat cheese galette with honey and thyme—and stake out a free barrel just off the dance floor. It's begun to rain, as the forecast promised, although I can't hear the rooftop patter over Hozier in the speakers, and it hasn't seemed to dampen our turnout. Rather, the corner by Val is filling with wet umbrellas while the hum of conversation and tinkle of glassware begins to swell. A short line has formed in front of the bar, where Mason is pouring glasses while gesticulating wildly.

Oddly, I don't see Logan—until I feel the warm brush of fingertips at my elbow. I turn, and there he is, tall and close, eyes steady on mine.

"Apparently I was 'killing the vibe,'" he explains with a half-crooked smile.

"Good," I say, returning it. "I wanted you to myself, anyway."

He takes me in with his severe gaze, but he still holds himself back, a few determined feet of space between us. Not for the first time this evening, I think about the curse. And the tree. And whether Logan will insist on going back to distance.

Then the song changes. It's Adele and she's singing about someone like you—timeless and emotional—but I'm hit with a different kind of nostalgia. A memory of this song, a couple of days before I was supposed to leave for Alaska. Those late afternoons, Logan and I would carry my portable speaker to the creek after we each finished our work. That day, we settled back in the sun-warmed grass and Logan's fingers tangled in my hair and clouds roved overhead. Adele's lyrics about heartbreak and yearning and a long-unspoken grief unspooled in the air between us.

"Is she singing about us?" I asked—pure adolescent self-centeredness, utterly sincere. "What's coming for us?"

Logan, who clearly hadn't yet developed his adult edge of realism, said, "I think she is."

And I sighed wistfully and he kissed my hairline and we both ached.

"Do you remember this song?" I ask him now.

"Ali," he chides.

"Steel trap memory again?"

"Only sometimes."

I smile, but there's an ache in my chest. "It wasn't about us, not exactly. But it wasn't entirely off base."

Something flashes in Logan's eyes as his throat works through a swallow. For a fleeting moment I'm convinced he's going to step away.

But instead, he offers a hand. "Dance with me?"

I feel that gesture like a steel rod through my sternum, and I put my hand into his. An electric crackle rides up my spine as our fingers meet.

"I didn't know you dance," I whisper.

Gently, Logan tugs me forward, one hand on my low back, steering us toward the entirely empty dance floor.

"Not usually," he says. Then his lips barely brush against my ear. "But tonight, I do."

He gathers me into his arms, and we're moving together. My cheek finds the slope of his shoulder. His hands settle at my waist. The music carries us in slow, unhurried circles and I breathe him in. Despite the suit, Logan's familiar smell meets me, that hum of cedar and wind-worn cotton.

Across the floor, I catch Mason at his bar, a glass in one hand and a watchful gaze trained on both of us. I have only a moment to register an oddness to the tilt of his head before Logan spins me again so I'm angled toward the barn doors instead.

"I talked to Val about the curse," I say softly. "And I was right."

"That it forces people to leave?" he asks, and even though his tone is soft, it carries the same quiet doubt he had about Saturn placements.

I nod into his chest, even though I still have more questions than actual answers. How strong is it? How fast does it work? What's the trigger? Does the person get an undeniable urge to leave or will circumstances eventually compel them to do so?

"That's what my uncle thought happened to your mom," I say. "And mine."

Logan hums thoughtfully, considering, but not quite relenting.

"And maybe," I say tentatively, "it's what already happened to us. When we were kids."

Now he does pull back, but only so he can look down at me. "You think?"

"I don't know. Val said Martin thought the curse only affects the owner, but she also said no one understands the full extent of it."

He hesitates before saying, "I would have left with you, if I could."

"And I would have stayed, if I had the choice," I answer softly. "It's what I wanted. More than anything else."

And even though he's leaving—*cursed* to leave—and even though this might be exactly the mistake I made fourteen years ago and again two days ago, I don't care. I ease in closer, my hand slipping higher on Logan's shoulder. I hear him draw in a breath as his fingers tense at my low back.

"You were the one who asked me to dance," I remind him.

"You're in that dress," he argues.

I grin. "I see you're not such a bastion of self-control in the face of my pockets."

He chuckles as we draw apart, and I feel his gaze skate down the length of the fabric before he curls me in close again. "I never stood a chance."

As we move, I'm too aware of my pulse. The strong planes of his torso. The cuff of his jacket tickling the inside of my wrist.

The music shifts, easing into something softer. A few other couples have drifted to the floor, but they barely register. All I feel is Logan—his hands steady on me, the warm press of his body, his earthy scent. I want to hold this sliver of time close, tuck it somewhere safe and let it thrum over my skin forever.

"What does this mean for us?" I ask, voice unsteady, even though I know there really isn't an *us*. It's only been a few weeks, and I still have so much to learn about this man who's holding me like he's afraid I might break. He's different than his teenage self—more assured, more stoic, more magnetic. But if this curse is real, then why would I submit myself to another heartbreak, knowing that our end is inevitable?

I watch him working over thoughts, cycling through unseen emotions and contingencies. There's a definable moment where something solidifies and he seems ready to speak, because his lips part.

But then two things happen in quick succession.

Over my shoulder there's a bang, followed swiftly by a loud curse.

"Damn it," Logan mutters as he releases me. Behind us, Mason is now trying to use an old rag to smother a keg that's spraying foam. "I'll be right back."

And just as Logan strides off, two figures at the door catch my eye.

A short woman with even shorter blond hair shakes rain off her coat. Behind her, a dark-haired man murmurs something to Val. And my aunt, who has always struggled with names and faces, is clearly oblivious to the identity of the two people in front of her. She marks her clipboard with no more than a perfunctory nod.

It's Blake and Liv. They're here together.

Chapter Seventeen

As Liv searches the crowd, one of her hands squeezes into a fist. It's a tell, the same motion she used to make when she was working herself up to text a guy or check her bank account. Then, Blake grabs her hand, Liv's fist relaxes, and their fingers weave together. The barn's twinkle lights brighten and fade and for a moment the whole scene strikes me as nonsensical. I can't understand why they're here. Or why they're holding hands. Blake doesn't even *like* holding hands.

But then they ease into the room and heaviness settles into my chest as everything catches up. They're here together. And they're looking for me.

What do I do? Hide? Help Logan with the keg? I can't imagine it will take more than two adults to get it under control, which means I'll just be standing idly and in open sight.

I certainly can't stay here. They'll intercept me in the middle of my crowd of guests and I'll be imprisoned in a spotlight of attention. These people paid good money to pull my farm out of its debt burden and I'm not going to punish that with a scene.

There's only one option.

Mustering the most natural smile I can, I stride toward the pair, angling to intercept them near a hay bale topped with pumpkins. I'll get this over fast. In and out.

This is fine.

From a few feet away, Liv's eyes catch mine. Her smile widens and she tugs Blake's attention in my direction. He releases her to cough into his fist.

"Ali!" Liv says, sounding almost breathless. "Hi."

Maybe it's muscle memory, or awkwardness, or maybe Liv genuinely thinks it's an appropriate greeting, but the next thing I know, she's diving in for a hug. Her woolen sweater scratches against my face as the familiar, sickly sweet smell of coconut shampoo strangles my nostrils. My body feels hot and tight all over, and I stand limply until she releases me.

When we step apart, Blake smiles.

"Hey, there," he says with confidence that pairs perfectly with his mirror-polished oxfords and tailored suit in a muted navy. "How are you doing?"

If he's uncomfortable, he's hiding it well. It's one of his superpowers—always knowing the appropriate thing to say with precisely polite phrasing, even when confronted with a demanding professor or a disagreeable neighbor. It's something I used to admire, but it feels different now. Less respectful and more disingenuous.

I clear my throat. "Hello. You're here. Both of you."

Liv bites the inside of her cheek. Her hair is longer than when I last saw her—just brushing her shoulders now—and a wisp sticks to her forehead from the rain outside. She tucks it behind her ear. "I know this might be a little out of the blue. But we heard about the fundraiser and we wanted to be supportive. You know, to show that we're—we're here for you."

"You . . ." My heart thuds low and hard in my ears as the world disintegrates into nonsense again. There are a dozen things I probably should be saying or asking, but it's like I'm scrambling around for thoughts on cue cards and every one of them is coming up blank. "You came to support me?"

They glance at each other, exchanging a small, textured look that twists like a corkscrew through my insides.

"Yes," Liv says. The word lifts with hope.

"And why are you really here?" a deep voice asks.

Solid warmth grazes my side. I twist to find Logan. His fingers brush my elbow, his gaze finds my face. There's a question there, like *Are you doing okay?* or *How can I help?* A rush of relief overtakes me, so staggering I nearly topple.

"Hi," I mouth as I lean into him gratefully.

Logan catches me around the waist, securing my whole frame. "Hey there."

Suddenly, everything makes sense again.

When I turn back to the pair, Liv's mouth is open. Blake's smile has faltered, his eyebrows pulled together as his attention latches to the spot where Logan's hand grounds my waist.

With a gentle shake of her head, Liv recovers first. She sticks out a hand. "I'm Liv."

Logan doesn't move. "I'm aware."

After a beat, she winces and withdraws. Her teeth saw against her bottom lip. "I know it was a bit rash to show up like this. Usually, you know, it's not something we would do. But we really wanted to talk to you, Ali. We really want things to be okay. And . . ." The words tumble out with the slightly out-of-control cadence of a ball pitching off the top step of a stairwell and finding itself hurling downward. "And . . . since you blocked me on social media, and you wouldn't answer my calls, this was the only way to get in touch."

"I—" I start. "What?"

"You wouldn't answer our calls," Liv says again. "You blocked me."

Logan's fingers twitch against my side. "And you figured the appropriate next step was showing up here."

Blake straightens, shrouding himself in a professional veneer again. "This event requires tickets, not invitations."

Logan regards him, expression flat. "Drawing that distinction is not the vindication you think it is."

Blake bristles. "Who even are you?"

"Someone Ali invited to be here."

Blake huffs a laugh, but I can tell he's uncomfortable because he crosses his arms and taps his fingers against his elbow, looking at me instead of Logan. "Can we talk privately? There's something we should discuss between the three of us."

It's almost convincing. Maybe because of Blake's smooth smile and deliberate eye contact. But more likely because it *has* always been the three of us. Blake, Liv, Ali. Brunch on Sundays at a café with mismatched dishware. Friday nights at a dueling piano bar where we shout Kelly Clarkson songs until our throats go hoarse.

Waking up at dawn. Climbing ladders. Splaying out in armchairs and slathering our sore backs with numbing creams.

Only those last ones? Those were supposed to happen but never did.

Because they left me.

"This is Logan," I respond. "And I would like him to stay."

"Ali," Blake says stepping toward me, "this is already difficult enough. Don't make—"

His fingers barely graze my forearm before Logan's arm shoots forward, plucking the offending wrist from midair. He steps forward firmly, without violence, but he's big enough that it crowds Blake out of my proximity.

"Don't touch her again," Logan says in a voice that could split quartz. Then he releases Blake's limb, straightens his suit jacket sleeves. He adds levelly, "Please."

Until now, Blake has looked too startled to be resentful, but the expression overtakes his face as he backs away and rubs at his wrist.

"All right." Blake's mouth twists into a smile that isn't quite convincing. "You don't need to make a scene."

I squeeze at Logan's fingers, which have returned to my side. "I think, what I'd like, is an answer to the question. Why are you here, really?"

This time I'm met with silence. Liv glances at Blake and they share a look, like an unspoken negotiation. Another twist goes through my rib cage, not only because of the casual familiarity in the gesture, but because I recognize it. I've seen them glance at each other like that before.

Blake clears his throat. "We came because we're hoping to find a way for things between us to be cordial. For the next time we run into each other."

I have a sinking sensation even as I ask the question I'm not sure I want answered. "Why would we be running into each other?"

"Because we're moving to Apple Valley," Liv says with a barely contained squeal of excitement.

I step back. Logan's hand tightens on my waist.

Liv is still talking. Something about how going back to Florida only proved how perfect Oregon was for them. How Blake will be volunteering with the ski patrol this winter. How she's already found a job at the farmer's market.

I can barely hear her over the roar of blood in my ears.

They left me, but they're going to live here. Together.

I don't know how to process this.

But I'm also out of time because Blake and Liv are looking at me expectantly—Liv with a hopeful smile, Blake with the edge of presumption—and all I know is I don't want to be here anymore.

Desperately, I spin toward Logan.

"*I can't,*" I mouth.

He grabs my elbow. "We're leaving."

Liv's mouth falls open. But I can't see any more of their reactions because Logan gently, but firmly, spins me away.

As we forge through the crowd, I feel the prickling static of collective attention. Val has lurched off her stool. Words die on June Hart's lips as she catches Logan's expression. Mason has his gaze locked on his brother's shoulders even as he fills an empty glass. Suddenly, the smell of hay and sawdust is thick in my nostrils, and every lungful of air feels too tight in my ribs.

"I just . . . I need a minute," I whisper so only Logan can hear. "Away from all these people."

He grabs my hand, braiding his fingers with mine and anchoring my knuckles with his thumb. With his massive frame forging our path, we march toward the back door. He grabs two oversize coats off the rack, engulfing my shoulders in one before we spill onto the soggy grass.

Music fades as the door slams, giving way to the steady roar of rain. It splatters against the heavy black jacket, wetting my face until I tug the hood over my curls.

Without pausing, Logan angles me past the pair of food trucks and through parked cars. He doesn't stop until we're under the canopy of the trees.

The only place that could help.

I hug myself and wait for my heart to slow its hammering. My dress sandals are already soaked from the sodden grass, and my toes are curling with cold. Around us, crystal pears sway in the driving wind. One loosens from its branch and shatters in a pulpy mess against the hard earth.

From the shadows, Logan's jaw throbs as he watches me.

"They had no right," he says. I've never heard him sound so angry.

"I don't know," I stammer. "It's just . . ."

"Don't say 'how they are.'"

"But it is."

His fingers flex closed as he levels a hard stare on the barn door. "I shouldn't have let them get off so easily."

My next breath catches in my throat. "I don't think it would have helped."

Logan's gaze tracks to my face. I can feel the tears bubbling against my eyes, a sob pushing on my chest. The fight dissolves from his posture. He steps swiftly toward me and cups my chin with his rough fingers.

"What do you need?" he asks, softer now.

Water invades my hood—so much I can taste rain. My cheeks are as soaked as if I'd already been crying. Still, I won't let myself. Not for them.

"I'm okay." I suck in a shuddering breath and with it more rainwater. "You don't need to worry about me so much."

Logan's thumb traces the curve of my jaw.

"You get to feel what you feel," he says.

I shake my head against his hand even as tears singe my nose and eyes.

They're *together.* I could have guessed it from the way they tried to apologize, the glances they exchanged as they rushed to pack. But having a suspicion is different from being confronted with a hard reality. Even worse, after spending years imagining a future with these two people, they have seamlessly moved on to an entirely different one.

Or, rather, the same future without me.

Because they're *moving* to Apple Valley.

My legs tremble as I shut my eyes against it all: the cold rain that's slicking the backs of my legs. The soaked, spongy earth under my feet. The cinch of betrayal.

"Hold me?" I whisper.

Logan closes the distance between us and scoops my body into his arms. His biceps are steady and warm and my chin sinks against his expanse of chest. My hands close into fists as I tremble against him, fighting back the storm.

"I've got you," he says softly. "You can let go."

I shake my head, rubbing my nose against the coarse material of his jacket. I can't. I'm teetering along a narrow ledge. I'm barely keeping myself from free-falling into an abyss where I'll lose everything. My farm. My home. Myself.

My mental attic is so packed that if I pry loose one box, the entire tower will collapse.

The wind picks up.

Over Logan's shoulder, the back door to the barn snaps open. Framed by a bright shaft of light, Val squints into the darkness. There's almost certainly something I need to deal with inside, like a dessert tray that needs to be refilled or a problem with the stereo.

I step out of Logan's embrace, but I'm flagging with the wind. His fingers brush against my elbow, and I fumble for his wrist to keep upright.

"I shouldn't be out here," I say. "There's a mousse in the fridge and—"

"The guests will be fine."

Pressure is mounting inside my chest, but I *can't.* Every muscle in my body is rebelling against my anger. My hurt. It's too big, too explosive. If it comes out pure and raw, it'll consume me.

"And . . . there's Blake and . . . everyone else. They'll notice I'm missing."

My breaths are coming in short gasps now. The rain intensifies, assaulting my knees and shins in cold droplets that are so hard they're nearly painful.

"You can let go." Logan's voice is a rumble against my ear, so low I nearly miss it. "You're safe. You aren't alone."

A sob wrenches in my throat. I can't. I can't.

I can't.

The rain intensifies, scoring the backs of my hands, the tops of my feet exposed by my strappy sandals.

It's so painful that it doesn't feel like rain.

And that's when I know it's not.

Hail.

Icy balls accumulate in the grass in a nearly instant blanket. Wind roars across the trees, violently stripping them of their leaves. Hail scores my face as I lift my eyes toward the branches still loaded with my precious, unpicked pears. Some of the few that the crystals haven't yet taken.

Hail will mark the rest of my fruit.

Hail will ruin my crop.

Hail is a death sentence.

Pears rattle on their stems. My chest quivers, then heaves. It's too much. I can't hold on anymore.

A sob escapes my throat. Shivers rip through me in waves as ruthless as the wind. Tears loose from my eyes, soaking my cheeks and mixing with the elements until I don't know what belongs to me and what once belonged to the sky. I fumble for Logan. He engulfs my hand with his, squeezing me back as my knuckles turn white from the pressure and the cold.

The hail is taking it all.

Everything that's left.

Logan tugs me into his chest.

My knees buckle. I go limp in his arms, clutching at the slick, wet fabric of his raincoat. The hail drives harder, slashing my skin with the same viciousness that's marking my fruit.

I cling to him as I sob. And let go.

Chapter Eighteen

Sometime later, I manage to extract myself from a shivering fetal position and, despite Logan's protestations, journey back to the barn. I'm not eager to rejoin the guests—my velvety dress now has the texture of wet papier-mâché, my cheeks are stained with mascara, and the hail is still actively tearing at my fruit—but this is my fundraiser for my orchard. I need to be there.

Only, I don't get past the door.

Val takes one look at me, glares at Logan, and says, "Get her to bed."

He cups my elbow even as I stay rooted to the spot. "I should help."

"You're a wreck," she says. "And there's nothing more to do."

Honestly, it's a relief. Despite all my practice, I'm not sure it would have been possible to summon a smile.

So, I cling to Logan's arm as we make our way back across the muddy grass. Once we're inside, he wraps me in a starchy towel. Rainwater drips from my hair as he helps me step into a pair of sweatpants and then thick wool socks. I peel off my sticky dress with his eyes fixed to the ceiling, then tug my arms through a dry sweatshirt Logan's holding out. It's his, clearly, because it smells sweet and clean and swallows me from shoulders to hips.

He pulls back my bedsheets and the mattress creaks as I sink under the covers, tug a quilt to my chin. The sleet has let up, but I still flinch every time a ball of hail snicks against the roof. I'm cold, too. A deep, sinking chill that's settled into my bone marrow.

Logan steps back to appraise me.

"I just need to get warm," I argue to his silent frown.

He hums. "Be right back," he says and then disappears behind the door.

When he returns, he's got a mug of tea, the smell of cinnamon and cardamom rising with the steam, and a plate filled with pear desserts. He's changed out of his suit and into a dry pair of sweats and a T-shirt clinging with his clean smell. He sets the plate on my bedside table, and I wrap my white-knuckled fingers around the warm ceramic mug.

"Better?" Logan asks gently.

I thought I'd shed all my tears outside, but another one escapes my pressed eyelids and drips off the crest of my nose.

Blake and Liv are moving to Apple Valley.

My trees are hurting.

My land is cursed.

I'm fated to a lifetime of solitude.

Every box in my mental attic has toppled loose and there isn't a smile big enough to Jenga them back together.

I shake my head.

The bed shifts as Logan sinks down next to me, a still weight. I lean into his frame.

"Want me to stay?" he asks.

I should say no. He might be here now, but he won't be forever. I don't want to depend on someone who I won't always be able to count on.

But right now, all I want is his comfort.

So, I say, truthfully, "Please."

Logan rounds the foot of the bed and lifts the covers, sandwiching himself under my thick pile of blankets.

I roll over so I'm facing him and he tugs me toward his chest, slotting my forehead below his chin and folding me in his arms. I inhale his smell: bright and earthy, grass after rain. Despite the devastation still being wrought outside, I find that comforting.

The shivers up my spine ease. The crackle of my mind quiets.

Eventually, I fall asleep.

Hazy morning light filters through sheer curtains. My hair, tacky with the residue of sweat and tears, is plastered to my cheeks. I force my eyes open and find one of Logan's arms cinched around my waist. My chin is planted into the dent of his sternum.

He brushes a curtain of my curls away from my face.

"Morning," he says softly.

Oh, my heart answers. *It's you.*

The ceiling fan turns gentle circles, ghosting my sticky cheeks with air. It might be the only thing that saved me from sweating through this pile of blankets.

"Did I dream it?" I whisper.

Logan shakes his head minutely, as though a smaller gesture will hurt me less. The plunging of an emptying drain pulls through my stomach.

"But the gala?" I ask.

"A success," he confirms. "The guests left happy."

"And how about . . . the two of them?"

Logan's expression hardens. "Mason told them to get lost before I had a chance."

I stare at a swirl of plaster on the ceiling. They might be gone, but this isn't over. If I'm lucky, that gala will be the last time they'll show up at my house, but this is a small town. I'll never be able to walk into a grocery store or the dentist's office without low-level anxiety. Every time I think I've moved on, there they will be, a sharp reminder of my fallibility.

When I don't say anything else, Logan asks, "Do you want to talk about it?"

"No. Yes. I don't know." A frustrated sigh rattles out of me. "Wouldn't it be weird?"

Logan hums under his breath and grabs my palm, starts tracing my lifeline with a callused thumb. "I don't think there's much you and I can't talk about."

In my mind, a tire swing creaks.

I nod and blow out a long breath, remembering that look Blake and Liv exchanged. I'm sure I've seen it before. Once in the car, when I was falling asleep in the back seat and they were up front. Once when I interrupted them cooking together and they startled apart by the oven. Once—across a crowded bar—when I was pulled away to greet an old client.

And all of these moments? They didn't happen in Oregon.

They're all memories from Florida.

"I think . . ." I begin. "I think maybe that whatever was going on between them, it had been for a while. And I ignored it until last night when they were standing in front of me."

Logan anchors his thumb to my palm. "I'm sure it was difficult to see them at all, and worse to see them together."

I shake my head. "Actually, no. I mean, sure, that conversation wasn't fun by any means, but them being together isn't what's really bothering me."

"What's bothering you?"

I stare at our joined hands for another long moment. Steady. Unyielding. "I was so certain that the three of us were happy. I believed that in my core. It was a lie, but what if it's not just a lie they told me? What if it's a lie I told myself? How do I know the difference between what's real and what I just want to be true?"

Logan doesn't answer. Maybe my question is unfair. Unanswerable.

But then he says, "My mom was a really good carpenter." When my eyebrows pull together, he smiles softly. "This will connect, I promise."

I snort and rest my temple on his chest. "All right."

"My dad was the one who taught me about framing and scale and sequencing, but Mom was the one who was passionate about the work. Somehow, I learned the most from her—that summer we built your uncle's barn. Sometimes, we'd find a measurement that was off by a hair or a part of the design that didn't fit as planned, and Mom would say something like 'The tape measure tells you the numbers. Your eyes tell you the truth.' Or 'If you stare at it long enough and something feels off, it probably is.'"

It reminds me of her language from the letter. "Do you think that was her thinking about leaving?"

"Maybe. But what I'm trying to say is that, after many years of experience, I've learned that her advice is right. You might use tape measures to set posts and build walls, but sometimes your hands know more than your brain does."

"That sounds like something my uncle would have said."

"He was a wise man."

I nod even though those words twist, too. "I'm sorry, but I don't really understand what this has to do with Blake and Liv."

Logan rakes his nails against his beard. "Sorry. This isn't as eloquent as I'd like. What I'm trying to say is that your mind is right about a lot of stuff, but at the end of the day, it can lie. All you can trust is your gut."

"That was very well said," I whisper. "I didn't know carpenters were so wise."

Logan eyes me steadily. "I'm wise about as often as I dance."

"So, quite a lot?"

"So, only with you."

Warmth spreads through me as memories surface. Whispered dreams on a tire swing. A careful kiss in a tightening eddy. The impossible blossoms of a pear tree in autumn.

And then.

A front door snapping shut. My house lapsing into silence. One mug of coffee. One pair of boots. The taste of rain as ice scores my skin.

Cursed to solitude.

Fated to be alone.

Leaving.

"How do you know," I ask, low, "what your gut is telling you?"

He tips his chin down. "How do you mean?"

"Like . . ." I smooth the quilt against my legs as I work through my tangle of thoughts. "I understand the metaphor about trusting your instincts when it comes to carpentry. And my uncle always tried to teach me to tend the land that way, too. But I don't know how to apply that logic to big, complicated life decisions. When your mind is racing with a million thoughts, what does 'trusting your gut' even mean?"

Logan frowns, ducks his chin. "Can't say I've gotten there yet. Let me know if you figure it out?"

I sink against his shoulder. "Yeah. Sure."

Somewhere downstairs, a door bangs closed. I glance out the window and find a flash of saturated, industrial green—a Gator parked where the grass gives way to dirt.

I sit up. "Val's here?"

"She's been out there for a couple of hours."

I should have known. No matter how late she stayed up last night, of course she came screaming back at dawn to survey the damage. She's probably careened over every hill in that Gator, repeatedly heaving off the seat to glare at the branches, no matter how much she's supposed to be keeping off her ankle.

"Did she say anything about how the pears look?"

Before Logan can respond, the creak of a loose floorboard draws our attention toward my door. I find Val there, arms crossed and leaning heavily against the doorjamb. There's dirt smudged against her worried frown.

"Want me to come back later?" she asks.

"No." I shuck the quilts off my lap. "I need to know. Let me get dressed."

After I brush my teeth, shove my feet into a pair of fluffy slippers, and spritz my curls with water, I pad down to the kitchen where Val is already grinding coffee beans while Logan fries a panful of eggs. When the low beeps of the toaster oven sound, Mason's snores from the living room cut off and he stumbles into the kitchen, hair wild as he rubs at his eyes.

"Morning," he says and plops into a chair. His smile drops as he glances between our faces. "Something wrong?"

I sigh and say without hesitation, "Yes."

Mason frowns, and his gaze lingers on my sweatshirt—Logan's sweatshirt that I'm still wearing—for a beat too long. "Okay, then. But if we're about to spelunk in some dark, emotional cave, I'm going to need caffeine reinforcements."

I pass him a mug of coffee. "Val was about to tell us just how severe the damage was from that hail. And the whole truth," I add to her. "Don't sugarcoat it."

"I've never coated anything with sugar in my life," Val says stubbornly as she pours pumpkin creamer into her mug. Instead of continuing, however, her eyes flick uncertainly between the brothers.

"Don't worry," I say. "They already know."

She lowers her chin. "Four generations of Reids managed to keep these secrets to themselves."

"You're not a Reid, and you know," I say.

"I'm as good as one," she retorts.

"It would have been a bit difficult not to notice the rainbow-colored rabbits," Logan adds.

Mason spills a bit of coffee down his front and smacks a hand against the table. "Oh, now we're talking."

Val scowls, muttering something about trusting strangers with secrets.

Mason crosses his heart. "You can share anything with us, Val. The Wright brothers have many times been called both dependable and trustworthy."

"That's just me and Andrew," Logan mutters as he scrapes an egg onto his brother's plate.

Val snorts and frowns for another beat before relenting. "Fine. Here's the deal. The storm last night was bad, but it was also weird. It turned to hail right over Ali's property, and nothing but. Right across the boundary, there isn't a single marked apple, but the pears are fucked."

My heart thumps, a slow, steady drumbeat that feels more like despair than disappointment.

"The curse," I say softly.

Things are such a mess, I can't tell which goodbye caused the storm. Maybe it happened because Blake and Liv showed up and disappeared again last night. Or maybe it was about Logan, like a precursor to something that's ready to happen or a signal about the decision he's already made.

There's still so much about how this works that I don't know.

"I've watched a load of storms in my day," Val says. "And, yeah, they sure can do weird shit, especially in this valley. But the one last night was something else."

"So how many pears are salvageable?" I ask.

"It took out every good pear."

My heart stalls. "*Every* piece?"

She nods, looking grave. "There might be an unmarked one here or there, but that hail was thorough. You can still pick the marked ones—that's about half the crop. But you won't be able to sell them for fresh pack. And the crystal ones are worthless."

I have to steady myself with an elbow as I digest that. Fresh pack pears are the highest quality ones—those that eventually end up in grocery stores and restaurants—and they have to be unblemished. Not because marked pears are unsafe, but because they look terrible. What starts as a small, clean puncture will eventually widen into an ugly, black bruise. Consumers don't want fruit like that, so the packing houses will only buy marked pears for stuff like cider and baby food. And they'll pay a much lower price.

I don't need to have gone through the ledgers in the office to understand what this means. Even with the proceeds from the gala, half a crop of low-grade fruit won't be anywhere near enough to make ends meet this season.

"What's our next move?" Val asks, looking to me for answers.

"I don't know," I whisper. "I genuinely don't know what we can do."

Logan bumps my knee with his. "Another fundraiser?"

"Or we go back to that pear jam idea," Val offers.

I shake my head. "There's no way Apple Valley is in the mood for a second fundraiser for my quirky farm. And, Val, you already said yourself the pear jam won't be enough."

I have no idea what the path forward is, but it doesn't seem like I have any options. Or, even if I do have some options, that the curse is going to let me make progress again.

Mason slurps at his coffee and tilts his head, his expression heavy with amusement. "What are you all talking about? It's obvious what Ali should do next."

Logan frowns at his brother. "If you have a suggestion, we're all ears."

Mason blinks back, eyebrows raised expectantly.

"Guys," he says, and the unspoken *duh* is clear. "We have to break the curse."

Chapter Nineteen

After much discussion, we settle on the only starting point that makes sense: the sprawling library at Mason's college. There, he promises we'll find plenty on the cultural significance of trees in mythological systems, including historical accounts.

Val has remained utterly unconvinced this endeavor will be fruitful. "Martin spent the better part of two decades obsessing over his curse," she protested, arms crossed. "Not sure what you lot are going to accomplish in the next week."

Mason puffed up his chest. "Clearly you haven't seen me in action."

Val gave him a slow once-over before her eyes landed—unimpressed—on the faded text across his wrinkled T-shirt: *Running Late Is My Cardio*.

He dusted off the letters. "Well, clearly I'm not in action right now."

Logan nudged him with an elbow. "Let us know when it starts."

Oddly, I'm about as optimistic as Val.

I keep waiting to feel energized again—Mason's enthusiasm should be contagious. Yes! We'll find a solution in Maplehurst. Yes! We'll break the curse.

But I'm not sure I believe it.

How do we even break a curse?

And if, by some miracle, we do, would it solve my farm's financial problems?

Still, it's our only lead. Plus, Logan needs to drive back to Maplehurst, anyway, both to bring Mason back to campus and for another meeting with the insurance company. Tagging along to do some research seems better than staying back in Apple Valley with Val and doing nothing.

So, we spend the rest of Sunday gathering empty cups and plates and scrubbing serving platters clean. On Monday morning, Mason, Logan, and I pile into Logan's truck, windows down to catch the crisp morning air. Soon, we're purring along a stretch of highway hemmed between towering basalt cliffs and a broad, silver-blue river. As usual, the gorge is stunning, but today it's dressed in autumn: the hillsides streaked with gold, amber, and rust.

On the drive, Logan and I explain everything we know about the curse and my family's history with it. This includes Logan gently recounting what we found out about Lydia: the letter, the possible (probable?) affair with my uncle, and the growing theory that she left Apple Valley because of the land's magic, which led to my uncle facing problems on the orchard for years.

When he finishes, Logan taps his thumbs on the steering wheel as he waits for his brother's reaction.

To my surprise, Mason rolls his eyes. "Figures."

Logan's eyebrows stitch together. "How does it figure?"

"Well. It wasn't the only mess she left for someone else to clean up, was it?"

His brow furrows, but he doesn't press his brother further.

"So," I ask Mason, "now that you know everything we do, do you still feel optimistic about breaking this curse?"

He loosens his seat belt and swivels to look at me over the

backrest. "'Cursed to solitude' does sound more serious than I'd expected."

Logan meets my gaze in the rearview window. I feel a shot of heat through my belly even as I say aloud, "I think the pears are the immediate problem."

A few minutes later, Mason instructs Logan to exit the freeway. When we hit a residential street, the truck slows to a crawl—despite Mason's complaints, Logan always drives the speed limit—and I take in deep pulls of crisp fall air from our lowered windows. Giant sequoias humming with crows line the street and delivery bikes zip around the car. (At this, Mason sighs aggressively. "Jesus, Logan, you're driving slower than the *bicycles*.")

Logan kills the engine in front of a stately building rimmed by manicured shrubs. Even after Mason throws off his seat belt and jumps out, Logan remains, swivels to look at me.

"How are you doing?" he asks.

"Oh, by all means." Halfway up the steps, Mason seems to have realized we aren't with him because he's tapping at his wrist and shouting, muffled through the closed windows. "Take your time! It's not like those pears are ripening by the minute or anything."

Logan ignores him. "It's been quite the few days."

And, genuinely, the first thought that springs into my mind, fully formed, is *I've only survived them because you've been with me.*

There's an ache in my belly as I say, "It has. And thank you."

Logan studies me for a moment longer before saying, "I'm here. And I'm with you."

My heart squeezes with both pleasure and pain, and I nod before we step out of the cab.

The library is solemnly quiet but for the faint scratch of a highlighter and stifled yawns from students huddled around glowing screens. At the far end of the third floor, we find the reference librarian: a woman in a high-neck blouse with bangs as blunt as her stare.

"The bigfoot section is in the back," she tells us when Mason asks for books on lived mythology.

"Sorry, no," Mason says, flashing a golden-ticket smile. "We're actually looking into trees."

Now she squints over her dark-rimmed glasses, lingering on me and Logan. She must be wondering what we're doing here—so clearly past the age of midterm exams.

"Mythology or folklore?" she asks. "Or, perhaps, I can direct you to the fantasy section?"

Mason rummages through the bowl of hard candy on her desk, foraging until he finds a red piece. "No, no. None of that. Historical accounts. But recent ones."

"Legends?"

"No, we want serious,"—he pops the candy into his mouth and smacks hard—"well-documented material only."

She appraises Mason's contradictions. "But not cryptids."

Mason hesitates, looking like he might just be curious about the bigfoot section after all.

"Trees," I interject. "Just trees."

The librarian nods, types something at her keyboard, then pushes off her chair and hooks a finger for us to follow. We wind around long communal tables pooled with warm light from antique lamps, past glass-walled study rooms, and take two more abrupt turns before stopping in a short aisle with humming overhead lights that don't quite reach the bottom shelves. The librarian directs us to a shelf of spines fading to gray and washed-out navy before turning on her loafers and marching away.

Over the next handful of hours, Logan, Mason, and I chase leads between the stacks, hunting through ecological magazines and bound journals. In the strained silence of the library, footnotes and bibliographies blur into white noise. And although I should be laser focused on breaking the curse and saving my farm, I'm far too aware of Logan's exact position in the stacks. The way he thumbs through pages, slow and deliberate. The way his gaze flicks toward me when he thinks I won't notice—except I always do. Not for the first time today, I wonder where on earth we stand.

Our first, most promising lead is in an excerpt from a mid-twentieth-century travel journal, long out of print, which Logan finds tucked among the Pacific Northwest regional writings. The author, a botanist from Montreal, recounts a visit to a remote coastal retreat outside Tofino—once a logging camp, now maintained by a small, reclusive community of spiritual naturalists.

The botanist describes a forest grove just beyond their main lodge where the trees, primarily old-growth Douglas fir, seem to shimmer faintly at dawn.

"The morning after a heated argument," Logan reads aloud, "the grove stood stiff and silent. But when someone sang—a woman's voice, cracked and shy—the moss clinging to the trunks suddenly brightened, not blooming exactly, but waking. Even the ravens returned."

"Sounds pretty," Mason says. "A sudden blooming."

"Yeah," I say and catch Logan's eye over the textbook, fire charging through my veins as I remember our own blossoms. "That would be pretty."

His lips lift, a crooked half smile.

A bit later, Mason finds a niche feature called "The Red Grove of Caldesia" in an ecological magazine. It describes a hidden grove where trees turn blood-red when certain family members are present. A local artist, descended from the grove's founders, says, "I painted there the day I left my husband. The trees turned overnight."

Given the connection to both trees and departures, this feels like the most promising avenue, and we spend another couple of hours searching through back issues of the same magazine, although it went out of print in the early 2000s. Once we reach its end, I try looking for other work by the author and find one last lead: a documentary that references his work.

It's called *The Land That Remembers*, and we're able to stream the film on one of the library's computers. After I listen to the introductory voice-over, I smash the pause button and grab Mason and Logan. We huddle around the screen, closed-captioning on, and I navigate back to the beginning.

"There are places where people claim the land listens," the narrator tells us. "Where storms roll in with your sorrows, and the wind sings back what you're afraid to say. The salt lands of the southern coast are among them."

The scene resolves to an older man wearing a faded windbreaker and jeans stiff with salt and age. Behind him, a long dock groans softly, and a five-gallon bucket sloshes at his feet. The caption identifies him as **Everett Miles, 82, Scald Bay.**

"I used to think the tide was just the pull of the moon." Everett's voice is rough and raspy, like he's been trying to shout over the wind for decades. "Science and all that. But then Mable disappeared. My wife. Forty-two years, and she just . . . left in the middle of canning peaches. After that, the tide stayed out for three days. Three whole days. No storm, no wind. The marsh looked like it forgot how to breathe."

The narrator's voice again. "Some said it was coincidence. Others said absence has a gravity all its own."

The video shifts again and the scene that unfolds has me tipping closer to the screen. It's an orchard. Rows of gnarled apple trees stretch down an uneven, sloping hill.

"Thousands of miles away," the narrator says, "in an orchard tucked into the Appalachian foothills, a woman named Lorena Fletcher tells a similar story."

Lorena Fletcher, 78, Hearthfield, has silver hair and a quilt across her knees. A rocking chair creaks as she glides forward and back, her eyes on the horizon.

"I was sixteen when my cousin died. It was sudden—he got thrown from a horse. We were close. He used to say the apples tasted better when we were laughing. Silly thing, but . . . I believed it.

"The day after the funeral, we got hit with hail. End of summer. No clouds before it, no warning. Just sudden, angry ice. The whole north grove was shredded. My uncle said it was a freak weather event. But the trees didn't bloom the next spring. Not a single flower. I remember thinking it felt like the land was angry with us for losing him."

I can barely process how eerily similar that sounds to my own experiences before the narrator claims our attention again.

"The orchard recovered, eventually. But Lorena never forgot that storm. Or the strange quiet that settled over the trees. It's not unlike another story, this one from a different orchard on the other side of the country. One where not a single apple will grow, in a valley where pears refuse to thrive anywhere else."

My back stiffens as the scene unfolds. Silver-gray pear trees underneath a hooked-nose mountain. A red barn with paint that's brighter than it is today.

I grab Logan's knee. "That's my orchard."

Then, a woman in the voice-over. "I don't know how to explain what I saw that summer, what I felt on the land. I worry it defies words."

When her face appears, I notice the laugh lines that have settled around her mouth, the wisps of gray in her hair. Logan tenses. His hand closes over mine.

"That's our mom," he says.

Her name, **Lydia Holloway, 47,** appears underneath her image. And, after it, a location.

Maplehurst.

Chapter Twenty

Mason pounds a button. We all stare at the frozen face, words still lingering on the screen: **Lydia Holloway, 47, Maplehurst.**

Distantly, I realize my mouth is agape. Logan is still staring forward, one hand covering mine. I squeeze his leg, just to remind him I'm here. Even his thigh feels tense beneath my hand.

"Maplehurst," he says through a tight jaw.

I recognize that look. This time, I can guess what he's thinking.

"Do you know what year she was born?" I ask as I lean forward to click back to the main menu, looking for a date this documentary was released.

"Nineteen seventy-four," he says.

"So . . ." I tap some fingers, doing quick mental math. Lydia must be significantly younger than I would have guessed. "This had to have been made four years ago."

He nods, then says what I'm already thinking. "She could still be here."

"Yeah, I've thought she might," Mason remarks.

We turn to him. He's got a temple tipped back on his chair's headrest, an ankle slung over a knee.

Logan's eyebrows pull together as he studies his brother's nonchalance. "You've thought what, exactly?"

Mason flaps a hand. "That Lydia could be around. There's a store downtown called Holloway Woodworking or something. I noticed it last year when this new pizza place opened up next door. It always seemed like kind of a coincidence that a carpenter with the last name Holloway would have a woodworking shop fifty miles from the place that woman grew up."

"And you never bothered to investigate."

Mason lifts a shoulder. "I have better things to do with my time."

"A month ago," Logan says carefully, "you spent an entire afternoon building an exact replica of the PNU campus in Minecraft."

"Exactly what I'm saying." Mason grins. He tips his chair back onto two legs and jams his hands into his pockets. "So, obviously, that's higher on the list. Plus, stuff that sounds way less painful, like deep cleaning the microwave and tweezing out my leg hairs."

He glances up, waiting for the joke to land. When it doesn't, he sighs and lets his chair slap back down. "Look. I barely remember her. She's always been hypothetical to me. I'm not sure why I would bother spending a bunch of energy and time hunting her down when she knew exactly where I was for more than a decade and never bothered to do anything about it."

"You weren't at all curious?" I interject, unable to help myself. Not after spending the last couple weeks witnessing the ways that glimpses of Lydia's past have affected Logan.

"Nah. I only had one parent I cared about."

"Dad was at least there," Logan concedes. "Physically."

Mason unwinds his legs so he can kick his brother on the shin. "I meant you, man."

Logan blinks.

Mason expels a sigh and pushes his hair back. "C'mon. There was only one adult around to clean up my bloody knees when I tried to skateboard down the front steps. Only one person who told off those monsters under my bed and made me dinosaur pancakes on Sundays and put drawings of my favorite cartoons in my lunch box. But it wasn't Dad and it definitely wasn't some lady named Lydia."

Logan stares at his brother for a beat longer and then grabs his forearm and squeezes so hard I wonder if Mason will yelp.

He just grins back, though, and pats his brother's hand. "Well," he says, "as much as I'm enjoying this moment of brotherly love, I think we have a pear farm to save, yeah?"

We watch the rest of the clip, taking in Lydia's familiar account of the orchard's magic: strange weather patterns, a glowing beetle, and of course, the forget-me-nots blooming in strange patterns. She doesn't mention the curse or her own decision to leave Apple Valley, but when her interviewer asks if these odd occurrences affected her, she freezes and says, "You promised not to ask about that."

The off-screen voice tries to press, but after that, Lydia clams up, barely giving more than one- or two-word answers. The interview ends with another shot of my land and a line from the narrator about unanswered questions. It seems that the documentarians were unable to get a firsthand account from the owners of the orchard, and although Lydia's story was too compelling to leave out, they had no way to independently corroborate it.

When we've finished watching the unsatisfying clip a third time, Mason sighs and switches off the computer.

"I guess we could have predicted she'd give us nothing," he scoffs. "As usual."

Logan is still bent forward in his chair, hands clasped between his knees. "We could ask."

I whirl toward him, eyebrows raised.

Mason clicks his tongue. "She doesn't deserve that conversation."

I ignore that. "Do you *want* to talk to her?"

Logan frowns as he massages the back of his neck. "I don't know, honestly."

"That's fair," I say. "You should take some time. Figure out what you want to do. It's your choice."

Mason's mouth twists in a skeptical frown. "Feels to me like an easy no right now."

I glance at him, uneasy with his tone, but it doesn't feel like my place to push back. So, lightly, I say, "I don't know. I struggle nightly with choosing between washing my hair and stretching the dry shampoo for one more day, so I think it's fair for Logan to take a minute on this one."

Logan's lips twitch in the first almost smile I've seen from him since Lydia's face came onto that screen.

Mason puts up his hands. "Your call, boss."

"While you're thinking," I ask Logan, "do you want to stew or a distraction?"

His lips curve from an almost smile into a full one. "Distracted, I think."

"Mason," I say. "What if we didn't go back to Apple Valley tonight? Any chance you know of something fun enough in Maplehurst to make us forget all this for a while?"

Mason's mouth explodes with a grin. "Hell yes. My whole life has led up to this moment."

After Logan has his meeting with the insurance adjuster downtown, Mason plies us with smashburgers at a place where the tables have crayons for doodling on white paper tablecloths. Then he convinces us to go to a house party, which to Logan's horror and my own surprise, is being held on a Monday.

"Monday is the new Wednesday," Mason quips.

"There are parties on Wednesdays?" I ask.

Mason grins. "Wednesdays are the old Thursdays."

Logan pinches the bridge of his nose. "I'm way too old for this shit."

But I elbow him and whisper "distraction" while Mason follows up with such an alarming mix of persistence and determination that he relents.

That's how Logan and I—both in our thirties and definitely way too old for this shit—end up shoving ourselves between tightly packed bodies in a low-lit basement that reeks of the chemical-sharp smell of spilled liquor and college student sweat. A kid with messy blond hair who calls me "bro" serves us beers from a keg and we take up a spot in the corner where Logan, empty-handed, crosses his arms and surveys the room.

"Cut that out, you look like a cop," Mason yells over the thud of music.

"That child could not be eighteen, let alone twenty-one," Logan says, uncrossing his arms to gesture at a man-size boy, fully sprawled out and snoring on a stained couch. "Someone should tell his parents where he is."

"Wake him up and ask for their number," I offer with a smile.

Logan narrows his eyes like he's considering it.

"Do not encourage him," Mason says elbowing me and glaring at his brother.

Logan puts up a hand. "Fine. I'll let it go this time."

"At least you're not thinking about Lydia," Mason says.

"Who knew underage drinking would be the best distraction Maplehurst has to offer?" I ask as I take another sip from my Solo cup.

Over the rim, Logan's eyes meet mine. "Or a close second."

Something bright and warm washes through my belly, and it has nothing to do with the cheap beer.

After Logan complains thirty more times about the volume, Mason steers us onto the lawn, where the air is fresher and the music dulled. We play cornhole, our hands smeared with orange from chips and Cheetos. Every time I sneak glances at Logan, meeting his gaze across the lawn, it sends a shock of pure adrenaline through my system.

Mason goes to get himself another beer—I didn't find it nostalgic enough to override the fact that it's also disgusting—and then harangues his brother until he joins a game of flip cup.

"You've got to see this shit, Ali," he says as Logan lines up next to a kid who barely comes up to his chest. Then, to my slack-jawed shock, he keeps nailing the flip on every try and Mason starts bellowing "check out my ringer" until a small crowd has gathered.

"Wait," I hiss to Mason. "Does Logan have a secret backstory as a frat bro?"

He laughs as he claps. "Nah, I discovered he had this innate talent a few years ago, probably something to do with those steady carpenter hands. But I've also made him do this pretty much every time he's come to visit sooo . . . he's had a lot of practice."

Eventually, we forgo the game altogether and the college students line up a full row of empty cups to see how many Logan can flip in one go. By the time he's midway down the row, the students are chanting his name so loudly it's drowning out the thumping bass from the stereos. He flips the last one and the assembled crowd dissolves into a fit of screams.

Logan breaks into a faint smile and takes a long sip of water.

Beside me, Mason sighs as he claps along with everyone else. "Name another man who is simultaneously so cool and so absolutely not."

"I think it's the plaid," I supply and Mason laughs again.

"Again," someone screams, eliciting a chorus of "AGAIN!"

Logan tries to wave them off, but the kids are so persistent he relents and starts lining up cups, strong hands dwarfing the red plastic. There's a faint smile on his lips and ease in his shoulders, and I think, against all odds and his own better judgment, maybe this evening is exactly what he needs. What we both need.

I feel Mason nudge me with an elbow. When I turn, he's taking a nonchalant sip of beer, but the tilt of his head has me wondering how long he's been watching me. "So, tell me, Ali. What are your intentions with my brother?"

I nearly choke on my next inhale. "Excuse me?"

"Clearly you two are doing it."

"Not that it's any of your business," I splutter, "but we are not."

That one time doesn't count as a gerund.

Mason frowns. "All right, either you're a really good liar or my brother has kept his perfect track record of always telling me the truth."

"The second one," I say.

"Sounds about right." Mason takes another casual sip. "So that circles us back to my original question."

I wrinkle my nose. This whole conversation feels squarely in the none-of-Mason's-business category. "Yeah? How does that 'circle us back'?"

The college students start chanting again and Mason taps my elbow with his, angling us back a few steps. There's no trace of his dimple-rimmed smile.

"My brother might be tough, but he's also been piloting our family alone for more than a decade. He has no one to look out for him—no one except me."

"I think Logan can look after himself just fine."

Mason shakes his head. "I'm talking about my *duty*, here.

That man gave up his entire life for me and Andrew. Everything. He thinks I don't know about it, but I do. He had these big dreams, Ali. Dreams of being an artist. Getting out of Apple Valley."

"I know that," I say softly.

"Good. Then you also know he didn't get to have that life he wanted because he was taking care of me. But I'm an adult now and that means it's my duty to look out for him. And that means making sure he's happy."

I don't quite know what to do with this information. On one hand, part of me admires Mason's fierce protectiveness. On the other . . . "What makes you think I'm interfering with Logan's happiness?"

Mason rocks back on his heels and lowers his chin. "You've pulled him into a lot. A whole damn curse, apparently. And I know it's not your fault that our shitty mom left us and all that is getting dredged up for him again, but that's what's happening. So maybe that's the reason this thing between you two is a lot deeper than I understood. But now that I can see it . . ." His lips go flat. "Look, Logan isn't quick to let people in, but when he does, he stands by them like a load-bearing beam. Which means I need to know what future you're picturing with him."

I suck in a breath as Logan flips his final cup and the kids dissolve in another round of cheers and fist bumps. I'm not entirely sure how much of an explanation I owe Mason, but I get why he's asking. And I grudgingly respect it.

"Your brother means a lot to me," I say. "He's such a good man. He's loyal and kind and strong and . . ." I trail off, thinking of the veneers of commitment and future planning I got from Blake or the instant, probably unhealthy adhesion from Liv. Logan is nothing like either.

"Steady," I finish. "He's steady."

Mason nods. "He is."

"He's also sacrificed a lot in his life," I continue. "And I want him to be happy. Even more than that, I think he *deserves* to be happy. Probably more than anyone I know."

Mason raises an eyebrow. "But?"

"Why do you think there's a 'but'?"

He scoffs into his next sip of beer. "Ali. I've known you for, what, forty-eight hours? And please don't take this the wrong way, but I've gotten a pretty good idea of just how messy your life is. You're full of nothing but 'buts.'" He grins. "You know what I mean."

I swallow. Despite the attempt at humor, I'm uncomfortable with just how accurately that particular missile has landed. "All right, fine. *But* I don't think I can be serious about him. I don't know what kind of future we have. The last he told me, he's leaving. And I would never want to stand in the way of that dream. But also, I'm always going to want to stay."

To my surprise, Mason's frown eases. Like, somehow, this is just what he wanted to hear. From across the pool table, Logan catches my eye. Maybe he clocks our serious expressions because his half smile fades and he strides toward us.

"My ringer!" Mason shouts as Logan lands beside us and nudges me with a shoulder.

"Everything okay?" he asks.

"Yes," I say, and let myself settle against his wide frame. "Your brother loves you a lot."

Mason elbows me. "You weren't supposed to go spilling my secrets, Ali."

"Oh, so I shouldn't tell him about your finsta?"

Mason snorts. "I like her."

Logan's lips hitch. "I do, too."

Eventually, Mason abandons us to team up with a raven-haired girl for a fresh round of cornhole and Logan and I flop onto one of the couches. I sag against the worn bolster, shoes off and legs crossed underneath me, and Logan positions himself on the center. He hasn't had a single sip of alcohol, but he lies back with his head against the upper cushion, looking considerably more relaxed than he was when we were in that library.

As I watch Logan, Mason's words echo in my ears, but so do my own. What I said was true—I don't know if we have any kind of future. But, also, what I want most is for Logan to look like he does right now: easy smile, shoulders loosened. I want him to be happy. And I can't help but wonder if it's not a coincidence that he looks this way after getting some distance from Apple Valley.

"This has been quite a day," I say.

He laughs through his nose. "That's been true every day since I moved onto your farm."

"That sounds suspiciously like an insult."

"It's not."

I raise an eyebrow.

"Really," he says. "Living in Apple Valley is like playing the same Hank Williams album on repeat. These days, I get to listen to Lady Gaga."

My fingertips tingle as music thumps under our seats. "I think this is actually Doja Cat."

Logan snorts. "We're still too old for this shit."

I lean a temple against the worn bolster, thinking about the millions of ways our lives have fragmented in the last forty-eight hours. The curse. The fundraiser. The hail. Logan's mom. "You still want to be distracted?" I ask. "Or is it time to stew?"

He tips his head, aligning our faces. "How about if I listen to how you're feeling?"

My sigh is a bit like a snort as hail pricks my memories. "I'm . . . I don't know exactly. What's the opposite of optimistic? Not pessimistic. Like, deeper than that."

"Discouraged?"

The word clangs with the jarring weight of truth. "Yeah. I think I'm discouraged."

Logan sits up and grabs my ankle, runs his hand up and down my calf in a soothing motion. It sends a frisson of electricity along my skin. "Ali. We're not going to let your farm fail."

And even though his confidence—and the word *we*—ignites a spark under my ribs, I can't help but feel frustrated for erasing the ease from Logan's posture. And I can't help but think Mason is right. These weeks on my farm have taken a toll on him.

"I think we should stay distracted," I say. "I don't want to bring you down."

He tugs on my calf, sliding my body closer to his. "I want to be with you, wherever you are."

My heart pulses, deep and rhythmic. Warmth radiates from his hand and up my leg. We're close enough that I can smell him—earthy and sweet—strong enough that it drowns out the tacky scent of this basement.

"Even if I'm falling apart?" I whisper.

"Lots of good things fall apart," Logan says.

"Yeah? Name one."

His lips twitch. "Tacos."

I feel a laugh bubble up in my chest. "Nice."

Our smiles drift as Logan watches me, thoughtful in ways that make my chest tight. He draws in a deep breath, then lets it go, slow and controlled.

I've seen this before.

"You're going to say something about how you don't want to hurt me," I say.

"Glad to know I'm still predictable."

"And, true to form, it's still working for me."

His mouth firms. "I haven't stopped worrying about that."

"Because I'm cursed to solitude?"

"Because you've been through enough."

I sigh, slightly exasperated. "And I already told you it's my choice if I want to go through it again."

Logan scrubs a hand against his beard. "But now I've seen it for myself. What they did to you. And I don't—I can't be the reason you look like that. I could never live with myself."

He's talking about the hail, my wracking sobs. Finally letting go. Even though I know he's not judging me for it, I still feel a whipcrack of shame. "That wasn't just about them. I've . . . The hail . . ."

Logan gathers one of my hands in his. "Ali. You get to feel what you feel. Whatever that is."

I swallow past a painful tightening in my throat and try again to explain. "They hurt me. I'm still hurting. But not because they left me. Not because they're together. It's that they upended my—my confidence in my own decisions. I believed in *us* so strongly. Not just me and Blake. Me and Liv, too. And I was so wrong. That's what hurt the most."

Logan considers me for a long moment. "That sounds like another reason for you to be cautious."

"Logically, I know you're right. And maybe this is wrong, but . . . I think you're different."

"How do you know?"

I thread my fingers between his, and although his hands dwarf mine, we seem to fit together. "Because sometimes your hands know more than your head."

His eyes flicker between mine. "Are you trying to use my carpentry wisdom against me?"

Gently, I tug his hand toward my body. "Is it working?"

"Keep talking. I'll let you know."

I tug again, but Logan is an unyielding wall and I'm propelled into his chest. Suddenly, without trying, I'm straddling him on a beer-stained couch in someone else's basement. I pin both elbows around his head and maybe for the first time, I'm looking down at him. Logan twists one of my curls around his finger. Our breaths tangle.

"The truth is that I don't know how to make big, complicated life decisions with my gut," I say, "so what if we don't?"

"We don't listen to our guts?"

"We don't make any big, complicated life decisions. We stop worrying about what's already happened or what could happen."

He doesn't answer. His hands cup the backs of my thighs, just along the hem of my dress where it flutters against my leggings. Music and electricity hum in the disappearing space between our lips.

Logan's pupils have nearly swallowed his irises.

"What do we do instead?" he asks.

"This," I whisper. My fingers pull at the short hair at the back of his head. "Just . . . this."

He draws me closer until I'm pressed against him, knees sinking into the collapsing cushion and hips driving into his torso.

"This." His breath is warm against my cheek. His voice low and rough. "And?"

I nudge my nose against his, angling his face higher, letting my lips graze his beard. "Maybe this too."

My lips sink to his.

Logan's lips part and his tongue scrapes against mine. He tastes like mint and he smells like soap and those two sensations are powerful enough to drown out everything else. His hand goes to the small of my back, securing me to his chest. My breaths grow shallow as he kisses me with an urgency I can't help but match.

Logan's hands ride up my leggings and there's a bonfire building under the thick material of my cable-knit dress. Our tongues tangle. My hand finds his cheek as his teeth graze against my bottom lip. A groan slips out of me.

Maybe I should care that this is messy. There are kids here, basically, and some might be watching. That's not to mention the fact that, twenty-four hours ago, I was curled in this man's arms, sobbing because I had to talk to my ex–best friend and ex-fiancé for the first time since I found them together. Or that I'm losing myself to a man who is supposed to leave the only place I want to stay forever.

Yet I can't summon the energy to care because in this exact moment, every part of me wants him and only him.

I tug at Logan's shirt and untuck it from his pants, not because I'm planning to screw him on this couch, but because I want to feel his skin against mine. The rough fabric pries loose and his skin is so smooth that I shudder as my fingertips race over the heavy lines of his body, wrought from a lifetime of working with his hands.

Both of us are breathless to the point of panting, trying to suck in air between the swipes of tongue and press of lips. Logan shifts, repositioning me in his lap, and I feel the hard lines of his erection straining against his jeans. My body flushes with desire. Nothing about this is restrained anymore—my moans, his hands, our hips. It's a whirlwind of touch and clumsy movements and chaotic kisses.

All noise has bled into the background: the music, the intermittent muffled cheers from outside, the dull roar of conversation.

Yet, somehow, two sounds pierce our pocket.

The bang of a door.

And a booming voice. "*Where's my ringer?*"

Chapter Twenty-One

We spring apart. I land on one end of the couch, threading my fingers through my hair as Mason weaves around the Ping-Pong table. My cheeks have been consumed by fire and I'm positive my curls are as wild as my eyes.

Logan is breathing hard, but he isn't tracking Mason's approach. He's staring at me, pupils blown out like I'm still straddling him. It sends another rush of desire and heat through me even as Mason lands in front of us.

"Whatcha doin'?" Mason cocks his head like he absolutely knows the answer.

"Nothing!" I chirp.

"A likely story," he bellows as he pulls up Logan by an elbow and squats like he's going to fireman-carry his (much larger) brother out of the room. "Time for bed, you assholes."

We saunter back to Mason's house through a campus maze of lampposts and sycamores, my arms prickling with goosebumps from the late-night air and Logan's proximity. Mason stumbles ahead, occasionally belting out off-key lyrics to a nearby trash can. In our pocket of shadows, Logan keeps bumping my shoulder and brushing the backs of my fingers with his. Each touch sparks like static under the streetlights.

"So, sleeping arrangements," Mason says, grinning, when we're in his living room. "Here's what I'm thinking—"

"Absolutely not," Logan says.

"You have to listen to my idea before you shoot it down," Mason protests.

"I know your ideas well enough to take aim in advance," Logan growls.

"I'll take the couch!" I say, trying to preempt an argument.

Mason wags a finger like a scolding TV judge. "Absolutely not."

I fold my arms. "I'm not breakable."

"No, you are a guest," Mason says as if I'm checking into his countryside bed-and-breakfast rather than crashing in his apartment with a giant hookah behind the couch. He straightens another few inches. "Besides, I was raised by Logan Wright. Courtesy has been etched into my bones."

Logan's lips crack. I want to add that he's a guest, too, but also my skin is still tingling from his hands and I'm not ready to fully commit to this argument until I know what Mason is planning to propose.

"*Anyway*," Mason continues, "as I was saying before my idea was preemptively and indecorously shit up, I will take the couch. Ali can have my bed. I have fresh sheets and everything. My eldest brother will take the top bunk."

"You have bunk beds?" I ask, even as I have a full-body reaction to the fact that, technically speaking, his brother just suggested Logan and I share a bed. A bunk bed, sure. But still.

Mason straightens the front of his T-shirt. "We got the furniture from the last dudes that rented this place. And it has a double on the bottom," he adds, as if this makes it a sophisticated bunk bed.

"Okay, fine," I say, "but I'll take the top."

Mason lends me an old T-shirt and a pair of boxers and I do everything in my power not to look at Logan as we take turns in the bathroom with Mason's surprisingly plentiful array of spare toothbrushes. When I push open the bedroom door, Logan is under a sheet on the bottom bunk.

I tiptoe into the room. The lights are out, but for a patch of warm light filtering through the open window, which casts a willowy shadow across the carpet. As I make my way to the ladder, I watch Logan's chest rise and fall, and I wonder if he's asleep.

My feet have only hit the first rung when Logan's fingers circle my ankle, his thumb on the divot behind my ankle bone.

I slacken, sliding back to the ground and resting my chin on the top rail. "My uncle always said it's dangerous to play on ladders."

His eyes darken as he props himself up on an elbow. His other hand finds my hip, fingers pressing just enough to make my breath hitch. "Then you better stay down here where it's safe."

He tugs me toward him, and I melt into the curve of his chest, propelled by much more than gravity.

As one, we seamlessly plunge back together like time had paused and is now resuming. Our bodies cinch together from wobbly knees to thumping hearts. Our mouths find each other like magnets in the dark, tongues slipping together like we've done this a hundred times and it's as easy as coming home.

My hands move under Logan's shirt. He runs his tongue across my jaw. It sends a frizzle of energy over my bare skin, goose-pricked from the open window.

We're already zippered together, but it's not anywhere near close enough. It's too frictionless, too easy. I clutch at Logan's wide back, my hips trying to gain purchase against one of his quads.

In the sliver of space between our bodies, Logan's hands travel up the loose fabric of my T-shirt. His fingers trace across the dip of my waist and the curve of my low back. Heat builds, an inferno of desire that grows with every shaky inhale of breath, every swipe of our lips.

I shiver as his fingers push under my bra. His thumb glides over my nipple. The motion draws a wobbling sound from my lips, not even a whimper.

"This time do we have a condom?" I ask into Logan's mouth.

"Yeah, I—" He lets out a shaky exhale. "Mason palmed me one. Then he tried to wink."

I want to laugh at that. I want to tear at his clothes and push his shirt over his head and claw at his boxers until they fall around his ankles. I want to feel him slide down my underwear until it's ringing my knees. I want—

Logan smooths a thumb across my cheek and I hear the word before it falls out of his mouth. "But."

I have never resented this man's self-control so much in my life. "But?"

"But this is my brother's bed," he says.

Logan lowers his face and his lips trace my collarbone.

I hook an index finger into the top of his pants. "Okay, but hear me out."

Logan chuckles into my hair. "Do you have an argument this time?"

"This time I do."

He waits.

"What if it's two different beds?" I ask.

He draws back slightly so he can see my face. "The top and bottom?"

"Yes," I say breathlessly. "If you want it to be."

His lips hitch. "That's a very good argument."

Then he hauls me out by the waist. In the next instant, we're frantically scrambling up the ladder. Logan nearly slams his head against the bed's trim. I do hit my chin against the top rung. Messy.

We peel away clothing like we're shedding every pretense we've ever worn. I straddle Logan and push his T-shirt above his head. I hear him murmur a curse as I tug off my own shirt. Then I yank down my underwear, kicking it off the railing when it gets caught at the base of one ankle.

Logan laughs, dark and husky. He runs his fingers across the skin of my clavicle, my throat. He gazes up at me, pupils blown out and eyes dark. Straddling him, his eyes on me—it's filling, empowering. Like the first time I trimmed a tree, drove a post. I'm heady with it.

Then we're back where we started, but with nothing left between us. I kiss him as his hands cup my hips, gently lifting me. He slides on the condom, and repositions himself. Slowly, I settle lower. We both draw in sharp breath as he sinks inside me. Almost tentatively, I move, sweeping experimentally, then driving down. Logan groans, his fingers curling into mine. It's full and taut, like the ringing note of a single string pulled tight on a harp.

We move together, at first slow and then faster. He rolls his hips and I find a rhythm to match. Sweat slicks down my back and our thighs lick together. I press both hands into his chest, pinning them to his pecs, and hope I'm not digging my nails in enough to leave a mark.

Logan runs his thumb over my cheek, glancing off the corner of my lips, then down my throat to cup my chest. The millions of emotions are still there, bubbling and churning under the surface, but that one touch is enough to drive one of them to the forefront. Pleasure. Intense, ringing pleasure. And so much happiness I feel like I'm in a free fall.

Our breaths are hard and fast. Sweat mingles with sweat. It's all heat and curves and naked joy. A crescendo building. We're moving slower now, but every stroke is hard and soaked. I clutch at his chest. The wave builds. Builds.

Breaks.

Pleasure rolls through me in an endless series of waves, the snapping of a thousand rungs on a thousand ladders. A bottomless ledge. A vibration and its infinite echo.

My chest keens, somehow simultaneously from both the gnawing pain of tattered life and exquisite happiness. It's messy, but it's also so, so good.

Chapter Twenty-Two

When I wake, I find myself curled against Logan's chest, my hair moving with his breath. Sunlight pours from an open window and, through the door, Mason's stereo plays something electronic and dancy.

Logan tucks his chin to look at me. The next beat of my heart trips over itself. It feels like I'm getting away with something, seeing him like this. There's a pillow line on his temple, framing his sleepy eyes. His hair is mussed. His smile soft and vulnerable.

"Hi there," he says.

I let my cheek settle on his solid shoulder. "How're you doing?"

He hums and presses his lips together, clearly consulting some physical sensation I can't see. "Well, obviously last night was . . ."

"Good?"

"I was going to say remarkable."

I smile. "That, too."

Logan's lips graze against my temple, like an unconscious kiss. "But . . ." His eyes glide back to the ceiling and I wonder if he's been awake for some time, contemplating it. "I've been stewing."

"It's time."

"It is. So, to answer your question, happy. But also . . . torn. Maybe a bit angry. And . . ." He runs a hand up the back of my arm, sending goose bumps along my skin. "Did I mention happy?"

I grin into his collarbone. "All that's missing is the salsa."

Logan smiles back at me so broadly it's almost a laugh. My skin tingles with that look. He draws me closer, tucking me back into his arms. I nudge his chin with my nose. He presses a kiss to my forehead. My body flushes again with warmth from his arms, tangled with memories of last night.

A ping from the windowsill hijacks our attention. I flop over, groping for my phone that's plugged into one of Mason's spare chargers.

It's Val. Progress?

She must be desperate enough for news to set aside her skepticism. I tell her: I'm not sure yet. How are things looking on the farm?

I watch as the message goes from unread to read. Then her dots bounce. Everything is the same here.

My grip tightens on the scuffed case before I sigh. Click off the phone.

Logan smooths a hand up and down my bare arm.

"Only one lead left," he says. When my frown deepens, he purses his lips. "Maybe I *want* to talk to her."

"You literally just said you were feeling torn."

"Right, but if it helps you . . ."

I shake my head firmly. I had a feeling Logan would do something like this—try to set aside his own needs for mine. "Absolutely not. You're not going to talk to your estranged mother for the first time in more than a decade because of my pears. If you decide to talk to her, that's one thing, but it will be because of what *you* want, not what I need."

Logan uses a fist to push higher in his seat, gaining altitude on me. "Look, Ali—"

"No, you look," I say, meeting his chest with my hand.

It's true I would like to talk to Lydia. I want to know how the curse works, how it forces people to leave. I want to know if it has any loopholes. I want to know if we can break it. And a twisted part of me wants to know exactly what happened between her and my uncle—and how much it mirrored what Blake and Liv did to me.

Despite all that, this has to be Logan's decision. My brief conversation with Mason about us only solidified that.

"You spent your whole life subjected to choices and life changes because of what other people needed or thought they wanted," I tell him. "Your mom. Your dad. Even your brothers. Trust me, I know what that looks like when I see it. My entire childhood revolved around the whims of my mom's vague vexations. But I got agency over my life after I left her. You still haven't."

My hand flexes on his sternum. "I think it's important that this one is your decision. Not what I need. What *you* do."

A long silence descends as Logan's gaze tracks over my face, looking a bit like he's memorizing the exact angle of my jaw, the contours of my cheeks. "What?" I ask. He swallows, then clears his throat. "I'm just not used to hearing that."

My chest warms in a confusing mix of pride and sadness. "Well, frankly, you deserve nothing less."

Logan draws me closer, nestling me into his arms, his lips on my hair. I settle into the warmth of his embrace, his comforting smell, relishing it even as I wonder how many times I'll get to enjoy this feeling.

A loud knock startles us both.

"T-minus five minutes, you little shits!" Mason yells from the hall.

Logan groans and throws a pillow at the closed door.

"No violence before noon!" Mason protests.

"Since when," Logan mutters.

"Five minutes until what?" I yell back.

"Breakfast burritos," Mason says, like this should be obvious. He could be remembering some conversation that I'm not, but only one of us drank more than half a beer last night, and it wasn't me or Logan.

"Sorry?" I call.

Mason beats against the door like he's open-palm drumming. "I have an exam in three hours and I need the brain food. Plus, they're delicious. Can't miss. But we have to get there while the beans are freshest."

Logan groans again. "He's not stopping until we cede to his demands."

"Terrorist," I mutter as I hoist myself onto the ladder.

"He's lucky I love him so damn much," Logan agrees, following after me.

Mason's spot for breakfast burritos is a graffitied yellow school bus with a chalkboard specials menu leaning against a wheel. A woman in a trucker hat takes our orders from a window framed by sunflowers. At Mason's insistence, we all order the breakfast special and find seats at a reclaimed wooden park bench. With the bus doors flung open, we're serenaded with vibey folk music and occasional curses from the chef.

It's the kind of place Liv would have loved.

There was a time that I would have reflexively shut down that thought. But now? It's sad, but it's also okay that it's sad. Sitting here in the dappled fall sun, sipping hibiscus tea, I let myself feel loss and pain even as my chest purrs because Logan has a knee pressed to mine.

"So," Mason says as he sops up some salsa with a chunk of potato. "Last night. Did I distract you or did I *distract* you."

Logan's gaze slides to mine. "Distracted might be putting it mildly."

Mason chokes and pounds a fist against this chest. "All right, man, that's enough information." He's still smiling, though. "And you, Ali? Sufficiently distracted?"

I want to make a joke, but the truth is I feel the weight of this question. Maybe because I haven't forgotten Mason's missile-like assessment of my problems. I have been distracted, but there's also so much waiting for me back in Apple Valley. The downed branches. The ruined fruit. All the bills I haven't opened yet.

I'm not sure there is a distraction big enough to stave off my feelings.

Logan must have read my expression because he grabs my knee and squeezes.

"You'll figure it out," he says. "*We'll* figure it out."

I swallow. Although I'm grateful for the sentiment, I'm not sure that's a promise anyone can keep. Even Logan. "I don't know if that's true."

Mason's head moves back and forth, attention pinging between us.

"I'm not leaving until we do," Logan says, full of confidence.

"You might not have a choice," I say quietly.

"Ali. Nothing is going to force me away."

Mason sets down his coffee cup. "I'm sorry. 'Force' you away?"

Logan frowns and I bite the inside of my cheek. When we explained the curse to Mason—how it affected my family, his mom, how it makes people leave—we never mentioned Logan could be part of it, too. Although, even with his leg pressed against mine and his fingers on my knee, it feels presumptuous to tell his brother that a generations-old curse could tear him from me because we might fall in love.

Or, in my case at least, because the fall already started.

Neither of us has spoken. Mason has a fork dangling from his fingers, breakfast forgotten. Clearly, he puts two and two together because he says, "The curse has nothing to do with Logan leaving Apple Valley."

I glance at my hands. "We don't know that."

Mason snorts. "I do. I know that. Logan has wanted this for years and always found a reason not to do it. He said he'd go after high school. After I left for college. After Dad died. Now he can. The business is gone. Andrew and I are grown. He has the money. That's what's changed. Not some curse."

Logan lifts a shoulder. "Other things can change, too."

Mason drops his fork. "What the fuck does that mean?" When his brother doesn't say more, Mason tips forward, elbows on the table. "I'm serious. What exactly could change your plans?"

Logan's gaze moves to me, sidelong. A tingle works up my neck as I busy myself with a bite of eggs.

"Not that it's any of your business," Logan growls, then says low, like the next part is only for me, "but my feelings could change."

It's like he's hummed those words directly into my sternum.

Mason takes a swig of coffee, his lips processing a frown as he swallows. "I see."

"Now let it go."

Mason stares at his brother for another beat before turning to me. His unbridled attention is about as uncomfortable as it looks from afar.

"I apologize in advance for the fight you're about to witness," he says, "but sometimes my eldest brother needs a swift kick in the ass and I'm really the only one who can do that for him. Plus, I think it's kind of important that you understand what I'm about to say."

Logan narrows his eyes. There's a warning etched in his expression that I, for one, would not defy. "Drop it, Mason."

"I'm just getting started," Mason bites back. "Unless you tell me clearly and unequivocally that you're not backing out."

Logan is silent.

Mason swears under his breath. Then, louder, he says, "I've seen this exact shit before, man. That doubt. That 'maybe I shouldn't.' You've gotten carried away by some shiny new problems to fix, and now you don't . . . Have you even been drawing?"

Logan blinks. "Why is that relevant?"

"You promised you would. After the fire."

"There hasn't been time."

Inwardly, I cringe. Even though I know this isn't entirely my fault—for the last few weeks Logan has also been focused on a lot of his own stuff—this pronouncement is disquieting. Just how much has he been setting aside to take on my problems?

Mason, far past disquieted, tosses up a hand. "Exactly. And the itinerary? The Atacama Desert? Seeing the Pacific Ocean for the first time? Mexico City? Or is this all stuff you don't have time for, either?"

Logan glowers, a line burrowing between his eyebrows. "It's not your job to look after me."

"If not me, then who? You've lived your whole life for us. Me, Andrew, Dad. And I've had to live with the fact that you gave up your future for mine."

"That was my choice."

"Doesn't change the fact that this is your opportunity," Mason insists. "You're always fixing everyone else's lives for them. When are you going to fix your own?"

"Damn it, Mason!" Logan pounds a fist against the table. "I'm not going to just up and *leave*. I don't bail when I'm needed."

I freeze, a sinking sensation pouring through my limbs as I realize he's talking about *me*.

"Logan . . ." I start.

But Mason must have some other, completely different interpretation of what Logan just said because he leans back on his bench, eyebrows drawn together in something that is no longer anger, but unmistakably concern.

"You're nothing like her," he says quietly.

I blink. *What?*

"What?" Logan asks.

"If you leave," Mason says, eyes lancing his brother, "it won't make you like her."

The hairs on my arms rise, like I've been hit by a cool breeze through sprinklers. Logan is still but for the rise and fall of his chest.

"I know that," he says evenly.

"But clearly you don't," Mason says, and the fight has drained from his voice. "You are not her. You could never be her. You were the one who stayed with us, raised us. You were the one who chose us."

Logan's fists are so tight that I see his knuckles turn white. "And if I leave now? If I start driving down the coast and you need something? You break an arm or get in a car accident or who knows what else? What will that make me?"

"I'm an adult now, brother. I can take care of myself."

I don't want to overstep, and I need to sort through how I feel about everything Mason is saying, especially my role in it. At the same time, I can see the pain and conflict in the tight throb of Logan's jaw. As a compromise, I nudge his knee with mine, a silent reminder I'm still here. He closes his eyes for a moment and leans into my touch, brief but deliberate, a thank-you he doesn't need to say aloud.

"I think you should meet her," Mason says abruptly.

We both look at him.

"I barely remember the woman," he adds. "And I have no desire to change that, but even still, *I* know you're nothing like her. That you could never be anything like her. I think if you talk to her, you'll figure that out, too."

Logan's face goes slack for a moment, but when he raises his head, his gaze doesn't go to Mason.

He looks to me.

I put a hand on his forearm and squeeze. "Whatever you choose."

He holds my gaze. "Together?"

"I'm with you."

Chapter Twenty-Three

The storefront's tall windows glow against the gray afternoon, HOLLOWAY WOODWORKS AND DESIGN spelled out in tarnished brass. A gust of wind scatters a handful of dry leaves across the sidewalk as a customer slips out the door with a twinkle of bells, letting out a slice of warm air. They pause to hold the door open for us, but Logan remains mutely fixed in place and I wave them off with a polite smile.

His eyes haven't stopped tracing that brass lettering.

"Don't feel like you have to do this," I say. "We don't even know for sure that this is your mom's shop."

"It is."

"The point is that you're not committed." Logan's mouth opens with a protest, but I cut him off. "And don't you dare say anything about cursed pears."

His fingers brush against the back of my hand. "What if I also care about cursed pears?"

"Do you?"

"You care about them, and I care about you." He grabs my hand, threading his long fingers through mine. "Let me care about you, too, Ali."

Warmth glides along my limbs as my heart cycles through pleasure and longing.

I let out a long breath and my hand relaxes into his. "Just this once."

Logan keeps hold of me as he pushes open the door, eliciting another round of chimes.

"One moment," someone calls.

Logan's gaze roams over the burnished concrete, antique workbenches that have been repurposed as display tables, and ambient lighting from bronze sconces. When he reaches the wood samples—fluted columns, mantelpieces, and crown molding profiles—his already tense shoulders stiffen, registering a significance I can't see.

A few moments later, footsteps signal the arrival of a woman with round cheeks, gray-streaked hair pulled into a loose bun, and a waxed canvas apron.

"Hello, there, what can I—"

Her easy, customer-service smile freezes, drops away.

Even if I'd never laid eyes on her before, I'd know this is Lydia. I can tell by the way her face has transformed, the way Logan's entire body has gone rigid. I tighten my grip on his hand and he holds on right back.

"Logan," she whispers.

Customers drift around the store, conversations buzzing around our pocket of frozen silence. Lydia's fingers twitch uncertainly and she takes a tentative step toward the son she hasn't seen in fourteen years. My mind goes red as I remember the sensation of Liv's coconut-scented hug at the gala. I shift, angling between them.

Lydia stops. Stuffs her hands into the pockets of her high-waisted trousers.

"Planned or accidental?" she asks, voice barely above a whisper.

"Planned," Logan says flatly.

Lydia's eyes flick to me, and I wait for Logan to decide how to introduce us.

He opts for simple. "This is Ali."

We've met before, but it was years ago and we're completely out of context, so I'm not surprised when Lydia says, "Nice to meet you, Ali."

I nod, remaining silent, because if Logan doesn't feel pressure to make this interaction pleasant and socially acceptable, then I'm certainly not going to.

Lydia fiddles with a measuring tape looped into her belt, then sighs. "Would you like to talk? I can close early for the day."

At Logan's curt nod, she leads us through a door to a small room dominated by a worktable, then forges back out, presumably to close up the front.

While we wait, I perch uncertainly on a high metal stool, and Logan remains upright, hands thrust into his pockets as he studies the wall. It's occupied by a huge slab of wood carved with hundreds of cutouts, creating an ornate and repeating trellis pattern. It's intricately done and . . . I would say beautiful, but that thought feels disloyal.

He's still sizing up the carved wall when Lydia steps back into the room, juggling a swing-top bottle topped with three overturned glasses. Her eyes tighten as she watches Logan's back for a moment, lets out a small breath, and closes the door.

"Fretwork," she explains as she joins him. "This one was made with a scroll saw. A common misconception about fretwork is that it has to be done with a fretsaw to count, but it's not like champagne or Manchego. What matters is what comes out, not how or where it was made."

Logan clears his throat. "I'm a carpenter. I know what fretwork is."

"Oh? Are you?"

"Not by choice," he says flatly.

Lydia regards the side of his face with confusion. I'm sure she can read his tone, but I also don't think she appreciates his textured meaning because she turns to the big worktable, arranges her glasses.

"Well," she says, popping open her bottle with a thumb and pouring out gently fizzing water. "The artist who made it is quite well known and lives here in town. I'd be happy to give you his name if you want to check out his studio."

She slides a glass across the table to me and extends one to Logan. He turns to face her, but doesn't take it. "You didn't make this."

"No, no. I just do columns, and mantelpieces, and such."

"So," he says flatly, "you're still a carpenter."

Pink slides into Lydia's cheeks as she retracts the glass, then takes a few swigs of it herself. She clears her throat, again reaches for a smile. "We call ourselves woodworkers around here, but mostly so we can upcharge the rich customers."

"You're a carpenter," he repeats. "In Maplehurst."

Now I think both Lydia and I see where this is going because Lydia's face has gone from red to a blotchy kind of purple. She takes a shaky step backward.

"If you came here looking for a compelling explanation for my life choices," she says carefully, "I'm sorry to say you're going to be disappointed."

Logan watches her for another beat. "No," he says finally. "That's not why we're here."

He rounds the table and takes the seat next to me. One of his hands goes to my knee and his gaze catches mine. There's something in there like a question. Or maybe an appeal.

I rest my fingers over his and clear my throat. "We wanted to ask you about the orchard. And the curse."

Lydia blinks as she turns to me, eyebrows climbing. "*Martin's* orchard?"

"Martin Reid died earlier this year."

"Oh." She sways and grips the edge of the table, then sinks onto a stool. The water trembles in the glass as she raises it and takes another shaky swallow. "Okay, just—I think I might just need a moment to process that."

"We're here to ask you about an interview you gave for a documentary a few years ago," Logan presses. "Ali took over the farm earlier this year and we're trying to answer some questions about it."

Lydia's attention rises to me again, recognition in her eyes. "Martin's niece. You're Ali."

I nod. "In the interview, you said you saw strange things on the land?"

She sighs and takes another trembling sip before answering. "I shouldn't have. Martin never wanted me to talk about it to anyone, especially not like that. But those documentary guys offered to pay. It wasn't much, but I needed the money. I tried to apologize later but . . ." She drifts off and her lips harden as her eyes find mine again. "Is it causing you problems? Martin thought it would one day. He said it . . . Well. He was very upset."

I blink as my stomach shifts uncomfortably. I hadn't thought Martin and Lydia spoke again after her letter. It seemed so final and I didn't see any evidence they were in touch before he died. She certainly didn't come to the funeral.

But now she's saying they talked again? And she never reached out to her sons.

I press a shoulder to Logan's, just in case he's having these thoughts, too.

"No," I say, "we're wondering if there's anything you can tell us that you didn't say in the interview. The clips were quite vague."

Without answering, Lydia uncertainly twirls a hair tie around her wrist.

"Whatever it is," I push, "we won't be surprised. Over the last few weeks, we've probably seen stranger."

"Oh? Even . . . even with Martin gone?"

"Yes? What does that have to do with it?"

She frowns at her glass. "Maybe nothing, I don't know. To answer your question, it was . . . subtle. Some of it so subtle that I don't think Martin even noticed it until I pointed it out. Maybe because he'd lived on that land all his life and he just . . . Well, he was a very accepting person."

My body tenses at the compliment. Martin's unequivocal acceptance of me—all parts of me—used to be my favorite thing about him. Is Lydia about to sour that, too?

She's still talking. "Some of it seemed undeniable. Trees that would bend without any wind. Sudden shifts in the temperature. Unexplained flowers."

"The forget-me-nots," I say.

She nods, and there's so much weight to the gesture I think she might be wondering how much we know. Or maybe she's assuming Martin spilled his secrets before the end. This thought gives me another spike of resentment. He *should* have told me what he knew.

"You say this is all happening again now?" she asks. "Even after he died?"

"It hasn't been exactly the same," I tell her. "But, yes, something supernatural is happening with the land. You're saying you believed Martin was the source of it?"

"He never agreed. But if he's gone and the magic is still there, then . . . I guess I was wrong after all."

My stomach drops with the edge of disappointment, and I'm not sure how to continue.

Logan, though, does seem to know because his expression is steady as he says, "Is the orchard's magic the reason you left?"

Her face snaps up. "How do you know that?"

This reaction is enough to make me straighten. "How, exactly, did that work?"

Lydia's lips firm as she considers, then spreads her hands out on the table, pressing her palms and splaying her fingers. "I . . . it's complicated. Give me a moment to think about how to explain." She frowns like we're looking at her impatiently. Maybe we are. "Not because I haven't thought about it. It's just that my understanding of what happened has changed over time and if you'd walked in that door a year ago or five years ago I would have said something different. I want to make sure this answer is the best I have to give."

"I don't need your best explanation," Logan says. "I only want the true one."

And even though he's holding his face neutrally, I can see the uncertainty there, the significance in the sweep of his mouth and the set of his eyebrows. Despite what he said earlier, it's clear Logan is not only asking this question because of the pears. At this point, I don't think it's about Lydia, either. After that conversation with Mason, I think he might be asking a question even closer to home.

I steady my leg against his knee. He shifts slightly, leaning into me.

"The truth of it," Lydia says, and draws in a steeling breath, "is that I was unhappy for many years. I got pregnant right before I graduated from high school, and then your father and I got married before I started showing. I wasn't ready to be a mother, not in the way people said I would be. I didn't know how to say no to the life that was already building up around me."

Logan swallows and I press my knee harder to his, like I can absorb some of this blow for him. Like I can shield him from the pain this woman has inflicted, and all the pain she's about to inflict.

"Your father . . . he wouldn't have admitted it, but he wasn't happy, either. He was young, too. Way too young for that life. Only his way of dealing with that was by disappearing. Sometimes into the garage or our workshop or, later, down to some bar. Sometimes farther. He never wanted to talk about anything, not what I was feeling and certainly not what he was. He'd only try to outrun it.

"I was the one who stayed," she continues, bravely meeting Logan's eyes. "For years, I stayed even though he was always leaving me. Then, we built the barn on Martin's orchard and I . . . Well, I don't know how much he told you already."

"We don't know exactly what happened between you," I say, and I can feel my body bracing itself, not just for Logan but also for me, and the image of my uncle.

The betrayal that maybe shouldn't feel personal but still does.

"We talked, mostly," Lydia says. "Martin was such a good listener. But, also, the land went still for us. For me. Suddenly, it was as if I had the space and the quiet to see things for how they were. It was like . . . I opened my eyes for the first time in years and, my god, I was thirty-seven. I was thirty-seven—the middle of my life—and where had it all gone? I'd sacrificed all those years so that my husband could avoid his own. I'd been trapped inside a vicious, unhealthy cycle. It had to stop. I told Martin all of that. Everything I was feeling. And on that last day . . . the day we finished the barn, we—he and I—we kissed."

My shoulders tense.

Logan's jaw is clenched tight, but he doesn't otherwise react.

Lydia takes another breath. Releases it slowly. "Something snapped. Or maybe everything snapped. It was like I had all these tiny threads holding my life together. For months, they frayed, and that last day, they came loose. I knew I had to leave.

"Was that the orchard? The magic?" She pauses, then nods. "Maybe it was. It showed me the truth of my life, my strengths and my flaws. It let me see everything in a way I hadn't allowed before. It changed me by revealing what was already true."

Logan's leg bounces once, then again. His thoughts are too complicated for me to guess, but I can imagine some of it, maybe. I lay my hand lightly against his thigh, and he stills, restless energy folding into my touch. Before I pull away, his hand covers mine, and he squeezes my fingers.

Are you telling me," Logan says slowly, "you left us because Dad left you first?"

She grimaces. "He didn't just leave—he was *always leaving* me. It's so much worse. I knew that if I turned that around on him, he would finally have to step up. It was his turn to show up."

"He didn't."

Her eyebrows pinch a fraction. "He did. He said—"

"You were in touch with him?" Logan asks so sharply that Lydia startles backward.

"Briefly. He told me to stop calling, but I— It was enough for me to know that everything was okay. He insisted. He said . . . he said that I was right. He said you were better off without me. He said not to come back."

Logan's fist clenches so hard it's shaking. I tighten my grip on his leg.

"I see," he says coldly. "Except none of that was true."

She opens her mouth to protest, but Logan plows forward. "Andrew started third grade right after you left. And I thought, he should just go to school. Be as normal as possible. Problem was, none of his teachers could get him to do anything but stare out a window. Dad was— How did you say it? Outrunning his feelings?

Certainly not around for parent-teacher conferences. So, I went instead. I was eighteen when Andrew's teachers started telling me that I was failing at home. And you were choosing not to be there."

I chance a glance at Lydia. The color has drained from her rose-tipped cheeks.

"Mason," Logan continues firmly. "Mason was six. He'd wake up at night screaming, drenched in sweat. Inconsolable. It got so bad he was afraid to go to sleep at all. I'd lie on the floor in his bedroom, every night, listening to him cry. And you were choosing not to be there."

"I—" Tears hover in Lydia's eyes. She blinks them back as her voice trembles. "You have to understand. It was *impossible* to come back."

Logan's eyes flash. "Difficult."

Her red-rimmed eyes lift to him in question.

"It would have been *difficult*," he clarifies, "to come back. Maybe you would have had to file for divorce and figure out joint custody or weekend visits. You would have needed to sit down your kids and explain. Maybe pay child support. There would have been awkward conversations with judgmental teachers and nosy neighbors. But none of that was impossible."

Lydia winds and unwinds her fingers together and apart, clenching at her knuckles intermittently as tears leave tracks along her cheeks. She's watching Logan with the air of someone inflicting pain on themselves. "I didn't— I couldn't come back. It was something I couldn't control. The decision had been made. Or maybe it was the influence of the land or—"

And for the first time since we stepped inside this storefront, Logan loses the tight grip he's held on his emotions. He pounds a fist against the table. Lydia jumps. "*No.* Maybe that felt like one choice or two. Influenced by the land or some shit Dad said on a phone call. But it wasn't. It was a thousand choices. A million.

You made a choice every minute of every day that you stayed away."

Lydia's mouth drops open, but Logan stands abruptly, sending his metal stool screeching. I immediately follow suit. He puts out his hand and I take it, letting my fingers collapse under his iron grip.

We forge toward the exit, but when Logan reaches the knob, he pauses. Angles his face backward.

"I'm glad I came here. I appreciate that you were willing to talk to me and that you explained as much as you could. But I don't forgive you. And you don't get to blame *anyone* but yourself for what you did."

With that, he jerks open the door.

Chapter Twenty-Four

Logan sags into the driver's seat of his truck and I climb in through the other door, tucking my leg so I'm facing him. Brown leaves cling to the windshield, wet and paper-thin, their stems trembling in a cold breeze. Logan twists the key and the wipers drag against the glass, smearing water and leaves and filling the cab with a rasping sound. Still, he doesn't shift the truck into drive. Instead, his clenched hands roll over the steering wheel, back and forth, as he takes deep, even breaths.

"Logan."

He turns to me. Even though his body is graphite-still, there's a storm churning in his eyes. I don't know whether to reach for him or give him space. The silence feels like a test I should know how to pass, like there's a right thing to say if I could only find the words. But I don't think I'm up for this task.

Which is maybe why I say, "Mason was right. You're *nothing* like her."

They're opposites in every way. Where Logan is slow to smile, Lydia is quick with one. She's warm and practiced, with a customer-service polish that I've never seen in Logan. But the important differences run deeper. Logan shoulders every burden within reach, especially the ones that don't belong to him. Lydia, meanwhile, could barely acknowledge her own.

"Was that the wrong thing to say?" I blurt out when he hasn't yet spoken. "I'm sorry, I just—"

"No, it wasn't. I've been thinking about the same thing since we walked into that store." His jaw muscle leaps, and he rolls his fists again. "I didn't recognize the woman in there. But then again . . . maybe I wouldn't. She wasn't exactly the most attentive mother, and the more I think about it, she wasn't always happy. But she was there with us. And one day she wasn't. You heard her. She wanted to leave for years and never did. That's how it's been for me, too. Thinking about all that made me angry. Too angry. I went too far."

I reach across the seats and grab his wrist, tighten my fingers onto the ridges of his forearm. "You stayed when you were needed. You heard her out today when you could have screamed instead. You are loyal and honest in every way she isn't."

His breath catches, barely audible, but enough to stir the silence in the cab. "Does it matter if I did those things even when part of me wanted something else?"

"It matters more," I insist to his uncertainty. "That's when it matters most."

His eyes close as he rubs at the bridge of his nose. "I still shouldn't have let myself get angry with her."

"*No.*" I scooch toward him and yank his hand away from his face. "You were brilliant."

His eyes snap open. Fly to me.

"I wouldn't have been able to do what you just did," I explain. "I wouldn't be able to . . . to tell her how I feel. You stood your ground and explained your perspective, and you didn't cross any lines, at least not any that I could tell. That kind of conviction in your emotion, it's . . . it's impressive. You're impressive."

Logan holds my gaze, and that storm in his eyes quiets. His

irises flicker, as if holding a scrap of refracted light. Then he reaches for me, his fingers brushing my elbow before settling there. "Ali."

"Logan."

"I believe you could, too. If you decided to."

My mom's flat expression ripples through my mind. "Maybe."

Outside the cab, a perfectly normal-looking cedar sways in a perfectly mundane wind. Maybe I should feel glad to be here, away from my complicated trees. Away from the stump where I split open my elbow and the strange weather and my ruined fruit. Instead, my chest twinges so abruptly it's almost painful.

"Do you think we could go back to Apple Valley?" I ask. "I think I need to be home."

Logan offers me a soft smile and turns on the engine. I let my head sink to the cool window and listen to the tires rumble as the college town melts into endless gray. The highway is slick from rain, making mirrors that reflect the cloudy skies.

After rows of harvested cornfields transition to evergreen slopes blurred with fog, Logan asks, "Do you blame the orchard for the way your mom raised you? Not that she left, but all the choices after. Moving from place to place. Never letting you settle."

I tip my temple against the seat's backrest and think about the impatient frown that would bracket Mom's lips every time something displeased her. Traffic congestion. Sporadic power outages. Chatty neighbors. Neighbors who left out their recycling bins for an extra day or who sped around corners. Overly strict teachers. Overly *lax* teachers. And every time that unhappiness started to register, she was already planning a new move.

Could that have been shaped by her upbringing? Maybe. But also that seems like the work of the mystical.

"I think my mom's choices came from her. Not the trees."

Logan nods, and ever so gently, he asks, "And Blake? Liv? Not just what happened in the barn, but everything after."

I swallow, remembering the familiar look they shared, the one that corkscrewed through my chest. Their decision to move to Apple Valley. Their decision to show up to my home. "I think that maybe us living together gave them an opportunity to do something they wanted to do all along."

He blows out a breath and nods, like I've just agreed with him about something. Maybe I have.

"They all made choices," he says. "Your mom. Mine. Blake and Liv. Not just one choice. Many. And I don't think they get to blame the trees for any of it."

Awareness prickles the back of my neck. "What are you saying?"

He glances at me sidelong. "I don't think the curse has forced anyone to leave. I don't think it has that power."

And even though Logan has expressed skepticism about the nature of the curse before, for the first time, I really see what he means.

Maybe none of them deserve the absolution that would come from denying their agency.

Not my mom. Not his. Not Blake and Liv.

Because they didn't just make one decision. They made a thousand. A million. And how can we blame the trees for that?

But if that's true then everything we thought we knew about the curse was wrong.

At the same time, the list of people who left stretches impossibly long, as my uncle discovered, across decades and generations. "It can't be a coincidence that all those people left the farm, though."

Logan runs a hand along the steering wheel, for the first time breaking his perfect ten-and-two grip. "I've been thinking about that. I think the answer is they aren't coincidences at all."

"How so?"

"It would be a bigger coincidence, more unexplainable, if no one who stepped foot on the land ever left. Think about it. If you run out a lifetime long enough, everyone leaves, eventually. In one way or another."

"I guess if you define 'leaving' broadly enough, that's true."

"Exactly," he says. "It's been true for me and there's no orchard to blame, at least not for the people who aren't my mom. My dad left years ago, over and over, before he really, fully did. Andrew enlisted in the navy and he only comes back to Apple Valley every six months or so. Mason went off to college."

I tilt my head, thinking about how the reverse is also true of my family. "And not everyone who my uncle loved left him. Val, most importantly. Their love wasn't romantic, but it was undeniable. She stood by him until the end. And everyone else . . . folks in town, friends and neighbors. Well, maybe Val was right about how he pushed them away, like a self-fulfilling prophecy. When he was convinced he'd die alone."

Logan flicks on his turn signal and we slip off the highway. Concrete and steel give way to rolling hills lined with apple trees. The road leans into a curve, and we begin the climb along a steep ridgeline toward my land.

"Plus, there's you," Logan says. "You left when you didn't have a choice, but you also came back. You came back to your uncle and the land, even when all you were ever taught was to leave."

I swallow past a lump in my throat as my uncle's face fills my memories. The gratitude brimming in his eyes as he held my hand with his cool, papery skin, and I said I'd do it—I'd take over the orchard. It still burns like a hot poker pressed against my chest, no matter how much my view of Martin has shifted.

"My love of this land has never wavered," I say. "The more time I've spent here, the more I've wanted to stay."

Logan hums. "That's how I knew we were wrong."

"Because I wanted to stay?"

"Because"—Logan's grip tightens on the steering wheel—"I've wanted to leave Apple Valley for as long as I can remember. I've spent years tormented by that dream. But the only thing that's ever really changed it—that's ever made me truly reconsider the idea—is being here, on this land, with you. You make me want to stay."

"Thank you," I whisper.

"I mean it," he says.

My rib cage expands until my next breath feels too tight. His words feel good, too good. It's everything I've wanted him to say. At least, before I talked to Mason. Before I understood how important it is for Logan to leave.

The truck rounds a corner and the farmhouse sails into view, canary yellow trim welcoming me home. Trees creep past the window as we scale the driveway. In the branches, crystal pears take languid turns, scattering prisms of blue and yellow across the ground.

Breathtaking.

Gutting.

My temple settles against the truck's cool window, and a new, complicated conflict gnaws at my thoughts. On the one hand, I'm relieved not to be cursed to solitude. On the other? None of what we learned in Maplehurst or decided on this drive solves my immediate problems. Half of my pears are crystallized. The other half are marked. I don't know whether I'll be able to pay my bills this year. I don't even know how big my bills are.

"I don't know what to do next," I say helplessly. "Maybe the land isn't cursed, but I don't—"

My throat ratchets around a shaky breath, and with it, words stumble loose. Words that I've buried for weeks. Words I haven't dared say aloud because they're too big, too terrifying. Too true.

"I think I could lose my farm."

I could lose it all: the new shoots that remember the old roots, the porch that remembers my weight, the branches that carry the scars of my childhood.

The trees that have marked me, just as I've marked them.

Pressure builds behind my eyes. Logan kills the engine, unclips his seat belt, and slides toward me, tucking me into his arms.

"I'm sorry," I say as I clutch at his shirt and choke on a sob.

He smooths back my hair. "Ali. Never apologize for how you feel."

A tear escapes my clenched eyes. "Even if it's messy?"

"Especially if it's messy."

"I'm just so afraid," I say. "I'm afraid I'll lose everything I have left."

Logan picks up my hand, braids our fingers together. I cling right back.

"I'm here," He says softly. "I'm with you. Wherever you are."

Tears track down my cheeks as the sun hovers above the ridgeline, casting the sky in softening gold. We remain in the quiet cab, suspended in that fragile hour before sunset, our fingers braided together, knuckles white with the grip neither of us will let go.

Logan squeezes my hand. "Ali."

I sniff. "Yeah?"

"I got my insurance settlement yesterday."

My stomach backflips as my head jerks up. "I thought it was just a meeting."

"I thought so, too, but they've given me the final payout amount. Once I sign, I'll waive any further claims related to the fire. The case turned out simpler than they thought, or maybe they had been keeping my expectations low."

Alarm kindles at the base of my throat. I thought we had weeks. A month. If he has the money—

Logan must see what's in my face because he squeezes my fingers. "What I'm trying to say is that it's going to be a big check. The workshop and house were worth more than I'd realized."

"Oh." My eyebrows pinch together. "What kind of more, exactly?"

A micro pause. "I can help you pay off your debts. Maybe not all of them, but enough to get you through another year, at least. Probably a few."

"You—" I swivel in my seat so I can lower my chin at him. "You can't just give me money."

"A loan, then."

"I have a million loans."

"From banks, which won't let you extend the terms or lower your interest rate."

I shake my head, partly in disbelief and partly because what he's offering is much bigger than he's letting on. If Logan gave me that money, it'd create a debt between us that would irrevocably alter our power dynamic. I'd owe him my entire livelihood and, regardless of what kind of future we might or might not have, we'd be tethering ourselves to each other in a serious and lasting way.

"That's a huge commitment," I argue. "What you're talking about is a long-term financial relationship where you are my creditor."

He stuffs a hand in his jacket pocket and lifts a shoulder as though he's offering to replace my half-functional toaster oven. "I don't see it like that. I have the money. I don't need it. Why wouldn't I help?"

It's tempting. It's absurdly tempting. In a world of no choices, this is a real choice.

Still. Saying yes right now feels consequential. Monumental. Not an answer to give when I'm half bleary from lack of sleep, sitting in a truck in my driveway.

"Let me think about it?" I ask. "Consider my options?"

He nods and tucks me back into his arms. On the windshield, a drop of water catches another, filling it, and they slowly slide downward. "Of course. Take all the time you need."

I settle against him, burying my nose into the soft folds of his jacket, even though that word—*time*—sticks.

How much time do we have?

"When do you think you'll leave?" I ask.

"I said I would help you pick. That hasn't changed."

"Thank you," I say, although I haven't missed the fact that he didn't answer. We start picking in less than a week. A few weeks later, we'll be done. And then what?

Maybe this is some kind of a test.

Last night I told Logan that I didn't want to make any big, long-term decisions. That I wanted to live in the moment instead. But that concept was much easier to accept when the end felt far off and intangible. Before I understood how important it is for him to leave.

I've spent my whole adult life clinging to people. Places. Stability. Specific versions of the future. And maybe, in a different way, so has Logan. But where has that gotten either of us?

I twist in my seat so I can unclip my belt, letting it curl away from my shoulder as my eyes find Logan.

He tilts his head. "Ali. You have that look."

"What look?"

With a thumb, he rubs the furrow between my eyebrows. "You get a little divot right here when you want to ask me something."

I grab his wrist, capturing his hand next to my face. His fingers splay and I let my cheek sink into his callused palm. "That's not my 'wanting to ask' divot."

"What is it then?"

I scrape my fingernails along the rough material of Logan's jeans, just inside his thigh. "That's just me wanting."

Logan's breath stills as he takes me in. His hand wraps around the back of my head, fingers riding into my hair. That look tells me he's memorizing, not just seeing. There's reverence in his expression—something that undoes me more than his touch alone.

Then he leans in and kisses me, slow and sure.

And, oh.

It's overwhelming how much I want him. Maybe it's the emotional roller coaster we've been riding over the last few days interrupted by the stillness of this driveway. Or maybe it's the fact that, somewhere deep down, my heart already knows that although Logan might not be cursed to leave or that I might not be fated to solitude, *this* is not going to last. One way or another, it can't.

Logan tugs me closer and I'm propelled into his chest. In a moment, I'm straddling him again, steering wheel brushing against my hip, and his hands in my hair. When I lower myself, I can feel how hard he is. My throat releases an involuntary sigh against his mouth. There's steam riding up the windows and we're pressed so close together that I feel, rather than hear, him groan.

"Ali," he says, that warning in his voice again.

"Don't tell me to stop," I say breathlessly between each kiss pressed close to his mouth. This isn't the time for his self-control. "I will get out of the truck if you tell me to, but I—"

Logan's hands move from my shoulders to the sides of my face, holding me steady in a tilting world. "I never want this to stop."

I sigh with relief as my lips crash to his. Every hesitation we've carried folds into this single, unstoppable pull. The truck seems to shrink around us. Our exhales fog the window. Logan's hands ride up my back, under my shirt. He unhooks my bra and his thumb catches my nipple. I feel the shiver all the way to my throat.

I want more of him. With each unsteady beat of my pulsing heart. Each swipe of my tongue. I want *time*.

"Is it too much," I say, breathless, "to hope you have a condom in this truck?"

"Mason gave me a few," he admits, hitching me upward so he can pull it out of his pocket.

And I practically laugh with relief. I reach down to his belt. It's awkward, messy even, because we're wedged in the tight space between his seat and the steering wheel. Still, somehow, I manage to unclasp his buckle and lift my hips while Logan pulls himself free of his zipper and rips open the wrapper.

I'm aching and pulsing with so much need and impatience that when I pull aside my underwear and lower myself again, he pushes inside me almost easily. I release a tight gasp, pulled in two with friction and pressure. Logan is watching us, watching me, eyes glued to my movements.

"Ali," he says again, and this time it sounds so different in his mouth. Full of reverence.

I lower myself farther, feeling the push of pressure higher still, and maybe it would be too much if it also weren't incandescently pleasurable.

"Logan," I say. He groans again at the sound of his name on my lips, unrestrained in a way that washes over me in glittering waves.

We move together rhythmically, each stroke drawing quivering breaths out of my lungs. Sensation builds and deepens, steadies into something wordless and inevitable. The sound of it—our breaths, my heartbeat, the quiet creak of metal—feels like the only thing left in the world. And when his next breath stutters and his hips follow the movement, it rips an explosion out of me so intense I nearly cry out.

When the vibrations finish passing through me, I lower my forehead to Logan's shoulder and rest against him, our inhales and exhales falling into the same slow pattern. His thumb traces a path through my damp hair, a small, grounding gesture. He kisses my cheek, my temple. Outside, everything is misted and blurred.

"Now," he says gently, "I think we get out of the truck."

But I shake my head into his shirt. Not only because I feel so limp that I'm not currently sure I can stand, but also because, out there, the night breathlessly waits with everything we've postponed. In the safety of this cab, the air is thick with warmth and stillness—the kind that can only exist right before everything changes.

Right now, I want to hold on to this moment forever.

Like a frozen bubble on the edge of a lake. A river stilled to silence.

A crystal pear.

Chapter Twenty-Five

Our days hang suspended like dust motes catching the light—twinkling, turning, and unthinkably still. Each moment I'm caught between yesterday and tomorrow, as if underwater or half asleep.

The night we get back from Maplehurst, Logan and I sip wine on the porch and watch the sunset melt from gold to violet, lingering until we're shivering because even a stack of blankets isn't enough to stave off the mountain chill. When I close my eyes, I can almost believe this is ordinary, impossibly mundane, just another night in a long stretch of nights that we'll have together. In my bed, Logan kisses me and holds me close and my chest aches with something that feels too big for pleasure.

Morning arrives with soft, pale light spilling through the curtains and the faint tick of the coffee maker beginning its slow percolation. I find Logan barefoot beside the machine, sweatpants low on his hips, fingers splayed wide beside a closed book.

When our eyes meet, Logan smiles softly and—

Oh.

It's you.

I round the counter so I can circle my arms around his waist, latch my hands together, and rest my chin on his firm shoulder. The warmth of his body seeps into my chest. Solid. Still here.

From this angle, I can see the book is actually a sketchbook—larger than the ones I remember from when we were teens.

"Mason gave it to me," he says. "Before we left Maplehurst."

"Are you going to use it?"

He tips his temple, touching mine. "It's a big part of who I was."

Somehow, I hear what he doesn't say. Is it still a part of who he's going to be?

Later, Val comes by to check in on the pears. Even before she digs the pressure gauge from her pocket, I can feel something is different. Maybe it's because of the color rising in the fruit, now a green that reminds me of moss clinging to the north side of a damp stone wall.

"Something's off," I guess as she lumbers down her tree ladder holding a marked pear.

She studies her piece of fruit, thumb brushing over a dark bruise. "Seems they stopped ripening."

I lean closer to see the reading. "Like they won't be ready by the end of the month?"

Val nods, lips pressed.

"But it's always been September thirtieth," I protest in stunned disbelief. "Every season for five generations. You can set your watch to it."

At my expression, an uneasy smile ghosts her face. She squeezes my shoulder. "No luck breaking the curse, then?"

My stomach sinks at her nonanswer. "Like you said," I tell her softly, "Uncle Martin tried for years. I don't think we were going to figure it out in a few days."

She purses her lips, looking like she's regretting her own words.

But Val was right, which means that if there's a way to save my farm's future, it lies not in the supernatural, but in the mundane.

It's in that office where antique desk drawers overflow with overdue bills. And maybe, it's in Logan's offer from the truck. Another loan—this one bigger than I've ever had before.

There's only one way to find out.

The next morning, fog drapes over the orchard like sparkling gauze and I brew a pot of coffee so strong it burns the backs of my eyes. I douse it with pumpkin spice syrup before filling my favorite mug and tiptoeing into the office. The first ledger is spiral-bound, with neat rows and columns across pale green pages. Across them, my uncle's nearly unreadable scribbles transition to Liv's precise handwriting. I run my thumb along a column of their notes and, instead of pushing the feeling away, I let my chest burn with everything this brings up. Loss. Hurt. Anger.

When those emotions pass on their own, I get to work.

I dump out the cardboard box full of bills and sort them into piles. I fire up my cashbook—the sole part of this accounting system that's actually on a computer—only to discover it's woefully out of date and riddled with holes. So, I start over from scratch, filling in what I know about prices and expenses. When I reach too many dead ends to count, Val stops by to pour two mugs of tea and alternates between squinting at Martin's handwriting and Liv's, guessing what they could have meant by some notation or another.

Hours later, I've made only a dent, but my eyes are crossing and my back feels permanently hunched, so I emerge, rubbing at a knot in my neck, but resolved to start again tomorrow. In the dining room, I find Logan at the wide antique table. The table runner is rolled neatly to one end as he steers a pencil across paper.

"Hey," I say.

He looks up from his page, lips hitching in that familiar crooked smile. It's been easier to come lately, I've noticed. I like that.

"Did you figure anything out yet?" he asks.

I rub at my cheek. "Not yet. But at least I've started."

I wonder if Logan will ask me again about the money, but he doesn't. Instead, he pushes the chair back next to him, and I sink to a seat, peering at his open sketchbook.

"You're drawing," I observe.

He tips up the page so we can both examine the sketch. It's not like the apples or mountains I remember from his teenage years. More abstract than still life.

"What is it?" I ask.

He drops the page and plucks up his pencil again, rolling it thoughtfully between thumb and forefinger. "I'm not sure yet."

In the afternoon, we meander through the rows with steaming mugs, carefully avoiding the honeybees chasing from clover to clover. Ostensibly, I'm out here to check the pears for progress, but I don't need to pull out Val's old pressure gauge to know nothing has changed since yesterday.

Instead, I let myself really see this place.

The trees lean toward one another, their branches arching into tunnels where the air smells of blossoms and honey. Between the limbs, motes hang in the sunlight, but not like ordinary dust. They shimmer and slowly drift, frozen like far-off stars. When I swirl my hand through the glimmering cloud, the motes startle, scattering in delicate arcs that curve around my fingers and twirl back into place. It's another tiny miracle, a moment of magic so subtle I wouldn't have noticed if I hadn't been looking for it.

My uncle would have loved it.

I lean against Logan's shoulder and let myself feel that, too.

The next day, when I emerge from the office, I don't find Logan hunched over his sketchbook. In fact, I don't see him again for hours. It's not until late that evening, when I'm curled on the couch, that he strides through the door, sweat rimming his collar and dirt smudged around his beard.

Without a word, he crosses the room to the couch and lowers his mouth to mine. I catch his neck and he hauls me up the stairs. We both plunge into the shower, water running his sweat-slicked chest clean. Our mouths fuse together and my heart feels like it's shearing in half and remaking itself.

That night, a pack of coyotes wanders onto the land. Frantic cries spike the moonlit air as I curl into Logan's chest. His fingers twist in my hair. My lips glance against his jawline, and, suddenly, our movements become both involuntary and deeply deliberate. My fingers find his waistband. His hands lift my nightdress.

And when he pushes into me, we are two mirrors reflecting each other: an endless feedback loop of fragility.

"What does it feel like?" I ask with my next lungful of air.

Logan shifts and smooths a hand down my collarbone, fingertips glancing down my spine. Then he draws me deeper into him, and I gasp as his breath warms my skin, pulling me taut.

"Like being made new," he whispers against my throat.

"Like I've been asleep," he says into my hair.

"And now," he breathes into my heart, "I'm awake."

We kiss, and it's everything.

"I like that," I whisper. "But I was going to say that it feels like coming home."

The next day, we do it all over again.

About a week after our trip to Maplehurst, I finish going through the farm's books. I haven't decided if I'll take Logan's money, but I do know that it might be my only choice to save my farm. Late that afternoon, he gets back to the house after another long, mysterious absence. Instead of kissing me or sinking to the couch, he tugs me toward the door.

"Let me show you something?" he asks.

Wordlessly, we pull on coats and scarves and walk hand in hand down the property, up the driveway, and past the equipment shed. In the golden light of late afternoon, the barn's sharp crimson red has deepened to rust, the weathervane still as stone. The door is newly hung, the windows unbroken. But, inside, the dusty floors still hold memories—some that have dulled, some that have tangled, and, on the night of the gala, some that have multiplied.

That's not what's changed.

What's changed is me.

Despite everything those walls hold, I don't feel like running or shoving anything away. Not because any single emotion has dried up, but because now I understand what that pain is in the first place.

It's a tree stump that left a half-moon scar on my elbow.

It's a branch, pruned to the trunk.

My pain has marked me.

And why would I turn away from the proof that I've grown back?

"I've been thinking about something," Logan says, startling me from my reverie. When I turn to him, he draws our joined hands into his chest, kisses the backs of my gloved knuckles. "Maybe the choice isn't between distraction and stewing. Or at least, maybe it shouldn't be. Maybe what we need is both, simultaneously."

"What's both?"

He pauses. Then, without letting go of my hand, he rolls open the door. "Evolution."

Inside, the smell of wood and fresh sawdust folds around me

as my eyes slowly adjust to the low light. It takes a moment before I see it: on the back wall, an ornate design. The style is familiar—the same kind of cutouts that we saw at Lydia's shop. Only here it feels alive, with carvings deep enough that butter-soft light threads through the seams of the barn's wall, scattering lacework shadows across the floor. I step toward the mural, holding my breath as the design sharpens into focus.

Intricate patterns spill across the wood—pears, hearts, rabbits, butterflies—repeating until broken apart with faces. Martin's exuberant grin. Val's unmistakable frown. Mason, lips tilted in that half-sly smirk. A boyish face with wide, trusting eyes that must belong to Andrew.

And then, mine. Smiling, radiant, caught in a shaft of light that seems to move as I stare.

"Evolution?" I ask, transfixed.

He moves to my side, arm brushing against mine. "I wonder if sometimes the only way to get over something is to go through it. To face it. And, also, I'm thinking that maybe Mason was right."

"Just don't tell him," I whisper. "About what, exactly?"

He runs his tongue over his bottom lip before responding. "That I'm always cleaning up other people's messes."

My lips twitch. "You're just noticing that now?"

He grunts a laugh. "It's always felt good to fix things. This barn, for example. My parents didn't build it right the first time, and it felt good to spend those weeks making that right."

"I remember," I say.

"But because it feels so right, I've never really thought to try something else entirely." He steps forward to run his thumb along one of the cutouts, blotting out the shaft of light, then releasing it again. "What would it mean not to fix it the way it should have been, but to do it over again for myself? To try it my way instead of theirs."

Affection surges through my chest. I'm blown away the self-reflection it would take to see this in himself. But even more, I'm witnessing the edge of something I haven't seen since we were teenagers and he sat on those hills with a pencil in his fingers, frowning at the trees.

"You know you're not her," I say softly.

He exhales through his nose, shoulders lowering. "More than that, I don't have to keep being the person who cleans up her mess." His chin dips and his thumb traces a half circle into the palm of his glove. "Although it didn't come out quite how I'd envisioned it. I didn't have all the right tools."

I step closer to grab his hand. "Hey," I say, and wait until he looks up. "You're incredible. And this is *art*, Logan."

He grunts. "This is carpentry." At my raised eyebrows, he adds, "I didn't make this with pencils or paints. This is just careful measurement and accurate cuts. Leveling and angles and material selection."

"That doesn't mean it's not art."

He doesn't look swayed. "What makes it art, then?"

I press his hand to my sternum, right above my heartbeat. Lacework shadows scatter across our faces. The scent of wood and dust mingles with all the emotions stirring in this place: grief, shame, pleasure, longing. None of them are covered by Logan's mural, only complicated by it.

"Because it's something I experience with my heart, not my head."

His next breath catches. Then he reaches for me with his other hand, fingers tangling into my coat pocket and yanking me into his chest. His mouth finds mine and I grip him tighter, fisting the fabric of his shirt and anchoring myself to his body. We stay like that for a long time, each refusing to break.

Because, deep down, I know that this is the last gasp of a desperate, bleating heart.

As much as I want to cling to him, something has breached my walls.

I know what I need to do.

Chapter Twenty-Six

I tell Logan we should talk over dinner. Two hours later, we sit side by side on the porch table benches as the sun sinks low, butter cooling on our fingers, salt still bright on our tongues. The sprinklers have started up their evening regime, sweeping in methodical arcs. They darken the earth and fill the air with their soft, predictable chorus: *pshhh-tick-tick-tick*. The orange sky catches on crystal pears, scattering light in shards of copper and pink. For a moment, it looks like the trees are burning from the inside out.

Instead of looking away, I let the beauty sting.

When we've finished eating, Logan pushes away our empty plates, tips the remaining few drops of wine into both of our glasses, and administers his full attention on me.

"You've made a decision," he guesses.

I nod, running my thumb along the stem of my wineglass. "I can't take your money."

An unsteady wind moves over the grass; branches rustle in faint protest.

Logan, however, doesn't seem surprised. "You figured out a better option," he guesses again, this time incorrectly.

As the books in my office have made clear, the financial situation of the farm is worse than I might have thought. I have very few options, none of them good. I could try refinancing my loans, but my uncle took most of them out years ago. It'd be impossible to get better terms, particularly given how much debt the farm has. I could lease, but that would only make the problem worse, adding another person—an outsider—who would also need a cut of the already slim profit. I could try selling some of the land, but it's already such a small acreage farm, and my fixed costs are so high that downsizing would make it even more impossible to generate enough revenue to support my expenses long term.

After going over all the numbers again and again, it's likely that, without Logan's money, my only option is to sell. The worst option of all.

It means losing the land, my farmhouse.

Losing the place where I belong and began.

"No," I say. "I don't have any better options."

Somewhere in the orchard, a pear drops, muffled in the grass.

Logan frowns. "Then why?"

I swirl the liquid in my wineglass, then drain the rest. I've been going over my answer to this question in advance because I already know that Logan isn't going to like it. I need to say it in a way that will force him to listen. "Because I don't want you to give up your future in exchange for mine."

A sharp line appears between his eyebrows, as I would have expected. "I don't see how that's a problem. You're about to lose your multigenerational farm because of money. I have money from a life that I inherited and never wanted. I can give you a loan, and you'll pay me back when you're able."

"It'll take me years to work myself out from under the farm's debt," I reason. "Even with a string of good seasons. But there's no guarantee I'll have that. Things were bad for my uncle for a long time, and there's no evidence that anything will be better for me. What if I can't start paying you back in a year?"

"I'll give you an extension."

"And if I need more and more of them?"

"Then I'll give those to you, too."

I blow out a long, slow breath. A bat dips through the trees, quick and certain in the fading light. It flicks between fruit—half crystallized, the other half marred. Beautiful, and nearly worthless. A complex entry in the reality that Logan is refusing to acknowledge but I can no longer deny.

"I might never be able to pay you back," I say. "If I default on a loan from a bank, it's one thing. If I lose your money? That's something else entirely. I won't let you take on a risk like that for me."

Logan folds his arms and lets out a heavy sigh that sounds like half a growl. "We're getting off track here. This isn't about me."

I tuck my knee onto the bench, turning so that we're facing each other head-on. "This is *completely* about you. At least it should be. It's your money and your future. But you're trying to sacrifice it for me instead."

Logan drums his fingers against the edge of the table. His face should be unreadable—he holds a poker face so well—but I know the signs. Frustration in the taut line of his mouth. Helplessness in the set of his shoulders. As much as I don't want him to feel those things, I know what I'm doing is right.

"Why won't you let me help you?" he says.

"I did. I have. Over and over. But that's not the point. This isn't about me or what I need. It should be about what you want." Here, I take a long breath, think about his mural. "You should have the life that's right for you—the one you'd choose if you weren't carrying everyone else's weight. You said you wanted to know who you are when you're not cleaning up other people's messes."

An emotion passes over his still face, this one inscrutable. "I did say that."

"And you deserve to find out. But you can't if you're still cleaning up mine."

Logan swipes his nails along his jawline. The orchard has gone still but for the hum of the insects and the creak of the porch swing. There's a weight to it, like the land is holding its breath with me—a silence that feels sentient.

"I can't read that look," I say. "Tell me what you're thinking."

"Can you usually?"

"Sometimes," I hedge. "I would like to say I'm getting better at it."

He smiles softly. "I was thinking that I don't usually do this."

"Do what?"

"Let someone else put me first."

My heart stutters. "You deserve it."

"And yet I don't know if I like it."

"You don't have to like it." I think about the orchard, slipping through my fingers. I think about losing Martin. Blake and Liv. "You just have to accept it."

The last light of evening slides unevenly over the trees, gilding one row, washing the rest in gray. A shifting line, already pulling back.

Then Logan says, "You could come with me."

My fingers tighten involuntarily, even though I've been expecting this. I thought we might get here, once it became clear Logan shouldn't stay. So, I've already mentally played out much of this conversation.

I've pictured it, too. Us. Holding hands by the gearshift as we cruise down the Pacific Coast Highway, arms hanging out the windows until they bronze in the sun. Lying together in the bed of Logan's truck, staring up at a starry sky and mapping constellations that Logan hasn't seen before. Passing through a coastal town and stopping to saunter down a pier before we sit on a bench, eating oysters with our hands.

It would be beautiful. Perfect.

But I can't.

Because Logan deserves the life he wants.

And so do I.

"I don't want to travel," I say. Before Logan can respond, I grip his thigh with both hands, forcing him to witness my sincerity. "I've tried it. I had it for over half my life. And if there was one person in the world who could make me want to try it again, it would be you. You're the only person I've ever met who makes me feel so stable and safe that it almost doesn't matter where I am. Being with you almost feels like being home. But even then, I already know I would be unhappy. I would be giving up something . . . something really important. Even if I don't have much more time here, I can't voluntarily leave."

Logan's lips flicker between a frown and a smile. "I wouldn't ask that from you."

"And I can't ask you to stay in Apple Valley and give up everything you've ever wanted just to be with me and this farm."

He studies me with penetrating eyes, and I know deep in my bones that if I shared even a shred of hesitancy about this, he *would* give up his entire future for us both. Which is why I say, "And I'm not going to ask you that."

He exhales and squeezes my fingers. "I should at least stay until the pears are ripe."

"I don't know when that will be." When I checked the marked pears this morning, they were still the same as yesterday and the day before. The same as the day we left for Maplehurst. "Plus, it's only half the crop. Val and I can handle it."

When Logan doesn't look convinced, I add, "This is all just stolen time. The longer you stay, the harder it's going to be to say goodbye. It's already going to hurt enough, but I think if I get any closer to you, if I come to depend on you more, it's going to be unbearable. It's going to be a pain I may never heal from."

The earth is dark where the sprinklers have finished their run. The puddles hold the fading light for longer than they should, stealing colors they have no right to keep.

Logan closes his eyes, and when they open, I know. His emotion is plain.

Acceptance, at last.

"I was afraid you would say something like that," he says.

"Not because you think I'm wrong?" I ask.

"Because it's the only thing you could say to get me to leave."

Tears sting the back of my nose. I sag against his chest—from both relief and grief—because even though I'll soon need to stand up alone, right now I'm desperate for him to hold me. He catches me around the waist and burrows his nose in my hair.

"I'm losing my orchard," I say. "I'm losing you for a second time, before we've even had a real chance. It's not okay. Maybe it's never going to be okay. All we can do is accept it."

Logan smooths back my hair. "Nothing about this feels right."

"I think, maybe," I whisper, "that's how grief feels."

He kisses the top of my head. A flicker of moisture seeps between my eyelids.

We stare into my ruined orchard and I let myself *feel*.

Everything. All at once.

Chapter Twenty-Seven

When I was a kid, I got really good at goodbyes. Not because they grew less tender with repetition. In some ways, the opposite was true. I learned that a goodbye isn't only about the pain of *now*, the pain of leaving, but also the pain of *later*. The disorientation in the face of an unfamiliar layout of a new school. The ache of loneliness as I waded through a cafeteria filled with strangers. The tug of homesickness at any thought of the orchard.

"Gainesville gets two-hundred-and-twenty-four days of sun each year," Mom once assured me, eyes fixed on the road as we charged past the Seattle city limits. "Much better for your mood."

As though the rain were the reason I had been miserable.

She broke her focus from the road to glance at me, monitoring my reaction.

I nodded stiffly, fighting back tears and keeping my eyes fixed forward like hers. Mom rolled her driving gloves against the steering wheel as she refocused on the road.

As Logan packs the next morning, my body aches to fall back into the familiar, well-worn grooves of muscle memory. But I don't let it. Tears leak down my cheeks as I dig through the cabinet for an old travel mug and a water bottle. My hands tremble as I fill one with coffee and the other with filtered water. A sob moves through me as I slice cheese and pears and pack them into an old takeout container.

"Ali."

I feel Logan's hand on my elbow, steering me around. When I blink, another tear slips down my cheek. Logan's grip tightens, and there's so much concern in his eyes that I have to fight, again, not to dry my face and paint on a smile.

He smooths back one of my curls, tucks it behind my ear, then catches my next tear with his thumb.

"Ali, I—"

"Listen," I say. My voice is thinner than I want it to be, but I need to head him off before he says something I might beg him to take back. "I'm going to cry for this. That doesn't mean you should stay. It doesn't mean you're doing anything wrong. I'm sad, but that's okay. Sadness is just—part of it. It just *is*."

Logan closes his eyes and tugs me into the hard planes of his chest. He holds me like he's trying to memorize the shape we make when our bodies fit together. I cling right back, not because I want him to stay, but because I love him enough to let him go. His jacket is cold against my cheek, but he still smells the same—like wood and earth and home. I take a shaky inhale and let my salty tears wet his collar, marking him one more time.

When we finally pull apart, I register that he's wearing something different: a dark jacket instead of Carhartt tan. A hoodie instead of one of his ubiquitous plaids.

At the tilt of my head, he lifts an arm, motioning downward. "Mason's. He thought I needed a change."

"It suits you," I say.

What I mean is *You do.*

What I mean is *You deserve to be happy.*

"Thank you," he says.

And I let myself hear: *I'm finally starting to believe it, too.*

"Have you decided where you'll stop first?" I ask.

He shoves his hands in his pockets and squints at the window. "Seaside, I think. To see the Pacific Ocean."

He deserves the ocean. He deserves the whole world.

"And then south?"

"Yeah, but I haven't decided where exactly. It's hypothetical on a screen. I think I have to experience it to know how I feel. What do you think?"

I look up at the beautiful man framed by my well-loved kitchen cabinets and force myself to picture him somewhere else. Cruising along the highway that rapunzels down the West Coast, his windows down, the din of wind and crashing waves flooding the cab. Pulling over at a scenic vista to squint at the sunset as he runs charcoal over a pad of paper. Wandering sandy beaches with his shoes off and jeans cuffed at the ankles.

Maybe these images don't make perfect sense to me, but if they make sense to Logan, then that's all that matters.

"I think I want you to be happy. Whatever that means to you." I extend the travel mug so I don't have to hold our eye contact. "Keep this. Use the handle, though."

Our fingers touch as he takes the mug, and my chest seizes. I yank my hand away to keep myself from reaching for him, closing myself in his arms one more time. Instead, I wrap my arms around my waist, digging my fingernails into my sides.

Logan's worried frown deepens. He cups my cheek with a tender, calloused hand and says, "I promised myself I wouldn't hurt you."

"No amount of pain could erase what you've given me."

"What was that?"

"The chance to feel safe enough to cry."

He screws his eyes shut, lips pressed in his own pain.

My eyes won't stop leaking.

"No," I insist, brushing the tears back with fingertips before reaching out to lightly shake his wrist. "That's a good thing."

Logan cradles the back of my head with one hand and leans his forehead against mine. His breath is warm on my cheek, and I press a palm to his sternum. I can feel his heartbeat—hard, steady—in my fingertips. For a moment, I let myself relish the shape of him, the feverish heat that reminds me of a college kid's basement. Mason's bunk bed. My quilts. His cherry-red truck.

"Tell me again," he says slowly, as a groan escapes with the last syllable. "Remind me why I'm leaving."

I don't need to think about this. "Because you deserve it. And because the longer you stay, the more it will hurt."

He nods, eyes dull, mouth firm.

My heart thumps so hard I can feel it in my fingertips.

Then Logan releases himself from my arms, moving toward the door.

I try to breathe around the shards of glass lodged in my lungs. This isn't okay. Maybe it never will be. I'll never fall for another man like I have for Logan. My home will never feel complete without him.

But I also know I'm strong enough to admit and accept that now.

Logan tucks the travel mug into his elbow so he can reach for the handle. I wait for the click of the mechanism, the groan of the hinges.

But as he presses on the lever, I watch it stick. A pause. Logan stares at the handle. His face turns minutely, angled down so I can't see his expression. I can see his lungs moving, though. Steady, long breaths.

"Drive safe, okay?" I say, heart hammering so hard I think I might collapse.

His grip tightens on the door handle.

This time it clicks open.

And then he's gone.

Chest heaving, eyes streaming, I take myself to the trees.

I clutch my jacket to my chest as the pain takes over. The valley's merciless wind claws at the hem of my dress. The light stutters over the leaves, fracturing over the crystal fruit, as my fingers tremble. When I take a shaky inhale, the smell is startling. Sweet with an edge, like the sting of pinesap that won't wash clean.

Blinking, I sink to my knees in the cool grass and Lydia's words stir in my mind—about how subtle the magic can be. How you have to pay attention to notice it.

How these trees made space for her to ask her questions. My uncle was like that—a good listener. When he was listening, even the birds would go quiet.

I think about that woman from Appalachia and the hail that wouldn't stop after her cousin died.

The man whose wife left him, and the marsh that forgot how to breathe.

What if . . .

What if the orchard's magic has never been about the people who left?

What if it's always grown from the hearts of the ones who stayed?

Not the land that remembers. The trees that *feel*.

Perhaps the forget-me-nots didn't bloom because of Lydia, but because my uncle fell in love with her. Then, his years of devastating, never-ending bad luck might have reflected his heartbreak, and also his increasing isolation from the rest of the world. A choice that he made, not something thrust on him.

My mom said the land reacted differently to each of my grandmother's husbands—but that might have had less to do with who they were and everything to do with how she felt about them.

And me.

The pears that started crystallizing after Blake and Liv left.

The tree that bloomed when I was bursting with happiness.

The hail on the day I finally released my bottled-up anger.

And the pears that have refused to ripen? Maybe they exist because I, too, have stalled since the gala. Frozen with Logan. Stealing time.

It is as Logan and I said—not forcing anyone to choose anything, but a reflection. It's a mirror held to that which is most deeply, intrinsically important.

My feelings.

The truest expressions of them all.

And with this realization, I lift on my feet and walk through the orchard. I feel. And I see it.

My chest lifts and falls with the rise and fall of buzzing bees. An ache curls in my chest like a lone leaf folding against the autumn wind. And when I tip my face toward the sun, the trees exhale.

Chapter Twenty-Eight

If the orchard is reflecting my emotions, then what, exactly, are the crystal pears? Although they started turning after Blake and Liv left, I'm not convinced they are only about grief or heartbreak. After all, that deep, hollow ache from the days and weeks following their departure has subsided. And, after the gala, my feelings toward them evolved.

As the sun starts to set, the air thickens, prickling my skin, and I sling myself upright. Pressure builds at my temples and in the pads of my fingers as the wind carries me into the rows. I think about my cluttered mental attic. The first day he was on the orchard, Logan observed that, at some point in the last fourteen years, I started smiling over the pain. At the time, I told him it helped.

That wasn't true, of course. But what if it's worse than that? What if I wasn't protecting my heart from the acute pain of grief, but *sharpening* it? What if, by denying my emotions, I only honed their edges?

A crow calls out, falls silent.

I tug off my gloves with my teeth and run bare fingertips along the smooth, cold surface of a pear. If I'm right, then these crystals aren't grief itself, but the denial of that emotion. A protective instinct gone terribly wrong. But now that I've stopped turning away from my feelings, shouldn't the crystals have cracked?

Goose bumps pebble my arms as I hear Logan again in my memory—his voice steady, his hand warm around mine.

Sometimes the only way to get over something is to go through it. To face it.

Evolution.

The word buzzes through me, as I yank that pear loose, trying to peer through its crystal exterior, wondering about the fruit inside. Maybe if the pears crystallized because I turned away from my emotions, then the only way to undo it is to face them fully. In some ways, I already have. I've gone through those ledgers. I talked to Blake and Liv at the gala. I unearthed my family's secrets, learned my uncle's uncomfortable truths.

But have I truly faced what hurts most? I've accepted things, yes, but passively—like standing limply in the rain.

Maybe it's time to steer into the storm.

The next day, I visit my uncle's grave.

He's buried, like the Reids before him, on the southern side of the property, just below a gnarled old fruit tree with unusual surface roots. As family legend has it, it's the oldest on the property and the first one planted by my great-great-grandfather, although that would make it preternaturally ancient. Still, in the eerie silence of its canopy—accompanied only by the skitter of windfallen leaves across a handful of stone plaques—I have no trouble believing the legend is true.

A tight handful of forget-me-nots trembles in one of my fists, a folded note in the other. The air is cold enough that my exhales fog my vision. The ancient fruit tree creaks as it sways, like the low keen of a dirge singer. At my feet, Martin's marker is simple: his name and dates of his birth and death divided by a dash.

Underneath, the words Val selected for him:

Loved. Always.

My hands tremble as I unfold the paper I'm clenching. I planned to tell him that I'm angry, betrayed. He should have warned me about the orchard and the magic. He should have trusted me to make the right choice while knowing the truth. I resent the role he played in Lydia's disappearance. His betrayal cuts deeper because I loved him and I'll never get to hear his side of it.

But now all I can think about is his wheezy laugh echoing down the rows.

Cruising around the orchard in a Gator, banking hard around curves, our twin screams of joy as I tossed up my hands like I was riding a roller coaster. Watching the trees from the porch swing while he wailed on his reedy harmonica.

His floppy hat bobbling as he gesticulated. Honeydew- and zucchini-blossom greens and yellows. The way he used to listen so intently that even the wind would hold its breath.

The way he always let me cry.

I drop to my knees. The grass is cold and damp, even through my fleece leggings, and my knit dress gathers in a caramel pool. I trace the carved letters of Martin's name, lingering on the year of his death.

"I loved you," I whisper. "I still do. You might not have been perfect, but you were a remarkable, wonderful man."

Then, I set the pale blue flowers against the plaque. And I stand, brush the dirt from my knees, and turn.

On Saturday, I pick my way through jars of apple butter, clusters of pumpkins in cream and orange, and past the Harts' cider wagon. Liv is beaming behind the flower stand's register, framed by neat rows of fresh-cut sunflowers and planters filled with marigolds in mahogany and tangerine. She's all easy smiles and effortless charm, her hair catching the light like honey.

My feet pause when I spot Blake. He's weaving between tents, a breakfast sandwich gripped in each hand and a bottle of hot sauce trapped under an armpit. When he reaches her, he holds her sandwich back until she kisses him.

I wait for the nausea—the quick familiar pulse of panic, the sharp edge of sadness. Any second now, it'll rise.

Oddly, though, it doesn't.

I feel . . . not happy for them, certainly. But, separate, I guess. Like I'm standing behind glass, watching them move through a world that no longer needs to include me.

Deep down, I know this is enough. Not that it'll fix my problems, but that there isn't more I need to do.

I'm about to turn away when I see Blake look up, his gaze meeting mine across the rows of golden flowers. Liv dusts off her hands and turns to help a customer.

For a heartbeat, we stand like that—neither hostile nor tender.

I nod once.

He nods back.

And then I walk away.

I leave the hardest conversation for last.

Attempting to ease us into it, I call Mom on Sunday five minutes before one o'clock. I know she'll be free, expecting me, and maybe even softened by predictability. Maybe that'll help me get through this without breaking down.

And then I remember that's not the point.

With a stiff quilt shawled around my shoulders, I sip at a half-finished cup of tea to stave off the October chill and dial her number. Although it's her preference, I don't use a video call. This conversation will already be difficult. The thought of her composed, expressionless face is too much.

"Ali?" she answers after a few rings. "This is a surprise."

So much for easing us in. "Hey, Mom."

The words land flat. "I hope nothing is wrong."

I take a bite of cookie from the tin on my lap and try to consider my response.

Is something wrong?

Emphatically yes.

But also. A curl of steam rises from my mug, smelling of cardamom. The hillside is brightening under midday sun, warming the grass and burning the trees in rust and copper. Even though I might not have much more time in this beautiful, perfect place, right now the answer is also no.

"I wanted to talk to you about something," I say instead of answering.

A brief pause. Then Mom says, "Go ahead."

"I haven't been fully honest with you about how I feel about some things," I say, my practiced beginning. As with my uncle, I have a speech prepared. This time, I need it. "But hiding all that has been making everything worse. So, I want to tell you the truth."

"I see," Mom says neutrally.

Every instinct in me screams to stop.

I'm six, walking through the door with a skinned knee and there's confusion in her eyes. I'm sixteen, on the phone begging her not to move us to Alaska, and I hear only a click on the other end. Eighteen, clutching a diploma in a borrowed city while she blinked, unsure why I'd be crying on a special day.

And then, through the static, I'm with Logan. Sitting in his truck, his eyes on mine. *I believe you could, too. If you decided to.*

I stand. Shuck off the blanket. Abandon my notes and move

down the porch steps. Grass presses cold against my bare toes, still slick from the sprinklers. Wind coils low through the tree trunks, rattling leaves in uneven gusts.

And I ride the wave.

"I'm so *angry* with you," I say.

Before she can respond or I can talk myself out of continuing, I press on. "I spent my entire childhood uprooted. Dragged from city to city, stranger to stranger. I stopped making friends because I always knew they were temporary. I never went to prom. Never had a homecoming. I graduated surrounded by people who didn't know my name. And when I cried, you looked at me like you couldn't understand why. I was engaged for more than a year and when it ended, when I told you what happened, all you could ask was when I was going to *leave.* You could never see how important this place was to me, because you can't see the things that make me *me.*"

Another gust of wind ripples through the trees, scattering brittle leaves across the strips of bare earth at their bases.

"That's what hurts most," I continue. "Not that we moved around or that you wouldn't tell me why, but that whenever I tried to tell you how I felt, you shut down. You rejected the parts of me that are most deeply me."

The wind picks up, hard enough to make the pears sway. A droplet of rain finds the earth, darkening the spot to black.

"That's why I started to bottle everything up. I covered my tears with a smile. I told myself that choosing happiness was a kind of strength. And all it did was rot me from the inside out."

I can feel the pressure of tears behind my eyes and bubbling up my throat, and I let the sob escape.

"And now look at me," I say, gesturing toward the darkened skies, heavy with rain clouds. The pale, incandescent crystal fruit, dull under a slate sky. The wind shifts colder, slicing across my cheeks. "My crop is ruined in more ways than one. I'm going to lose this farm and the one place I've ever called home. This is what comes from pretending. This is what comes from trying to be fine when I'm not.

"And maybe it's too late for me to save anything but myself, but if that's the case then so be it. What's important is that I don't want to live like that anymore. I don't want to be afraid of how I feel. Or of how you'll look at me if I show it."

Silence fills the line. The trees creak. My heart thunders in my ears.

"I'm—" Mom starts. She doesn't usually stumble over her words. "I'm sorry."

For the briefest of moments, hope buoys my heart. I've gotten through to her. I've broken through the vacuum seal that she keeps around her heart.

And then she says, "I'm sorry, Ali. I can't do this."

My heart free falls. My knees fold. "You . . ."

"I'm not good at this," she says, voice hard and cold. "I never have been."

"I don't need you to be good at it," I try, fingers on my forehead, desperation crawling into my voice. "I just need you to try. You just need to talk. You just have to be here with me."

"I'm sorry I'm not the person you need me to be."

The silence that follows is absolute.

She hangs up.

Cold droplets of rain patter across leaves, prickling against my face and hands. My chest trembles, then heaves, and a stream of my tears joins the elements, running along my jaw and into my mouth until I taste salt and rainwater.

Briefly, I worry the rain will turn to hail again, like the night of the gala. But as I let my chest heave, let the tears mingle with the elements, the droplets only drum on the canopy, a steady, inevitable roar.

Chapter Twenty-Nine

In the morning, the pears are still crystal.

And I'm out of options.

I find the number for a real estate agent who specializes in agriculture. She's an efficient woman with a steady manner and, after a fifteen-minute phone call, we agree to meet at a coffee shop in town the day after tomorrow.

Then, I enjoy the time I have left. I wander through the rows in a statement-print dress and fleece leggings. When I get hungry, I eat a sandwich on the porch and consider my beautiful ruin. I climb into the attic and flip through old ribbons from a county fair in which my great-grandfather was awarded a prize for *Most Unusual Fruit*. At the bottom of the box, I find a sepia-toned photograph of a man who looks vaguely like Uncle Martin holding up a pear shaped like a heart. I clasp the photo to my chest and try to imagine what he could have been feeling.

That evening, I fall asleep wrapped in a blanket, curled on the porch, trying to soak in the beauty of the place I live.

For now.

I wake to my name.

Knocking at the door.

I rub the sleep from my eyes, unravel myself from the pretzel that I slept in, and drag my stiff body through the house. I'm massaging the back of my neck and longingly thinking about anti-inflammatories when another rapping knock, smart and firm, hastens my steps.

"Be right there!" I call as I yank open the—

Mom.

Her hair, usually smoothed into a precise middle part, is creased on one side, and flying out of the hair clip on the other. Her blouse is rumpled, like maybe she slept in it. Her eyes are wide and bloodshot. There's a sedan I don't recognize in the driveway behind her, shiny enough that it must be rental.

"Mom," I say, too stunned to say anything else.

"Ali." She smooths down the front of her shirt. Presses shaking fingertips to sweep back the wisps of hair near her temples. "I believe your doorbell is broken."

My mouth is open. I snap it closed. "It hasn't worked in years. What are you doing here?"

She swallows again. "I would like to come inside. If that is all right."

I widen the door.

Mom steps through the entrance and into the kitchen, landing uncertainly on the linoleum. She smooths down the front of her shirt again. Her gaze darts around the room, touching briefly on the portraits, the old fridge rattling in the corner, the gingham wallpaper. I think this might be the first time she's stepped foot in this house since she was in her twenties.

I still have no idea why she's here.

"Are you thirsty?" I ask uncertainly. "Can I get you a water or something?"

Mom swallows. "Tea, if you have it."

I nod and pull down the tea bags from the cabinet while she

lowers herself to a countertop stool, back ramrod straight. We wait for the kettle to boil, the room silent and unsteady until the steam screeches. I fill a ceramic mug—the one with a pickle for a handle and *Kind of a Big Dill* printed on the side. It couldn't look more out of place in her manicured hands. Still, she takes a grateful swallow, then lowers the mug uncertainly, not letting it touch the counter.

I'd never once seen my uncle use a coaster and the kitchen countertops have the panoply of stains to prove it.

"You can just, uh, set it down," I tell her.

She eyes the counter and, as though exerting great effort, releases the ceramic onto the Formica.

I lean against the sink, again wondering why she's here. But Mom's uncertainly fingering the tea's paper tag, and even though I remain more confused about her presence than happy with it, I don't want her to bolt.

"Do you . . ." I start, just as Mom clears her throat and says, "So, I—"

She snaps her lips closed as I trail off.

"Go ahead," I say.

Her eyes go slightly wide, like I've just caught her off guard by asking her to continue the sentence she started. She clears her throat again. Is this the first time I've ever seen Mom at a loss for words and experiencing what seems to be unmistakably *discomfort*? Or am I now recognizing something I haven't before?

"You mentioned a problem with the fruit?" she asks.

I blink. "Yeah. It's, um, hard to explain. I can show you instead?"

She draws another steeling sip of tea before pushing to her feet. "Please."

Chapter Thirty

Mom toes off her loafers and cuffs her linen pants at her calves. I hand her my smallest pair of boots, which fit adequately when paired with a double layer of wool socks. A few minutes later, we trudge into the trees, and her back stiffens. Refracted light in yellow, sapphire, and rose scatters across the front of her white blouse, where her jacket parts. Her eyes flicker wider, and I encourage her onward with a small nod.

With me trailing a few paces behind, Mom picks her way through the rows, occasionally turning tight circles to peer higher in the branches. Starlings flit from tree to tree, disturbing the crystal pears. They spin and shake like Christmas tree ornaments in a drafty room, clinking together and filling the air with their discordant song.

When we crest the first hill, Mom pauses to tug off one of her gloves and lift a pear with her fingertips, as though testing its weight.

"I guess you never saw anything like this when you were a kid?" I ask.

She holds the pear for a moment longer, then retracts her hand and replaces her glove. "No. The orchard's affliction was never this obvious before." Abruptly, she wheels on me. "Why has it happened?"

My neck prickles under the sharp question and her harsh scrutiny, especially because the answer is so tender.

I swallow and fold my arms, burrowing deeper in my down jacket. "It's complicated."

Mom regards me, lips pursed, as she picks a lint ball off her jacket.

"Is it—" She coughs into her glove. I have the distinct impression she's processing something or trying to find the right words for something difficult. Finally, she says, "They remind me of something my mother used to collect."

"Oh." Given all that buildup, I was expecting her to say something more significant. Then again, it's Mom, so the fact that she's voluntarily bringing up her own mother is notable. "You mean like figurines?"

She still looks like she's working herself up to something. "I believe they were paperweights, although she never had them holding down paper. They sat on almost every windowsill and end table in the house. Some clear, some colorful. There was one—a pear. It was smoother than these, more like glass than a crystal. It was her favorite."

I'm not sure why we're talking about this. "I haven't seen them in the attic."

"Martin told me she smashed them all. After I left."

I take a surprised breath. "That's a bit extreme."

She crosses her arms and smooths her fingers against her jacket sleeve. "He took her side, actually."

I try not to let my surprise show. Not, I suppose, because Uncle Martin's position in this argument surprises me. Rather because I can finally see the edge of where this is going and I don't want her to recoil from it.

I'm rewarded for my patience because she adds, "He told me . . . he said that Mom losing me was worse than all four of her husbands combined. He told me that things started happening—terrible things. It went on for years. He said it was my fau—"

She inhales sharply through her nostrils, eyes closed.

"He said it was your fault?" I encourage.

To my surprise, she nods and continues. "I knew the land molded itself to the presence of the people who lived on it, but I didn't think *my* presence or absence could have been that influential. I was certain he was exaggerating. I believed he was only attempting to make me feel guilty so I would move back. I shut him out."

I lean against a tree trunk and pick at a sheet of loose bark. It's easy to empathize with my uncle's side of this story. I can imagine him by my grandmother's side, watching everything spinning out of control—elements and diseases wreaking havoc on his precious trees. I can imagine his anguish, feeling he knew *why* but also powerless to fix it. "I think it was really hard for him when you left."

Her lips bracket with a frown. "I suppose."

An uneasy current of wind rides over our hillside, sending leaves shivering and crystals jangling. This very well could be the end of the conversation. Mom will zip up her jacket, and we'll trudge back to the house in stilted silence and endure an awkward conversation over a cup of tea before she gets back into her rental car. We'll go back to our calls on Sundays that I'll often neglect to answer.

But even though I don't fully understand the gesture yet, Mom showing up here with a wrinkled blouse and mussed hair was clearly an olive branch. Also, even though this place is the right one for me, I've come to understand why someone would want to leave it.

So, I extend a branch of my own. "You were happier, though. When you moved away."

She blinks, and the rigid set of her shoulders softens slightly. "It was the happiest I'd ever been in my life. Even though I'd left so much behind. More than—" She cuts herself off. "Just. A lot."

"Did you ever think about coming back?"

"Mother and Martin and . . . and everyone else, they were all so angry with me. It only made it harder. Even after Mom died. Even after Martin got sick."

I think about Lydia, her millions of choices. "Did you try to talk to him, though? Before the end?"

She closes her eyes for a moment before nodding. "I called when you told me about his diagnosis. And again after you said—when you were sure the end was coming. Last winter. But, both times, Martin told me it was too late. And I—I didn't push. Perhaps I should have come anyway, to try to get him to talk to me. Perhaps if I'd come back, I could have—" She takes a sharp inhale, almost like a gasp for breath. Like she's never spoken this much in one swoop before. "I couldn't do it. It had been too many years."

It's painful to imagine what that conversation might have been like for them. Then again, I'm not sure a reconciliation at the end of his life would have been possible or fair for Martin. It would have taken time and energy that he might not have wanted to spend, not when there were so few days left. "He was dealing with a lot at end. I think he felt abandoned by the people who cared about him. I think him pulling away wasn't only about you."

She frowns. "I see. But that's not why I'm telling you this."

"Oh. Why, then?"

Despite the cool October air, the tips of Mom's ears have gone pink. She takes a deep, even breath and, although I can see how much it costs her, she holds my eye contact. "I know I've never—I've never been able to say the right thing to you. Especially when you're upset. I've never been the person you need me to be."

I'm tempted to say it's okay, but it's not. It never has been. "I know."

"I very much doubt I ever will be that person."

I swallow, and the air feels thin. "I know that, too."

She flexes two gloved fists, in and out again, like she doesn't quite know what to do with her hands. Then, she closes the distance between us with two staccato steps. Her fingers find my forearm. My throat releases a startled *oh*.

"But I want to *try* to be that person," she says. "And I can be here with you. If my presence can help, if I can fix anything by staying on the farm, I will do it. As long as it takes."

My breath stills. Distantly, I hear a faint popping sound, but I don't turn to investigate because Mom's fingers still cling to my arm.

"I—" I start. "Thank you."

She nods and releases me. "You're welcome."

I shove a curl off my forehead. "The thing is, though, that's not the problem. The problem isn't about who is here or who isn't."

"No?"

The conversation has hit another crossroads, but this time I take a breath and plow forward. "It's mirroring the emotions of the person who owns it."

Mom's back remains ramrod straight, but her eyes tighten around the edges. Her gaze runs between me and the trees without ever quite touching my eyes.

"Like, you said there were field mice all over the place when my grandmother was married to Martin's father," I explain. "And the soil turned up gemstones when she was married to yours. I don't think that was about those men. I think it was about how she felt about them. And then"—I remember what Val told me about my grandmother's personality and what I vaguely remember myself. Her high highs and low lows—"there was what you said about how the land was mercurial when you were a kid. The sudden changes in weather and the erratic birds. That was about her, too. Her feelings changing quickly."

Mom draws in a breath but still doesn't respond.

"Does that make sense?" I ask, because even though my theory fits, it's still new, and I haven't found a way to confirm it.

Above our heads, a crow lands noisily on a branch and shrieks out its disdain. Mom flinches.

"Mom?"

She composes herself, straightening her jacket, smoothing back her hair. Finally, she says, "My mother's feelings ruled our lives."

"Because she would get upset a lot?"

"When we were younger, we accepted them. Perhaps we didn't know any better. Later, Martin started trying to talk her through her . . . rages, as we called them. But it all became more and more difficult for me. I suppose I . . ."

She shakes her head and instead of continuing, tips her chin to study the branchful of pears—marked by hail, but not yet ripe. In a practiced motion, her hand shoots out and snaps one free. It's so scarred I doubt I could sell it, even at a discount.

Her thumb runs over a blackened puncture mark. "Hail?"

"Yeah. A few weeks ago. I was . . ." It's complicated, so I opt for simple. "Angry."

She squeezes the fruit. "And yet far too firm."

"They stopped ripening a couple of days after." I pause, but if I'm strong enough to admit my emotions to myself, I can admit them to my mother, as well. "Maybe hopelessness. Or fear of the unknown."

"And the crystals?"

"That happened after Blake and Liv left but—" I rub at one of my temples. This is complicated, too. "They might have been the catalyst, but I think that happened because I've been holding it all in. Refusing to face how I feel. Like I said when I called . . . I've been doing that for a long while now."

Mom's hand slackens. The fruit slips from her fingertips. Rolls across the ground. Falls still between us.

She draws in a long breath. "I'm sorry."

"For what?" I say, even though I think I know. I want to hear her say it.

"For whatever I did that made you—that hurt you like this."

A sharp breeze ruffles my curls, sending a prickle up the base of my neck. Even though I know my eyes are red, I hold her eye contact. Pears draw together and apart, a rolling tinkling through the branches. It's punctuated by another far-off snapping sound, like a distant firework or the crunch of glass underneath a booted foot.

"You once tried to tell me," I say, throat tight, "that those moves were for me."

"Yes."

"But you never really told me why."

She hesitates. "Nothing seemed good enough for us. There would be a teacher you didn't like. Or the neighbors would drive too fast. Or the school district wasn't quite the quality I'd expected. Often, I'd tell myself that you'd be happy if only there were more sun or better parks. Or that I was giving you opportunities I never had—a life that I'd always wanted as a kid.

"The truth is I think I was—I was trying to find my way back to the only time in my life I had been completely . . ." She trails off.

"Happy?" I guess.

She thins her lips. "Free. Although, at the time, it felt like the same thing. We had plans, your father and I. We were going to see the world together. Experience everything that I didn't have as a child. And when he was gone, it was like—" She blinks and runs her thumb over the plain wedding band that still sits on her finger. "The longer I stayed somewhere, the quicker all that pain came back. Not just losing him, but all of it. My mother's rages. That feeling of being trapped in a place I hated."

"Mom," I whisper as I step toward her.

She pulls me into a firm hug. Her arms hold tight, her temple against mine.

"I know you said my presence wouldn't help, but I'll stay, Ali. If you need me, I'll stay as long as you want."

Still letting her hold me, I wipe my cheek with the back of my hand.

"Okay," I say.

The next morning Mom has swapped out her linens and merino wools for a crisp cotton blend. She puts the coffee maker on without asking how to work the finicky buttons and levels the scoop with a precision that reminds me of Logan, standing barefoot in my kitchen, hands dwarfing a coffee mug. That thought is tender, but it's a clean kind of ache. Earned from a life worth living. Like sore shoulders after a hard day of pruning.

With the *Kind of a Big Dill* mug back in hand, Mom braces the other against the kitchen counter and squints at the unruly grass beyond the window.

"Where do you keep the mower these days?" she asks.

"In the equipment shed," I say. "But I need to go to a meeting in town, so I can help you with it when I get back."

She hands me a mug of coffee. "A meeting?"

"With a Realtor."

"To sell the farm," she clarifies.

I nod.

She sets down her mug and watches me for another beat before saying, "Cancel it."

"Sorry?"

"I don't think it's time to accept defeat yet."

Later that day, we ride the mower together with the blade set low. Occasionally, Mom jumps off the seat to make precise edges with a string trimmer or to test the firmness on the marked pears, looking for clues about their quality.

When we finish, she wipes her brow with a grass-stained sleeve, peers out into the trees, and says, "I want to take another pass on the Sheppard block tomorrow."

Over her shoulder, I hear another faint popping sound.

The next day, Val bursts through the door unannounced. She comes to a sudden, skidding stop when she catches sight of Mom, standing over the sink with rubber gloves up to her elbows.

They stare at each other. Mom unblinking. Val running her tongue over her teeth.

"You're back," Val says flatly.

I clear my throat. "Sorry, I was going to mention that."

But Val doesn't break her stare. Oddly, the prolonged eye contact doesn't make Mom flinch away.

"I'm here for Ali," she says, lifting her chin, her voice just below breathless.

"Yeah? For how long?"

Mom draws in a breath. "As long as she needs me."

"Fine, then," Val says, although it sounds like its not.

That night, when we're alone again, Mom washes her hands like a surgeon before she makes a caprese salad with mozzarella and slices of tomatoes from the vegetable bed that Liv planted and I forgot I had. The plant's leaves are yellow and curled and there are only a few tomatoes clinging to its stems, but Mom still harvests them and trims back the diseased leaves. When we finish eating, I tentatively ask her about Val.

She doesn't answer for a long time.

Then she says, "Val is the first person I ever loved. But she wanted to stay in Apple Valley forever and all I wanted was to leave. So, I chose your father instead. I left here with him and I—I didn't even say goodbye. I'm not sure she'll ever forgive me for it."

I consider that before I say, "Maybe she will. She just needs time."

Mom nods.

"And," I venture, "possibly an apology."

She swallows. "Yes," she says. "I suppose she does."

Later, when I clear our plates, I find a new potted plant on the kitchen windowsill. It's a healthy cutting from the tomato plant, rooted in new soil, with a label in Mom's simple block letters:

FOR NEXT YEAR

I stare at the words for far too long.

Over the next few days, Mom walks the irrigation lines to check for leaks and flush the filters and sediment traps. She asks to look over the books and finds three mistakes, which she corrects in precise script. The morning I wake to the first glimmer of frost clinging to fallen leaves, she visits Martin's grave. I don't join her, but she returns in the afternoon, her cheeks and ears tipped with pink. I'm leaning over the counter, waiting for the kettle to boil, and she squeezes my shoulder without a word.

That evening, Mom and I sit by the fireplace, legs tucked under my grandmother's quilts, and I venture to tell her about Logan. About falling in love with him, his past dredged up on the land, his art. How I now understand why he needed to leave. Not because of a curse, but so he could live the limitless life he deserves. She remains still, but for this moment, when my words land heavier than I intended.

She blinks hard and wipes her ring finger against the corner of her eye. Then she asks, "Show me his art?"

Even though it's late, we pull on boots and plod toward the barn, surrounded by crystal pears that reflect the moonlight and bathe the ground in a pale glow. When I roll open the doors, Mom inhales sharply.

Logan's mural is even more beautiful in the moonlight. Pinpricks of light scatter across the surface like stars, drawing shadows from its divots.

Mom's hands go tight as she steps toward the portraits. Her lips tug into a soft smile at Val's frown before she angles toward my face. My portrait's expression, so bright in the daytime, has taken on a different cast in the muted twilight. Serene, but thoughtful. Complicated.

Mom traces a gloved finger along the wooden cheekbone. "I've never seen anything like this before," she whispers. "It's beautiful."

There's this *tug* in my chest, like a wave of homesickness even though I'm already home. I might be happy for him, but that doesn't stop me from missing him.

I can feel the pressure of tears building behind my eyes. "I know."

Mom turns. I ignore the urge to hide my red-rimmed eyes. A tear trips down my cheek. Her fist tightens by her side. Then she strides toward me. She cups my cheek, catching my tear with her gloved thumb.

"*You're* so beautiful."

My heart nearly shears in half.

Outside, I hear a pop. Then another. The sound is loud and close, like a cork firing off a champagne bottle.

We glance at each other before hurrying out of the barn.

The air is still until a third pop draws our attention to a tree with a cockeyed branch. As we step toward it, a pear crystal bobs, as if springing loose from an invisible hand. A rough sound scrapes from it as a jagged line moves through its center. Then, with another loud *pop*, glass-like shards split apart. The pieces, like the fragments of a splintered lightbulb, catch the moonlight as they rain down and dissolve in a shimmering puddle.

Mom's arm edges out, angling me behind her as she strides toward the pear, newly emerged like a butterfly from a chrysalis, bobbing gently on its branch.

I reach around her to snap it loose.

Under my fingers, the fruit is full and firm with just the right amount of give. It's like the other uncrystallized ones: fern green, just on the edge of ripe. But with no markings from the hail. Ensconced, but protected.

Mom takes the pear from me and inspects it carefully, turning it over in her gloved hands. Then she presses her lips into something that almost looks like a smile. "We're going to need to start picking soon."

"We?"

She pats my shoulder. "I'm quite good on a tree ladder, you know."

And I hear more pears burst clean.

It takes another week for the crystals to shed and the pears to fully ripen. By the time we're ready to pick, the leaves have turned scarlet and the days are rapidly shortening. On our tree ladders, Val is in a quilted vest, Mom has donned a utility jacket, and I'm in overalls, having conceded to nature for the season.

"Still the weirdest shit I've ever seen," Val says as she dismounts her ladder to lumber over to the bin, kicking at a huge pile of fallen leaves for emphasis. "Picking pears at the end of October. Unnatural."

Mom is already standing over the white bin, carefully releasing her own bag in a way that somehow avoids bruising even a single piece. With uncharacteristic patience, Val waits before taking her place. I catch them glance at each other before abruptly turning apart.

It reminds me of the look they exchanged the first day of harvest, when Mom showed up to work without her wedding ring.

"I don't want to damage the fruit," she said primly.

But as I turned away, I saw her raise her eyes to Val.

"More unnatural than crystal pears and technicolored bunny rabbits?" I ask now, bracing my shoulder against a central bough as I reach high into a branch.

"Absolutely." Val cups her fingers and blows into her callused hands. "None of them ever gave me frostbite."

Mom's lips tick like she's considering smiling and as I pluck another perfect pear, my chest aches with pleasure that feels so familiar and yet so incomplete. That same nostalgic tug is in the whispery scrape of branches moving in a light wind, weaker without the full canopy. It's in the drone of an occasional insect, buzzing thinner in the cooler air, a holdover as fall turns toward winter. It's in the steady, familiar rumble of tires against gravel that carries through the leaves.

It's everything I've ever wanted, only missing the one person who would make it feel whole.

Val, scaling her ladder again, tugs at her beanie and glares down at me, the look she always gets when the trees or weather do something unexpected. "Cut that out."

I snap a pear loose. "Can't help it."

Mom eyes Val, who's still gripping at her rungs.

"Take a breath or something," Val insists.

"I'm really not doing anything this time," I protest because the wave of longing has passed and I don't hear the trees groaning anymore.

Mom sucks in a breath. And I follow her gaze to the trees.

Then I drop the pear clutched in my fingertips.

And my brain catches up with what my hands already knew. That familiar rumble of tires on gravel? It's the sound of a red truck, streaking through tree trunks.

"Ali?" Mom asks.

But I've already dumped my picking bag. I'm already running toward the driveway.

Chapter Thirty-One

Dust rises behind the wheels of a familiar cherry-red truck rounding a corner. The entire orchard thrums—leaves quivering, the ground faintly vibrating.

The cab comes into full view as I screech to a halt.

The wheels stop. Then the engine.

Logan swings out of the cab, stepping onto concrete.

Everything goes still with me. The branches. The bird songs.

Despite the cool air, he's got his shirt rolled up to the elbows. His left forearm is slightly tanner than his right. He's shaved at some point because his face is smooth. I think maybe he's even more beautiful like this: the strong line of his jaw more prominent. The curve of his cheekbones even higher. His eyes are the same, though.

And when they grab me across the pavement, his expression lifts like a question, unasked.

I mean to say something simple, like *Hello,* or meaningful, like *You're back.* But instead I blurt out, "You shaved."

Logan's smile hitches and he rubs a wide palm against his chin like he's still getting used to an unfamiliar sensation. "Mason held me down and attacked my face with a razor. The beard or the jugular, he said."

I let my smile spread as my heart beats—one, two—heavy with anticipation. The wind picks up, tossing my curls into my peripheral vision. "It looks good."

Logan steps toward me, eyes traveling down my dirt-stained overalls. "You're picking."

I consider telling him about my mom's return, the bursting crystals. But there's something far more pressing to attend to first. As though in agreement, a lick of wind nudges me forward. I take a few steps until I'm nearly an arm's distance away from Logan.

"You're here," I say, the words more breathless than I'd expected. Another question without a question mark, this time mine.

Logan's hands flex by his sides. "You kept telling me I should have what I want, that I deserve it."

I nod, nose stinging, unsure if this is relief. "I did. You do."

He closes the distance between us, cups my cheek. My breath hitches as he lifts my face toward his eyes, as warm as a backwater pool. "It took a week on the road to realize that what I want is right here."

My eyes flutter closed. Suddenly I'm too full of everything—hope, relief, *Logan*—and looking at him is too much. "Really?"

I feel his forehead touch mine. "I've always known what it feels like to stay too long in the wrong place. I never knew how it felt to walk away from the right one."

"Aren't those the same places?" I whisper.

His head shakes against mine. "Not at all. Everything changes when you're here."

And, oh.

A breeze shudders over the orchard as my heart surges so fiercely it feels like it might wrench free of my chest. I feel like I'm floating, weightless, riding the gusts of wind.

I open my eyes to the fizzes of gold in Logan's irises, the curl of his eyelashes brushing his skin. And even though everything is full and close, it's the right amount of both.

"So, if you figured that out in a week, what did you do for the other three?" I ask, breathless.

He loops a finger through one of my curls. "I forced myself to be sure. I was worried that I felt that way because I missed you or because I was still rebelling against the idea of leaving. I didn't want to come back until I could look you in the eyes and tell you I'm sure."

"And are you?" I ask. "Sure?"

"Endless travel always seemed like a good answer to the riddle of what to do with my life because it was so different. But I know now it's not right for me. I might not want to build barns, but I don't want to be a world traveler, either."

I reach for him, rooting my fingers to his. "What do you want instead?"

Logan tugs on my hand. He pulls me forward, leading the way through silvery trunks. Together, we forge across the grass, crunchy with the cold, until the barn crests into view.

The doors are open—we've been in and out all morning—so I can already see the constellation of my own face, framed by butterflies and pears.

"I stopped in Maplehurst on my way back," he says as we come to a stop, "and found that designer in town. He's about to retire and willing to take me on as an apprentice. I can study under him for a while, and then hopefully start my own shop."

I go still. "It's perfect."

His lips quirk, something between a smile and a frown. "You think? I've been worried it's a bit . . ."

I tilt my head, concerned he's going to say juvenile.

"It's carpentry in Maplehurst," he finishes.

I grab his hand and force him to look me in the eyes. "It's art, Logan."

He flashes the smile he reserves only for me: open and vulnerable and exquisitely him.

"Art in Maplehurst," I whisper, not only proud of him, but hopeful for myself.

"Maplehurst," he confirms.

"It doesn't bother you knowing Lydia will be so close? I imagine it's a small community. You'll run into her, surely."

"Maybe if I'd seen her without warning. But I think the fact that I went to her first makes it easier. If I see her again, it'll be on my terms."

"That makes sense," I say, thinking of the farmer's market. I've caught glimpses of Blake and Liv in town a couple of times since and, even though we haven't talked, I haven't flinched, either. They're here, and it's not what I'd choose, but also, it's okay.

Logan pulls back slightly, surveying the nearby trees, the branches already losing their scarlet leaves and dotted with unblemished pears. Mom, Val, and I have gotten down most of the fruit, but it's slow going, especially with the shorter days.

"I won't start the apprenticeship for a few months," Logan says, "and I still owe you some time on a tree ladder."

"Hey," I say, grinning. "You want to help me pick pears in exchange for a room in my house?"

"I was thinking . . ." Logan brushes his nose against mine. "Maybe this time, we share."

I close my eyes. "I'm a little messy, you know."

"I wouldn't have it any other way."

My heart wobbles as the world splinters, light and shadows shifting. A butterfly lands on Logan's shoulder, wings the color of spilled sunlight. I pull back to find another twisting around our bodies, flashing peacock blue. A third, as silver as moonlight on crystal pears, drifts between us, scattering the light to pieces that dance over our skin.

"Remarkable," I whisper.

"Not just the butterflies."

Then Logan's hands close around my waist as he lifts me into his arms. He tilts up his head and I lower my mouth to his. And as we kiss, it doesn't matter where in the world I am, because in his arms, I feel at home.

But, even better than that, I'm with him *and* I'm home.

Three Seasons Later

Golden light slants through porch railing, casting shadows across the sun-bleached boards and gilding our confetti cake. Insects hum in the grass like a winding-down engine, and the faint musk of dust and soil fills the air between the scrapes of forks, carrying voices, and laughter.

At the head of the table, Mom sits primly, expression hovering between a smile and a frown as she watches Val gesticulating with a fork and monologuing about pruning best practices. Logan's hand rests on my knee. Across the table, Mason and Andrew track Val's windmilling arms like they're watching the progress of a Ferris wheel.

"And Ali here," Val says, pointing a fork at me, even as she steers her voice to the rest of the table. "Never listens to my advice."

"I listen to literally all your advice," I protest. "What advice didn't I listen to?"

"In the spring, I told you to prune aggressively while the trees are young and flexible. Otherwise, you'll be in your seventies and wrestling with stiff wood."

I roll my eyes. Val sits back triumphant, eyeing my mom, and I wonder if that entire speech was a setup to garner her reaction.

Mom, to the surprise of the entire table, crosses her arms and retorts, "Valentina. What on earth do you know about stiff wood?"

Mason guffaws, Andrew laughs, and Logan chuckles as Val blinks with barely repressed adulation before leaning in to kiss her temple. Mom flushes with pride.

"Damn," Mason says, sounding half impressed. "Even I wouldn't have dared a genital joke in this company."

Andrew leans toward Logan and says, under his breath, "Now that the floodgates are open, though . . ."

"*But now that the floodgates are open,*" Mason bellows, "I have about—"

Logan clears his throat. "Another time, big guy."

Mason falls silent with a pout, and Andrew's lips twitch like he's torn between brothers, unsure whether to laugh or frown. I've met him only a few times now—he's only home twice a year when he's on leave—but he strikes me as the middle ground between the other brothers: as quick with a smile as he is with a courtesy. The kind of man who I fear may have his heart easily broken.

"Also," I say, trying to redirect the conversation well away from anyone's anatomy, "the trees I've planted are still too small to prune. Who knows what will happen with them."

Val's eyes tighten around her smile.

"I know," she says. "Don't you?"

My gaze wanders to a row of trees even as Logan's arm cinches tight around my waist. The last three years haven't been easy. Since the crystals cracked, production has improved, but even with the aid of the supernatural, a farm's fortunes don't turn around overnight.

That first year, Mom, Val, Logan, and I got nearly all of the fruit down, both marked and unmarked, but that was still only enough to make minimum payments on my debts and avoid losing the farm. It wasn't enough to replace my broken machinery or to make serious headway on my financial problems.

That came in the next years, though. The soil, as Val keeps telling me, has turned supernaturally productive. In fact, through some mysterious process that no one fully understands, the more mature trees have started growing without the need for irrigation water. Val thinks it's because their roots are so extensive they're tapping into deep recesses of groundwater.

It would be impossible, but so are many things.

"Yeah," I say as I eye Val steadily. "You're right. I know it, too."

Not an irrational optimism that I'm clinging to because I'm terrified of confronting reality, but a steady, filling kind, rooted in truth.

Mom's lips tip into another soft smile before she busies herself with a forkful of cake. As I look away, she and Val share a smile. Mom hasn't moved back to Apple Valley yet, not officially, but her trips to the orchard—harvest in fall and thinning in late summer—keep getting longer. Just last week, I overheard her telling Val she's ready to add her name to the lease at the retirement community. A move that, once she makes it official, will almost certainly be her last. She hasn't told me about this yet. But that's how she is, I guess. It takes her time to work up to talking about things, especially when it's this big.

I feel Logan kiss my temple, and I squeeze his knee.

"More cake?" I ask as I lift the knife and carve another piece, careful to avoid the words nearly sliced away: *Congratulations, Logan.* And even though we're not alone—Val has gone back to gesticulating, drawing alternate laughs from Mason, a kind of choking chuckle from Andrew, and gasps from Mom that I think might be the real goal of her campaign—it feels like the two of us are in our own understory.

He groans good-naturedly. "How many pieces do I need to eat before you're convinced I've celebrated enough?"

I scoop another slice onto his plate. "How many pieces will it take for you to admit you're proud of your art?"

It took weeks to convince Logan to have this party, which he protested felt "self-indulgent." He flatly refused after he finished his apprenticeship, even though that was nearly a year ago and we'd fully moved in together, turning our irregular weekends and part-time trips into one fully merged life. At the time, Logan claimed he couldn't celebrate because he was still making ends meet with odd barn jobs around the valley. But a couple of months ago, he signed on to his first big contract—a gazebo roof lattice for a community park pavilion in Portland—making enough money that he's nearly ready to transition fully to art. Finally, he relented on a party.

Logan's lips twitch, then he takes a bite. "I guess if five didn't work, we might as well try our luck on the sixth."

"Good," I say. "You deserve it."

Mason laughs again, a ringing sound that bites over the rasp of Val's voice, and this time Andrew and my mom join in. I grin across the table as the orange glow of the sunset bakes the porch wood. There's a sense of rightness again that feels like another steady blast of that rooted optimism.

Logan nudges me with an elbow, and I realize he's been watching me. He leans over to whisper in my ear, so close that it draws warmth up the back of my neck.

"Marry me."

I whirl on him. "Did you ask me what I think you just asked me?"

His eyes are on mine in a way that feels like pulling myself through the keyhole into a secret garden.

"I had a whole plan for asking," he says, "and it involved saplings and the irrigation system and going down on one knee. I have a speech, too."

"A speech?"

"About how I lived a whole lifetime in darkness. Shades of gray were all I knew. I was so adjusted to it that I thought that's just how life is. But then, there was you. And it's not just that you're bright and colorful where everything else is gray, although that's true. It's also that you light up everything else. You're so bright, you put the rest of my life in technicolor. I want that, Ali. I want technicolored butterflies and bunnies. I want you."

My heart fills so fast that I have to reach for his hand to keep from toppling over this bench seat.

A wedding. *Our* wedding.

Trees as an aisle, a mountain as our altar. Mom firmly gripping my elbow as I make my way down blossom-specked grass. Andrew officiating. Val somewhere off to the side, grumbling about allergies as she uses a knuckle to wipe away a tear. Mason, stock still and uncharacteristically serious.

And Logan, there in front of me. His soft smile. Broad chest. Walking toward him and a future that feels right, not just in my head, but in my heart, too.

I grin. Sunlight spills over the green canopies as the trees glow in agreement. The light catches a flash of silver—a butterfly rising on a draft of wind, flickering as it dances across gleaming leaves.

"You should give more speeches," I say. "You're very good at them."

Logan's smiling. "Well, there's more if you want it. And also, a ring. And a down-on-one-knee proposal. I can—"

"No, Logan. It's a lovely speech, but I don't need any of the rest of it."

"No?"

"I just need you."

Logan sifts a hand through my hair, rough fingers finding the back of my neck. "I'm with you. Wherever you are. Always."

He tugs me into his arms, and I burrow my face into his shoulder and inhale his clean scent, and it all feels complete.

A circle, closed. A cutting, replanted. A pear tree, cycling between white and green.

Change that feels steady if you stick around long enough to see it.

Because often people leave.

But, sometimes, they come back.

Acknowledgments

Everyone says your sophomore book is the most difficult, and good lord I hope that is true. I have never experienced so many dark nights of the soul with any piece of work, and I would not have made it through a single one of them without the people named here.

To my agents, Lauren Spieller and Hannah Teachout: I am endlessly grateful to have you as my partners and champions. Lauren was the one who—brilliantly—suggested this book needed magic, a change that moved it a giant leap closer to what it was always meant to be. Hannah brought her sharp, thoughtful editorial eye to the draft and helped me dig into the story with the depth this story demanded. Thank you both for believing in this book and in me, and for advocating so fiercely for us both.

To my editor, Sydney Collins, who pushed this story into new territory and higher heights. It takes a brilliant mind to be an editor, but an ever rarer one to see what a story should be—and to trace the map for getting there. I'm so grateful for your insight, your challenges, your trust.

I feel so lucky that another of my stories benefited from the meticulous eye of Whitney Bak. Whitney, I am fully convinced you are the best copy editor in the business. Thank you also to proofreaders Hope Clarke, Frieda Duggan, and Emily Zebrowski.

I'm deeply thankful to the talented team who brought this magical orchard to life on the cover. To the indispensable cover director,

Carlos Beltran, and illustrator, Georgie Stewart—thank you for the artistry, flexibility, and patience you brought to every turn as you shaped the visual heart of this book. And thank you to Elizabeth Rendfleisch for the gorgeous interior design.

As always, a book takes a village, especially on the production side. My sincere thanks to production editor, Annette Szlachta; managing editor, Saige Francis; and production manager, Meghan O'Leary, for shepherding this book so carefully into the world.

I'm grateful to the team who works to get the word out about my books, especially my publicist, Brianna Kusilek, and marketer, Emily Siegmund. Your enthusiasm and care mean so much to me.

To the booksellers who showed early love for my debut—and especially to the folks at Knotty Novels, Capital Books, and Wild Sisters—thank you. Julie, Kat, and Katie: I'm so grateful for your support and friendship.

This book went through many (many) iterations, which means it had many (many) early readers. A special thanks to those who read multiple versions, particularly Bri and Lauren, who each read this book (I'm quite serious) no fewer than three times. Your insights were indispensable. Lauren, thank you especially for your long phone calls and emoji reactions. I'd be lost without you. I'm also so thankful to the rest of my early readers: Rebeca, Natalie, Fija, Gabrielle, Ari, Stephanie, and Emma. Your time, care, and thoughtful feedback shaped this story in ways both big and small.

This book is a love letter to my favorite place in the world—a pear orchard in Hood River, Oregon—and to the people who make it feel like my second home. Thank you especially to Bobbie and Kristi for helping me get my pear facts straight and for being so generous and supportive. I am so lucky to have you.

I'm endlessly thankful for the people in my life who lift me up not just as a writer but as a person, too. Thank you to Hannah, book bestie and wonderful human. You're the best (tied with Lauren). Thank you to BASK for loving me exactly as I am and, somehow, not finding me insufferable. I viciously love you all. Thank you to my mom, my biggest cheerleader, always. Thank you to my best friend and sister, Lauren, for championing this book like nobody's business—and apologies that this one, too, has no dragons. We're getting closer, though!

And finally, to my husband, partner, and the love of my life, Cam. This one is for you, but more importantly, I am for you.

Ann Adams is a former athlete and current writer, reader, and wonk. She lives in Sacramento, California, where she spends her time analyzing public policy and going for moderate hikes with her husband and overly enthusiastic cockapoo. Mostly, though, she's writing stories—especially those about women falling in love and finding their power.

annadamsbooks.com
Instagram: @annadamswrites

ABOUT THE TYPE

This book was set in Electra, a typeface designed for Linotype by W. A. Dwiggins, the renowned type designer (1880–1956). Electra is a fluid typeface, avoiding the contrasts of thick and thin strokes that are prevalent in most modern typefaces.